For My Family:
Wayne,
Jane,
& Andrew

EXHIBIT: MURDER

1977

Chapter One

Pedalling as hard as he could, Peter Morgan forced his red rental bike up East Chop Drive. This was by far the coolest bike that Peter had ever ridden. It was a five-speed Schwinn Sting-Ray with handle-brakes, a headlight, and an awesome banana seat. He had never ridden a bike with more than one speed before. He still hadn't quite figured them out but he was working on it. His bike at home didn't have handle-brakes either; he just pushed backward on his pedals and the brakes kicked in—same as all of his friends' bikes. His parents said his bike at home was "just fine" and Peter *did like* his bike—he loved it in fact—it was cool, or at least, it had been cool before they got to Martha's Vineyard and rented this one. The Sting-Ray was the only bike left in

Peter's size, so they got it. The cheaper standard bikes were already gone. Peter was fine with that. He even loved the colour too—metallic cherry red. It was *totally* decent. Going back home to his regular one-speed bike was going to be tough even if it was black with yellow gas tank and fenders. The fenders and gas tank made it look awesome like a motocross bike but it wasn't really. Still, when Peter used a clothespin to clip a baseball card to the rear fork, it sounded pretty cool when the card hit the spokes.

With quick glances, Peter turned his head to the right and looked out over the Atlantic Ocean thirty feet below. There were hints of deep, translucent blue but mostly the ocean shimmered like diamond dust, all white light too bright to hold any colour at all.

Finally, at the top of the Chop, the road flattened out and Peter coasted for a while, steering under the hot June sun. He turned to look behind him and then returned his attention to the road ahead. He squinted to see as far as he could. There was no traffic on the road at all. Crossing the streets down in Oak Bluffs had been a lot trickier than navigating his route up East Chop Drive. In town, he had walked his bike across the intersections like he had promised his Mom, weaving through tourists as he went. This was the first trip that Peter had been allowed to go out on his own and he didn't want to blow it. He had grown up a lot since last summer and he needed to prove to his folks that he could handle the responsibility. This was the beginning of a whole new kind of Vineyard vacation for Peter. It was exciting and a little scary.

His Dad had given him a dollar for an orange soda and a frozen Mars Bar. He was planning to stop at the store on his way home. First, he wanted to get a picture of the Chocolate Lighthouse. Both his new camera and his new binoculars were slung over his shoulder, banging against his back with every pedal. Peter figured the Chop had to be the best place to use binoculars. Gay Head would be wicked too—it was way higher than East Chop—but there was no way he could ride his bike all the way down there and he didn't want to wait for his parents to take him either. This was the first year that his parents had rented a gingerbread cottage in the Oak Bluffs Methodist Campground, so East Chop was the perfect place.

Every summer before this one, his family had pitched a tent at one of the island campgrounds. Over the past winter, Peter had heard the conversations here and there and he knew that it had been his mother who had wanted to try something new. She said that she still liked camping but Peter could tell that she didn't like it as much as Peter and his Dad did. She still wanted to come to the Vineyard but she didn't want to have to sleep on the ground to do it. Both of his parents liked the cottage appeal of the gingerbread houses, so they had found one to rent. Of course, Peter had been through the Methodist Campground lots of times—you couldn't really visit Martha's Vineyard without looking at the gingerbread cottages and eating an ice cream, at least you couldn't with his parents—so he was just as happy to be staying in one of them. He hadn't known which cottage until they arrived but when they got there and he saw that on this vacation—not only was he going to have the Schwinn Sting-Ray to get around on—he was going to have his own room to sleep in to boot, Peter had been pretty excited.

Peter lifted two fingers from each grip and curled them around the chrome brakes as he approached the lighthouse. He squeezed them gently, applying equal pressure. The right handle controlled the front brake and the left controlled the back. Peter had tried using them individually and almost flew over the handlebars using the front brake alone. He decided then and there to try and get into the habit of always using them together. Just in case, he figured out the 'right' and 'front' both had five letters and 'left' and 'back' both had four. There was a high-pitched squeal as the rubber brake pads pressed against the spinning metal rims. The bike began to slow. Peter stretched out his legs and skidded the soles of his white and blue Adidas in the dirt beside the road. Clouds coughed up behind him as he came to a full stop. He looked past the white picket fence at the lighthouse and smiled.

The East Chop Lighthouse was by far Peter's favourite lighthouse on Martha's Vineyard. He liked that it was painted brown which was why the locals had dubbed it 'The Chocolate Lighthouse'. He didn't know why he thought that was cool but he did. All of the lighthouses on Martha's Vineyard were different. The West Chop had a house attached to it, so that was pretty cool too; The Edgartown Lighthouse was white—boring! The Gay Head Lighthouse was red brick and on top of a cliff—it was probably his second favourite. There was another lighthouse too but Peter couldn't remember where it was or what it was called. He had never been there. Being on a cliff was one of the things that he liked so much about this one. Peter liked that he could see so far. He shaded his eyes with his left hand and watched a seagull squawk by. *That's it exactly*, thought Peter. *Up here, I have the same view as the seagulls! I can even see the Cape!* That was why he had wanted to come with his binoculars. He couldn't wait to see how far he could see with them! That would be really decent, for sure!

Peter dismounted. He walked the Schwinn Sting-Ray a few steps, leaned it against the white picket fence, and turned to read the sign by the gate. In bold black lettering the sign read 'Telegraph Hill'. It also said that the East Chop

Lighthouse was a 'Semaphore'—whatever that was. Peter reached for the camera case that hung over his shoulder. He unsnapped the metal clasp and flipped open the black leather top. He inhaled deeply. The inside of the case smelled like leather and faintly of his Nana's car. Peter didn't know what that smell was. His Dad said it was "moth balls" but Peter didn't know what that was either. It sounded rude so Peter didn't ask. Nana had given him the camera just before they left for vacation. It was a nice smell. He took the camera out and, looking through the viewfinder, aimed it at the sign. He pressed down with his forefinger until he heard the click. Reflexively, he wound the film so that it was ready for the next shot. He knew he wouldn't remember the word 'semaphore' and he wanted to look it up later. He didn't know if Oak Bluffs had a library but he knew where the library in Edgartown was. He could look it up there. Pleased with himself, Peter turned toward the lighthouse and took another photo. He put the camera back in its case. Reaching over the fence for the latch, Peter opened the gate and stepped across the threshold.

* * *

Using both hands, Judie Tate turned the wheel gently starboard and felt the twenty-one-foot wooden catboat slice through the waves beneath her. They had left Edgartown Harbor very early. Once they were out on the sound, she had picked a spot on the horizon and that was where she pointed the bowsprit. The *Warlock* was heading northwest following the Vineyard shoreline. The Edgartown Lighthouse behind them, the June sun was heating her already bronze shoulders. The summer weather had come early and Judie picked up colour quickly. The day was two or three degrees past hot. The weather forecast predicted a wind of about ten knots with gusts up to fifteen—perfect for a leisurely day of sailing. Every time one of those gusts picked up, a mist of saltwater sprayed across Judie's face and semi-clad torso. It was intoxicating.

Judie wore a white bikini top and cut-off jean shorts. Her bare feet were already brown and smooth from early summer days on the beach—days that started with jogging on South Beach and ended with clam and lobster bakes on Lucy Vincent. She could never get enough. All winter long Judie ached for summer. The icy grey of winter that chilled her to the bone left her desperate to be wrapped in a warm island breeze, fragrant with salt water and wild roses. There was a time when she would have headed out to South Beach, Wasque, or even State Beach on a day like today and been quite content to while away the hours with a few Jackie Collins or Harold Robbins and a cooler full of cold beer and sandwiches. If that was all that her summers had to offer, it would have been fine with her but that was before she had discovered sailing. Sailing changed everything for her. It changed her whole Martha's Vineyard experience. Sailing changed her life.

She wasn't sure what it was about sailing. Judie had grown up around boats. Her family had always owned several motorboats. At the cottage, they had gone for sunset cruises on the lake and they had gone waterskiing, but it wasn't the same thing at all. She loved being at the helm and feeling the power of the wind. She loved the strength involved in hoisting sail or adjusting the gaff. The illusion that she was controlling the elements was thrilling. The fact that all of her sailing experience had been on an antique wooden catboat meant that there was an element of history that went along with it. The catboat was a New England classic. The more Judie read about them, the more she felt like she was a part of a simpler time when she was on board. She didn't even have to be at the helm. There was a glamour in its cedar plank on oak frame design. When she was aboard a wooden boat, listening to the ocean lap at the hull and the winds slap the canvas sail, she was Jackie Kennedy, Lillian Hellman, or Carly Simon. Out on Vineyard Sound, on a wooden catboat, very little had changed over the years. There was no politics on the ocean. There was no city skyline, no traffic, no pollution, and no noise. All of the modern stressors were hazy memories at best. The only skyline that she could see was that of Edgartown and it had changed very little in the last four hundred years with its white captain's houses and the Old Whaling Church. The Chappy Ferry had changed over the decades. In fact, at one time, it too had been a catboat but other than that... With any luck, it wouldn't change for the next four hundred either. She turned her face away from the horizon, up to the sun. Eyes closed, the sun burned bright orange through her eyelids and she felt the corners of her mouth curl up in a reflexive smile. She could stay out on the water all day. As long as the weather held out, she could stay out on Vineyard Sound forever.

*   *   *

From the galley, Alan Quaid watched Judie at the helm and smiled. She was so beautiful. Her sun-streaked hair blew around her face and she didn't seem to notice. Her skin—the colour of caramel—was a rich contrast to the white bikini top that tied in a knot behind her neck. Hidden from view, her nipples pressed against the thin white cotton. Her stomach was taut and covered with fine white hair. The shorts she wore were slung just a little too low and cut just a little too high to be deemed acceptable by polite society—their white cotton pockets hung out below the frayed denim. Shorts that short on legs that long always gave the illusion that you were seeing a lot more than you should without showing you anything at all. It had been nothing at all for her to talk him into sailing. They had gone out sailing before. Alan and Judie had done a lot of things before. It was his boat. His family was known all over the island for sailing. They all sailed. The Edgartown Yacht Club displayed many a plaque and trophy with brass nameplates engraved with his family name. His uncles, his grandfather, great-grandfather, and his father—all of the Quaids were all up there. Some people were natural born sailors and the Quaid family certainly fell into that category. Judie was beautiful—of that, there could be no question. She was beautiful eating eggs at The Black Dog and she was beautiful in front of a campfire on South Beach but out with him, at the helm of Warlock—she positively shone. Beautiful women and sailors had gone hand in hand since time immemorial. Alan and Judie weren't sleeping together—at least not yet. Alan wasn't really sure what they were. At present, they were probably just friends, but he'd like it to be more. It felt like there was an intimacy there that wasn't present in his other friendships. He was pretty sure that Judie felt the same way. Alan was never sure how to bring that up. When he was a teenager, he thought for sure that talking to beautiful girls would get a lot easier when he was an adult. Well, here he was full adulthood with his own tour company and his own sailboat, but talking to beautiful girls still completely and utterly sucked.

Alan bent down, opened the orange Coleman cooler at his feet and pulled out two gold and white Narragansett Lagers. He kicked the cooler closed and stepped back up onto the cockpit. He passed a beer to Judie.

"Thanks," she smiled, accepting the beer. "I like your Aviators."

Alan adjusted the sunglasses on his nose at their mention. He returned the smile. "You do?"

"I do," Judie took a mouthful of beer. "They're very Robert Redford."

Alan laughed, "I guess I could do worse than Robert Redford."

"Everyone could do worse than Robert Redford," Judie said. "I hear he likes to sail too."

"Well, he's okay in my books then." Alan sat down on the orange seat cushions and took a sip from his beer. "Does he have his own sailboat?"

Judie shrugged. "I'm not sure."

"So, he might not?"

"He might not." Judie grinned at him. Even with his Aviators on, she knew she was staring him straight in the eye.

"So, what you're saying is—there's a chance I'm cooler than Robert Redford?"

Judy laughed out loud. "You might be pushing it!"

"I don't know… If he doesn't have his own sailboat…" Alan stretched out on the bench and kicked his bare feet up on the cushions. He lay back until the sun caught his sunglasses.

"He's Robert Redford! He was Gatsby for crying out loud! He was that pool guy too—that was a good movie. He was Butch freaking Cassidy!" Judie, feeling that she had made her point, took another mouthful of beer. She had to admit, the Narragansetts were going down pretty easy.

"No, he wasn't," Alan said, without getting up from his languid position.

"No, he wasn't what?" Judy asked.

"He wasn't Butch Cassidy. Paul Newman was Butch Cassidy. Redford was The Sundance Kid."

"Whatever. That was like ten years ago. Who can remember a movie that's been gone for ten years?"

"I'm definitely not as cool as Paul Newman. Nobody is as cool as Newman."

"Yeah, that's probably true. Did you hear what he said to that reporter when he was asked if he was ever tempted to cheat on location?"

"No. What did he say?"

"He said, 'Why would I go out for a hamburger when I have steak at home?'"

"He's a class act," Alan sat up a bit and looked at Judie again. "More men should be that respectful. As I said, I am not as cool as Newman but I think I might be as cool as Redford. There might be a chance...couldn't there be? Even a little chance?" Alan was trying not to laugh but he couldn't help it. His own sun-kissed torso began to vibrate and beads of sweat rolled down his well-rounded shoulders.

"Maybe a little one," Judy conceded. She steered the wheel a little further and the boat shifted port. "Where are we headed anyway?"

"Wherever you want," Alan said. "The day is yours. You're becoming an excellent sailor."

"Really?" Judie asked unable to contain her excitement.

"Yes, really," Alan said.

Judie turned her head and watched the people jumping off the bridge that separated Vineyard Sound from Sengekontacket Pond. "Check it out," she said and pointed toward the bridge with her beer in hand. "It's the JAWS

Bridge. That's what everyone's calling it now. Did you see that movie?"

"I think everyone saw that movie. I guarantee you everyone on this island did. Hell, almost everyone on the island was in it! I saw it at Island Theater when it opened. It was great!"

"It was good. It scared the crap out of me! I wasn't even sure that I would go swimming again after I saw that little boy get eaten on the raft. You know on the beach? The part that scared me the most wasn't seeing the kid get eaten but the music and looking up at all the swimmers from underneath. The shark's perspective?" Judie shuddered. *"Jesus...that music!"*

"They're back in town, you know," Alan said.

"Who are?"

"Those Hollywood people. They're making JAWS 2, here, now, on the Vineyard."

"They are? That's so exciting!" Judie said. "In Edgartown?"

"Yeah, down at the harbour. I read about it in the paper." Alan got up, went down to the galley, and returned with two more beers. "Apparently, there's a mechanical shark there and everything."

"Will you take me down to check it out?"

"You want to go with me?" Alan felt himself blushing. He hoped she couldn't tell behind his tan.

"Of course. I thought we were kind of a team. We do lots of stuff together, don't we?"

"Yeah, I guess we do," Alan said softly.

In response, Judie spoke softly as well. "I think that's pretty cool. Don't you?"

"I think it's really cool," Alan said.

2

Peter coasted back down East Chop without pedalling at all. The hill was steep enough that there was no need. Quite the contrary—he kept a firm grip on both brakes, gently squeezing when he felt that he was picking up a little more speed than he would like. The ride back down the hill was easier but it was nowhere near as interesting. He was on the opposite side of the road from the ocean view. He could see it in the distance but it wasn't right there, so close that he felt he could jump into it at any moment. The inner-side of the road was home to steep driveways that led up to large east coast houses of the traditional weathered cedar shingle. Occasionally one was painted a different colour—

there was a baby blue one that Peter thought was cool—and there were a couple of white ones, but for the most part, the greying shingles prevailed. Peter could hear his father in his head, "I'm glad I don't have to shovel those driveways! Why would someone buy a house with a driveway like that?" That's exactly what his father would say. Eventually, East Chop Drive levelled out. When the Sting-Ray began to slow, Peter began to pedal again. With a quick glance left and right, Peter crossed the street and coasted through the parking lot of Our Market. He pedalled a little faster and rocks spit up in his wake. He was along the harbour now. Boat after boat lined his path. Sleek fibreglass speedboats—some with cabins and some without—and smooth wooden sailboats that looked like they had been there for one hundred years, still gleaming like new.

Peter loved the harbour. He loved the water. He didn't know why but there was something cool about being on the ocean. Was it just that he didn't see it everyday at home? Did the people who lived on the island think it was as cool as he did? Peter decided that some of them did but some of them probably didn't give it a second glance. Peter couldn't imagine that. Every year that his family came to Martha's Vineyard, it was the idea of seeing the ocean that always got him the most excited. The thought of swimming in the waves of South Beach and bridge jumping at State Beach kept him up nights. The night before Peter and his family left for their Vineyard vacation was even better than Christmas Eve and Peter definitely got even less sleep.

    Peter pedalled past the harbour and the gingerbread cottages and the Wesley Hotel on the hill until he came to the base of Circuit Avenue. The foot traffic was getting thick and Peter—hearing his mother's voice in his head—dismounted his bike. The Corner Store wasn't far up, so after crossing the street, he continued to walk his bike up the hill. He looked up at the Island Theater to see what was playing and his heart leapt into his throat. They were showing JAWS. The movie was a couple of years old now but he had never seen it. He had begged his parents to take him but they hadn't budged. His mother had been adamant—"You might not care if you're up with nightmares every night but I don't feel like getting up with *your* nightmares. Nice try, kiddo." Peter loved sharks. He went to the library and got out every shark book he could find. He had even impressed his folks with some of the science books he had read about sharks. Sharks were totally decent. Peter was a lot older now. Maybe his parents would take him to see JAWS now that he was older. Maybe the fact that they were on vacation would soften them up. Would it help that they were on Amity Island itself? Peter paused for a moment and stared up at the red, white, and blue poster. He felt electricity prickle its way across the fine hair on his legs and arms. His eyes moved over each and every long triangular tooth in the shark's mouth. He felt like he almost fell into the shark's black eyes. Everything about the shark was directed toward the naked woman swimming on the ocean's surface. She seemed so small—so helplessly small. Was that how big the shark was in the movie? Did she know that the shark was there? Did she know that this was the end for her? The poster filled him with a dread and excitement that he couldn't explain. Maybe he was old enough to go and see it with his parents now. Maybe...

Peter walked his bike up to the small courtyard in front of The Corner Store across from Seasons Restaurant. He leaned it up against one of the wooden planters and went inside. The man behind the cash looked Peter over as he entered. He was heavy set, balding on top with white hair on the side. Peter thought he looked like Mary's boss Lou on TV. Peter smiled and the man returned his attention to the woman at the counter. Peter could hear enough to know that she was complaining about crowds on Edgartown Harbor. This didn't come as any surprise to Peter; he always remembered the harbour being crowded every time he and his family went down there. He walked over to the ice cream freezers and looked inside. Finding what he wanted, he slid the top open and pulled out a frozen Mars bar. They didn't sell them like this at home. They were strictly a Martha's Vineyard treat—at least they were for Peter. He had tried to make one at home, but he didn't have the patience. He had put one in the freezer a couple of times but they had barely gotten cold let alone frozen. "Peter, you're going to have to leave it in the freezer until tomorrow if you want it to freeze, buddy," said his Dad. There was no way Peter could do that. So, he only had them on the island. They were like eating the chocolatiest Fudgsicle imaginable—and they lasted forever! They just kept getting gooier and gooier. The malted nougat and caramel pulled out in strings as they thawed. Frozen Mars bars were perfect on a hot summer day. Closing the freezer, Peter walked over to the coolers, opened the door and went for an Orange Crush—his favourite—but quickly changed his mind when he caught a glimpse of red and white cans decorated with green palm trees. Tahiti Treat! *You almost never see Tahiti Treat anymore*, thought Peter. He picked up a can and looked at it for a moment. The palm trees were cool. Peter closed the cooler door and went to the cash.

The woman was still at the counter complaining about the crowds at the harbour but Peter could see that her bags were in hand and she had finished her business. Still, Peter stood behind her. His mother had told him that it was rude to interrupt grown-ups and Peter didn't want to get in trouble from these strangers. So, he waited. He tried not to hold his frozen Mars bar in a way that it would start melting in his hands. He wanted to tear it open and get it while it was completely frozen! The woman didn't even seem like she was stopping to get a breath and the man hadn't said a word. Finally the man looked over to Peter and winked at him. Peter smiled but stayed silent.

"Alright, I'd love to stay and chat all day, Lee but I have a business to run. You know how the tourists are!" He nodded toward Peter. "This young man seems to need my attention! What do you have there, son?" The man turned his attention toward Peter. The woman looked down at him and scowled. Clearly, she hadn't finished and was not happy with Peter for bringing her chat to such an abrupt ending. With a curt "Good-bye," she walked out of the store. The man chuckled. "Thank you for being so patient. What's your name son?"

"Peter, sir. Peter Morgan."

"Well, Peter Morgan, you're a very polite young man."

"Yes sir," said Peter. "I mean, thank you sir." Peter put his frozen bar and his soda on the counter.

"One Tahiti Treat and one frozen Mars bar—that'll be thirty cents, Peter," the man said.

Peter reached across his back and pulled a dollar bill out of his camera case. He passed it to the man.

The man opened the till and then passed Peter his change. "Looks like you've got a nice camera there! Did you take any good pictures today?"

"I think so sir. I was up at the Chocolate—I mean—the East Chop Lighthouse. I went on my bike," said Peter.

"That's a great place to take photos," said the man. "Do you like liquorice?"

"Yes sir," said Peter.

"Black or red?"

"Red sir," said Peter.

The man reached into a plastic container on the counter, pulled out a long red twisted rope of liquorice, and passed it to Peter. "Thanks for being so well-mannered with that chatty busy body. We need more youngsters like you."

Peter took the liquorice and put it in his camera case. "Thank you sir!"

"Now, go eat your bar before it melts, Peter. I've got customers." The man winked again.

Peter waved and walked back out into the sun. He sat beside his bike and opened the Mars bar. He slipped one end into his mouth and began working it with his tongue. It was still frozen but there was just enough give in the outer layer to start a chocolate swirl melting in his mouth, filling his cheeks. Perfect. This was turning out to be a really good day.

* * *

The Warlock sailed into Oak Bluffs Harbor in the early afternoon. The sun was high in a virtually cloudless blue sky.

"Turn on the motor," directed Alan.

Judie reached below her and started it up. Then she pushed the throttle gently into forward. "Good?"

"Perfect," said Alan. He gave her a thumbs-up and smiled. Alan walked the gunwale of the boat and with a firm grip on both the peak and the throat halyard, began lowering the gaff.

"How do you know how to lower the gaff?" asked Judie.

"Well, I usually let out the peak halyard until the gaff is parallel to the boom and then I lower the peak and throat together." Alan shrugged but kept his eyes focussed on what he was doing. "I don't know if that's what other sailors do, but that's how I do it."

"I want you to teach me next time," Judie said.

"Sure!" said Alan. "I'll give you Captain Quaid's Sailing 101!"

Judie laughed, "That would be totally cool." She strained to look around the harbour. "Where do we tie her up?"

"I'll call the Harbor Master," Alan said. "Oak Bluffs has free day moorings which is amazing. Edgartown charges."

"Oh, that *is* cool," agreed Judie. She inhaled the ocean air deeply and looked around the harbour. It was busy but not full. A deep horn bellowed and she turned to see the Steamship Authority ferry coming in to dock just outside the harbour. She smiled. It was such a Vineyard-esque thing to see.

Having tied up the sail, Alan jumped down into the cabin and picked up the handset on the CB radio. Judie watched as he adjusted the dials and called for the Oak Bluffs Harbor Master. After a short exchange, he stepped back up to the cockpit and pointed toward Nancy's Restaurant. "We can pull up to the mooring fourth in from Nancy's," he said. "Can't ask for better than that!"

"Perfect!" Judie said.

Alan watched Judie's face lose all excitement and go blank. "What's the matter?" he asked.

"Are you going to do it?"

"Do what?"

"Dock her?" she asked.

"No. You are," Alan said. "You'll be fine. You're the one who wants to learn how to sail. Well, here we are—Captain Alan Quaid's Sailing 101!"

Judy furrowed her brow. "Somehow, that's not as funny as it was a moment ago."

"You'll be fine," Alan walked up and stood beside her. "Let's go."

Judie wove between the harbour moorings until Warlock's bow aimed directly at the slip.

"Okay," said Alan. "Be sure you're allowing for the force of the water. Can you feel how we're being pulled to port? You want to compensate for that by pulling starboard just a little—very little."

Judie adjusted the wheel.

"Excellent. Now just before we enter the slip, put her in neutral and let the momentum glide us in. If we stay in forward, we'll come in too strong," Alan directed.

Judie reached down and cut the engine. Just as Alan predicted, the Warlock slipped into the mooring with almost no effort at all.

Alan leapt up, tied her in place at the bow. Then, he walked the gunwale back and tied the stern. He looked at Judie and smiled. "I couldn't have done better myself!"

Judie blushed with pride. "Thanks!"

"Now let's get some food. You're buying right?"

"Why am I buying?" Judie raised an eyebrow.

"Well, we never did discuss the entrance fee for the sailing course..." Alan gave her his best Cheshire Cat grin.

Judie shook her head. "Isn't that always the way? These things always seem like a good deal at the time and then after you sign up, they nickel and dime you all the way!"

Alan stepped up onto the dock and reached out his hand for Judie's. "Well, maybe it's negotiable."

Judie stepped up onto the dock beside him and with her face close and her green eyes fixed on his, she said, "Are you thinking of taking it out in trade?"

This time it was Alan's turn to blush.

Judie smiled, "C'mon, I'm starving!"

The two of them walked barefoot down the dock toward Nancy's Snack Bar.

3

Charles Williams walked down Circuit Avenue wearing navy blue shorts and a white JAWS t-shirt. His red flip-flops smacked the cement sidewalk under his feet. He was heading to The Corner Store. He had left his parents on Seaview Avenue and crossed Ocean Park. Charles' Dad had given him some of his allowance to get a drink as long as he promised to be quick. It was hot and Charles was dying of thirst. His parents told Charles to meet them at the car. The three of them had spent the last couple of hours on Inkwell Beach. The water had been awesome but they had wrapped it up for the day. Charles had been hungry for a while, then his Dad, finally when his Mom had decided she was hungry too, they had packed it up. They were going back to the campsite to barbecue hot dogs.

Beside the entrance to the store sat a boy Charles' age. In one hand he held a Tahiti Treat—Charles' favourite soda—and with the other he was working hard on a frozen Mars bar—also one of Charles' favourites. Charles checked out the kid's bike—red with handle brakes and more than one speed. It was a seriously cool bike. The boy looked up at Charles as he walked by. Charles looked away before their eyes met—he didn't want the guy to think he was staring at him—and walked into the store.

It would be cool to have someone to hang with, he thought.

Even though the doors were propped wide open, the store was a little cooler than outside. The owner had turned off all of the lights. The store was a little bit dark and that was enough to keep the temperature down. The indirect sunlight lit the store surprisingly well. Charles walked straight back to the cooler and grabbed his own Tahiti Treat. He walked to the counter and paid for his drink before walking back out to face the hot afternoon sun. Charles popped the top of the can and took a long chug of the cold drink. The cold pop was so refreshing that Charles sighed audibly when he took the can away from his lips.

The boy with the cool red bike was still sitting outside working his Mars bar. He looked up at Charles and at the can in his hand.

"It's cool that they have Tahiti Treat here, isn't it?" the boy said. "You can't hardly find it anywhere these days."

"It's my favourite," said Charles.

"Mine too," said the boy. "I don't know what flavour it's supposed to be though. It doesn't really taste like anything that I can tell."

"I think its fruit punch," said Charles.

The boy thought about it for a second, took a sip, and then his eyes widened. "Oh yeah! I think you're right! It's fruit punch. I didn't even think of that. Cool!"

"What's your name?" asked Charles.

"Peter. What's yours?"

"Charles."

"Do you live here Charles?" asked Peter.

"No. I'm here from Toronto for like two weeks," Charles said. "What about you?"

"Same," said Peter. "I mean, I'm here for two weeks. I'm not from Toronto. We're from Blairstown, New Jersey."

"I've never heard of Blairstown. I know where New Jersey is though. Is Blairstown small?"

"Kinda small, I guess," said Peter. "Toronto is in Canada, right?"

"Yes," said Charles with a nod.

"That's far," said Peter.

"It's pretty far," said Charles. "We drive here and it takes *forever!* It always feels like we're never going to get here."

"Same here."

Charles made a mental note to go to the library and find out which was farther from Martha's Vineyard, Toronto or Blairstown. He looked up Circuit Avenue and back down at Peter. "I gotta go. My parents are waiting for me over by The Flying Horses," Charles shrugged and started to walk away.

"Where are you staying?" asked Peter.

"Martha's Vineyard Campground," Charles said. "You?"

"One of the gingerbread cottages." Peter paused and said, "I'm going to State Beach by the JAWS Bridge tomorrow morning if you want to meet me there."

Charles thought about it. "Yeah, maybe." He started up Circuit Avenue. "See ya!"

Peter waved. "I like your shirt!"

Charles looked down reflexively at the shark on his chest. "Thanks!" He turned around and picked up his pace. His parents would definitely be wondering what happened to him. He couldn't help but smile though. It would be cool if he had a friend to hang out with—especially one with an awesome bike who liked JAWS.

*   *   *

Peter could barely contain his excitement. Charles seemed to be wicked cool. He never met other kids on the island in all the times his family had been coming! Making friends was a lot harder than people always said it was. To hear other people talk about it, you'd think they were just walking up to strangers all over the place and making plans to go to the beach or movies or grab a burger. Adults were the worst. They always thought that all kids could be friends just because they were kids. The truth was introducing yourself to someone and saying you wanted to hang out was scary. It was the absolute worst. What if they said no? What if they thought you were a total loser? A freak? Peter had been scared to talk to Charles but he decided that any embarrassment that he might feel being turned down by this stranger would be way easier to take than another vacation without a friend. Besides, he had been wearing a JAWS shirt! Peter didn't want to sound like a dork and bring up how badly he wanted to see the movie. What if Charles had already seen it and would think he was a baby for not being allowed? Would he think it was funny that his parents thought he would be too scared? Peter would have to feel out the situation before he told Charles any of that. He would ask a few choice questions next time. He had yelled out that he liked Charles' shirt and probably sounded like a complete idiot doing it too. Too late now. Hopefully, Charles would come to the beach tomorrow morning and they could talk about JAWS then. He couldn't wait to get home and tell his folks!

*   *   *

The production team for JAWS 2 had moved into Edgartown about a week before Craig Upland had hooked up with them. He had gone down to The Kelley House to audition for one of the smaller roles. The front page headline in the Gazette on June 7th had read, "*JAWS Tightens Its Grip Here: Happy Confusion Ensues As Our Favorite Movie Company Is Off Again! Casting Goes On For Small Parts*". Craig never had a problem with the ladies on-island so he figured that he totally had a shot as an actor. He would get a role in JAWS 2 as a bartender or something equally lame, but they would see his talent, he would look good on camera, and the casting agent would take him back to Hollywood with the production company and he would get a real agent—nothing to it. Before he knew it, he would be at

Hollywood parties with Jacqueline Bisset and Farrah Fawcett. It hadn't worked out that way though. Universal had turned him down as an actor but because of his muscular build, they had offered him a job as a grip with the crew. He didn't even know what a grip was but they said it was very physical work and it would mean long hours. He took it. Even as crew, if he worked hard enough to impress the company, he could secure a position and they would take him back to California. Once he was on the west coast, he could get an agent and do everything else as planned. Craig knew one thing and one thing only: he needed to get off of this godforsaken rock.

Craig Upland was an islander. He was born in Martha's Vineyard Hospital and he grew up in the house where his family still lived. His father Dr Tom Upland had delivered him. His father had delivered most of his friends too. Dr Upland was held in high regard on Martha's Vineyard. As the only child, Craig had been expected to live up to the same standard. He hadn't. Dr and Mrs Upland had set the bar way out of Craig's reach and no matter how hard he tried, they never let him forget it. The whole island reminded him of it.

Craig had tried in school but it just wasn't his bag. He didn't fail but C's and D's were the norm. He got a B+ once in art and had raced home to show his father. *"Art class?*

What are you going to do with that? Show me a B in a real subject. Then you'll have something to talk about." Craig had never shown his father anything again. He started throwing his report cards in the trash on his way home from school after that. His parents hadn't noticed or if they had, they didn't say anything. Craig would be the first to admit that he wasn't perfect, he never had been. He had made mistakes. The time he had been pulled over in a car and been busted for smoking pot with two of his friends hadn't gone over well at all. It had spread across the whole goddamn island in a day too. There was no such thing as a secret on the Vineyard. Craig hadn't even been the one driving—his friend Ross was driving. He had been smoking, sure he had, but the weed had been his buddy Doug's. None of that mattered to anyone. It sure hadn't mattered to Officer Kramer who busted them that's for sure. The three of them spent the night in jail. Peggy who worked on the desk in the police station had seen to it that the news got around as fast as possible. She had dashed for the phone as soon as she saw that it was Dr Upland's boy they were bringing in. She had covered her mouth with her fat, pasty hand while she spoke into the receiver so Craig couldn't hear what she was saying, but she kept her beady little eyes on him the whole time. Everyone knew what had happened before he even got home. That was a year ago. No one on the island remembers that Doug and Ross were even there, even though it was Ross's goddamn car. Both of their fathers were local fishermen; Doug's mom was a cashier at the market and Ross's mom didn't work. They both ended up working long hours on their fathers' boats and Craig hadn't really seen much of them after that. Nobody did. Maybe that's why no one remembered that they were even involved. They had been dragged out to sea and off of everyone else's charts. Besides, they lived so far up-island that people barely remembered who they were anymore. All the down-islanders remembered was that Dr Tom Upland's boy had been caught with drugs and held in Edgartown jail. All of the middle-aged housewives in Edgartown still whispered it over their coffees when he walked into Dock St Coffee Shop. They murmured it when he walked by on the beach, *"Dr Upland must be so disappointed... Poor Mrs Upland... That Upland boy really squandered his opportunities...such a good family too."* They could all go to hell. Craig Upland was going to make something of himself and then his parents and this whole stupid island could kiss his hairy white ass.

With work-gloved hands, Craig reached for a heavy coil of cable, picked it up, and threw it over his tanned, muscled shoulder. Universal had been right—Craig was strong. His shoulders and arms looked like tan boulders.

His feathered hair was light brown, bleaching out in the summer sun by the day. It stuck in places to his thick dirty bronze neck. He walked the cable over to the barge that was draped with a heavy canvas. Craig thought it looked like one of the doctor's tents in M*A*S*H. KEEP OUT was painted on the outer wall in a broad uneven brush stroke. He was dying to take a look but he had been told in no uncertain terms that it was one-hundred-percent off limits. He knew what was behind the canvas, what was housed in the makeshift tent. It was a shark.

"Where's that going?" asked a voice behind him.

Craig turned around. It was his boss, Mike. Mike was heavy-set, grimy, and always seemed slightly disgruntled. He didn't smell or anything but Craig always got the impression that Mike could use a bath. "I was told to take this over to Mr Hancock's boat," said Craig. He tapped the coil with his free hand in case there was any question what he was talking about.

"Who told you?" asked Mike.

"The A.D.," said Craig. He twisted slightly and pointed toward a tall skinny guy with a moustache. "That guy."

Mike snorted his disapproval. "Goddamn assistant directors. They're not real directors yet but they want it so badly they can taste it." He shook his head. "They're supposed to go through me when they want any manual labour done. Assholes. Well, you'd better go do it then."

Craig smiled and walked toward the production boats tied up in the harbour. *What the hell was the point of all that?* He wondered. *If you were just going to tell me to do it anyway, then just let me do it!* Craig walked out onto the dock and stopped in front of the boat where the director was talking to the head of production. He hadn't actually had the chance to talk to the director yet and this could be his big chance to make an impression. A third man leaning against the stern with a clipboard in his hands, looked up as he approached.

"I was told to bring this to Mr Hancock," said Craig.

The third man motioned with a flattened spread-out palm for him to lower his voice. "SShhh! Quiet!" the man said. "Thanks man but we don't need it anymore. Today's pages have changed. You can take it back."

Craig looked warily at the man and then looked in the direction of the director.

As if reading his mind, the third man spoke again. "Don't even think about interrupting Mr Hancock now. That won't win you any points, handsome. You're going to have to be discovered another day." The man chuckled acerbically. "Just go away."

Craig felt his face flush. If they had been anywhere else, this little faggot would be getting his clipboard rammed right up his goddamned ass right about now. Craig adjusted the heavy coil on his shoulder, turned and walked back down the dock. The movie business sure wasn't what he thought it would be. He thought it would be fun but so far, it was one giant pissing contest. So far, the movie business sucked.

* * *

Peter pedalled through the multi-coloured gingerbread cottages as fast as he could. The pathway that wound its way through the houses was barely a road. One car could fit on it and occasionally one did crawl through but it was rare. Mostly, it was filled with tourists wandering on foot, picking the most colourful of houses to use as backdrops for their family photos. A heavily leafed canopy of branches danced overhead. They flashed a strobe of sunlight across Peter's face as he made his way toward the family rental.

Peter was going a good speed when he reached the front steps. He grabbed the brakes and screeched to an abrupt halt. The front tire latched onto the ground. The Sting-Ray bucked. Peter felt the back tire lift off the ground. His centre of gravity jolted forward and his stomach leapt into his throat. For a moment, he thought he was going to go over the handlebars—he didn't. Peter felt his weight shift back onto his seat and the bike once again found its place on solid earth. Peter's skin prickled and he felt his palms moisten with sweat.

"Whoa!" he exclaimed. Peter planted his feet firmly on the ground. The feeling of the solid ground beneath his feet was reassuring. He curled his toes inside his shoes looking for extra purchase. His heart was beating just a little too quickly. He took one deep breath and then another. He had been so excited about telling his parents about his new friend that he hadn't really been paying attention to what he was doing. "Jeez, calm down, Peter," he said to himself. All of a sudden he felt kinda stupid. All this over meeting some kid. He didn't even know him yet. He did love the idea of hanging out with a buddy this summer though; that would be so awesome.

Like all of the gingerbread cottages in Wesleyan Grove, their rental house was small. Each house was almost uniform in size—one and a half storeys with a small front porch. What set each one apart from its neighbours was the colours. Peter loved the colours. Each and every cottage in Wesleyan Grove was painted with vibrant colours. The one right beside their rental was all different shades of pink! Peter was glad they weren't in that house. He thought it was

47

really pretty if the truth be told but there was no way he would be able to make friends and bring them home to a pink house! That would not be cool.

His family's house was a kind of greeny-blue with white and orange trim. He thought it was turquoise but his Mom had said, 'It's teal'. Peter had never heard of *teal* before. The porch and steps were painted grey. The wood walls were *teal* but the window frames, the shutters, and door jams were white. The gingerbread trim on the roof was white too but with orange details. The front double doors, behind the white screen doors were also orange. All of the railings and trim were white and orange. Peter would never have suggested that anyone should paint their house greeny-blue, orange, and white but now, seeing it in front of him, he thought it might just be the coolest house he had ever seen. There were lots of flowers planted around the front and sides of the house too. A lot of orange tiger lilies. Peter figured that the tiger lilies had been chosen because they matched the orange paint. There were other colours of flowers too. His Mom *loved* the flowers. She spent a lot of time outside, crunching on a glass full of ice, and admiring them. Peter suspected that she would have been quite happy staying at the campground in a tent if there had been lots of flowers at their campsite. He chuckled at his own joke.

His heartbeat back to normal, and his breathing under control, Peter climbed the stairs to the porch and pulled the screen door open. The rusted metal springs groaned in resistance. Once Peter was inside, the almost weightless door clacked loudly in its frame. *Groan...clack! Groan...clack! Groan...clack!* The screen door sounded like the one at his grandparents' cottage on Sand Pond in New Jersey. Peter smiled. Those were sounds he always associated with summer.

"Well look what the cat dragged in!"

When Peter walked in the front door, his Mom looked up from the sink where she was washing vegetables. The kitchen was at the back of the house but the house was small and most of the wall separating the kitchen from the living room had long been taken down.

"Did you get the photos of the lighthouse that you wanted?"

"I did! It was really cool! I could see forever on the cliff with my binoculars too. I can't wait to tell Nana!"

"No doubt she'll want to hear all about it. You know you could write her a post card," Peter's mother said. "She'd love that."

Peter nodded. "That's a good idea." Peter shrugged off his camera case and his binoculars and set them on the table.

"Peter that's not where those go. I don't want any of us to get into the habit of leaving things all over the place. This house is too small. It will drive your father crazy. Put them up in your room, please."

"Okay Mom but you'll never guess what happened!"

"You can tell me after you put those things away. It will take two minutes—not even. Now, go!"

"Mom, can't I just—"

"Go!" Peter's mother laughed and pointed upstairs. "I'll make you a sandwich and then you can tell me all about it when you come back. Bologna and ketchup?"

"Yes, please," said Peter. He collected his camera and binoculars off the table and walked up the narrow staircase to the second floor.

Peter's bedroom was white. The inside of the house was all painted white. His Mom said it was to make it seem bigger. She said that was why the wall between the kitchen and living room had been taken down too. The floor was painted the same grey as the porch. His Mom said that was to help hide the dirt. Peter liked his room a lot. There was a fan in the room's only window and it did a pretty good job of bringing the breeze in. That was good. Peter was already noticing that it was starting to get hot. He dropped his camera and binoculars on the robin's egg blue chenille bedspread and went back downstairs.

Peter crossed over to the kitchen and sat up on a barstool. The wall dividing the two main rooms of the first floor had been turned into a counter with room enough for two to sit. Peter's Mom put a plate in front of him with a bologna sandwich cut in half diagonally. She had pulled the two halves apart and between them, she had piled the plate with potato chips.

"Thanks, Mom," Peter said.

"You're welcome," said his Mom. "So what's your big news?"

"I met a kid at the store!" exclaimed Peter.

"You did? That's nice. What's he like?" asked Peter's Mom. She leaned forward, propping herself up with one hand on the counter, and straightened her son's hair with the other.

"He's really cool."

His Mom laughed. "Well, that doesn't tell me anything. Tell me something about him. What's his name?"

"His name is Charles," said Peter. He took a big bite of his sandwich.

"Charles—that's a nice name. I've always liked that name. Is he an islander?"

Peter shook his head. *"Heef fum Cahaha!"*

51

"*Heef fum Cahaha?*" Peter's Mom laughed again. "Gee, what a wonderful quality in a friend! Let's try that again without a mouth full of bologna and Wonder Bread. Okay?"

Peter chewed quickly and swallowed most of the food in his mouth. Enough that he could speak clearly anyway. "Charles is from Canada! He's from Toronto."

"Oooohhh! He's from Canada! Well, he probably really is nice. His family is here on vacation?"

"Uh-huh," said Peter.

"Pardon?"

"Yes," said Peter.

"Are you guys going to *hang out* or whatever you kids call it?" She asked.

"He's going to meet me on State Beach tomorrow morning. At least, I hope he is. He didn't say anything but I could tell he really liked my bike! Maybe he has a bike too. Oh and Mom?"

"Yes?"

"He was wearing a JAWS t-shirt!" Peter said.

"And there it is," his Mom said. "Now, it all makes sense." She shook her head. "You and that movie—you haven't even seen it yet!"

"I know but sharks are just *so cool*, Mom. If Charles is wearing a JAWS t-shirt, he must think so too."

52

"I'd say that was a pretty good guess. Well, sharks are everywhere around this island. Let's see how cool you think they are if you bump into one while you're swimming on State Beach. You two should have lots to talk about. After you guys get tired of hanging out on the beach tomorrow morning, why don't you bring Charles back here for lunch? I'd like to meet him."

"Ok, Mom. I'll ask him!"

"Make sure it's okay with his parents too."

"I will," Peter turned his attention to his sandwich. He didn't realise how hungry he really was until he started eating. The bike ride up East Chop had really given him an appetite. Even after his frozen Mars bar, he was starving.

4

With a cardboard tray containing two tall drinks, Judie sat down on one of the benches that faced Oak Bluffs Harbor. Before getting comfortable, she slid down to make room for Alan. Warlock rocked gently in her slip in front of them while cars full of tourists drove by on Lake Avenue behind them. The harbour traffic had increased since they had gone up to Nancy's Snack Bar. Sailboats and motorboats danced back and forth across their watery stage and Judie couldn't help but be enraptured by the show.

Alan rolled open the top of the large paper bag on his lap. He reached inside and pulled out a foil wrapped package. "Here you go," he said.

"Mmmm! Yummy! Thank you!" said Judie accepting the foil roll. "I owe you one vanilla milkshake!" She reached across her lap to the tray of drinks and pulled a tall wax paper cup out of its holder and passed it to Alan.

"Thanks," he said. He immediately wrapped his lips around the straw and sucked hard, pulling the thick sweet milkshake through the straw.

Judie laughed. "You look like your head is going to cave in!"

"That's the sign of a good milkshake. If you don't nearly have an aneurism getting it up the straw, they didn't make it right," Alan stated.

Judie peeled back the foil wrap in her hands revealing white bread stuffed with large chunks of lobster meat, mayonnaise, lettuce and celery. She stuffed the exposed end into her mouth and bit down hard. Juices filled every corner of her mouth. She moaned with delicious ecstasy.

This time it was Alan's turn to laugh. "Is this the first time you've eaten this month?"

Judie tilted her head up toward the sun and chewed her sandwich.

"I take it, it's good?" Alan asked.

Judie nodded and moaned again.

Alan reached back into the bag and pulled out a second foil wrapped package. He unwrapped it, exposing a cheeseburger fresh off the grill. He took a bite, tossed his head back, and moaned in mimicry.

Judie managed to swallow most of her lobster before laughing out loud. Playfully, she kicked at his leg. "You're an ass!" She looked at him, smiling through his mouth full of burger. He was so handsome.

"What?" Alan asked with innocence. "Didn't I do it right?"

"I didn't do it that bad!" Judie said. Her mouth was completely empty now and she pulled her chocolate shake out of the tray. She sucked hard. She could feel her cheeks caving in and her eyes bulging.

"I told you it was thick," Alan said. "Suck harder."

She looked up at him. Their eyes met. There was a pause before the two of them exploded into laughter. Alan doubled over, wrapping his arms around his stomach. Judie flung her head back and screamed with delight. Out of the corner of her eye, she caught passers-by staring at them with mild concern and that made her laugh even harder. She felt the tickle of tears rolling down her cheeks.

"Oh my god!" Alan said. He gasped for air and tried to regain his composure. *"That did not come out right!"*

Judie straightened up on the bench. "One second later and that milkshake would have come out of my nose!"

"I haven't laughed that hard in a long time," Alan said. He slid his free hand behind his sunglasses and wiped his eyes.

"Me neither," Judie agreed.

They looked at each other and smiled. Neither of them spoke. They just smiled. Then, in unison, they both took another bite of their sandwiches. They ate in silence watching the boats play their parts on Oak Bluffs Harbor. Seawater lapped at the dock not three feet in front of them.

"There is nowhere else in the entire world that I would rather be," said Judie.

"Me neither," said Alan.

"That's quite the statement, isn't it? I mean, if you really think about it." Judy picked up her milkshake again. "It's pretty heavy."

"I guess so, yeah." Alan said.

Judy put down what was left of her lobster roll and wrapped her hand around the lid of her shake. Gently, she pried the lid off, tilted the cup up, and took a mouthful—smooth, chocolaty, and cold.

Alan chuckled. "Aren't you going to give the straw another go?"

Judy joined in the chuckle. "Not a chance," she said.

*   *   *

Craig Upland walked up Main Street Edgartown after his shift. He looked around town with a wry smirk. Shots were being set up at Main and Water; equipment and crew were blocking traffic with large signs that read, *Universal Studios Filming Site For JAWS 2 Sorry For The Inconvenience.* It was this sort of thing that had so many of the locals pissed off. Universal was bringing a lot of money to Martha's Vineyard but nobody on the island ever wanted anything to change. There must never be any inconvenience of any kind. Hotel owners were thrilled, Bob Carroll of the Harbor View Hotel and his ilk. They were making money hand over fist. Everyone else was pissed.

Craig didn't see the problem himself. Nothing ever happened on Martha's Vineyard. From October through May it was dead. You could shoot a cannon down Main Street and not hit a soul. The restaurants were mostly closed and so were half of the shops. Then, June through August, maybe part of September, the place was pandemonium. Tourists descended on the island like locusts on a cornfield. Locals were in a bad mood if business was slow in the summer and they were stressed and upset if they were overworked. Nine months of living in a coma every year didn't prepare them for the hectic pace of summer. What Craig couldn't figure out was why they cared if the movie company was here causing chaos? It's not like they would all be happy if the company left. They'd just be mad and complaining at the town hall that JAWS 2 left and took all of its money with it. As Craig saw it, there was no pleasing islanders—just one more reason for him to get the hell out.

Craig walked past the red brick Edgartown Bank and Edgartown Hardware. Both signs had temporarily changed to Amity Bank and Amity Hardware respectively. The tourists had all become lookie-loos, straining their necks in the hopes of catching a glimpse of Roy Scheider or Lorraine Gary. On the other hand, islanders walked by pretending not to be interested in the slightest. Craig thought both groups were ridiculous. He really wasn't interested in the slightest. His shift was over and he wanted nothing more than to get the hell out of 'Amity'. He crossed Main Street and headed up toward the parking lot on Summer Street.

Craig's brand new 1977 GMC Jimmy High Sierra was his pride and joy—blue and white with a white hard top, blue bucket seats, and automatic transmission. He had worked hard for the money to buy this truck and it had definitely paid off. Getting chicks to drive out to South Beach and watch the sunset was a breeze and totally decent. He would drive right out onto the sand on Norton's Point and they'd stretch out in his carpeted flatbed with some beer and blankets. It was a pretty amazing way to spend the evening. Craig might not have a boat but a truck with tires deflated for beach driving was the next best thing on this island. Craig stepped up into his truck, put the key in the ignition and turned. The engine roared to life. Boston's *WBCN—The Rock Of New England* pumped "Blinded By The Light" by Manfred Mann through the built-in speakers on his dash and doors. He reached behind his seat for his cut-off denim shorts. Craig pulled off his boots and socks and his t-shirt and threw them in the backseat. After taking a quick look around and deciding he was more or less alone, Craig pulled off his jeans and tossed them in the back. Naked, he shook his shorts to make sure they weren't full of sand before sticking his bare feet through the legs and pulling them up to just below his hips. One by one he did up the buttons on the fly but left the button at the waistline open for comfort. Craig backed out onto Summer Street and turned right onto Davis Lane. He was heading toward Beach Road and Oak Bluffs. Oak Bluffs would be just that—Oak Bluffs. He needed food but most of all, he needed to leave all of this Amity Island and JAWS 2 crap far behind him. He turned up the radio and began to sing along, *"Blinded by the light! Revved up like a deuce another roller in the night!"*

*   *   *

Alan took the trash from their lunch and disposed of it in one of the bins on Lake Avenue. It was really turning out to be an amazing day—one for the record books. They had started out reasonably early, had great weather for sailing, and Judie was being more than just a little flirty. It was true that they had been seeing a lot of each other lately but Alan had never really been sure what was going on between them. She didn't see any other guys. If she did, Alan would have known about it. She would have brought it up; she would have told him. But that was just the thing—they were always together. Even if she wanted to see another guy, she wouldn't have time. No, Alan knew that he was the only man in Judie's life and he liked it that way. The food had been good, the laughs had been great, now he figured they would get back into Warlock and either sail back to Edgartown or continue on to Vineyard Haven. He didn't care either way as long as he was with Judie.

"Shall we get going?" Alan motioned toward Warlock rocking in her slip.

"Actually, as long as we're in O.B., I wouldn't mind looking around a bit. Is that okay with you? We could even have a drink at Boston House if you like!"

"Oh..." Alan looked back over his shoulder toward Circuit Avenue. "Um, okay. Sure!"

"Oh, you don't want to. We don't have to. We can get back on the boat," Judie said.

"No! No! It's cool," Alan said. "I just wasn't expecting it. Ya know what I mean? You surprised me." He reached out and took her hand. "C'mon. Let's go check out Circuit Avenue."

Judie beamed at him. "Totally cool!"

The closer they got to the foot of Circuit Avenue, the thicker the crowd got. "I think this is why they call it *Circus Avenue*!" said Alan.

"Ha! Definitely."

At Circuit Avenue, Judie jumped in excitement and clapped her hands. "Oh, let's get some popcorn at Darling's!" she exclaimed.

Before he knew what was happening, Alan felt their arms untwine. Her hand pulled out of his. He had no choice but to let go. As their connection loosened, his stomach tightened. "Wait!" he said.

Judie began to cross Lake Avenue toward Island Theater and Darling's Candy Shop with a little more enthusiasm than her feet could handle. She tripped and fell forward onto the street. Her whole body hit the pavement. She looked up just in time to see the silver grill of the GMC Jimmy coming at her at full speed. Judie screamed.

* * *

Charles Williams sat at the picnic table on his family's campground reading Edith Blake's *On Location On Martha's Vineyard (the making of the movie Jaws)*. He had scraped the last of the beans and wieners off of his paper plate and finished his milk. Milk was the only thing that wasn't better camping than it was at home. Charles loved camping. Eating cereal was cooler because it was the only time he was allowed to get the variety packs that you ate right out of the box. Cooking on the fire pit or on the Coleman stove was definitely cooler than cooking at home in the kitchen. Picnic tables outside were definitely better than sofas inside. He'd also take a tent over his normal bedroom any day. Charles always slept best in a tent. He loved the faintly musty smell of the tent. Even though his Dad always set it up and 'aired it out' a couple of days before they left home, the earthy, canvas scent was always there. The fresh air lulled Charles into a perfect night's sleep every time and waking up early to the sunlight beaming in through the canvas was the best. He would unzip the tent flap (how cool was that sound?) and creep out without waking his parents and choose his cereal in a box. Carefully, he would cut open the side of the box and the wax paper bag inside, splay them open, and get the carton of milk from inside the cooler and pour some on. This was the weakness of camping as Charles saw it. No matter what, the milk was never cold enough. Everything else was fine—great even. His parents didn't notice because his Dad didn't drink milk or eat cereal and his Mom only used milk in her coffee. It was probably a good thing that the milk wasn't that cold if you were only pouring it in your coffee but if you were pouring it on your cereal or drinking a glass, warm milk was not good.

Charles looked up from his book. "Mom?"

"Yes?" Charles' Mom looked up from her book.

"I met a kid at the store when I went and bought my pop," Charles said. "He asked me if I could go and meet him on State Beach tomorrow morning. Can I?"

"I don't see why not. I don't think we have any major plans for tomorrow morning." Charles' Mom looked over at his father. "Do we?"

His Dad looked up from his book. "Do we what?"

"Have plans for tomorrow morning," said his Mom.

Charles' Dad shook his head. "No. Why? Is there something you wanted to do?"

"I met a kid at the store. His family is visiting from Blairstown, New Jersey. We were going to meet up on the beach. He had a really cool bike and he liked my JAWS shirt," said Charles.

His parents both laughed. "Well, if he liked your JAWS shirt, he must be cool right?"

Charles felt his face flush. His parents were teasing him but the truth is that's exactly what he had figured. He hoped Peter liked JAWS as much as he did. "I just thought it would be cool to have a friend to hang out with this summer instead of...well..."

"Being stuck with us all the time?" asked his Mom. "I don't blame you. I think it will be fine. Make sure you wear your watch when you go and be home by twelve-thirty for lunch."

"I promise," said Charles.

*   *   *

Craig jammed his foot onto the brake pedal as hard as he could. His tires grabbed the road but the truck skidded forward out of pure momentum. The girl disappeared from his view and he heard her scream over the howl of burning rubber on pavement. Craig pulled the handle and his door swung open before his truck had come to a complete stop. Barefoot he leapt down and ran around in front, terrified at the thought of what he might find.

The girl was wide-eyed and wedged between the front of his tires and the pavement. His wheels seem to have pulled some of her hair under them but other than that—from what he could see—she looked okay. Miraculously, she looked fine. Craig got down on one knee and reached for her hands. She was shaking. "Ma'am! Are you okay? Jesus Christ! Can you move?" He felt her squeeze his hands in hers and he exhaled. He wasn't even aware that he had been holding his breath but he had been. He was sweating too. His heart throbbed in his chest.

She looked up at him, her eyes open almost to full circles then she blinked. "I'm stuck," she said almost in a whisper.

Craig ran his hands through her hair and found that a good chunk of it was indeed under his front wheel. "Are you hurt otherwise?" he asked. "What's your name?"

"Judie," she said. "No. I don't think so."

"Hi Judie. Try to stretch your legs. If it hurts—stop."

Gingerly, Judie extended first her right leg and then her left. Then she did the same with her arms, one at a time. "I think I'm okay."

"Judie?" a voice called from over Craig's shoulder. He turned to find the source. A tall, wiry man with sandy blonde hair peered down toward the girl under his truck.

"Do you know this guy?" Craig asked Judie.

"Yes, he's my friend," she said. "I'm alright Alan," she said in a marginally louder voice than she had been using. It was the first time that Craig was able to get an idea of what she really sounded like. It was a nice voice.

Craig extended his hand to Alan. Alan hesitated and then shook it. "She seems to be okay, man. Her hair is stuck under my wheel though. I want to do something but I'm going to need your help. Okay?"

"What do you want to do?"

"For starters, crouch down so I can explain to you both what I'm thinking of doing." Craig got back down on one knee.

Alan looked around. A crowd had started to gather. He propped himself against the grill of the Jimmy and got closer to the pavement. Craig had already started his explanation.

"I don't want to take my truck out of park. Your head is too close to the tires. What I want to do is get you to wiggle around a bit, make sure you are fully mobile, and then I will lift the truck up just a bit and you're going to roll forward while your buddy here pulls you forward as hard as he can. Got it?"

"*Buddy?*" Alan said. "My name is Alan, *buddy.*"

Craig looked at Alan quizzically and then nodded. "Nice to meet you Alan. I'm Craig. Can we do this later? Can you roll Judie forward so we can get her out from under my truck?"

"Of course," said Alan.

Craig reached out for Judie's hands once more and took her hands in his. "Will that be okay, Judie?"

"I can do it," she said.

"Okay," said Craig. "Give us a little wiggle. Let your body know that it's about to move and move fast. It might not be too happy with you right now." He smiled at her. She smiled back.

Judie moved her feet and then her legs. She rolled her hips as much as she could and shrugged her shoulders a few times. "Okay," she said. "I'm ready."

Craig turned toward Alan. Alan was glaring at him but Craig ignored it. "Okay, Alan. Place one hand on her shoulder and one hand on her hip. As soon as you see that wheel start to lift even a little pull her out." Craig stood up and grabbed the front of the wheel well and the inner fender, dropped to a squat position, and lifted with his whole body. Every muscle in his back, legs, and glutes bulged as he began to straighten lifting the truck with him. Out of the corner of his eye he saw a flash of movement.

Alan yelled, *"She's clear!"*

Craig strained to see over the truck and when he saw Judie sit up, he dropped the truck. The truck landed its weight back onto the front wheel and bounced. Craig straightened up and exhaled audibly. There was a cheer from the crowd. Craig stepped around to Judie and crouched beside her once more. "Can you stand?"

"Oh sure, really, I'm fine!" Judie started to get to her feet and her legs wobbled beneath her. "Oh! Maybe I'm not fine."

"Alan can you go into Giordano's and get her a water?" asked Craig. "I'll carry her to the bench in front."

"Yeah...okay," Alan said. He stood up and pushed through the crowd toward the restaurant.

Craig slid one arm under Judie's knees and wrapped the other around her shoulders. He stood up with considerably less effort than he had with the truck in his arms.

"A little lighter than the truck, huh?" Judie smiled at him.

"Just a tad." Craig looked her in the eye and smiled. She was the kind of girl The Beach Boys would sing about.

5

Peter woke up to the soft whirring of the fan in his bedroom window. Beyond the fan, he could hear birds chirping in the trees surrounding the house. Lying on his back, he stared up at the peaked ceiling. The ceiling didn't look like the ceilings they had back in the city or like any of the ceilings he had ever seen in a hotel either. It looked like they were just boards painted white and the other side of those same boards was the roof. There was no insulation, no wall stuff. He couldn't remember what that was called—the stuff they made walls out of. Whatever it was, it was missing. It was like someone built the outside of the house but didn't bother finishing the inside. The walls were the same. Peter wondered if all of the cottages in Wesleyan Grove were like that. Did people live in them year round? There was no way anyone could live in a house like this all year. It would be freezing in the winter…wouldn't it? It must be. It certainly wasn't helping to keep the summer heat out, that's for sure. Back home Peter slept in pyjamas but he couldn't do that here. Granted in New Jersey, his parents had an air conditioner in their bedroom window and that kept the second floor of their house pretty cool, good enough for sleeping anyway. At home, he even slept under the covers sometimes in summer—not here though. It was far too hot for covers in this bedroom. Regardless of the heat, Peter had still slept with a sheet over him. Sleeping completely uncovered was scary somehow. He didn't feel safe which was kind of ridiculous but it just wasn't comfortable. He had also slept wearing only his underwear. It was just too hot.

Peter pulled back the sheet and stepped out of bed onto the grey wood floor. The wood felt slightly cool under his feet. He had almost expected it to be hot to the touch. He padded his way to his suitcase, which sat flipped open on the only chair in the room. He pulled out his blue bathing suit and his Boston T-shirt. He didn't really know any songs by Boston but he liked the yellow and red spaceship in the picture and he liked that the band was called Boston. He had been to Boston the city with his parents lots of times and it was always fun. That's where his Dad had bought him the shirt. He pulled on his clothes and ran down the narrow staircase for breakfast.

The house was quiet. "Mom?" called Peter. There was no answer.

Peter walked over to the kitchen and pulled himself up onto the countertop. He reached into the cupboard over the sink and got out an orange bowl. There was a collection of bowls and cups in orange, yellow, and green. They were the same as the ones his grandparents had at the cottage. They had made his mother laugh when she saw them. She called them "Melamine" and said everyone had them when she was Peter's age. Apparently, a lot of families had them because they were hard to break. That was their big selling feature— you couldn't break them. Peter wanted to test that theory by smashing one to the ground. It was so tempting. How could a bowl or a cup not break? That was impossible, wasn't it? He jumped down and put the bowl on the table. Peter pulled open the fridge and took out the milk carton and the box of Cocoa Krispies that he had talked his parents into buying at Reliable Market in Oak Bluffs. His Dad said he didn't have "a snowball's chance in hell" of getting them at home but they were on Martha's Vineyard and if Peter wanted "to eat that junk for breakfast", his Dad wasn't going to stop him.

Peter noticed that even though they had just bought it yesterday, the box was already open and a good portion was missing. Clearly, Peter wasn't the only one eating "that junk" for breakfast. He filled the bowl until it was almost overflowing and then added as much milk as possible. Armed with a spoon from one of the drawers, he sat down at the round kitchen table and dug in.

* * *

Judie woke up with a throbbing headache. She started to open her eyes but decided against it. She started to bring her hand up to shade her face from the morning sun shining through her thin yellow curtains but when she tried, she decided against that too. Her arm and shoulder screamed at her when she moved them. *What the hell have I done to myself?* She thought. Then she remembered her fall on Lake Avenue and her near death experience under the wheel of the truck. She must have fallen a lot harder than she realised. That poor guy. What was his name? Craig? He had felt awful. She had his phone number somewhere. He told her to call him if she needed anything. He had even said that his Dad was a doctor. If she needed one, he would help her out. Judie tried to think through their entire conversation. The whole scene had been entirely her fault.

Had she told him that? She had tripped and fallen in front of his truck. She hoped he didn't think that he had hit her. Did he think that? That would certainly explain his doting on her like he had. Did she tell him that she had tripped over her own two feet and landed smack on the pavement? What an idiot. She and Alan had been having such a good day too. The sailing had been beautiful. Alan had not taken to Craig though. Even in her state, that much had been obvious. Judie didn't know what his problem was. The guy had been so nice. Maybe Alan had just been freaked out by the entire situation. Judie could totally see that Alan had been pissed that she hadn't sailed back with him but he must have understood that it made more sense for Craig to drive her home in his truck. He really hadn't liked it though. Judie didn't blame him. She was going to have to make some apologies. First, she was going to have to apologise to Craig and make sure that he knew that he hadn't hit her—she had tripped. He had to know that. Judie *needed* for him to know that. Second, she was going to apologise to Alan for screwing up their beautiful day. If she had just gone back to the Warlock like Alan had clearly wanted to, none of this would have happened. Before any of that, she needed a couple of Aspirins and some water. That was going to take some doing.

* * *

Craig woke up in the apartment above his parents' carriage house in Katama. The day had just begun but he could tell already that it was going to be a scorcher. He rolled over and checked his watch. It was early enough that he had time to go for a swim on South Beach, then breakfast at dock Street before work. He needed to clear his head. A swim would do it.

The accident the day before had really rattled him and he hadn't slept very well because of it. He had never hit anyone or anything before—not even a deer or a rabbit! Nothing! The memory of watching the girl disappear beneath the hood of his truck came back to him and he stopped breathing for a moment. For a split second, he wasn't sure if he was going to throw up or not. He had puked the night before. As soon as he had the girl home in her pink gingerbread cottage, Craig had driven away, stopped the truck on Beach Road, and vomited. There were people all around but he hadn't given a rat's ass. Tanned young guy with long hair and almost naked—they probably all thought he was drunk. Let them think it. He'd rather that got around the island than the fact that he had almost killed a beautiful young girl by crushing her skull onto Lake Avenue. Confident that he was not going to be sick, Craig sat up,

75

swung his legs out of the bed, and stood up. The cut-off shorts from the day before were lying on the floor. He scooped them up and slipped them back on. Remembering that the rest of his gear was still in the truck, Craig picked his keys up off his nightstand. He was headed for the beach. *Judie...* he thought. *Her name was Judie.*

His phone rang.

*　　*　　*

Alan stepped off of the On Time ferry and onto Chappaquiddick. He walked down to the beach on the harbour side where he kept his dinghy. There were five or six dinghies lying in the sand, flipped over, their fibreglass hulls bleached out from the sun. That always made Alan chuckle. It was pretty ironic really, the bottom of a boat being bleached by the sun but they were—each and every one of them. Alan's was red—the hull bleached to a baby pink—and painted free hand across her stern was *Seas The Day*. Alan had painted it himself about ten years ago when his parents had first given him the dinghy for rowing around the Vineyard. He had spent long days rowing up and down State Beach and rowing through Edgartown Harbor and Vineyard Haven Harbor. There had been one point when he thought that he could row all the way around the island but he had started out on Chappaquiddick and by the time he got around to Wasque he was fighting serious currents that almost swept him out to sea. He had been lucky to make it back to shore. His back and shoulders still ached at the memory. That had been the last time he had tried anything quite so foolish—at least until recently.

Alan was starting to think that pursuing Judie was just as foolish. He really thought that they had a good thing going until yesterday. That Craig guy almost killing her should have pushed Judie even closer into Alan's arms. Shouldn't it? It didn't. She had gone home with him or rather she had decided to let Craig drive her home instead of going back home with Alan in his sailboat. Yes, it had been a scary experience but again—wouldn't that push her toward him if she was into him? *She just met that guy!* Not to mention the fact that he was practically naked. He had jumped out of his truck wearing denim shorts that barely contained his junk. Then he started showing off by lifting the truck off the road. There were enough of them there to roll it back from Judie's head. He didn't have to lift the goddamn truck off the road. Who does that? Assholes with their brains in their goddamn biceps, that's who. He did get her out though. Alan had to admit that much. Is that why he was so pissed? Alan hadn't even seen what happened exactly. He thought she was walking out onto the road and he tried to stop her. Next thing he knew she was down and the truck was practically on top of her. He froze on the spot. He had been terrified. Alan thought Judie's skull had been crushed under the wheel of the Jimmy! Probably everyone else on the corner did too. Then Craig had jumped out of the truck and was down there at Judie's side before Alan could even figure out what to do. Alan just remembered looking down at this muscular tanned back and head of feathered hair kneeling over Judie and holding her hands. *He was holding her hands for Christ's sake!* Craig was holding her hands and Alan just stood there. Then he finally called out to her and when he did, clear as day, he heard Judie tell Craig that Alan was her "friend". That was it. That's what was really bugging him. That's what was really sticking in his craw. Judie told this muscle bound model type with the hair and the teeth and the new truck that he, Alan, was just her friend and it had knocked the wind out of his sails.

Alan flipped *Seas The Day* upright and picked up the two oars that were lying underneath her and tossed them into the boat. Without even thinking about it—a decade of seamanship under his belt—Alan grabbed her bowline and dragged her across the beach to the water. He pushed her afloat and with a single step, he was in and sitting on the bench. *Seas The Day* took a moment to adjust to the new weight and then glided gently toward the centre of the harbour. Alan picked up his oars, fixed them in the oarlocks and started rowing out to Warlock's mooring. He needed to think. Alan always did his best thinking on Warlock.

*   *   *

Peter eased his Sting-Ray to a stop on the JAWS Bridge using both brake handles. He swung his leg over the bike, walked it over to the Oak bluffs end of the bridge, and leaned it up against the Edgartown sign. Like the day before, he was loaded down with binoculars, and his camera case slung over his shoulder. Making his way around the traffic barrier, Peter followed the sandy path along the large breakwater that ran out into Vineyard Sound and made up the south end of State Beach. There was another beach on the other side of the bridge, on the Edgartown side, but Peter didn't know what that was called. Maybe it was State Beach too. It didn't matter. What interested him was this side of the beach.

Peter undid the clasp on his camera case and pulled out a well-worn paperback. In an elaborate font across a sepia photograph was written *on Location..... on Martha's Vineyard (the making of the movie Jaws) by Edith Blake*. Peter had thumbed through this book hundreds of times. He had propped it open on the floor and drawn pictures based on the photographs Edith Blake had taken that were featured in this book. He had read it several times—sometimes all the way through and sometimes just his favourite parts. He hadn't seen the movie yet but he could tell from photos in the book that a lot of it had been filmed right here on this beach. He wanted to see if he could figure out where and maybe get some pictures. Figuring out exactly where the filming had taken place using small black and white photos in a paperback was going to be tough—especially considering that the beach tents and food stands were no longer there. According to the book they were just props. They were never there in real life. Still, Peter was standing on one of the beaches in JAWS and that was pretty cool. He turned and looked out to sea. The water sparkled under the morning sun. It was still kind of a yellow gold out by the horizon but closer to shore, the water was as blue as Peter had ever seen it. Were there really great whites out there? Were they really lurking off the beaches waiting for him to jump in and go for a swim? Peter looked down the beach and saw a woman swimming alone. Wasn't she scared? She must know about JAWS. Everyone knew about JAWS! Still, she swam casually out to sea, away from the safety of the shore. She was the only other person on the beach. The two of them were alone. What would Peter do if she suddenly started screaming? What could Peter do if the ocean turned red, if it filled with blood? Nothing. There was nothing he could do. He would have to stand there and watch her get torn apart by a great white that he couldn't even see. An enormous fish hidden beneath the surface. Somehow, that made it even scarier. Peter watched her like a hawk. He didn't want to take his eyes off of her. He wanted to make sure she was okay at all times. If he lost sight of her, if he couldn't see her, Peter would never stop wondering what had happened to her.

"Hi!" said a voice behind him.

Peter screamed and jumped. He turned around to see Charles standing behind him in the same JAWS t-shirt that he had been wearing when they had met the day before.

"Jeez!!" said Charles. "Jumpy, are you? I didn't mean to scare you."

Peter caught his breath and started to laugh. "No, it's not your fault. I was watching that lady swimming and I kinda freaked myself out. It's stupid."

"You were thinking about sharks?" asked Charles.

Peter looked at him in astonishment. "Yeah!" he said. "How did you know?"

Charles shrugged. "I did the same thing yesterday when I was here with my folks. Well, we were further down on the Inkwell but every time I went swimming, I was always thinking about sharks. Well, actually, I was thinking about

81

that shark in particular." Charles pointed to the book in Peter's hand. "Stupid, right? I would picture that shark."

"Do you have this book?" asked Peter.

Charles nodded. "It's my favourite. I have Carl Gottlieb's book too. It's cool but the pictures in Edith Blake's book are way cooler."

"I know!" Peter handed the book to Charles. "Which picture is your favourite?"

Charles took the book. "Well, it has to be either *The Star* or that one at the beginning of chapter sixteen. What's it called?"

"Out In A Blaze Of Glory!" Peter exclaimed. He couldn't contain his excitement.

"That's it!" Charles grinned. "I love that one."

"I bet I know why," Peter said.

"Why?" Charles challenged.

"Because you like how big the shark looks next to that guy's head!" Peter said.

Charles started to laugh. "You're right! Oh my god, I can't believe you knew that!"

"I love it for the same reason," Peter said. "Hey, I was coming here this morning to try and take some pictures like the ones from this book..." Peter's voice lowered and he looked down at his feet in the sand. "I haven't seen the movie yet," he admitted.

"I haven't either," said Charles. "My parents won't let me."

Peter brightened. "Really? Mine neither. Well, I thought with my new camera that my Nana gave me, we could try and take some pictures like the book. I mean, we haven't seen JAWS but we know it was filmed here on this beach and that's still cool, right?"

"Absolutely!" said Charles.

"Great! Why don't you pick the first photo?" Peter handed the book back to Charles again and the two of them thumbed through, looking for the perfect picture to replicate. Peter could barely stand still. With Charles as his co-conspirator, this vacation was going to be the best one ever.

6

Craig Upland drove over the JAWS Bridge in the direction of Wesleyan Grove. He remembered exactly where Judie was staying. Her house was hard to miss—it was bright pink. A few different shades of pink but all pink, all over. It was even surrounded by rhododendron bushes covered in bright pink blooms. The house looked like something out of a fairy tale. All of the Oak Bluffs gingerbread cottages had that feel. At any moment you could imagine Hansel and Gretel walking up and talking a bite out of any one of them. Craig had grown up on Martha's Vineyard but he had never gotten used to them. He doubted that anyone ever did. There was nothing else quite like it, at least no place that he had ever seen.

As he drove by State Beach, Craig looked out over the Atlantic. It was blue, sparkling, and calm. It would have been a perfect morning for a swim. He really wanted to dive in and clear his head but when Judie had called, it had refigured his priorities. Not only did he want to make sure she was okay—it wasn't everyday that he almost ran over someone's skull with his truck—there was something about this girl. Craig knew that he didn't want to say goodbye to her just yet. State Beach was virtually empty. There were a couple of kids running around but other than that—no one. Maybe after he had talked to Judie, he could still get his swim in. He didn't need a lot of time, just enough to dive in and completely submerge himself in the bracing salt water. The ocean had restorative powers that human beings still didn't understand. Of that, he was sure.

Craig passed Ocean Park and turned off of Seaview Avenue onto Lake Avenue. He shuddered. Goosebumps covered his tanned skin making the hair on his chest stand up. The scene of the crime, so to speak. As he passed the foot of Circuit Avenue, Craig turned on the radio and tried not to think about it. Steve Miller was singing *Fly Like An Eagle.* Good tune. That was exactly what Craig wanted to do.

85

He wanted to get away; he wanted to fly like an eagle. He turned it up.

*   *   *

Judie made her way down the staircase with a mild limp. She was in pain. She had found some Aspirin in her medicine cabinet upstairs and taken a couple but they hadn't kicked in yet. She didn't know what she needed but she needed something. Her head hurt. No surprise there. When she had gone to the bathroom for the Aspirin she had discovered a pretty good bruise on the left side of her face. It indicated a hard enough bounce off the pavement to give anyone a headache. Funny, she didn't remember her head hitting the ground. She thought that she had successfully blocked her head with her hands. The heels of which were pretty scuffed up. Clearly she did hit her head though. Is it possible that she had a concussion? Didn't they say that you shouldn't go to sleep if you're concussed? Well, too late for that now. It was kind of like she was hungover. Right down to waking up in the same clothes she had been wearing the day before—bikini top and cut-offs. She had slept remarkably well considering all of her aches and pains this morning.

Judie had called Craig from bed. She hadn't planned on seeing him—or anyone else for that matter—that day but he had offered to come by and check on her before she even got to the reason she was calling. She thought that was very thoughtful of him. Perhaps it would be a conversation better had in person. He had dropped her off the day before so he knew where she lived. It's not like Edgartown was all that far away either. Ten minute drive? It had forced Judie to get up anyway. She had washed her face with cold water and that had felt really good. She would be doing that again before the morning was over that was for sure. Maybe after Craig left, she would have a cool shower. She wished that her house had an outdoor shower but it didn't. Most of the houses on Martha's Vineyard did but the cottages were pretty short on property. They had been built almost on top of each other. If Judie started showering outside, the kid next store would have to hold a textbook in front of his crotch all summer. The thought made her chuckle to herself. *You're thinking about giving twelve-year-old boys boners—exactly how hard did you hit your head, you pervert?*

The rumble of a truck engine got louder and louder out front before cutting out. It had to be Craig. Judie walked across the living room and opened the front door. The house was pure white on the inside but the outside was all pink. When the door opened, the hue of light in the front room changed from a cool sky to that of a young hydrangea. Judie stepped out onto the porch and watched as Craig stepped down out of the truck.

"Hey," she said.

Craig looked up at her. He did nothing to conceal his surprise. "Whoa!"

"Normally," she said. "I'd say, you should see the other guy."

Craig nodded and smiled. "But I am the other guy."

"Exactly," Judie said.

"Do I ask how you're feeling?" asked Craig.

Judie shrugged gingerly. "You can if you like."

Craig reached out and lifted her hair from her face. "Ouch," he said. "Is that your only bruise?"

"I think so," she said. "I'm not all that sure."

"Let's have a look," Craig said. "C'mon—arms out."

Judie straightened her arms out to the side and didn't fight when Craig started to slowly turn her all the way around.

"Your knees are scratched up," he said. Once she had turned completely around, Craig got up on the porch and gently brushed through her hair around her crown.

"I have a headache," she said.

"I'm not surprised," said Craig. "Your head is pretty red back here. It's not swollen or anything—just red."

"Is that good?" Judie asked.

"Not swollen is always good when you're talking about your skull." Craig cupped her head gently in his hands and then held the back of his hand to her forehead. "You don't have a fever and you don't sound confused." He walked around in front of her.

"You sound like a doctor's son," Judie said with a smile.

"Christ, I hope not," Craig said. "Do I sound like that much of an asshole?"

Judie blushed. "That's not what I meant."

Craig looked her in the eye and then turned away. This time it was his turn to blush. "I know you didn't. I'm sorry. That was a stupid thing to say." He was anxious to change the subject. "Are you nauseous at all?"

Judie shook her head. "Not in the slightest. I just feel like crap. Ya know? I feel like I just need a really good shower. I'm sure I'll be fine."

"You want to go swimming?" he asked.

"What?" she asked.

"Swimming," he repeated. "You can swim, right? Nothing fixes me up better than a swim in the ocean. That's where I was headed when you called me. I was going to go to South Beach but I can just drive us over to State Beach instead. We're two minutes away. You're already dressed for it."

Judie smiled broadly for the first time that day. "You're on."

* * *

Charles flipped through the book until he came to chapter nine, On The Beach. "These could have been taken anywhere along here," he said. "It's too bad that those cabanas weren't still here or the hot dog stands. That would be really cool."

"Do you think they were put here just for the movie? Like props?"

Charles nodded. "Definitely," he said. "But look at this picture." He handed the book over to Peter. The photo was mostly of crew and bit players but in the distance was the JAWS Bridge. That was still there. Using the bridge as a marker, they could definitely recreate the picture in the book.

"That one is perfect!" exclaimed Peter. "Let me get out my camera."

Charles stepped back and watched as Peter walked around in the sand, the camera viewfinder held up to his eye, trying to find the proper angle for the shot. Charles heard the slam of a car door and looked up to see a young couple stepping out of a blue and white truck on the Oak Bluffs end of the bridge. In fact, they were right in front of where Peter had left his bike. They disappeared beyond the dunes and Charles focussed on his new friend once again.

"There!" said Peter. "Got it!"

Charles turned and looked up the beach toward Oak Bluffs. "You could just take some photos looking up the beach. I mean, we don't know exactly where they were filming but it's right around here somewhere. You'll totally get the right spots if we climb up on the rocks here and snap some beach pics." Charles looked at Peter. "Don't you think?"

Charles and Peter both climbed up onto the breakwater that began under the JAWS Bridge and jutted out past the end of the beach and into the water.

Peter shrugged. "Probably, right?" He lifted his camera into position.

Charles raised his hand to block the sun and looked down the beach. The young couple from the truck were the only two on the beach.

* * *

Alan tightened the cover on his sail. The forecast wasn't the greatest and he thought that he would take this opportunity to get Warlock ready. A landlubber wouldn't know it from the current conditions. The water was calm and the sun was shining. It had been a beautiful sunrise too; however, the sky had been spattered with pinks and reds. There was a lot to be said for the old adage, *'Red at night, sailor's delight! Red at morning, sailor's warning!'* Alan and his family put a lot of stock in those old adages. Besides, there was a fair wind picking up and winds always meant change. A storm was coming.

Preparing the boat gave him something else to think about besides Judie and Craig. He had probably expended too much energy on them as it was. Judie didn't even know Craig anyway! Hadn't she spent the whole summer with him? Hadn't it been Alan that she had been flirting with just before the accident? Surely, he was overreacting. "He's my friend," she had said. What had he expected her to say? Boyfriend? He wasn't her boyfriend. They had been spending more and more time together and neither one of them had ever classified their relationship—*they sure as hell hadn't had sex or even come close!* So what the hell did he expect from her?

Alan stepped down into the Warlock's cockpit and surveyed his handiwork. The sail was secure, the cushions were all stowed in the cabin, and she was tied tightly to her mooring. He'd done as much as he could do here. Alan hopped down into his dinghy with the effortlessness that can only come from a life spent on the ocean. He untied it from Warlock and started rowing toward Chappaquiddick.

Why didn't he go over there? Judie had been through a lot. Why didn't he stop at Dock Street Coffee Shop, pick up a couple of coffees and breakfast sandwiches and head over to her place in Wesleyan Grove? As soon as he saw her, he would feel better. The two of them could sit together, have breakfast, and have a good laugh over yesterday's goings on. That was the best idea he had come up with ever since all of this began. Alan took a deep breath. He could feel some of the tension leave his body. He felt better already.

* * *

Judie walked stiffly over the sand of State Beach. She was certainly having an easier time of it than she had coming down the stairs less than an hour ago. She didn't know whether it was the Aspirin kicking in, the sea air, or just moving around, but whatever it was, she was definitely on the mend. Stepping down out of the truck hadn't been all that easy but it had been okay. Her hips were creaking and her back was stiff. She had expected her feet to hurt with each step but they didn't. Even when she had followed Craig over the uneven dunes to get to the flatter, smoother beach, they had been okay. Judie lifted her arms up and gently lifted her hair with her hands. She could feel the sensitive areas of her scalp where her hair had been wrenched under Craig's truck less than twenty-four hours ago. There was a throbbing warning as she moved her hair, but it was manageable. Judie raised her elbows as high as she could in a delicate stretch. It hurt but it felt good.

Craig turned around and looked at her. "You alright?"

The sun was low behind him and the light made his hair look like spun gold. She nodded.

"Alright," he said. "Let's go!" Craig turned and ran directly into the water. When he was knee deep, he lifted his arms and dove beneath the surface. The ocean wrapped around him in a white froth as he disappeared from sight.

Judie could tell from the way her muscles felt that there was no way she could jump in with such reckless abandon. Reckless abandon was how she had ended up so banged up. Although, it was also how she had met Craig and she didn't think that was such a bad thing.

Slowly, she waded into the ocean. The shallows lapped at her feet and then her ankles, coolly welcoming her in. The deeper she got, the better she felt. The salt water stung her knees at first but only for a second. The cold washed away her aches and pains almost instantly. Craig had been right—this was exactly what she needed. Once the water began to lap at her shorts, Judie lifted her arms, brought them together, took a deep breath, and dove.

The sea accepted her without question. All at once, it covered her stomach, her breasts, her shoulders, and face. She felt the ocean weave its way through her hair, and press her injuries with cold relief. Blindly, she kicked herself deeper before pushing against the water in a breaststroke. She had expected the effort to be met with screaming, aching muscles but instead she felt nothing but smooth salty exhilaration. She exhaled through her nose and when she had no more air to give, Judie came up and broke the surface. Her nervous system was overwhelmed with the sudden change. She didn't know how to react, so she laughed.

"Good, right?" she heard Craig's deep voice beside her.

Judie opened her eyes and turned toward him. "You didn't hit me."

Craig's smile softened. "What?"

"Yesterday," she said. "With your truck. You didn't hit me. I wasn't paying attention. I tripped and fell. Your quick reaction saved my life. I needed you to know that. That's why I called this morning. You seem like a really nice guy— you were so thoughtful and attentive yesterday while I was under your wheel. You made me feel so much better—I just really needed you to know that you didn't hit me. It wasn't your fault." Judie could feel her eyes welling up. She wasn't sure why. She didn't know whether it was shame, embarrassment, or just nerves in general. She started swimming toward shore. "I'm sorry."

"Hey!" Craig called after her.

Judie swam until she got close enough to shore to walk out onto the beach. She slicked her hair back with her hands and noticed that even that brief swim had increased her mobility tenfold. Her joints didn't ache and her head didn't hurt. Her headache was gone. One brief swim had brought on a lot of changes. Judie was crying. She wiped her eyes with the back of her wrist, her wet wrist. She searched the beach for the towel that she knew she hadn't brought. God, why was she crying? It had come out of nowhere.

Craig came out of the water and turned her to face him. "I'll be right back. I've got towels in the truck." He sprinted over the sand dunes and in a moment, Judie could hear the door of the truck being slammed shut.

Christ, she felt like an idiot. What Craig must think of her. Yesterday he thought he hit her with his truck and he takes her through it like a gentleman, then this morning he shows up at her house to see if she is okay, only to find out that she had tripped and fallen out into the street and now she was blubbering like a child in front of him on the beach. Judie felt a bubble of snot forming under her nose and quickly wiped it away just as Craig reappeared on the beach.

"Here," he said and wrapped a large navy blue towel over her shoulders.

"Thanks," she said. "I don't know why I'm crying."

"You don't?" asked Craig. "You almost got run over by a truck yesterday in downtown Oak Bluffs! I don't think you have really had enough time to process that information. I mean, you went straight home to bed last night. You were almost asleep before I left. You were wiped out. Now, I dragged you out of bed and out of the house, and threw you in the ocean!" Craig chuckled sardonically. "You've been through a lot. Let yourself go through it."

Judie looked up at him. He really was handsome. "You've been through a lot too. How come you're not bawling your eyes out on the beach?"

Craig smiled softly. "I've already done my processing." He paused. Then he said, "I had to stop driving and puke on the side of the road last night after I dropped you home."

"You did?"

Craig nodded. "Yup. Right over there." Craig pointed over her head toward the truck and the bridge. "In fact, I can prove it to you right now if the seagulls haven't eaten it all."

"Eww!" Judie grimaced and laughed. "That's disgusting!"

Craig laughed with her. He reached out and with both arms, he pulled her in toward his chest. Judie all but disappeared against him. "I'm really glad I didn't hit you."

* * *

Alan Quaid drove up Main Street Edgartown in his black Firebird and when the road split into Edgartown Vineyard Haven Road on the left and Beach Road on the right, he steered right. The traffic was still minimal. The occasional car passed him coming down from Oak Bluffs but just a few. It was shaping up to be a beautiful day. Maybe they wouldn't get the storm after all. Maybe it would skip the Vineyard altogether and Nantucket would get the brunt of it. That had certainly happened in the past. Sometimes, Alan was amazed that Nantucket was still there. It was a very small island that had been through a lot. It was hard to believe that all of those fishing shacks and houses that were built right on the harbour hadn't been washed right out into the sound. Crazy. Still, they had been there for four hundred years and they probably would be for another four hundred. As Alan passed Bend-In-The-Road Beach, the road straightened out. The ocean was in full view. It was calm. Shallow waves rolled in and lapped at the shore with an almost orchestral timing.

    Alan looked down at the passenger seat. He smiled. There were two white paper coffee cups with plastic lids and two tinfoil wrapped sandwiches balanced snugly in the centre of the red vinyl seat. Steam was still leaking out of the coffee cups. That was good. He wanted everything to still be hot when he got to Judie's. Judie had gone through a lot yesterday and admittedly he hadn't been the biggest help. He should have jumped right in when she fell but Alan thought—as did everyone else on the corner—that she was a goner! He froze. He had fully expected to watch her skin and skull explode into a red frothy pulp like that time his cousin had hit a watermelon with a baseball bat. He could still hear that crunch and pop and that was exactly what he had expected to hear again—*crunch! Pop!*—but he hadn't. Craig had stopped his truck just in the nick of time. Judie had tripped and fallen right out in front of Craig's truck and he had stopped just before she had been crushed under his wheel. When he looked at it that way, he actually owed Craig a thank you. He hadn't said thank you. In fact, he hadn't said anything complimentary at all. Immediately, Alan had felt threatened by Craig. There was no question that Craig was good-looking anyone could see that. It would be ridiculous to try and deny it but that wasn't it. Alan wasn't bad looking either. Hadn't Judie told him that he looked like Robert Redford yesterday morning? That wasn't insulting by any means. No, it wasn't Craig's looks that had Alan's back up. It was something else.

When Judie had fallen in front of the truck, Alan froze but Craig leapt into action. He got right down by Judie, as close as he could. He had taken her hands in his. Instinctively, Craig knew exactly what to do to make Judie feel better. Alan didn't.

Alan wasn't smiling anymore. His face wasn't even relaxed and expressionless. Alan could feel the muscles in his face were tense and his mouth scowling. He had to let it go. He had to stop comparing himself to that Craig guy and move on. Yesterday was an accident. It didn't have to change anything between Judie and himself. Judie would probably be a little freaked out now but Alan would be there for her and they would move on. Neither one of them had ever seen Craig before and it was very unlikely that they would ever see him again.

As Alan got closer to the JAWS Bridge, the sun brightened. He reached over to the glove box and pulled out his sunglasses. When he straightened in his seat and fixed his eyes back on the road, Alan felt all of the blood drain from his face. His arms went cold. Alan's jaw slackened. Parked right at the end of the bridge, beside a red kid's bike, was Craig's truck.

    Alan slowed. His eyes scanned the road but there was no sign of Craig. The Firebird crawled across the bridge. The wood rattled under his tires. Craig strained in his seat to look over the dunes to the beach. There were two kids hopping around on the rocks but they were the only ones— There he was. Craig was standing on the beach with a girl in his arms in a towel. *Figures*, Alan thought. *That guy probably had dozens of them.* As Alan drove past, the girl pulled away and it was Judie. There was no mistaking her. His Judie was on the beach with Craig. Alan screeched his car to a halt. The two coffees tipped forward with the jolt and steaming creamy brown liquid shot across the passenger seat and on to the floor.

7

Judie pulled away from Craig. She pulled the towel from her shoulders and tossed it at him. He caught it and smiled. She was feeling much better. She returned the smile. "Are you ready for another swim?"

Craig looked out at the beckoning ocean. "I really should be going. I need to get to work. I can drive you home though."

"Just one more quick dip. Okay?" she asked.

"Well..."

"C'mon! You know what they say about the last one in!" Judie pushed off into a run, but stumbled. She modified her gate and continued to the water. With as much strength as she could muster, Judie propelled herself into Vineyard Sound. She bent her arms and used her body to thrust her way in deeper. When she was waist deep, she dove in.

Craig laughed and called after her, "Well you feel a lot better!"

"Yeah," said a voice behind him. "I wonder why."

* * *

Peter clicked the shutter and lowered his camera. Instinctively, he wound the film. He squinted to try and get a better view of what was happening down the beach.

"What's the matter?" asked Charles.

Peter pointed. "That guy down there...he just punched that other guy."

Charles turned and looked in the direction Peter was pointing. "What guy?"

"That big muscle guy in the shorts," said Peter.

"He hit that skinny guy? Not much of a fair fight, I'd say," said Charles.

"No," said Peter. "The skinny guy hit the big guy!"

"Seriously?" Charles rolled his eyes. "That wasn't very smart. Where did he hit him?"

"In the face. Like, on the chin," Peter said.

"Wow. And he's still standing?"

Peter nodded.

"Probably not for long."

The two boys stood on the beach transfixed by the goings on less than twenty yards away. Peter's stomach had butterflies. He didn't like it when people hit each other, he never had. On TV it was okay because he knew it was all fake but in real life, it wasn't exactly scary but it felt like it was. He didn't like it. He thought for sure the big guy was going to knock the skinny guy's block off. Peter was expecting to see the little guy go flying through the air and land on his back like something out of a cartoon but it didn't happen. He could hear that they were yelling but he couldn't make out what they were saying. Then there was another voice. A girl's voice.

"Oh, it's them," said Charles.

"Who, them?" asked Peter.

"Well, I don't really know. I just saw the big guy and the girl get out of their truck earlier over there by your bike. They were alone. I saw them on the beach like they were going swimming. It was just the two of them though—there was no skinny guy."

"She kinda looks familiar," said Peter. "I don't know why though."

"Well, if the big guy was going to hit the other guy, he would have done it by now. Don't you think?" asked Charles.

Peter nodded.

*   *   *

"What the hell is your problem, man?" Craig rubbed at his chin. The little son of a bitch had just clocked him. *Clocked him!* Was he high? If Craig wanted to, he could snap the guy's neck with one arm tied behind his back. "You're lucky I don't beat the living shit out of you, here and now!"

"I saw you!" Alan said. "I saw you with your arms all over her. Just now!"

"Look, I don't know what you think you saw but you got it all wrong, man. Not that I particularly like the idea of having to explain myself to total strangers who think it's okay to run up the beach and punch me in the face." Craig stretched his mouth and moved it from side to side. Then he cracked his jaw. He was fine. He'd done worse to himself slipping in the shower. It was kind of funny really.

"*What?*" Judie waded out of the water and Craig gave her the towel again. "*You did what?*"

"Yeah," said Craig. "Your boyfriend here went into some sort of jealous tantrum and punched me across the goddamn chin."

"*Alan what the hell did you do that for?*" Judie demanded.

Alan stared at Craig and Judie blankly. He didn't say anything.

"You punched him?" Judie repeated. "Since when do you go around punching people?" Judie looked Craig up and down. "Especially one that looks like this? You're damned lucky you're not eating sand right now." Judie turned and looked at Craig's face. "Are you okay, Craig?" She lifted her hand gently to Craig's chin.

Craig laughed. "Oh hell, yeah. I'm fine," he said. "I just think this has been a really weird twenty-four hours and everyone is wound really tight. Alan saw us hugging when he was driving by and he kinda freaked out—that's all. I probably would have done the same thing if I had been driving by and saw my girl wrapped in a towel with some guy on the beach. I get it." Craig extended his hand to shake Alan's. "Let's forget the whole thing. Just don't hit me again, alright? Next time, I hit back."

"I'm not Alan's girl," said Judie.

"You're not?" asked Craig. He retracted his hand before Alan could take it. "*Then what the Christ, man?*"

Craig could feel his blood pressure going up. To have some asshole hit him over his girlfriend was one thing but to be hit for no reason? His patience was wearing thin.

"I'm not," Judie repeated. "Am I, Alan?"

Alan looked from Judie to Craig and back again. His face was flush. "No," he said. "You're not my girlfriend," he spoke softly. "We're just good friends."

"Alan, you owe Craig an apology. Seriously," Judie said.

"I'm sorry, Craig. I don't know what I was thinking. I shouldn't have hit you. That's not me. I've never hit anyone before."

Craig spoke but in a voice much deeper than before. There was a menace about him. All three of them could feel the energy on the beach change. Judie stepped back. Craig's face reddened and he seemed to swell in size from head to toe. He fixed his eyes on Alan and for the moment he saw nothing else. The morning light was gone. Craig saw only Alan and darkness. "That's fine. As I said, we've all been through a lot. But listen to me and listen good—you touch me again and I'll break off your goddamn fingers. Judie, I'll call you later." Craig walked toward his truck without looking back or saying another word.

* * *

Charles lifted his head from Edith Blake's book and watched the big man walk off the beach. It wasn't the same casual walk that he had when he got there. When he and the girl had arrived to the beach, they had been laughing and walking like they didn't want to be anywhere else. They had all the time in the world. This was a different walk. It was quick and strong. Now, it seemed like the man wanted to be anywhere but on State Beach. He couldn't wait to get away from here. When he got to his truck, Charles heard the door slam hard. His parents probably heard it at their campsite! The truck revved to life and did a U-turn. It disappeared over the JAWS Bridge and into Edgartown.

"That guy might not have hit the skinny guy," said Peter. "But he sure wanted to!"

"I think you're right," agreed Charles.

"I wonder what the fight was about?" said Peter.

"Search me," said Charles.

"I bet ya it was the girl," Peter said with confidence.

"What makes you say that?" Charles asked.

"That's why guys are always hitting each other in movies," Peter said.

Charles thought about it. Peter was right. Guys were always hitting each other over girls. How stupid was that? First of all, Charles could never imagine hitting anyone period, but hitting someone over a girl? That's the most ridiculous thing he ever heard. "Yeah, you're right."

"What do you want to do now?" asked Peter. "I think we've taken as many pictures of the beach as we need."

"Yeah, I agree," said Charles.

"Oh, my Mom wants you to come over for lunch," said Peter. "She wants to meet you."

"Today?" asked Charles.

"I think so but you have to ask your parents first. It has to be okay with your Mom," said Peter. "You know how parents are."

"My Mom would say the same thing," said Charles grinning. "but it's not lunchtime yet."

"I know, I'm just saying."

"We could go to Edgartown," said Charles. "There are some pictures in this book that were taken in Edgartown. Do you think you could double me on your bike?"

"Definitely!" Peter exclaimed. "You could sit on the seat and I'll peddle standing up. I think it's all downhill to Edgartown. It'll be a cinch."

* * *

"What the hell was that all about Alan?" Judie demanded. "Craig saved my life yesterday. So to show your gratitude, you take a swing at him?"

Alan could feel his face burning. His stomach was in knots. What the hell had he been thinking? Did he really think that Judie was going to come running into his arms after he punched Craig on the jaw? That is, if Craig didn't put him in the goddamn hospital first. There was no possible outcome that made any sense. He had no explanation. At least, he had no explanation that he was willing to share with Judie. What was he supposed to say? That he was in love with her? Or even better that he was jealous of everything about Craig? Could he stand there and explain to Judie that he was jealous of the ease with which Craig had slipped into the whole emergency situation, the way he had taken control and known exactly what to do? He sure wasn't going to tell her that he was jealous of the way Craig looked. Craig was one of those guys who just didn't give a shit how he looked and for whatever reason, women found him all the more attractive because of it. Alan, on the other hand, looked good because he did his best to look his best all the time. Craig didn't do a damned thing—Alan wondered if he even brushed his teeth.

"Well?" Judie said. "I'm waiting."

"I don't know," Alan said. He slumped down onto the beach and put his head in his hands. "I haven't been thinking straight since the accident yesterday. Craig is right. It really messed me up." He took a breath before continuing. "I really didn't like it Jude."

Judie sat down in the sand in front of him. "Well, I didn't like it either, but it didn't make me start punching people."

"I know, and I'm sorry. I really am!" Alan pleaded. "I was so scared. I thought you were dead. I was afraid to move. I kept thinking your head was going to explode under the wheel of his truck! I know that sounds messed up but it's true. All I could see was you—dead. It scared me bad." Alan looked up at her with damp eyes. "That's why I was going to your place now. I knew if I saw you, everything would be okay. If I could just see you and talk to you then I would know that you were alright and then I would be alright," he paused. Then he half-smiled. "I was bringing us breakfast."

"You were?" asked Judie. Her tone softened. She reached out and put her hand on his arm. "That was sweet of you."

"I was out on Warlock. We're supposed to get a storm so I was just making sure she was okay. I picked up a couple of sandwiches and coffees at Dock Street. The coffees spilled all over the car but the sandwiches were wrapped pretty good. They should be okay. You want one?"

Judie nodded and smiled weakly. "I'm starving."

Alan brightened a bit. "I'll be right back." He jumped to his feet and sprinted over the dunes that separated State Beach from Beach Road. Once at the car, he opened the passenger door and inspected the mess on the seat. The coffees had spilled forward leaving the sandwiches wrapped tight and dry. Alan picked them up and placed them on the roof of the car. He checked each coffee. The lids were still intact and they were both still about half full. They were only lukewarm but better than nothing. He hadn't realised it earlier, but he was pretty hungry too. He felt like an idiot. He didn't know what was going to happen now but the return of Judie's smile and her decision to eat breakfast on the beach with him was definitely a good sign. They would feel better after they ate. Maybe they would go for a swim together after breakfast. Alan had a lot of damage to repair but Alan had overheard Craig say that he had to go to work. With him safely out of the way, he and Judie could make up for time lost the day before.

Alan picked up the sandwiches with one hand and the coffees with the other. He pushed the door closed with his hip. Judie had mentioned wanting to check out the JAWS 2 production. He could take her there. She'd like that. He would too.

8

Craig parked his truck in the same spot that he had parked it the day before. Still behind the wheel, he stripped off his shorts and reached behind him for his jeans and shirt. Before he put them on, he took a whiff—they'd still be good for one more day. Not that he had much choice now, he didn't have enough time to go home for clean clothes. As it was he was cutting it pretty close. He didn't want to be late for work and he hadn't eaten breakfast yet. He'd take a quick detour over to Dock Street Coffee shop and pick up one of their breakfast sandwiches on his way. They pre-made loads of them for the local fishermen to grab on their way out, so he wouldn't have to wait. They were gems the girls who worked in there. Craig reached back for his boots and socks. He took a whiff of them too. The socks were a bit ripe but once they were in his boots he'd be fine. He made a mental note to remember to do his laundry that night when he got home. He could probably use a shower too. He didn't shower much in the summer. He swam in the ocean almost daily and he usually found that did the trick. Sometimes, he took a bar of biodegradable soap with him. He had even washed his hair in the ocean from time to time. It was way better than a shower—even better than an outdoor shower. An outdoor shower was the only kind of shower that Craig really liked. If he could figure out a way to keep the outdoor shower going all year without his pipes freezing up, he would do it. He knew a lot of other islanders who would too.

Dressed, Craig got out of the truck, closed the door behind him and started to jog down Main Street, Edgartown. His stomach was rumbling. He hadn't realised just how hungry he really was. He had been so distracted by all that crap on the beach. *What the hell was that all about?* His head was still spinning. It wasn't spinning from the punch—that had almost been comical—but just from everything that had happened in the last twelve hours! He'd almost killed a girl with his truck in Oak Bluffs, who actually fell in front of his truck—that was a good thing. At least he hadn't hit her. Also Craig thought he might have a thing for her. He barely knew her but something happened as soon as he saw her. He had never experienced that before. Was it true there was such a thing as love at first sight? Was that actually a thing?

Craig crossed Main Street toward Tashtego and Edgartown Hardware. He looked quickly and jogged across North Water Street. When he got to the corner of Dock and Main, he ducked into Dock Street Coffee Shop and came out a minute later with two breakfast sandwiches wrapped in tinfoil. He unwrapped one and took a bite that took off half of the sandwich. The bread, egg, bacon, and cheese squished deliciously into his mouth. He chewed quickly already eager for his second bite.

Clearly, that Alan guy had the hots for Judie. What's more, Craig thought that Judie was blindly unaware of the fact. She might have an inkling that he liked her but she didn't realise just how much. Girls like that never did. They didn't realise their effect on men. A beautiful girl can wind a guy up so tight that he will do and say just about anything that he believes will make her like him back. That's exactly what had happened this morning. Now that Craig had given it some thought, Alan had done what he did completely in a jealous fit. Ironically, he would have acted a lot more rationally if he had been in a real relationship with Judie. If Judie and Alan were in a real relationship, he wouldn't have felt so threatened. Oh he might have been pissed but he sure as hell wouldn't have taken a swing at Craig. Craig kinda felt bad for the little guy. Alan might be a bit of a goof but he was getting his heart stomped on pretty good right about now. Yes, Alan was wound up pretty tight. Guaranteed it had all started when Alan thought that he was about to see the girl he loved get killed by a truck, then he saw Craig—not a bad looking guy all things considered—half-naked on the beach with her the next morning, and finally, guaranteed she was tearing a strip out of him at this very moment. Craig had been there with more than a handful of women. Craig might have been the one who got punched on the jaw that morning but he wouldn't trade places with Alan for anything. That poor bastard was wound so tight he didn't know whether to scratch his watch or wind his butt. His mouth full of sandwich, Craig crumpled up the tinfoil and threw it in the trash. He opened the second wrapper and without waiting to finish the first, took a bite of sandwich number two.

* * *

Most of the way into Edgartown Village, Peter just had to coast. That worked out well, because peddling with the added weight of his new friend Charles was a lot harder than he thought it would be. Thankfully, he would be on his own peddling back to Oak Bluffs. The plan was that Charles would take the bus to the campsite and Peter would bike it home. If it was okay with his folks, Charles would either get his Dad to drive him to Peter's or he would take the bus again. This was turning out to be a wicked day. They really had a great time on State Beach. Having a best friend on Martha's Vineyard made all the difference. Having a best friend on Martha's Vineyard who was as into JAWS as he was—that was more than Peter could have ever hoped for! They coasted down Main Street into Edgartown. Traffic picked up as they passed the Old Whaling Church and Peter used a driveway to turn off the road and onto the sidewalk. Normally, he would stay on the road but with the passenger, the sidewalk seemed like the safer choice.

Charles tapped Peter on the shoulder. "Let's stop in at the store to get some snacks."

Peter nodded. As they came up to the drug store, Peter slowed his bike with both brakes and skidded to a stop with the soles of his sneakers. Charles got off first and then Peter. Peter rolled the metallic cherry red Sting-Ray to the white shingled outer wall of the drug store, and propped it there.

"Do you have a lock?" Charles asked.

"Yeah," said Peter. "but we'll only be a minute."

The two boys went inside.

One section of the candy wall was devoted to one-cent candies. The sign also said you could fill one of the small paper bags provided for a quarter. Charles and Peter went to work filling their bags with marshmallow strawberries, mojos, saltwater taffy, caramels, and gobstoppers. When neither of them could get anymore into their bags, they went up to the cash and handed over their money.

The lady looked down at both of them and smiled, "You got your money's worth today! Didn't you boys?"

The two friends responded in unison, "Yes, ma'am." Then walked toward the door.

"Are you headed down to watch those movie folks?"

"Ma'am?" asked Peter.

"Those movie people—isn't that why you're here?"

"I'm sorry, ma'am. We don't know what you're talking about," said Charles. "Are they filming a movie?"

The woman laughed. "Well, then you two must be the only two people on this island who don't know about it! They sure are! They're filming that JAWS 2 down there! You do know that they filmed the first one here, don't ya? Just about the biggest thing that ever happened on this island. Every islander and his mother was in it too! You boys should go and see what you can see. Word is they even have one of those big rubber sharks down there! Go on!"

Peter and Charles stared at each other, their mouths gaping. Then without saying a word, the two boys ran out of the store at top speed.

* * *

Judie stepped out of Alan's car in front of her cottage in Wesleyan Grove. She hadn't been sure about leaving the house that morning but Craig had been convincing in his argument about swimming and there was just something intriguing about Craig in general. The swim had been magnificent. She was going to make a point of going for a swim first thing in the morning from now on. She could walk to Inkwell Beach from her cottage; she didn't have to go all the way down to State Beach although she certainly could. It had been a great morning until Alan had come out of nowhere and attacked Craig. What could he possibly have been thinking? She still wasn't sure what to make of that. Judie knew that she wasn't exactly mad at Alan but if she was being honest with herself, she wasn't exactly thrilled with him either. Still, she and Alan had been having a really good time over the last little while. None of them was perfect. Look at the fiasco that had happened the day before—that had been entirely her fault. In fact, if she looked at it that way, it was Judie's fault that Alan had punched

Craig...kinda...wasn't it? Judie decided that the best thing to do was to just move forward. Craig hadn't been in a very good mood when he had left them on the beach and she couldn't blame him really. He did say that he would call her later. She hoped he would.

"Are you going to be okay?" Alan asked.

Judie turned around and looked at Alan. He looked somewhat sheepish but still handsome and friendly. Alan was a good guy. "Yeah, thanks. I'll be fine. I'm just going to lie down for a while. I'm really tired and my headache is back."

"Sorry," Alan said. "I'll stop by in a few hours and bring you some soup and a drink."

"That sounds nice," Judie said. "Thanks Alan."

"I was thinking—if you're feeling up to it—that we could go down and check out that JAWS 2 production. You know… if you still wanted to."

"I do want to," Judie said. "but only if I'm feeling better."

"Okay. Well get some sleep and I'll see you in a bit." Alan got back into his Firebird. The engine started to rumble and slowly he made his way out of the Methodist Campground.

When Judie could no longer see him, she turned and went inside her very pink house.

* * *

Peter ran down Main Street guiding his cherry red Sting-Ray with both hands. Charles ran along beside him carrying a bag of candy in each hand. Neither boy spoke a word. Peter's mind was racing and he knew instinctively that his friend's was too. *JAWS 2 was filming just a few yards away! There was a mechanical shark just a few yards away!* It was almost too much to fathom. *Was Roy Scheider there? Lorraine Gary? Murray Hamilton?* Peter had no idea what to expect. He had never been on a movie set before. They'd never film a movie in his hometown—Blairstown, New Jersey. Would they even be allowed to hang around? How close could they get? They stopped running when they got to Water Street and walked across the road with all of the restraint they could muster. Once across, without consulting each other, they broke into a run again.

Finally, at the bottom of Main, when they hit Dock Street, they slowed down. Peter was breathing fairly heavily and looking over to Charles, he was relieved to see that his friend was doing the same.

The Edgartown Yacht Club was across the parking lot from them and it marked the end of the working harbour on their right.

"I guess we go this way," said Peter. He pointed left up Dock Street.

Charles shrugged. "Guess so," he said. "Let's walk. It can't be that far. It must be hard with the bike. We should have ridden it."

"We really should have," Peter agreed. Peter was glad that Charles wanted to walk. He didn't know if Peter wanted to walk because he was actually tired or if he was doing it for Peter but either way, it was fine with him. It was hard to run with a bike. They should have ridden it but they didn't know exactly where they were going and they had been so excited that they just grabbed the bike and ran.

As they passed Larry's Tackle Shop, it was obvious that there was something going on up ahead. Peter felt butterflies in his stomach. He looked over at Charles. Charles returned his look, grinning from ear to ear. Peter returned his focus on the hub of activity in front of them. People ran back and forth. Some ran with clipboards and folders, while others lumbered under the weight of heavy equipment. Some people were well-dressed and others looked like hippies in t-shirts and shorts. There didn't seem to be any order to any of it. Was this the movie set? It had to be. The entire scene seemed ridiculously out of place. As a group, they just didn't fit in. These were not Martha's

Vineyard people. They weren't tourists and they definitely weren't islanders.

"This must be it, I guess," said Peter. "Is this what a movie set looks like?"

"It is," said Charles with confidence. "I see them in Toronto all the time."

Peter felt a pang of jealousy. It must be exciting to live in a big city, even if it was in Canada. "How can you tell?"

Charles pointed toward a series of folding wood and canvas chairs. "Movie people always sit in chairs like that. I don't know why. Movie stars and important people will have their names on the backs of their chairs so no one else will sit in them."

"Really?" said Peter. "So, no one else is allowed to sit in their seat even if they're not there?"

Charles shook his head. "Nope. If they do, I think they get fired."

"Jeez!" said Peter.

"Let's go over and see if any of the actors' names are on the chairs!" said Charles.

"*Like Roy Scheider?*" exclaimed Peter.

"Exactly!"

"Hey!" Peter pointed to a large sign in the road that read: *Universal Studios Filming Site For JAWS 2 Dock Closed During Filming We Are Sorry For The Incovenience*. Peter looked at Charles with a smile that almost hurt. "We are definitely in the right place!"

"They spelled 'inconvenience' wrong," said Charles.

*   *   *

Judie woke up from her nap feeling considerably better than she had when she got up the first time that day. For starters, it didn't hurt to open her eyes. That was always a good thing. She could feel the bruising on the side of her face. It ached a bit, and felt kinda hot, but mostly it was just stiff. Rolling over was still painful—sitting straight up was far more manageable—and standing was more than a little bit tender. Her feet hurt and her ankles were sore. Under normal circumstances, Judie would have decided to have a shower but now, she knew that a shower wasn't going to cut it. It would help, but there was no way that a shower was going to have the same purging effect that the swim in the ocean had that morning. The cold of the ocean, the healing of the salts, and whatever else was in there. Mother Nature knew what she was doing when she created the oceans. That's for damned sure. Isn't it where all life came from? Well, what was stopping her from going for another swim? Why not? Craig was right; Inkwell Beach wasn't far away.

She could grab a towel and be there in ten minutes. That's it—Judie made up her mind—she was going swimming.

Judie pulled open the top drawer of her dresser and rummaged around until she found a bikini. It was brightly coloured with uneven stripes across the top and bottoms. She pulled the bottoms on and then the top, which she then tied behind her neck. The towel that Craig had given her to use was draped over a chair. Deciding that it still needed to be washed before she could return it to him anyway, she picked it up to take with her. Judie raised the towel to her face and inhaled deeply. The towel smelled like Craig. Not like his aftershave or cologne—from what she could tell, Craig didn't really wear any—but rather just like him. She wasn't sure what the smell was. There was the briny smell of the sea; there was also that smell she got in her hair when she had been on a long ride in a convertible, that fresh air smell; sweat was there—that musky male scent. Salt water, ocean air, and sweat, maybe a hint of the wild roses that were everywhere on the island, sounded like anyone on Martha's Vineyard or even the Cape and Nantucket for that matter, but this scent was distinctly Craig. Judie liked it. She smiled.

Judie walked out of her pink house and stepped gingerly down the two front steps at the front of her porch. As she hit the path, a car pulled up beside her. It was Alan.

"Hey! Where are you going?" Alan poked his head out the driver's side window.

"I'm going for a swim at Inkwell Beach," she said. Judie scanned Alan's face. She was surprised to find that she was genuinely happy to see him. "Come with me!"

Alan hesitated. "I brought you some soup," he said.

"That's great. Thanks Alan," Judie said. "I'm sure I'll be famished when I get back, but right now, I really need a swim to sort myself out. I'd like you to come."

Alan paused for a moment. "Well, I don't want to intrude or anything."

Judie understood his hesitation now. "Alan, I'm going alone," Judie replied.

"Oh! Well, that's different! Hop in!"

"Leave the car or meet me there. I really want to walk. I need to move around. I'm sore but more than anything, I'm stiff. Walk with me?"

"Sure!" Alan turned off the ignition and hopped out of the car. "I'm glad to see you're feeling better." They started walking.

"Alan, I'm really sorry I ruined our day yesterday," Judie said. "It was all my fault."

"It wasn't your fault at all. It was an accident—plain and simple," he said. "Today is another day."

"Thanks," Judie said. She smiled at him genuinely.

"Let's have a swim, eat some soup, and then check out the JAWS 2 set down in Edgartown!" Alan said.

"You're on!"

9

Craig rolled a large spotlight on castors up into the back of a truck. Once in place, he secured the breaks on the wheels to prevent it from rolling around. There was something fishy going on. He chuckled at his small pun. People were stalling—even he could see that. He had figured out pretty early in the game that the movie business was a lot of waiting around and doing nothing but this was different. There was an air of unease floating around the set that was palpable. There was still a shark there and the second unit was going to film a shot of the shark swimming through the harbour the next morning but that was it. There were a lot of second unit shots like that planned but nothing first unit. They were killing time. Lorraine Gary was there, he had seen her but they didn't seem to be using her much. Apparently they had used her and Murray Hamilton more in the beginning but not now. There were a lot of discussions going around between the big shots from Universal. Craig had seen Zanuck and Brown walking around although he didn't know which was which. Nobody ever mentioned one without the other. Apparently, they had just flown in from "the coast". That's what everyone called California—*the coast*. That really frosted Craig's balls. Didn't they realise they were on a goddamn coast now? The more Craig got to know these movie guys, the less he liked them. Craig had also heard Florida mentioned more than once. Something big was going down but apparently no one knew what. Certainly no one at Craig's pay grade.

Craig seemed to be doing a lot of grunt work for no particular reason. His boss, Mike, was ordering him around and a couple of whiny assistant directors were too but they all just seemed to be justifying their jobs. Busy for busy's sake. One thing's for sure—Craig wasn't going to be offered a job on the *west* coast doing crap like this. He was just about ready to tell them all where to go.

In fact, the thought of telling them all to do just that was becoming more and more appealing now that he could be spending time with Judie. Before yesterday, his options were working on the movie or sitting around on Martha's

Vineyard with his thumb up his ass, fighting with his parents, or getting drunk at The Boston House or worse—The Seaview. Things were different now. In a very short time, Judie had changed things around for him. He didn't even know how long she was on-island. Was she here to stay? How much time did he have with her exactly? She could only be here for the week for all he knew. There was a genuine possibility that he might never see her again. He had told her that he would call her but that didn't mean that she would be there to answer. He had left the beach that morning in a huff. It hadn't exactly been his greatest moment, but what the hell was he supposed to do? Alan had come up behind him and clocked him on the chin. Craig had been willing to be understanding when he thought Alan was Judie's boyfriend *but they were just friends!* Not cool. Alan was damned lucky that Craig hadn't hit him back. Craig knew that if he had hit Alan, Alan would have been hurt—badly. Craig didn't need that kind of grief and he knew that punching Alan would not have endeared him to Judie either. Losing his temper might have freaked her out as it was, but Craig hadn't eaten anything yet—he had been starving. That's why he stomped off. He knew he needed to get the hell out of there and get something to eat. The two sandwiches from Dock Street had gone down pretty goddamn smoothly. He could have eaten at least four more.

Craig loved to eat. Maybe Judie would like to head out to the beach in Craig's truck when he was finished for the day. They could take some scallops, clams, and a few beer and watch the sun go down. They could even drive out to Menemsha. That was the best place to watch the sunset.

Craig jumped down from the truck and surveyed the scene. A lot going on about nothing. Off to the edge of the production there were two kids watching with the widest eyes Craig thought he had ever seen. He smiled. Being a kid that age on Martha's Vineyard had been alright. When he had been out away from his family, riding his bike with his friends, there had been good times. He watched as the two kids cautiously made their way toward the row of canvas chairs. One of them excitedly pulled out a camera and started taking pictures.

"Hey! You kids!"

Craig turned in the direction of the voice. It was Mike.

"Get away from there! You're not supposed to be here!" Mike yelled. "Put that camera away!"

Jesus H Christ, thought Craig. *They're not working for The Goddamn National Enquirer! They're just kids!* Craig started walking toward them. The two boys froze for a moment and then started to run. They stopped when they got to a red bike. Craig picked up his pace. He shot Mike a look. When Mike met his gaze, he opened his mouth to

133

speak but seeing the look on Craig's face, he thought better of it.

The two boys looked up at Craig. He was approaching quickly. Their faces were white. Their eyes were almost full circles, the whites visible all the way around. Craig smiled and beckoned them toward him. The boys didn't move. Craig continued in their direction. He looked over at Mike who was watching him intently. Craig shrugged at him. "Relax!" he yelled.

When Craig got to the boys, he crouched down. "Ignore him," Craig said. "He's a jerk."

"We don't want to get in trouble," said the boy holding the bike.

"You're fine," said Craig. "You like JAWS?"

Both boys nodded. The boy with the bike spoke again. "We haven't seen it but we've read the books about it and we love sharks!"

"Yeah, sharks are the coolest!" chimed in the second boy.

"Well, I tell you what," Craig said. "Why don't you come back tomorrow morning? There's nothing much going on right now. I don't even think the actors are still here."

"*Who was here?*" the boys almost shouted in unison.

Craig laughed. "The only one I saw was Lorraine Gary," he said.

"Did you talk to her?" asked the boy with the bike.

"Is she nice?" asked the second boy.

Craig laughed again. "No, I haven't talked to her but I'm sure she's cool. She seems to be smiling and laughing a lot. That's usually a sign of a nice person, I think," he said. "Anyway, if you come back tomorrow morning early—like six o'clock—we're shooting a scene with the shark. You won't see any actors at that time of day but I'll be here and I promise, you'll get to meet the shark! Now, get out of here before I get fired." Craig stood up and walked away.

*　　*　　*

Charles was so excited that he couldn't even eat any of the candy in the paper bags he was carrying. "Can you believe it?" he said to Peter as they walked back toward Main Street. "Tomorrow we're going to see one of the sharks from JAWS 2!"

"Where do you want to meet?" asked Peter.

"At the triangle?" suggested Charles.

"Where's the triangle?"

"The triangle is where Beach Road and Edgartown Vineyard Haven Road turn into Main Street—well, kinda. It's where Beach Road branches off anyway. If you come down

Beach Road from Oak Bluffs, I can meet you there because I'll be coming from Vineyard Haven," explained Charles.

"Okay," said Peter. "That sounds good. Five-thirty?"

"Oh man, that's so early!" said Charles.

"I know but we have to!" exclaimed Peter.

"Agreed," said Charles. "Do you think they're using the same sharks that they used in JAWS? *Do you think that we're seeing a JAWS shark tomorrow?*"

"Oh, I don't know! That's a good question," said Peter. "I guess we'll find out. If it's a JAWS shark, we'll know. We'll recognise it."

"Definitely," said Charles. "Oh, what time is it now?" Charles looked at his watch. "I should get on the bus if I'm going to make it to your place for lunch. What's your phone number?"

Peter reached into his camera case and pulled out a pen and paper. He wrote down his number and handed it to Charles.

"Okay," said Charles. "I'll call you from the campground phone and tell you whether I can come for lunch or not."

"Sounds good," Peter said. "I can't wait for tomorrow!"

"Me neither!" said Charles. He turned and ran up the street toward the bus stop.

* * *

Alan parked the car in the parking lot just below North Water Street behind The Fligors Gifts. The morning had gone really well. He had been hesitant to go swimming. Well, first he had been hesitant because he had thought Judie was meeting Craig on the beach. Craig and Judie had been swimming together that morning—something that he was never likely to forget—so when she had said that she was going for a swim, he had assumed... It seemed a reasonable assumption. When Judie had told him she was going alone, he had felt like a bit of a tool. He had forgotten that Craig said he had to work. Also, Judie seemed to genuinely want him to go with her. He had seen it in her face. She could have said that she wouldn't be long. She could have suggested that he wait or come back in a little while, but instead she had been insistent that he park his car and walk with her to the beach. That felt good. That had been the first step toward putting all of the negativity of the last day behind them. The swim itself had been good too. Judie had been right, there was something restorative about the ocean. Not only had it done her the world of good physically, the swim had definitely improved his mental state. It had cleared his head. The car accident, the jealousy, the punch had all dove right in with him but they had been stripped away beneath the surface. The briny salt water acted as an astringent, rinsing away all of the unwanted toxins that Alan had been carrying around with him. When he broke the surface a few feet from where he had gone under, inhaling fresh lungs full of oxygen, he had felt considerably lighter in spirit.

Craig's name hadn't even come up. It was like the accident had never happened. Not that Alan was able to put it completely out of his mind. Every time he looked at Judie and saw the bruise on the left side of her face, it all came back. But the conversation between them was back to normal. They swam and laughed and carried on like they had most of the summer. Alan did notice that the flirting they had begun before the accident was gone, but Judie was probably still settling back into her own skin. Going through an experience like that was bound to put flirtatious thoughts on the back burner for any woman. Women weren't like men. A guy might decide to have sex to take his mind off of his head being stuck under the wheel of a truck. *Some men would decide to have sex while his head was still under it!* Women were different. Women were looking for comfort, safety, and security. That might not be all they were looking for but those things certainly had to be in place before they were going to start feeling romantic. It would take a couple of days for the two of them to get back into the groove that they had shared before the accident; however, Alan could tell that they were off to a good start. Checking out the JAWS 2 production would help. A little movie magic never hurt. Hollywood was exciting and romantic for sure.

"You ready?" Alan asked.

"Absolutely," Judie said.

Alan stepped out of the Firebird and stretched. It was a beautiful day. The forecast had been for rain, a full storm actually, but so far it was great. Martha's Vineyard weather was completely unpredictable. It was entirely possible that there was a storm going on up-island and a big one. Just because one side of the island was sunny, it didn't mean the other side was.

Judie walked around the car. Alan offered his arm and she accepted. Neither of them said anything as they walked.

Alan noticed that the wind had picked up. It was still a beautiful day but there was something blowing in for sure. The sun still shone and there were still boats out on the harbour, but the waves were a little choppy and clouds were beginning to swirl overhead. It wasn't a cool wind—it was hot. Whether it was true or not, Alan always believed that a hot wind meant a meaner storm. "Maybe I closed up Warlock a little too early," he said. "We could have gotten in a quick sail before things get too crazy."

139

"That would be great! After?"

Alan shrugged and smiled at her before looking up at the sky. "Maybe," he said.

When Judie and Alan got to the end of Kelley St, they were met with a large sign that read: *Universal Studios Filming Site For JAWS 2 Dock Closed During Filming We Are Sorry For The Incovenience.*

"This must be the place," said Alan.

Judie laughed. "They spelt inconvenience wrong!"

Alan reread the sign. "Oh yeah! That's hilarious!"

Alan looked around. There seemed to be a lot of people running around but not a whole lot of movie-making happening. No one was yelling *"Action!"* or *"Cut!"* or *"Places everyone!"* or any of that crap. Assuming that all of those things really happened on movie sets. Truth be told, the only place he had ever seen a movie being made was in a movie. They would get it right, wouldn't they?

"I don't see Roy Scheider or Richard Dreyfuss anywhere," said Judy. "I don't even see a shark."

"No," agreed Alan. "Neither do I." He could hear the disappoint in Judie's voice. He had to admit, he was disappointed himself. He didn't know exactly what he expected to happen but he had expected to see something.

"Hey!" Judie exclaimed. "Look who it is!" she pointed excitedly across the production.

Alan turned, following her finger. Had she spotted Roy Scheider? Lorraine Gary? Then he saw him. Alan felt all of the life drain from his body. Standing beside a large truck amidst coils of cables, boxes, and sets of lights, was Craig. Alan's face burned. His chest tightened. Once again, they had been having such a good time and then, out of nowhere, they were blindsided with Craig—son of a bitch! *No wonder the sign was fucking spelled wrong*, Alan thought.

* * *

Peter hung up the phone on the wall in the kitchen of their gingerbread cottage. After untwisting the cord as best he could, he turned toward his parents with a slightly deflated look. "Charles can't come for lunch," he said.

"Oh, that's too bad," said Peter's Mother. "I was looking forward to meeting him."

Peter got up onto one of the stools at the kitchen counter. He opened Edith Blake's book and looked over the pictures that he and Charles had tried to replicate that morning on the beach.

"Who's Charles?" asked his Dad.

"He's the boy I met in Oak Bluffs yesterday," said Peter. "We hung out on State Beach this morning and took some pictures of where we think JAWS might have been filmed!"

Peter's Dad laughed. "Of course, you did! What else did you do?"

"Then we went down to Edgartown on my bike—Charles doesn't have one—*and you'll never guess what they're doing!*"

"Filming JAWS 2?" said his Father.

Peter stared at his Father in disbelief. "Yeah! How did you know?"

"There's a big write up about it in the paper today," his Father said. "Check it out, bud." Peter's Father tossed the paper onto the counter in front of Peter.

Peter stared at the newspaper almost too excited to move. Taking up almost the entire page, swinging from a crane, its belly leaking cables, was the JAWS 2 shark. After a moment of silence, Peter said, "Whoa!"

"I thought you'd like that," said his Dad.

"I assume that you didn't see the shark when you went down there today?" asked his Mom. "You would have come in screaming it at the top of your lungs—if you came home at all." She laughed.

"No, we didn't," confirmed Peter. "But we did talk to this guy who works on the movie and he said that they were going to film a scene with the shark early in the morning tomorrow, and if we came back, we could see it for sure!" Peter absorbed every detail of the photo. The shark was right down in the harbour. *Right where they had been!* He could see Memorial Wharf in the background. He and Charles could probably stand up there the next morning to watch all of the action. "Wait until Charles sees this!" Peter said. "He's going to flip!"

* * *

Craig looked around. He could hear his name being called. It wasn't Mike—thank Christ. It was a female voice—that was odd. There were no women ordering him around on set. Then he saw her. It was Judie. She was standing over by the sign that warned people to stay off the set. Craig felt himself straighten. He felt his chest puff out. He grinned so broadly that his face almost hurt. Just looking at her made him feel good. He waved and walked in her direction. Then he noticed Alan. Alan looked considerably less thrilled to find Craig there. Craig didn't care. That was Alan's problem, not his.

"Well, hello you two," Craig smiled. "Is it me who keeps turning up like a bad penny or is it you guys?"

Alan snorted.

"I think it's definitely you," said Judie. "This is where you work? *You work for Universal Pictures?*" Judie almost sang with excitement. "You didn't tell me that!"

Craig shrugged. "It's not as exciting as it sounds," he said. "It's just a job. I'm hoping that they keep me on after production is over and take me back to California with them. At least that had been my plan when I applied for the job. Things change all the time though. Now, I'm not so sure."

"Have you met any of the actors? Have you met Roy Scheider or Richard Dreyfuss?" asked Judie.

"Richard Dreyfuss isn't in this one," Craig said. "I've seen Lorraine Gary but I haven't talked to her. She seems pretty cool."

"That's so exciting!" Judie said. "Isn't that exciting Alan?"

Craig looked at Alan. He seemed to be shrinking by the second. His face was dark, his eyes narrow.

"Yeah," muttered Alan. "Exciting."

Craig turned his attention back to Judie. "Jude, there isn't much going on at all right now, but if you come back early tomorrow morning, you'd see us filming a scene with one of the sharks. That might be kinda fun."

"That would be so cool!" exclaimed Judie. "You want to Alan?"

Alan took a moment to answer. "I'm busy tomorrow morning. Sorry."

"Aw, that's too bad Alan," Craig said with all of the sincerity he could muster. "It should be pretty cool." Once again, Craig turned back to Judie. "Why don't I pick you up on my way to work tomorrow morning? We can go for a swim first and then come down here and make some movies. It'll be a laugh!"

"It's a date!" said Judie.

"Fantastic!" Craig looked at Alan. Alan was seething. "Well, I should get back to work. Have a good afternoon you two. It looks like a storm is coming!" Craig turned and walked away.

*   *   *

Alan marched back in the direction of the car. He didn't offer his arm for Judie to hold and he didn't wait for her. He could feel his temperature going up. His hands were in tight fists. Without looking, he could tell his knuckles were white. His neck was rigid and coursing with blood. He wanted—needed—to get away from the movie set, away from *him*. All he could do was move forward.

"Alan?" called Judie. "Where are you going?"

Alan didn't respond. He just kept going. He had no idea what to say.

"*Alan?*" Judie called again. "I thought we were going to get something to eat and maybe go sailing?"

"I'm going home!" he barked.

"Why?" Judie ran to catch up with him. When she did, she grabbed him by the shoulder and turned him to face her. When she saw his face, Judie took a step back. She folded her arms across her chest. "Alan? Why are you so upset?"

"*For Christ's sake! Why does that guy have to be everywhere we go on this island?*" Alan yelled. "*The Vineyard is one hundred square miles and he has to be in every square foot that we're in!*"

"You're this pissed off because Craig works for the movie studio?" Judie said incredulously. She shook her head. "He can't even leave. Now, you know exactly where he is all day, everyday."

Alan started to feel stupid. The reality of exactly how wrong he had just played the whole situation started to wash over him and he felt like a fool. If anything, he was pushing Judie toward Craig.

"I don't know what your problem is with Craig. He has never been anything but nice to us," said Judie. "I'm starting to see you through different eyes, Alan. Maybe you're not as cool as I thought you were." Judie turned and started to walk away.

Alan felt mild panic as he watched her walk up Dock Street alone. "Judie! Wait!"

Judie turned around to face him but continued walking away backward while she spoke. "You said you had to go home. You should go. I need to be alone for a while." Then she turned around once more and didn't look back.

10

Alan sat in the car with both of his hands on the steering wheel. The key was in the ignition but he hadn't started her up. He just sat there. He had done it again. He and Judie had been having a really nice morning. If he had cooled his jets, they would have made some brief small talk with Craig and then walked away. Craig would have gone back to work and Judie would still be with him right now. But that's not what had happened—and she wasn't with him right now. He had blown a gasket like some kid in high school and Judie had left him. She hadn't even left him for Craig. Judie had decided that being alone was better than being with him. Somehow, that was even worse. If Judie had walked away with Craig, then at least he could blame Craig.

He would have been able to tell himself that Craig had seduced her away from him but Judie's walking away to be by herself. That meant that he had no one to blame but himself.

Craig had been able to stay cool when they were all together. Clearly, Craig didn't see Alan as a threat. That meant one of two things. Either Judie was Craig's for the taking and there wasn't a damned thing Alan could do about it or Craig wasn't actually pursuing Judie and he had made up this entire competition in his head. The former made him feel like a loser; the latter made him feel like a nut bar. At the moment he didn't know which he preferred.

A sharp tap on the windshield broke Alan's train of thought. He looked up expecting—hoping—to see Judie standing over his windshield, peering in at him. There was no one. *Tap! ...Tap! ...Tap!* It was rain, hitting the glass in large heavy drops. The storm was coming in after all. Alan got out of the car and made a run for The Newes From America. It was his favourite pub and he could definitely use a Guinness. He ran across the parking lot to the front door of the pub. As he pulled it open, thunder cracked overhead.

* * *

The skies opened up and within a matter of seconds, Judie was soaked through. *Doesn't that just figure,* she thought. The day had started out beautifully. She had truly been having a good time with Alan on the beach and even on the walk to the beach and back. They had laughed and talked about sailing and bonfires. Alan had talked about what he was going to do when the season was over and she had been genuinely interested in what he had to say. Judie had been trying to sort that out herself. Hearing someone else talk about the plans they were mulling over helped. Their plans would be different but little things Alan mentioned had been triggers for her. Maybe she would travel for a bit. There was nothing saying that she had to stay on Martha's Vineyard. She planned to make the island her permanent home but a couple of weeks here and there during the off-season might be good. In fact, she would have embraced the idea of travelling without any question until Craig had come into the picture. Craig. With very little effort at all, Craig was making everything exciting and miserable all at the same time. He had turned everything upside down. Judie had been having one of the best summers of her life until Craig had come along. Not just because he almost killed her with his truck either. Judie's summer had been fantastic but it had been with Alan. In a very short period of time, Judie had made room for Craig in her summer but there was certainly no room for Craig in Alan's summer. That much was obvious. Judie didn't blame Alan. She wasn't stupid. She recognised jealousy when she saw it. Alan was increasingly jealous of Craig but that wasn't Craig's fault. It wasn't even Alan's fault. Judie felt guilty about it but really, it wasn't her fault either. It was so frustrating how people were so determined to assign blame whenever something didn't turn out the way they planned. Yes, she had been flirting with Alan—Alan had flirted back. They had been enjoying each other more and more but that was before Craig had come into their lives. She hadn't planned on being excited by Craig. She hadn't planned on meeting him at all. Judie could still see him kneeling into her line of vision when she was pinned under the truck. She had been so scared—her cheeks wet with tears—convinced that her life was ending. Then Craig had kneeled down. He was so big. If she had been walking toward him at night, she would have crossed the street just to get away from him. Then he had started speaking to her in that deep and soothing voice of his. He had sounded so calm that Judie knew deep in her heart that nothing was going to happen to her. She was going to be okay because Craig told her she would be. He had taken her hands in his. She remembered their warmth. He had stared at her with his piercing eyes. It had been impossible for her to look away. Then, he took complete control of the situation and before she knew it, she was free. Craig was carrying her across the street and ordering Alan to go to Giordano's and get her a glass of water. It was when he was carrying her in his arms that she first noticed just how handsome he really was. He had teased her and laughed. He made her laugh. Craig had a broad smile and perfect teeth. If asked, Craig would probably say that he had brown eyes—everyone who had brown eyes said that—but he didn't. His eyes were copper.

Then, they had gone swimming and there had been something very intimate about it. Judie had called him to thank him. She had called him to apologise for the day before, embarrassed by her own actions. The last thing on her mind had been to get in his truck and go swimming but she had. Yes, Craig had held her in his towel and she had smelled his scent, his ocean clean body, but the swim had been intimate before that. There had been a closeness, a tension, long before they even got anywhere near each other. She had felt the chemical charge coursing through her body, especially when they were both out in the water. Was that possible? Could salt water increase, even conduct, a chemical reaction between two people? Was that why there were all of those romantic scenes on the beach in movies?

Movies—who knew that Craig was going to be working on the set of *JAWS 2*? Judie actually felt sorry for Alan.

Craig even said it himself; he did seem to be turning up like a bad penny for Alan. Judie couldn't help but feel like Craig was her lucky penny. That was fate trying to tell her something. Yes—Judie and Alan had been having a really great summer but they hadn't talked about a relationship or even dating. Yes—that is probably where it would have been heading. That is until Craig showed up. The fact that he showed up was nobody's fault. It still might be nothing. Judie liked him though. Judie liked him a lot.

Judie walked up Main Street with her arms wrapped around her chest. She was shivering. Rainwater streamed over her bare shoulders, her hair slick to her neck. Torrents of water ran over her feet and down the red brick sidewalk toward the harbour. Wet sandals were making her steps uneasy. Someone pulled up beside her and stopped. She squinted to get a look at the driver. Large water drops on her eyelashes made it next to impossible. She could see a shadow but nothing else. She recognised the vehicle.

The door was pushed open from the inside. Craig leaned across the passenger seat. "Get in," he said.

*   *   *

Peter sat out on the front porch of the teal and orange gingerbread house. He was watching the rain thunder onto the grassy park that stretched out across the centre of Wesleyan Grove. Wesleyan Grove was a big circle. There was an outer circle of cottages, and then a smaller circle of cottages, and then a smaller circle and in the centre of all of them was the Tabernacle. Peter wasn't exactly sure what *Tabernacle* meant but it looked like a big outdoor church. There were small paths connecting them all and there were cottages on off-roads here and there, but essentially, the campground was a great big circle. The trees were huge in the campground so Peter figured that they must have been planted around the same time the cottages themselves were built. *The Campground*—Peter found that confusing as well. It wasn't a campground as far as Peter could see, but that's what people called it. They called it "the Methodist campground". *Methodist Campground* explained the big church in the middle but it didn't explain anything else. He knew that a grove was like a clump of trees or a meadow. That worked because there were tons of trees and flowers and bushes, but there were no tents so *campground* didn't work at all. The best name was when people just called it *The Gingerbread Cottages.* That made all the sense in the world. There was nothing but gingerbread cottages everywhere he looked.

Peter watched puddles form in the lowlands of the park. Small green grassy lakes. Hydrangeas of every colour drooped with the heavy burden of water. The lilies in front of the house hung low. Peter was getting antsy. How long would this storm last? Would it be gone by morning? Would they still be filming with the shark the next day? There was no way he could miss that. He would just die. Peter knew that his new friend Charles would feel the same way. To have a JAWS shark so close and then ripped away would be too much to bear. Surely this kind of heavy rain would disappear soon. Wouldn't it? He hadn't heard anything on the radio about a tropical storm or a hurricane or anything. They had just said rain. It was windy too! That was a good thing. His Dad always said that if it wasn't windy, that meant that the storm was looking to set up shop and stay a while. Wind meant that it was just passing through.

    Headlights turned onto the path about ten houses down from Peter. They lit up the rain like a silver curtain. He watched them approach slowly. It was a truck. It was the same truck that Peter and Charles had seen on the beach earlier that morning. Slowly, it rolled up in front of the pink house beside Peter's and stopped. The lights went out and the engine shut off. The rain hit the truck like a steel drum. Watching from the front corner of the porch, he began to edge toward the railing. The closer he got, the wetter Peter got but he didn't mind. He was more curious than anything else. The driver's door opened and a large man stepped out.

It was the guy from JAWS 2! It was the guy who had told Charles and him to come back! He would know whether or not the shoot was still on in the morning for sure! Peter felt butterflies in his stomach. He was scared to shout out and ruin everything but he couldn't help himself. He just had to know. This man would know. This man would know if Peter was still going to see his shark.

"Hey!" Peter managed weakly. He tried to sound cool but instead he thought he sounded like an old lady. The man looked up.

"Well, look who it is!" the man said. "It's my shark guy!" The man smiled and walked casually around to the passenger door. Even though he was wearing nothing but a pair of denim shorts, the man seemed completely oblivious to the fact that it was raining. "Where's your friend? Or is he your brother?"

Peter cleared his throat and tried to sound cool one more time. "No, he's not my brother. He's just my buddy." *Buddy? Who says 'Buddy'? God, I sound like such an idiot. This guy is going to think I'm a total loser and not think I'm cool at all.*

"Right on," said the man. He opened the passenger door and lifted out a woman. "Your brother from another mother. I can dig that."

Peter watched as the man tossed the woman over his shoulder with one arm and closed the truck door with the other. Peter was alarmed but then he heard the woman laughing and didn't know what to think. "Is she hurt?" he asked.

The man laughed. "No," he said. "She's wearing sandals and it's pretty muddy. I'm trying to be a nice guy…sort of." He winked at Peter.

Peter didn't have a clue what was going on or what the man was talking about. He chuckled politely. "Are you still going to be filming with the shark in the morning? I mean, it's raining."

The man looked up at the sky as if this was the first he'd heard of it. "This will pass right over us tonight. Don't you worry. Besides, sharks don't mind getting wet."

Peter laughed nervously again.

"What's your name kid?" The man set the woman down on her pink porch, walked over, and reached his hand up to Peter. The man's hand could have picked up Peter's head like a basketball.

Peter stuck his hand out and watched it disappear inside the man's. For a split second he wanted to pull it back for fear of never seeing it again. "I'm Peter."

"Nice to meet you Pete," said the man. He gave Peter's hand one solid pump and released it. "My name is Craig. My friend is Judie or do you two already know each other?"

"Hi handsome," Judie waved at Peter from her porch. Peter waved back.

"Hi Judie," said Peter. He could feel himself blushing.

"I'm going to go down to watch the shoot too!" said Judie. "Hey! Why don't you ride down with us?"

"Oh, that's okay," said Peter. "I have my bike and I'm meeting my friend."

"Okay," said Judie. "Well, you come knock on my door if you change your mind. Okay?"

Peter nodded. "Yes, ma'am."

"Great!" Judie waved as she opened her door and walked inside. Craig followed.

"See you tomorrow, Pete," Craig nodded as he went inside.

Peter puffed up his chest. He was beaming. The shoot was on. They were going to see their shark tomorrow morning as planned. That Craig guy was cool. No one had ever called him 'Pete' before. He liked it.

*   *   *

Craig closed the door behind him and followed Judie into the kitchen. He took in his surroundings. He had been there before, when he had brought her home directly after the accident, but he hadn't really looked around. That first time, his focus had been one-hundred-percent on Judie—getting her settled upstairs on her bed, making sure she was alright. On his way out, he had been mildly uncomfortable being in her house. Judie had been a stranger then and he had felt like an intruder. The context was different now. Now, Judie was someone in his life, someone important.

Judie walked toward the staircase that wrapped up against the wall of the cottage to the second floor. She turned to face Craig before she ascended. "I'm going to put on some dry clothes. I'll be right back."

Craig nodded. "No problem," he said. "Can you throw down a towel?"

Judie smiled. "Sure," she said as she started up the stairs. "I owe you one anyway. I'm sorry but yours is in Alan's car." She continued from the second floor. "I want to wash it before I give it back to you anyway."

"You don't have to," said Craig. "I've got other laundry to do. I can just throw it in with that." Craig walked around the small main floor of the cottage. It was very neat and tidy. There were the usual Martha's Vineyard trinkets—ceramic lighthouses, seagull mobiles, and a shell collection by the front door including a rather impressive pink conch shell, but it didn't come across as a rental. For starters there were family photos on the bookshelves and there were a few of a young awkward girl at varying stages of adolescence who had to be Judie. "You own this place?"

Judie came back downstairs in a white peasant shirt and a pair of jeans that had been rolled up to mid-calf. "I don't. My parents do. They never come out anymore though. No one uses it but me."

"Where are they?" Craig asked.

"New York," Judie shuddered. "I hate that place. You can't go out on the street for more than five minutes without being covered with a layer of grime or smog or whatever. It's disgusting. The noise is deafening—even when it's quiet in New York, it's loud. That's not how we were meant to live."

"I guess you have a point," said Craig. "Where do you want to live?"

"Well, if I can find a job," Judie said. "I'm hoping that my parents will give me this place. I love it here—the ocean, the clean air, the peace and quiet. You want a beer?"

Craig nodded. "Sure, thanks. Have you been here in the off-season? You'll get more than enough peace and quiet. You might want to try it before you commit."

"This is going to be my first winter on-island. We'll see how it goes. I'm really looking forward to it to be honest. Are you from here?" Judie opened two Coors and passed one to Craig.

"Yeah, I'm an islander," he said.

"Well, then you must know Alan," Judie said. "I mean, how many schools can there be on Martha's Vineyard?"

"What's his last name?" asked Craig.

"Quaid," she said.

Craig whistled. "He's one of the Quaids! No wonder I don't know him. My parents are friends with his parents though—guaranteed."

"So why don't you know him then?"

"Well, for starters, all of the Quaids went to private schools over in America. I went to good old Martha's Vineyard High. My Dad might be a doctor—that gives him clout—but it doesn't give him private boarding school kinda money. Believe me, they would have jumped at the chance to ship me off if they could."

Judie sat on the white cotton couch and patted the seat beside her. Craig sat down.

"So, that's for starters...what else?" Judie asked.

"I'm the black sheep," Craig said with a certain amount of pride. "My friends aren't *'the kind of people that one should be associating with'* to quote my mother. There's a class system alive and well on this island. It's not all sailboats, lobsters, and lighthouses like you see on the postcards."

"What are your friends like?" asked Judie.

"I don't know," Craig shrugged. "Like me, I guess. I don't really have a lot of friends."

Judie put her beer down on the table. "I think I'd like your friends." She moved in her spot until Craig had no choice but to stare directly into her eyes.

"Yeah, you probably would," he said.

Judie crawled forward until she was on top of him.

Craig put his beer down. As her weight pressed onto his lap, he became more and more uncomfortable in his cut-off shorts. He tried to shift her but she was holding on now. Her thighs were tightening around him.

Judie took his head gently between her hands and moved in until her mouth found his. There was a heat between them now, replacing the chill of the rain.

"Are you sure about this?" asked Craig.

"Absolutely," Judie said.

Craig slid his hands up under her blouse and cupped her breasts for a moment before sliding his arms all the way around her and lifting her up. He turned and lay her down on her back on the couch. Craig stood up and pulled off his shorts.

Judie lifted her top up over her head. Craig grabbed the cuffs of her jeans and slid them off of her. She laughed out of pure joy.

Craig got on top of her and for the first time in a very long time, he didn't want to be anywhere else.

11

Peter woke up before his alarm had a chance to go off. Truth be told he had been waking up, almost every hour on the hour, all night. It felt like Christmas Eve—he was too excited to sleep. Finally, at twenty past five, he got out of bed, dressed, and made his way downstairs. Peter hadn't really thought it through, being up this early. It was still dark out. Would it be any brighter when he met Charles? He wasn't a little kid anymore but riding his bike alone in the dark and then waiting around by himself would be kinda scary. He hoped Charles would be on time. If he wasn't, how long did Peter have to wait? He didn't want to be late for the shoot. There was absolutely no way he was missing the shark being lowered into the harbour and swimming around—would it have to come out of the water and open and shut its mouth? *Would the shark attack a boat? Would they get to see that?* That was probably too much to hope for. Still, he wasn't going to see anything unless he got down to Edgartown Harbor on time. Charles had better not be late.

Peter turned on the kitchen light. After pulling himself up onto the counter and getting one of the melamine bowls out of the cupboard, he started to pour himself some Cocoa Krispies. The heavy flow of sugary cereal that he had been expecting was a trickle at best before it stopped altogether. Peter looked down into the empty box in disbelief. *How could the box be empty?*

"I'll get you another box, bud."

Peter turned with a start. Sitting in the dark living room was his father, munching a bowl of Cocoa Krispies. His father grinned at him.

"What can I say?" said his Dad with a mouthful of Krispies. "They're good!"

"You ate the whole box?" exclaimed Peter.

His Dad chuckled. "Quiet—you'll wake your Mother. *You had some.* Besides, I told you, I'll get you some more. I'm going to pick up some fresh pastries for your Mom after I drop you off anyway. I'll stop into Your Market and get some more cereal when I go." His father took another spoonful and crunched.

165

"You're dropping me off?" asked Peter.

"I'd like to meet this friend of yours," his Dad said. "We'll put your bike in the trunk and I'll drive you and your friend to the set. I'd also like to meet this guy you've been talking to who works there too. Just to make sure everything is on the up and up."

"He's friends with the girl next door," Peter said.

"I know," said his Dad with his mouth full of cereal. "I haven't met him yet."

"Oh Dad—you're not going to embarrass me!"

"Of course not!" said Peter's father. "I am going to say hello and then I'm going to leave. I just think it's a good idea that I meet him and see his face, get a name, that sort of thing. Sorry, Peter but I have to be a father once in a while. If he kidnaps you to sell you to the gypsies, I would like to be able to give the police a description."

Peter rolled his eyes. His Dad was going to say something goofy; he just knew it. Still, a ride sounded pretty good and less scary. At least that way he knew he wouldn't be late for sure. "Okay, thanks," said Peter. "We should probably get going then."

"Okay, just let me finish your cereal." His Dad winked and grinned at him. "Make yourself some toast and peanut butter."

* * *

Craig woke up and for a minute, he didn't know where he was. The frilly curtains, the yellow and green floral wallpaper were definitely not his style. Then he remembered—Judie. He was in Judie's room. He turned and looked beside him. Judie was still sleeping. She looked like the little girl in the photos downstairs. The tension and worry of daily life were all gone. There wasn't even the tension of joy. Just peace. Her hair splayed across the pillow like a princess in a Disney movie. Craig wondered if he looked that peaceful when he was asleep. He sincerely doubted it. For one thing he had been told that he snored. Had he snored last night? He hoped not. They hadn't really had anything to drink; he hadn't even finished his one and only beer. It was probably still sitting on the coffee table.

Craig swung his legs out of the bed and sat up. He squinted through the dark, looking for his shorts. They were downstairs with the beer. He smiled again. It had been some evening. Craig had been with his fair share of women but last night had been very different. Last night there had been an intimacy in their lovemaking. There had been a tenderness that he had never experienced with anyone else. He had made love with Judie to get to know her better, to be as close to her as he possibly could. In the past, he had been with women because sex was fun. It felt good. The women had been with him for the same reason. They had found themselves at The Ritz or at The Sea View after a late night of live music and heavy drinking or maybe they had been drinking on the beach, watching the sun go down— either way, he and those women had sex because they were alone and for just one moment they didn't want to be lonely anymore. Last night had been different. He had needed to be as close to Judie as he could be. He needed to touch as much of her as he could, smell her and taste her, but most of all—just know her, really know her. He could tell she had felt the same way. Craig was under no illusions; he had not taken her virginity, far from it. Craig liked that. How else could she be sure that he was the one for her? It was important to live a little in order to decide on the life you want to lead. Craig didn't know if he wanted to spend the rest of his life with Judie but he did know that never before had he been closer to making that decision. It felt good.

Craig rolled back across the bed and gently shook Judie's shoulder. "Hey you," he whispered. "Sleeping beauty..."

Judie fluttered her eyes open, looked at him, and smiled. "That's my favourite Disney movie," she said.

"Are you still coming to work with me? If you are, we have to go," he said.

"Oh, yes! I would like to," Judie stretched her arms above her head. "Do we have time for a shower?"

"A very quick one," said Craig.

* * *

Judie stepped into the tub and moved forward to let Craig follow her in. She turned her face up toward the hot water and let it cascade over her. It felt good. A hot shower used to be her favourite thing in the world—or at least one of them—but now it would never compare to an invigorating early morning swim in the ocean. Still, right now the hot water felt good. Judie knew that a big part of that was Craig standing behind her. He was a big man and she could feel him brushing up against her. He began to wash her back and the electricity she had experienced during their swim in the ocean returned. Not a sexual electricity, not like last night, but an electrical connection. She felt like they were completing a circuit. This was new for her. There was something about Craig that was so compelling. Judie had enjoyed the company of other men. She had enjoyed them in her bed and she had enjoyed their company in life but Craig was something different. There was a greater power than herself telling her to be with him, telling her to spend time with him. When Craig stroked her back with a lathered face cloth, she wanted to push into his hand and get as close to him as she possibly could. It was the same need that she had felt the night before. Ever since they met, Judie thought there was something different about Craig but she had been wrong. There was nothing special about him but there was something special about their connection. Judie didn't like to think in terms of forever. She never had before and even in her brain, she could feel herself dodging the thought and the word like a bullet. But it kept coming. Kept shooting at her. Judie couldn't help but smile. She turned around to face him. She looked down and her smile broadened. "You said we had to go."

Craig smiled back at her, "I said it would have to be a quick one."

*   *   *

Alan drove the Firebird down Vineyard Haven Edgartown Road. He was sure he was doing the right thing. After all, Craig *had* invited him to watch the movie shoot and he had acted like a jerk. Judie was mad at him and she had every right to be. *He was mad at himself.* Ever since Craig had shown up, he had been acting like he was still in grade nine. Stupid, stupid, stupid. Last night in The Newes From America, he had given himself a stern talking to. He still liked Judie. He still loved her. The best way to prove that he was worthy of her time was to fight fire with fire. The only way to give Craig a run for his money was to beat him at his own game. Alan could be pretty damned charming when he wanted to be. Hadn't he and Judie been having a great summer together before the accident? They had history. That worked in Alan's favour. Now, he just had to remind her exactly why she had been spending so much time with him in the first place. Alan the sailor, Alan with the Robert Redford sunglasses, was still there—still waiting for her—and he wasn't giving up without a fight.

As he headed toward Edgartown, the sky started to lighten. It was a foggy morning—thick and grey. Even though Edgartown Harbor was on the southeast point of the island, there wouldn't be much of a sunrise. There would be no streaks of gold across an ever-changing canvas of orange and pink this morning. No, this morning there would be one even grey slowly lightening around them. It wouldn't even be a grey sky; it would be fog, swirling around them. They'd be lucky if they could see Chappaquiddick across the harbour. Alan wondered what kind of an affect that would have on the movie shoot. A little part of him—maybe not that little—hoped that the fog screwed everything up, squashed the movie magic that Craig was dangling in front of Judie, hopefully dulling his appeal in the process. Craig would be stuck at work and Alan could whisk Judie away for a big breakfast and a sail. Sailing in the fog was exquisite, almost ethereal. Alan would love to be able to share that with Judie.

Alan turned down Main Street and headed toward the harbour. He was hungry. It might be worth his while to stop at Dock Street Coffee Shop for breakfast before he headed over to the set. Surely, it was still too dark to be filming out over the water.

* * *

"That's him," said Peter. "Standing on the corner. That's Charles."

"He looks like a nice kid," said Peter's Dad. He pulled the station wagon to the curb, slowing until the rear passenger door was next to Charles.

Peter rolled down the window and stuck his head and hand out with a wave. "Hey! It's me!"

"Oh! Hi!" Charles spoke with a nervous warble. "I didn't know you were getting a ride." He opened the door, slipped into the seat, and pulled it shut behind him.

"You must be Charles," Peter's father looked back at him in the rear view mirror. "It's nice to meet you, son. I'm Robert Morgan—Peter's Dad. I've heard a lot about you."

Peter rolled his eyes.

"Thank you, sir. You've heard a lot about me?" asked Charles.

"*No! He hasn't!*" said Peter. "Dad, you promised me you wouldn't be embarrassing!"

"What did I say?" asked Peter's Dad. "Charles I heard that you are also a big JAWS fan like my son. What is it about the movie that you like so much?"

Peter waited in silence. He actually wanted to hear the answer to this question too. It was a good question and one that he hadn't thought to ask Charles himself, surprisingly.

"I think it's because it was the first time I ever heard of a shark, sir. I remember seeing the advertisement in the newspaper—you know, the picture on the poster—and thinking, 'Holy cow! What is that?' I asked my Dad and he told me it was a shark. I didn't even know what a shark was, so my parents made me look it up in the encyclopaedia. They're always doing that."

"Doing what?" asked Peter.

"Making me look stuff up in the encyclopaedia! Every time I don't know what something is or how something is spelled, I have to look it up. I don't know how much those books cost but it must have been a lot because my folks are making sure they get their money's worth!" Peter shook his head.

173

"I doubt that it's the encyclopaedias' monetary worth that your parents value but rather the education the books hold," said Peter's Dad.

Charles looked up and met Peter's Dad's eyes in the rear view mirror. "Yes sir."

Peter got up on his knees and turned around in his seat to face Charles. "My Dad brought home a book about sharks—well, a shark expedition. They weren't hunting them though. Were they Dad? They weren't hunting the sharks, were they?"

"Which book?" asked his Dad.

"Blue Meridian: The Search for The Great White Shark," said Peter.

"No, they were just studying them and taking pictures," said his Dad.

"It had amazing pictures in it!" said Peter. "And there were the pictures on the JAWS album cover. Do you have the album?"

Charles shook his head. "What's on the album?"

"It's all the scary music from the movie. Well, it has the poster picture on the cover but on the back it has some pictures too and one of them is of a shark's mouth coming up to bite something but all you can see is the mouth. I could stare at that picture for hours." Peter smiled with relief. It felt like he had needed to get that off his chest ever since he had met Charles. "Anyway, that was how I fell in love with sharks and JAWS."

"Maybe I need to get that record," said Charles. "It sounds cool."

Peter turned back in his seat and looked out the window. They were in Edgartown Village now. "We're almost there!" he said.

"Where are you supposed to meet this guy?" asked his Dad.

"Kind of by Memorial Wharf," said Peter. "You'll see it. It's all blocked off with a big sign that says *JAWS 2.*"

"A big sign that *reads JAWS 2*—signs don't talk," corrected his Dad.

"Yes Dad," said Peter.

Robert Morgan continued down Main Street until they hit Edgartown Harbor. He turned left onto Dock Street and stopped. "There it is alright." He looked around and made a sharp turn up Mayhew Lane and parked in the small parking lot below North Water Street. Turning off the ignition and pulling out the keys, he turned to the boys, "Okay! Are we ready to go?"

"Where are you going?" asked Peter.

"Peter, I told you, you're not going anywhere unless I meet this guy. For safety reasons, I think it's important that he knows that one of your parents has seen his face and knows his name. That's the way it is. After I meet him, I'll take off but not before." Peter's Dad opened his door and stepped out into the cool, foggy morning. "Are they even going to be able to shoot anything in this weather?"

The boys stepped out on the other side of the car and closed their doors.

"Craig assured me last night that they would be," said Peter slinging his camera case over his shoulder.

"You saw him last night?" asked Charles.

"I did. I think his girlfriend lives next door to me," said Peter. "I was on the porch out front when they came home. His truck was still there this morning when we left." Peter grinned at Charles. Charles grinned back.

"Alright you two—god, you're gossiping like two old ladies," Peter's Dad laughed. He walked in the direction of the set and the two boys followed.

* * *

After parking his Firebird behind Fligor's Gifts, Alan stepped out into the cool, foggy, morning. While the sky had lightened a fair bit, it was still pretty dark. Alan decided to take a quick stroll past the production site and then, if there was nothing going on, he would grab breakfast at Dock Street. The harbour was quiet. No doubt there were a few fishermen heading out over by the Yacht Club but there was no foot traffic to speak of at all. On a sunny morning, there would be a few tourists out with their coffees and cameras but the weather seemed to be getting everyone off to a slow start. Alan got closer to Memorial Wharf and the sign came into view. He squinted past it for signs of life. There were a few. People did seem to be setting up for something. Whatever they had planned to shoot that morning seemed to still be on. Alan decided that was a positive. It meant that Judie would be there and she would be excited and happy. She might even be happy that he had changed his mind and come around. She might be happy to see him. The thought put a smile on his face and a little bit of a spring in his step. He took a deep breath. He was nervous about seeing her and about seeing Craig but the more he put a positive spin on it in his head, the better he felt. Alan turned on his heel and headed toward Dock Street Coffee Shop. He really was starving.

*　　*　　*

"That's Alan's car!" exclaimed Judie.

"Which one?" asked Craig as they drove into the parking lot.

"The Firebird," she said pointing a finger.

"He might be a jerk but he's got good taste in cars—I'll give him that," Craig said in a matter-of-fact tone.

"I wonder what he's doing here?" Judie said nervously. "I hope he's not here to cause a scene. We didn't exactly end on a high note the last time I saw him."

Craig shrugged. "Maybe he's here to apologise."

"Maybe..." Judie said almost under her breath. "Look, do me a favour, okay?"

"Of course," Craig turned the wheel of his truck with one hand and backed smoothly into a spot. He turned off the engine. "What's up?"

"Don't tell Alan that we slept together," Judie looked at Craig.

"That's not how I usually start a conversation. It's tacky," joked Craig.

"Just promise me—okay?"

Craig turned in his seat and looked at Judie with both eyes. He felt his chest tighten a little and he didn't like it at all. He spoke in a very serious tone. "Babe, I really like you. I like you a lot. I know we haven't really talked about it yet, but I think we should—we're in new territory for me here. If you were in a relationship with this guy at all or you have feelings for him that you're not sure about, you need to tell me right now. I need to know straight up."

Judie waved her hands in front of her face. "No! No! It's nothing like that! I just don't know how he's going to take it and he's already hurting—I can tell by the way he's acting. Alan's a good guy; he's not usually this crazy. I just want to wait until the timing is better that's all. Really."

Craig stared at her for a moment before speaking. "Okay. I can do that. I guess that makes sense. But don't wait too long. I firmly believe that if you have to keep your relationship secret, you shouldn't be in it."

"I know. I agree," said Judie. "I just want a couple of days." She leaned forward and kissed him. Thanks... *Babe*." Judie pulled back and grinned. "You sure are cute."

Craig rolled his eyes and hoped that Judie couldn't see him blushing in the dim light. "C'mon. Let's go see what's up."

They both stepped out of the truck and started in the direction of Memorial Wharf.

"Craig!"

Craig stopped and looked in the direction of the voice calling from a couple of cars down. He smiled. It was Peter and his friend. The two boys ran toward him followed by a man walking casually behind them.

"It's my shark buddies!" Craig laughed. "How's it going men?"

"We're good," they said in unison.

"Are you still shooting?" asked Peter.

"Absolutely!" said Craig.

"Craig, this is my friend Charles. Charles, this is Craig," Peter said. Behind him, Peter heard his Dad clear his throat. "*Oh yeah*, Craig this is my Dad. He wanted to meet you." Peter spoke this second introduction with far less enthusiasm that the first one.

Craig's Dad reached his hand forward between the two boys and offered it to Craig. "Bob Morgan," he said.

"Hi Bob. I'm Craig Upland and this is my friend, Judie Tate. It's nice to meet you," said Craig, shaking his hand. "Peter's a really cool little dude."

"Thanks. We like him—most of the time. We're considering keeping him." Bob smiled. "He's taken quite a shine to you. I just wanted to come down and put a face to the name."

"Makes sense," said Craig. "We're all pretty excited. We're shooting some shark footage this morning. Are you going to hang around?"

"No thanks," said Bob. "I just gave the boys a lift. I have to get home with some breakfast pastries for the wife and me. We've rented the cottage next to Ms Tate." Bob smiled at Judie. "I guess you know that."

"It's nice to finally meet you," said Judie. "I should have come over and introduced myself when you got here. Are you here for the summer?"

"No. Just a couple of weeks," said Bob. "It's a beautiful spot though. Are you both islanders?"

"I am," said Craig. "Judie's a washashore."

"What's that mean?" asked Peter.

"It means she wasn't born here but she washed ashore from some place else and never left," Craig said with a grin.

Judie laughed. "You're such a snob, Craig Upland."

"Bob, I need to get these guys situated and get to work. It was nice meeting you. Thanks for bringing them down," said Craig.

"Thank you," said Bob. He turned and looked down at Peter. "You mind your manners and do what Craig says. Okay? He's being very generous with his time."

"Yes Dad," said Peter.

"Good," said Bob. "You come home right after. Charles, you're more than welcome to come with him."

"Thank you, sir," said Charles.

With a wave, Peter's Dad turned and walked back toward the parking lot.

Charles and Peter waved back at Peter's Dad.

"Hey, look!" said Charles. "Craig?"

181

"Yes Charles?"

"Isn't that your other friend from the beach?"

12

Alan had barely started walking down Dock Street when he spotted Judie and Craig. Even the fact that they were with two young boys didn't throw him. He would recognise Judie anywhere. His heart rate picked up immediately; he felt his face flush. It had been easy to tell himself to play it cool—give Judie the opportunity to remember what she had liked about him—when he had been alone in The Newes last night, or even driving down Beach Road early this morning. But now, seeing Judie and Craig together in person was a very different story. As Alan grew closer, one of two boys pointed at him. The group looked in his direction and Alan saw Judie take a step away from Craig—not a big step but a step nonetheless. What did that mean? Was she trying to tell him something or hide something from him? As he got closer, he forced a smile. His lips pulled across his teeth and stuck painfully in place with invisible tacks. Alan winced at the feel of it. A smile should be an involuntary eruption of joy and happiness bubbling below the surface but this one was not. He couldn't feel it anywhere else. There was no smile in his heart, and there was no smile in his eyes. Alan hoped that it was still too dark for anyone else to notice.

"Hey guys," said Alan in as casual a tone as he could muster. "Surprise!"

"It *is* a surprise," said Judie. "I really didn't expect to see you this morning, Alan."

"I didn't expect me either," said Alan. "After I acted like an ass—" Alan shot a glance at the two boys. "...jerk yesterday, I went to The Newes and had a long talk with myself."

Alan watched as Craig and Judie exchanged glances.

"I owe you both an apology. Especially you Craig," Alan said with complete sincerity. To his surprise, the more he spoke, the better he felt. "Ever since we met you, I haven't been myself. For whatever reason, you have been pushing every insecure button I have and I have just been making things worse...for all three of us." Alan took a breath. He really was feeling better. "You have no reason to but I'm hoping you'll accept my apology. You did invite me here this morning, so I thought I'd show up. Fresh start, new day, and all of that." Alan looked at Judie; she was beaming. Alan hadn't seen her that happy for a while. Alan extended his hand toward Craig. "What do you say?"

Craig's face was almost expressionless for a moment. Then he smiled and shook Alan's hand. "No problem. Glad you showed up Alan. It should be a fun morning."

"When is the filming starting?" Peter asked.

Alan looked down at the two boys. "Who do we have here?"

"Oh, sorry," Craig said. "Alan, these are my buddies—Peter and Charles. They're big JAWS fans. They're going to help me out with a couple of technical references. Right guys?"

The two boys nodded in silent agreement.

"Alan, why don't you head over to Memorial Wharf with Judie? I'm going to wrap up some business with the guys here. Then, I will send them over to hang out with you. Okay? If you sit on top of the Wharf, you'll have a great view of everything."

"Got it," said Alan. He looked at Judie. She was still smiling. "Ready to go?"

"Absolutely," said Judie.

*   *   *

Most of the harbour was quiet. The water was still and the roads were empty. Fog licked around the corners of the grey cedar buildings, wet from the morning mist. There wasn't even the foot traffic of islanders and tourists eager to catch a glimpse of the excitement going on behind the Universal Production sign. The sign acted as a magic barrier. On one side of the sign, there was Vineyard calm but beyond it, the hurried action of any Hollywood movie set. At least, that's what Peter imagined. The JAWS 2 movie set was his first. No one had ever filmed anything out by his house. Who would ever make a movie in Blairstown, New Jersey? Peter's heart was racing. He watched as young men walked back and forth carrying equipment or pushing lights across the pavement. The mumble of young male voices was constant but Peter couldn't make out a word. As far as he could tell, there were no actors on the set. He couldn't even see those folding wood chairs with the actors' names on them that he and Charles had seen the day before.

"Alright guys, stick close to me," said Craig. "Let's go!"

"Is it okay?" asked Charles. "What about that guy who yelled at you last time?"

Craig laughed. "Mike? He'll be here soon but he's never here this early. All of these guys are too busy and they won't care as long as we don't get in their way. You want to see the shark up close, don't you?"

"Yes!" said the boys.

"Alright then, follow me," said Craig.

Craig led Peter and Charles through the production. He pointed out large cables to step over as the three of them walked single file between crates taller than Peter or Charles. It was impossible at times for Peter to make out where they were going. The butterflies in his stomach increased. They must be getting close to the water. Peter could smell the salt water and rotting wood of low tide. He was sure he was going to take a wrong turn and end up in the ocean. Craig would have to drag him out, everything would grind to a halt, and they would be kicked out. Craig moved swiftly in front of him, clearing a path but also blocking his line of vision completely. Craig stopped and stepped aside.

"Well?" Craig asked. "What do you think?"

Peter made his way around Craig. He could feel Charles slip out of his place in line and step up beside him. Without looking at him, Peter could feel Charles' body stiffen. His friend was standing at attention like his Mom was inspecting him on school picture day. Peter's stomach dropped. His eyes widened. He could feel his palms get clammy. The light was still dim—the harbour encased in fog—but in front of Peter's face, not three feet away, was the gaping maw of an enormous shark.

*   *   *

The shark stared at him. Large black eyes were focussed on him with an intensity that made it hard for Peter to breathe. It was impossible but it was true. The monster of his nightmares was right in front of him. Its large mouth, lined with rows of teeth as big as his fist, open in a constant threat. Peter knew it was mechanical—In fact, he could see metal works deep in the shark's belly when he looked down its throat—but that didn't take away from the visceral affect the rubber skin, eyes, and teeth were having on him. With minimal body movement, Peter forced his eyes away and looked at Charles beside him. Charles was standing very still, not blinking. Peter knew that Charles was thinking the same thing he was. If they moved, if the shark smelled weakness, it would lunge forward. It would attack. Peter could feel the shark's mouth closing on him like a trash compacter, each and every one of those teeth puncturing his skin one by one. Peter started to feel a little dizzy. Realising that he had been holding his breath, he gasped for air.

"Hey! Pete!" Craig grabbed him by the shoulder and shook him gently. "Are you okay buddy?"

Craig's voice was enough to break the shark's spell. Peter felt foolish. "Huh? Oh...yeah, I'm fine," he said. "I just didn't expect it to be so big. That's all. Did you Charles?"

Charles shook his head, "No."

Peter stepped forward and to the side. He looked down the length of the shark. The fish was so long that he couldn't see the tail in the fog. After the large dorsal fin, the shark tapered off into the swirling mist as if it were leaping out of the ocean at them.

"It's not the same," Charles said finally.

"What do you mean?" asked Craig.

"As the first movie—It's not the same shark. This is a new shark," said Charles.

"From what I've heard on set, the sharks from the first movie were all thrown in the garbage. I don't know why. They could have saved themselves a bundle if they still had them for this movie. These babies can't be cheap," said Craig. "Still...he's pretty cool, eh?"

"*He's amazing*," said Peter in the hushed tone that he usually saved for church. Slowly, he reached out a trembling hand and laid his palm flat on the shark's skin between the mouth and the gills. It felt like it was alive, humming with energy.

"Get out your camera, Peter! Let's get a couple of photos and then you have to get out of here before Mike shows up. Okay?" Craig said.

Peter reached into the camera case and pulled out his camera.

"Here," said Craig. "Hand it over and I'll get a picture of the two of you with the shark."

Peter passed Craig the camera and stood up close beside the shark. Charles took a position on the opposite side. As excited as he was, Peter wanted to get away from the shark. It scared him. He hadn't expected that. He hadn't expected the shark to stir up the emotions that it did. When he looked at the photos of the shark in Edith's book, he felt an electrical current; the photos stirred something in him. He loved the images of that mechanical shark in JAWS even more than he loved photos of *real* great white sharks. There was something about it. Now, here, in person, it was the same charge but amplified to the highest degree. He could feel it pounding through his chest and screaming in his ears like feedback from a blown speaker. He was fascinated, thrilled, and completely terrified. He knew that it was metal and rubber—no different than the dashboard in his father's car—dials, springs, gears, pistons, all covered in smooth plastic—but somehow it was different. He could feel it.

"Here, let me take a picture of you guys," Charles said.

"I can dig it," said Craig.

Before he knew what was happening, Craig was kneeling down and putting his arm over Peter's shoulders. Charles was taking their picture. When he stood, Craig gave Peter's shoulder a squeeze.

"Make sure you get me a copy of that, Pete. Alright?"

Peter blushed. "I will." Craig was probably the coolest guy that Peter had ever met. The fact that he thought of Peter as a friend was the best thing ever.

"Alright," said Craig. "Let's get out of here. We need to get you two over and standing with Alan and Judie on the Memorial Wharf. You'll get a good view of everything from up there." The two boys turned and Craig led them back to the Universal sign. "You guys know how to get over there, right?"

"Absolutely," said Charles.

Peter gave him a thumbs-up.

"Great," said Craig. "See you guys later."

* * *

As he and Peter ran toward Memorial Wharf, Charles' mind was running almost as fast as his feet were. He was still trying to process exactly what had just happened. He had just been face to face with the beast that had consumed almost his every waking moment since he had first seen a commercial for JAWS. Since he had read Peter Benchley's novel in secret, since his Dad had brought home Edith Blake's book as well as Carl Gottlieb's. Okay, so it wasn't the one from the first movie. It was pretty darn close! Peter had been right—*it was so big.* A lot bigger than he had expected. Standing there, in front of that shark, he had been unable to move, or even speak! His central nervous system wouldn't allow it. The shark was nothing but an inanimate piece of plastic, but all of his senses registered a major predator. In a calm and soothing voice, the rational side of his brain told him the shark wasn't real, told him that he was looking at rubber and metal; however, at the same time, the other half of his brain was screaming in a panic that he had never before experienced. It screamed that a black eye the size of a cereal bowl was focussed on him, that a mouth fitted with rows and rows of serrated white knives was stretched open and about to take him. That second voice may not have been the more rational of the two but it had been the louder, and impossible to ignore. Charles' fear had almost made the whole experience difficult to enjoy. His fear had overridden his excitement. Charles blushed from embarrassment. He wondered if Peter felt the same way.

Once they were at the foot of the steps of the Wharf, the two boys stopped to catch their breath.

"That was the scariest thing that's ever happened to me!" exclaimed Peter.

Relief washed over Charles. He plopped down onto the wet bottom step and Charles sat down beside him. "Gosh, I'm so glad you said that. I was so freaked out but I didn't want to say anything," said Charles.

"Why not?" asked Peter.

Charles shrugged. "Embarrassed, I guess," he said.

"Why?" asked Peter.

"Well, it's stupid isn't it? I mean, it's just a big chunk of plastic!" exclaimed Charles. He could still picture every detail of the shark in his mind. It would be some time before he forgot anything about this morning.

"I guess, but it's supposed to look scary. It's supposed to be scary," said Peter. "Isn't it?"

Charles nodded. "Yeah, it is."

For a moment, it was quiet. Neither boy said anything. They just sat on the step looking out toward the Universal barges being rigged for the shoot.

"Charles?" asked Peter.

"Yeah?" asked Charles.

"When you would look at the pictures of the shark in Edith's book...," Peter struggled before continuing. "...did you feel anything?"

Charles thought and then said, "What do you mean?"

Peter looked down at his running shoes. "I don't know exactly."

Charles felt his belly start to shake. A grin spread across his face. He chuckled and then before he could stop himself, he laughed.

Peter started to laugh too.

Charles wasn't sure why he was laughing but he liked it. He felt nervous but he was happy too. Parts of the shark, the harbour, Craig, images from Edith Blake's book were all trying to fit together like a jigsaw puzzle in his brain. He didn't have the words to articulate the feelings he was having and he could tell his friend was experiencing the exact same thing. They were both on the same rollercoaster and they had just survived the steepest drop. Charles wrapped his arm over Peter's shoulders. Peter followed suit.

"That was pretty freaking awesome," said Peter.

Charles nodded. "Definitely."

"Hey, you two!"

Charles and Peter looked up to see Alan and Judie looking down from atop the Wharf at them.

"Are you two coming up or what? They're moving the shark out into the harbour!"

* * *

Charles and Peter scrambled up the stairs to the top platform of the Memorial Wharf. Judie couldn't help but laugh at their exuberance. "Be careful!" she called out, surprised at the maternal tone in her voice. The whole morning was taking on a surreal vibe that Judie hadn't anticipated. Waking up with Craig in her bed had filled her with a warmth that she couldn't remember ever feeling in the past. There had been boyfriends—of course there had been boyfriends—but Craig was different. Their connection was different. Craig had even spoken about carving out a future together and Judie knew that she could see it too. She looked at Alan and felt a pang of guilt. She needed to tell him. She wasn't sure how he was going to take it, but she knew she needed to tell him. Judie had been genuinely happy to see Alan reach out to Craig on Dock Street and offer his apology. Over the last couple of days, she had watched as Alan tied himself up in knots over the growing closeness between Craig and herself. She didn't blame him. She and Alan had been getting closer all summer but Craig had changed things and after last night, things would never be, could never be, the same. That wasn't Alan's fault, her fault, or Craig's fault. It was just the way things were. Judie was going to have to find a moment to tell Alan the truth. She was going to have to let him know that they could never be more than friends—Judie and Craig were a couple.

"Christ, that thing is huge!" exclaimed Alan.

Judie turned her attention to the harbour below. A large wood platform was being towed out toward the Edgartown Lighthouse. Every six feet, braces built out of two-by-fours arched over the barge. Together they held the monster shark in place. There were four men aboard the barge; Craig was one. He looked up in her direction and gave a casual wave. Judy watched as the two boys waved back with frantic excitement. She waved back as well. Alan gave a nod. Craig turned abruptly as if he had heard his name, crouched down and flipped open a large box in front of him. He started passing things to one of the other men who in turn started working on the underside of the mechanical beast. As they glided farther away over the smooth glassy ocean, Judie could no longer make out any details. All she could see was the shark. Just past the lighthouse, the boat stopped. The fog swirled around the barge and thickened. The view became more and more faint like trying to see through a frosted windshield. Judie had no idea what they were doing but after about twenty minutes, the shark began to submerge until only the dorsal fin and top of the tail were visible. Another barge slowly left the dock and headed out toward the shark and the first boat. Judie could see there was crew and equipment aboard this boat.

"That looks like the camera to me," said Alan.

"How do they get the shark to go where they want it to go?" asked Judie.

Alan shrugged. "Beats me."

"In the first movie, they ran it along a railroad track on the ocean floor," said Peter.

"Seriously?" asked Judie.

"They did!" said Charles. "That was the main reason they chose Martha's Vineyard. The water doesn't get really deep around here and the bottom is flat and sandy."

"So they're just going to tow it along a track that they've already laid down?" asked Alan incredulously.

"Probably," said Charles.

"How cool is that?" said Judie. "I wouldn't have guessed that in a million years. I would have thought it just floated but now that I think of it, the thing probably weighs a ton."

"Several tons," agreed Alan.

Judie looked at Alan. She wasn't sure what to make of his sudden change of heart. Was he just caught up in the magic of filmmaking? She certainly was. The boys *definitely* were. If Alan had decided to feign forgiveness just to see the making of JAWS 2, she wouldn't really blame him but she hoped that there was more to it than that. She hoped that he honestly had decided that he had been giving Craig a raw deal and that nothing Craig had done had been with malicious intent. In fact, the whole situation was absent of malice. Maybe Alan had come to the conclusion that he and Judie could really be friends. God, Judie hoped that was the case. That would make everything so much easier. If Alan had done some soul searching and decided the best man had won and they could all be friends, that would make everything so much easier—easier on her, easier on Craig, but most of all, easier on Alan himself. Alan turned and looked at her. He smiled at her and she smiled back. So what were the odds that was the case?

The boat that had hauled the barge turned around in the outer harbour and headed back in toward the wharf. On the deck of the second boat, spotlights were lit. There was no sign of the shark. It was underwater...somewhere. The second boat moved slowly, making very little wake on the glassy surface, and then stopped halfway across the harbour. The ripples of water behind her rhythmically made their way toward shore. The boats were motionless. Everything was still. The fog began to swirl back into place, casting a white-blue glow over the harbour. It was still quite dark except for the spotlights on the second boat.

All at once the first boat started to move. The shark's dorsal fin broke the surface in a clean slice right in line with the spot light. From their vantage point on the harbour,

Judie, Alan, Charles, and Peter could see the cameraman on the boat following the shark as it glided toward the docks.

Judie felt a shudder go up her spine. The presence of the boats, the lights, and the camera crew didn't make any difference. The sight of a great white shark swimming into Edgartown Harbor made her uncomfortable. The enormous fin cutting its way toward her was frightening. Sure this was a fake shark but sharks were real. They really swam around this island on a regular basis. She didn't give them any thought but who's to say that a great white hadn't swum past her when she was out swimming on South Beach, State Beach, Lucy Vincent? How would she know? As the shark got closer she could just make out the shape of it under the water's surface. A real shark—even one that size—could swim just a few feet down and no one would ever know until it decided that it wanted you to know. Then, it would be too late.

The boat stopped. The skipper walked toward the stern and spoke into a walkie-talkie. After a moment, he waved his hand in the air and headed back to the wheel. The boat turned back in the direction of the barge taking the shark with it. There was a rumble and a groan. The shark lifted up on a mechanical arm. Out of every orifice—gills, mouth, and underbelly—a grotesque waterfall pounded the surface. The men on the barge waited for the drainage to stop before guiding the great fish back toward its wooden hangar.

"Is that it?" asked Alan.

"I guess so," said Judie. She looked down at the two boys. They were completely engrossed. She wasn't even sure they were blinking. Their shark-infested brains were determined not to miss a single swish of that mechanical tail. Every detail was being filed away. Judie smiled. She loved that they were so passionate about sharks, about JAWS, the whole thing. It was endearing. If there had been something that had held her attention so completely when she was a kid, she couldn't remember what it was.

13

Peter looked over at Charles. His friend's focus on the goings on was unwavering; he stood perfectly still. Peter smiled to himself and turned back toward the shark. Still dripping, the monster hung on its barge and was now being towed back to the dock where it had been just a few minutes ago. The fog was lifting and the whole harbour was brightening in the early morning sun. The Chappy Ferry, which had paused for the shoot was now back on course, delivering islanders from one side of the harbour to the other. The day was getting underway. In fact, when Peter looked out over the harbour at the Edgartown Lighthouse, it looked like any other vacation day on Martha's Vineyard. It was only when he looked directly down that everything changed. The thirty-foot great white shark changed it all. Even out of the water, even on a wood barge surrounded by men, the shark gave him goose bumps. It triggered something instinctive deep inside him and the instinct was to run.

"Did you get any pictures?" asked Charles.

"I got lots!" said Peter. "You were standing right here!"

Charles grinned sheepishly. "I wasn't really paying attention to anything but the shark."

Peter laughed. "Me neither. I think the lighthouse could have exploded and I wouldn't have noticed. This is the coolest thing that has ever happened to me."

Charles nodded in agreement. "Me too. I'm never going to forget this as long as I live!"

"I'm really glad you were here to watch it with me, Charles. It was way better to watch it with a best friend who likes JAWS as much as I do."

"Thanks," said Charles. "This whole vacation is going to be the best I've ever had."

"Mine too."

"Hey you guys," Judie put her hand on Peter's shoulder and crouched down until they were eye to eye. "Alan and I are going to take off. Are you two good? We're going to get breakfast. You can come with us if you want."

Peter looked at Charles. "No. We're going to go and hang out."

Charles smiled. "Yeah, we've got some stuff to do."

"Okay, we'll see you around then." Judie ran her fingers through Peter's hair, tousling it. "My handsome neighbour," she said. Then, as she stood, she kissed him on the forehead.

Peter felt his face flush red. His whole body tingled. A pretty girl like Judie had never kissed him before. He didn't know what to do or say. Finally, as Judie and Alan made their way down the stairs toward the parking lot, he sputtered, "Thank you." but they were too far away for him to be heard. Peter turned toward Charles. Charles was adjusting his camera case and hadn't seen the kiss at all. Peter decided not to mention it. It occupied a warm spot in his chest and he wanted to keep it there. He took a deep breath and cleared his throat before he spoke. "What stuff do we have to do?" he asked.

Charles grinned and shrugged his shoulders. "I just said that so we didn't have to go with them. I'd rather just hang out. We will find some stuff to do though—so it wasn't a lie exactly."

Peter laughed. "Well then let's go find some stuff to do! Aw crap!"

"What's the matter?" asked Charles.

"I forgot to get my bike out of the car. We don't have any wheels!" said Peter.

"There's a bus," said Charles. "I know where to catch it and where it goes."

"You do? That would be cool. Want to get on the bus and go to Oak Bluffs? We could go to Circuit Avenue—play in the arcade, get popcorn at Darling's."

"Sounds good!" said Charles. "Should we say good-bye to Craig?"

Peter walked over to the southwest end of the Wharf and peered over the railing at the goings-on of the production crew. He scanned the crowd looking for his friend. Craig was carrying one of the shark's pectoral fins off the barge. Peter turned and headed back toward Charles. He shook his head. "I don't think so. He looks busy and he's surrounded by a bunch of other guys. I don't want to get him in trouble. That Mike guy is probably there."

"Yeah, you're probably right," Charles said. "Let's just go then."

"Do you have money?" asked Peter.

"I have five dollars," said Charles.

"Me too," said Peter. "That'll be enough to hang out."

"We could get a burger at Nancy's for lunch!"

"What do you want to do in the meantime?" asked Peter. He could still feel Judie's lips on his forehead. Where she had touched him, his skin felt different.

*   *   *

Alan and Judie walked down Dock Street toward the Dock Street Coffee Shop. Judie could hear herself talking about the shark and the movie. She heard herself talk about how much she had loved the original JAWS and she heard herself speculate on whether the sequel would be or could be anywhere near as good but in her mind there was a whole other conversation taking place. It was like she had subtitles that didn't match up with the dialogue. Inside her mind was racing. She had to tell Alan that she and Craig had become more than friends. She had to tell him now. She had been quite surprised to see Alan's car in the parking lot that morning—she and Craig both had. Even more of a surprise had been Alan's attitude, his act of contrition down on the dock. As happy as it had made Judie, the irony was if he hadn't done it, telling him about her romantic involvement with Craig would have been a lot easier but now, things were as complicated as they had ever been. Alan's sheepishness and self-reflection had given her a glimpse of the Alan that she had known all summer. She liked Alan, in fact she liked him a lot. If she was being entirely honest with herself, Judie was pretty sure that she loved Alan but she was not in love with him. She never would be either. She was convinced of it. She had been toying with the idea as the summer progressed. Judie had truly enjoyed Alan's company all season. In fact, she had enjoyed it more and more as the season continued and there was a moment when she thought that it just might grow into love. Then, with no warning, she had been struck across the face with love and she knew right from the get go that she was in love. She also knew that she had been entertaining the possibility of falling in love with Alan because she had no frame of reference. Only when faced with actual love did Judie realise that she had been wrong. She didn't see her time with Alan as a waste. No friendship or relationship of any kind was a waste. She still enjoyed being with Alan. Alan was a good friend. She only hoped that he would still want to be when he knew the whole truth.

"Judie?" Alan asked.

Judie's attention snapped back to the present and she realised that she had no idea what she had been talking about. Just in front of her to the left was a window with a brown awning and white muntins dividing it into nine panes. Alan stood to the right of the window, holding the screen door to Dock Street Coffee Shop open. "Huh?" she said.

"I said are you coming in?" Alan's smile faded. "Judie, are you okay?"

"Oh, Alan I'm sorry. Yes, I'm totally fine," Judie said. She felt her face flush. "I think I just really need some coffee."

"Well, you're in luck—this is a coffee shop!" Alan laughed.

Judie laughed too but it sounded forced and she stopped. "Good. Let's eat."

Judie stepped into the coffee shop and looked straight down the very familiar counter. Dock Street was a long narrow room with the entrance at one end and a long counter down the centre. On the left of the counter was a row of chrome stools each topped with a red vinyl cushion. On the right of the counter was the kitchen/workspace for the servers and cooks. White boards were posted on the walls with menu items and prices hand-written in black ink. The room was filled with the inviting smells of breakfast—coffee, bacon, eggs, and grease. Judie's mouth was already watering. She chose a stool about half-way down the counter and spun into position. The little girl inside her loved the spin and she continued to rotate back and forth long after it was necessary. Alan sat down beside her.

A plump waitress in a tight t-shirt walked up to them. "Coffee?" she asked.

"Yes, please!" said Judie.

"Yes, please," said Alan.

The waitress placed two identical paper cups in front of them and filled them from a steaming glass pot. "I'll give you a second," she said before walking to the cash register. Judie watched her hand a paper bag to a local fisherman and accept a paper bill. She punched a few buttons and the register rang and spit open its drawer. The fisherman told the waitress to keep the change before walking out with his parcel. Judie was engrossed. She loved the local colour. She always did. She particularly enjoyed it at the moment because it distracted her from the task at hand.

"Where are you this morning Jude?" Alan asked.

"I'm sorry Alan," Judie placed both hands around her cup. It felt good. It was warm. She hadn't realised how chilly it had been outside. "You're right. I am distracted. There is so much going on. I'm really glad that you and I are here alone. I've been wanting to talk to you."

"I don't blame you," Alan said. "I've been acting like an asshole lately. You have every right to be pissed off at me. I'm just glad that we're here now and that you're giving me a second chance."

Judie looked away from her cup and up at Alan. "A second chance?"

"Well maybe that isn't the best way to put it." Alan shifted awkwardly on his stool. It spun more than he expected and he had to grab the counter for balance. "I just mean that I'm glad to be back in your life and to have you back in mine. We were having a great summer until…until the last few days."

Judie could feel her eyes starting to well with tears. She felt hot. "Oh, Alan. I'm so sorry. I know that you and I have been having a great time—we really have—but things have changed. They've changed and it's not my fault, it's not your fault, and it's not even Craig's fault. It just happened. It is what it is—damn! I hate it when people say that. Forget I said that." Judie pulled a napkin out of the stainless steel dispenser and blew her nose. She pulled out another. Wiping her nose, she looked at Alan and his face was blank. *Did he get what she was saying at all?*

Alan sat in silence for a moment and then cleared his throat before speaking. "What are you saying? I'm not sure I understand why you're so upset. What's not my fault?"

Judie straightened up a little and wiped her eyes. "I'm sorry. I am upset. I feel really badly. Alan, you and I were heading toward something more than friendship. We were getting really close—I still feel close to you—but Alan, we will never be more than friends. You and I are really good friends. If we get through this, you will probably be my best friend! I love you Alan...I'm just not in love with you." Judie took a sip of her coffee. It was bitter. She added a little bit of milk from a metal creamer. "I'm really sorry, Alan."

"So, you and Craig are..." Alan said quietly not finishing his sentence.

Judie wondered how she would have finished that sentence if she were him. She didn't have a clue. She wasn't even sure how she would finish it herself! "Well, we think we would like to make a go of it. I like him Alan. He likes me too."

Alan nodded.

The two of them sat in silence drinking their coffees. Bacon and hash brown potatoes sizzled on the grill not four feet in front of them across the Formica counter.

"Are you okay, Alan?"

Alan nodded. "Sure."

"Do you think that there will ever be a time when you could be happy for us?"

Alan looked at Judie just as the plump waitress stopped in front of them with her pad and pencil at the ready. For the first time, Alan read her two sizes too small t-shirt. Large round red letters read *I'm A Pepper* across a grease-stained, white cotton background.

210

Alan started to laugh.

*   *   *

The two boys stepped off the bus in Oak Bluffs and made their way toward Circuit Avenue. It was still early and a lot of the businesses weren't open. The Flying Horses carousel was still closed up tight and so was Darling's Candy. There were adults walking around the streets but each of them had a coffee in their hand and some had a pastry.

"What time does everything open?" asked Charles.

Peter shrugged. "I don't know," he said. "Nine, I guess." Quickly, Peter glanced both ways across the street and then ran across to The Flying Horses. He read the sign on the front door and looking both ways again, ran back to Charles. "The sign says nine o'clock. Everything is probably the same."

Charles looked at his watch. "It's quarter-to-nine now. We have fifteen minutes to kill. What do you want to do for fifteen minutes?"

Peter didn't answer him. He was distracted. His eyes were focussed far past Charles and the ruddy wooden walls of The Flying Horses. "Why are there people going into the Island Theatre at eight-forty-five in the morning?"

Charles turned to look toward the base of Circuit Avenue. A short line of young people was slowly making their way inside the pale yellow theatre with white trim. "They don't show movies in the morning...do they?"

The two boys ran toward the Island Theatre. They reached the front doors just as the last couple bought their tickets and disappeared through the double doors.

"Well?" barked a voice from behind a Plexiglas booth. "Are you coming in or what boys?"

"You show movies in the morning now?" asked Peter.

"Just this movie. We're doing a weekend marathon. All day, every goddamn day—JAWS, JAWS, and more JAWS," said the teenage boy behind the glass. "It's on account of them filming JAWS 2 down in Edgartown. It's stupid if you ask me. Everybody's seen the damned thing by now, *especially* on this island but...*whatever.*"

"We haven't seen it," said Charles.

"Well you must be the last two," The young man ran his hands through his long brown hair and gave a long bored sigh. "So, are you coming in or what? It's a buck-fifty each."

"Are we allowed?" asked Peter.

"It's the Vineyard kid—I don't give a shit—just figure it out. If you're coming in, it's three bucks for the two of you. If you're not, beat it."

Peter and Charles looked at each other.

"We weren't going to do anything anyway," said Charles.

"We haven't seen it and we really have to!" said Peter. "It's JAWS!"

Charles nodded. "It's JAWS."

The two boys dug into their pockets. They each pulled out a five dollar bill and passed it through the window to the cashier. He handed them each a ticket and their change.

Peter pulled open one of the heavy wooden doors and they entered the darkened vestibule. Before the door closed behind them, they heard the teenager yell out, "When you're too scared to swim on the beach this afternoon ladies, don't come crying to me!"

* * *

Craig sat on a bench under Memorial Wharf sipping a coffee. He always enjoyed a break but this time he really needed one. He had put on a brave face when Alan had showed up—at least he was pretty sure he had—but where the hell did that guy get the nerve showing up there that morning. Craig was sure that after his last performance, Alan was out of his and Judie's life for good. So much for that. Craig had wanted to punch each and every one of

Alan's teeth out when he came strolling up full of apologies. Craig had invited him but he sure as Christ hadn't expected him to take him up on it! *'I had a good long talk with myself at The Newes'*—what a load of crap. He didn't believe it for a minute. Oh, Alan may have had a think and realised that his little temper tantrums weren't going to get him anywhere with Judie but there was no way Craig was going to believe that he had had a realisation or a moment of clarity and was now a decent guy. Craig felt like he had spent his entire life being fed a load by people who thought they were better than he was. What's more, they always expected him to thank them for it. He wasn't going to do it anymore.

"Hey handsome!" Mike yelled at Craig, breaking his train of thought. "You coming back to work or what?"

Craig got to his feet and tossed his coffee cup in the trash. "Yeah, I'm back. What are we doing?"

"We've gotta crate that son-of-a-bitch up. They're shipping everything to Florida," said Mike.

"Why? What's going on?" asked Craig.

"The director's been fired," said Mike.

"What?" Craig really was shocked. "Can they do that?"

"It's their goddamn money; they can do whatever they want with it. It just came down the pipe. Zanuck and Brown and Hancock had *artistic differences*."

"What does that mean?" asked Craig.

"How the hell should I know? I don't give a rat's ass. I'm still getting a pay cheque and that's all I need to know. You'll figure that out if you stick around."

"Am I supposed to go to Florida too?" asked Craig. He hadn't even thought of that. Did he want to go to Florida? What about Judie? She was planning to set up roots on-island for the first time.

"Do you want to go to Florida?"

"I don't know. I've never thought about it."

"Well, think about it. We won't know where all the dust is settling for a couple of days. My advice to you is to keep your head down and work hard."

"I can do that," Craig said.

Florida…Jesus.

14

Peter followed Charles into the dimly lit lobby of the Island Theatre. There was always a certain amount of excitement about entering a theatre. He and his parents didn't go to the movies all that often. When he did go, it was a real treat. This time, being in a movie theatre on Martha's Vineyard, finally seeing the movie he had been obsessing over for years with his new best friend—no adults—was almost as thrilling as the early morning's events. This would definitely be a day that he wouldn't forget. Peter looked around as his eyes adjusted to the surroundings. Occasional sconces shot weak sprays of light up and down the walls brightening the room just enough to ensure people didn't trip over their feet on the way to the bathroom. Most of the light came from behind the concession booth to their right. A middle-aged woman was pouring Coke from a fountain behind the counter. After popping on a lid and inserting a straw, she slid it toward a cardboard container of popcorn. A young woman picked up both and walked through one of the double doors that led into the theatre.

"Are you going to get something?" asked Charles.

"Do you want anything?" asked Peter. "I was thinking we could share? I'll buy a drink if you buy a popcorn."

Charles nodded. "Deal."

The two boys walked up to the counter and the woman looked at them warily. "You fellas are going to see JAWS? Don't you think you might be a little too young?"

"We're both already big JAWS fans!" said Charles.

"We just saw them filming JAWS 2 in Edgartown this morning!" said Peter. The enormity of that experience still hadn't processed completely. He read the nametag pinned to the woman's smock. Her name was Dolly.

"Oh, you boys have already seen JAWS?" Dolly raised an eyebrow.

Neither boy said anything.

"What can I get you?" Dolly asked.

"We're going to share," said Peter. "May I please have a large coke, ma'am?"

"And I'll have a large popcorn," continued Charles.

"Coming right up," said Dolly. She turned toward the popcorn maker and reached in for a large metal scoop. "You know JAWS premiered here at Island Theater when they released it on the Vineyard back in '75. I was working that day and the line-up went all the way down the block!" She scooped two scoops into a striped cardboard container that read 'Popcorn' in big red letters. "That was an exciting day!"

"We wish we could have been here for that," said Peter.

Dolly laughed. "You would have been babies at the time." She handed Peter a large coke. "You're babies now. I wouldn't let my kids see JAWS and they're older than you two. You'll never swim again. I'm telling you right now—oh, that's right—you've *seen* it before. I forgot." She winked at Peter. "That'll be $2.00 fellas."

Peter handed Dolly the money. "Thank you," he said.

"Thank you, hun," she said. "Have you been to this theatre before?"

Peter and Charles shook their heads.

Dolly pointed up. "The best seats are in the balcony. You should go sit up there. Just take one of those staircases."

"Thanks!" said the boys in excited unison.

Peter walked up the winding staircase that led to the balcony seating. He didn't like the staircase at all. It was too dark to see his feet and the stairs were sticky. The smell was a mixture of popcorn, cigarettes, and old wood—a homely smell. The light was brighter on the balcony than in the staircase. Peter looked around. The balcony was empty.

"Sit in the centre," said Charles.

Peter walked to the centre of the balcony and pulled down one of the red velveteen and vinyl seats in the front row. He sat down and looked out over the gallery. The seats were divided into three sections divided by two aisles. Everything directed toward a stage and an enormous white movie screen. Peter thought it looked like a sail on a pirate ship. Charles sat down beside him.

"She was right!" Peter said. "This is pretty decent! Have you ever sat in the balcony at the movies before?"

Charles shook his head. "No. Have you?"

"No," he said. "It's cool though."

"I can't believe we're going to see JAWS! Are you scared?" asked Charles.

"I don't know," said Peter. "I don't think I've ever seen a scary movie before."

"Me neither," said Charles. "We've seen the shark in pictures though. We already know what it looks like."

"True," said Peter. They did already know what the shark looked like. Would that make a difference? Would their familiarity with the shark take all of the scariness

219

away? Peter didn't really understand what it was like to be scared by a movie. He didn't get it…it was just a movie.

The lights started to dim and the projector whirred into action far behind them. "Here we go!" exclaimed Peter. He reached for a handful of popcorn and stuffed it into his mouth.

The Universal logo started spinning across the screen. When it disappeared the screen went dark. There was a faint noise coming from the speakers that Peter couldn't identify. It kinda sounded like the whales that he had seen on Jacques Cousteau but not quite. Then he heard it—a single bass note boomed out of the front of the theatre. Peter felt a smile broaden across his face until it almost hurt. He turned to look at his friend. Charles twisted in his seat and met Peter with an equally ecstatic look. They had just boarded their first rollercoaster and neither one of them wanted to get off. A second bass note followed by a quick third. Then the screen lit up with a moving shot of the sea floor. The familiar music kicked in—du-dun-du-dun-du-dun—and in large thick white lettering, in the centre of the screen, appeared one word: JAWS. The scene switched abruptly to a beach party—young people kissing and drinking beer by the flicker of a large fire. The ocean roared in the background. Peter recognised it as South Beach in Edgartown. He had swum on South Beach lots of times with his Mom and Dad.

He had never been to a cool party like this though. This looked like the kind of party that Craig and Judie would go to. This was already the coolest movie that he had ever seen and he hadn't even seen the shark yet!

A blonde woman jumped up from the party and ran across the sand. A man got up and followed her. Peter laughed; the man was drunk. He could barely walk. *Idiot*, thought Peter. *Why do grown-ups do that? It's so stupid!* The woman started taking off her clothes and Peter felt a bit funny. It was kinda the same feeling that he had when Judie kissed him that morning. He couldn't describe it. It was uncomfortable but nice at the same time. The woman ran completely naked into the water and the man collapsed on the beach. Peter chuckled again. "Come on in the water!" the woman called. *He can't even walk lady!* Peter thought. The shot changed and Peter found himself looking up at the woman from deep in the ocean. The music started. Peter held his breath. Surely it couldn't be happening already, could it? The music got louder. Peter's heart began to beat faster. They were getting closer and closer to the woman. They were back above the water again—looking at her smiling face. Peter noticed for the first time just how pretty she was. The music burst into a loud crash and the woman dunked quickly under the surface. Peter and Charles both jumped. The woman came up sputtering. Something started pulling at her, dragging her. She was screaming louder and louder as she was being thrashed about. Peter had never heard anyone scream like that before. He didn't like it. His mouth was dry. He couldn't swallow. Strange and terrifying noises came out of her. Peter wanted to put his hands over his ears. The woman grabbed onto a buoy before being pulled away once again and disappearing under water. This time, she didn't come back up. The music began to fade. Without even realising it, Peter had shrunk deep down into his chair almost onto the floor.

*   *   *

Judie stared uncomfortably at Alan. She wasn't sure what to do or say next. She had prepared herself for a lot of reactions to the news about her and Craig being lovers but laughter had not been one of them. It kind of scared her. Had he snapped completely? She couldn't tell. So, she decided to just sit very still and wait for Alan to make his next move.

"Laughing and crying, you know it's the same release?" said Alan finally. He looked away from Judie and down at his coffee. "Isn't that what Joni Mitchell says?"

Judie smiled weakly. "People's Parties—I love that song," she said.

"I know," said Alan. "Does Craig know that?"

Judie winced. She knew what he was saying. "Alan I can't pretend that you and I haven't become very close lately. I'm grateful for that closeness. If at all possible, I'd like it to continue. I'd like that very much but we're going to have to be friends. I hope that's okay."

Alan sat quietly.

Judie continued, "I would rather have you in my life than not at all but if that doesn't work for you, then I totally get it."

Alan nodded. "I would rather have you in my life than not at all too."

"Oh, I'm really glad to hear you say that," Judie smiled even though Alan was still starring at his coffee. She reached out to put her hand in his back—thought better of it—and placed it on his arm. Alan pulled away.

"How do you figure we proceed?" asked Alan. "I mean, is this one of those things where we both say we'll still be friends but then never speak to each other again? It's a small island Judie. Are we just going to exchange awkward 'hellos' at The Black dog and go about our lives?"

"That's up to us. Don't you think?" said Judie.

"You mean me—It's up to me. I mean I'm the injured party here, right?" Alan looked up and faced Judie. His eyes were wet.

This time it was Judie's turn to look down at her coffee. "Yes...I guess so...God Alan, I feel so bad about all of this."

Alan looked over Judie's shoulder out the front window of Dock Street Coffee Shop. The sun was beaming in through the gingham curtains. "It looks like the day is clearing up," he said. "At least for the afternoon. If the wind isn't too bad, we could probably get in a sail...at least in the harbour. What do you think? Sailing always makes me feel better. I still owe you sailing lessons."

Judie stared at him, dumbfounded. "Sailing?"

Alan shrugged. "Sure, why not? Does Craig like sailing?"

Judie shook her head. "Umm...I don't know?" She kept staring. She wasn't even sure she was blinking anymore.

"Well, find out. If he does, we'll go. You know us Quaids, we sail. When in doubt, go sailing. Sailing fixes everything."

* * *

Craig walked off set toward the parking lot. He had a lot to think about. Florida? He was going to have to talk to Judie about that one. Life was funny. A week ago he would have jumped at the opportunity no questions asked but now? It almost seemed like he was building a life on this damned rock. He could see himself living with, even marrying Judie and being very happy. They could make a life working odd jobs as a lot of islanders did—construction, waiting tables, bartending—and live in that little house of hers. They could pack picnic lunches and hike up Abel Hill or Great Rock Bight, they could play it lazy and swim naked at Lucy Vincent Beach. Craig didn't need anymore of a plan than that and although he and Judie had never talked about it, he got the vibe that she didn't either. As soon as Judie had her talk with Alan and he was out of the picture, the two of them would have to have a serious talk about the future and what they were going to do. This Florida trip would only be temporary—a couple of months tops—and it would definitely pay him a lot more than any on-island job would. Maybe Judie could stay here and get a job while he went to Florida for a couple of months to get some cash behind them. Universal would put him up somewhere and probably pay for his food too. When he came back, they would have a nice little nest egg to get them started. Not a bad plan at all. That would leave Judie on Martha's Vineyard with Alan. Craig didn't like that idea at all. He laughed out loud. *I'm feeling threatened by Alan now?* He thought. *Wouldn't he just love that.*

Craig pulled his car keys out of his pocket and twirled them once around his finger before catching them in his palm. He began to whistle. The sky was clearing up although it was windy as hell. He could go for a swim. The waves would be high on the south shore. There wouldn't be many people there except for a few surfers. He didn't have a board but some body surfing might be just the thing. A few tumbles in the sea, trying to ride the waves while Mother Nature showed him who was really calling the shots was always exhilarating. South Beach was only a five-minute drive away. Craig stepped into the parking lot behind The Fligors and stopped whistling. What the actual fuck was Alan doing leaning against his beautiful blue GMC Jimmy High Sierra with Judie?

* * *

Peter could barely breathe. He wasn't even sure when he last blinked. He sat in the dark theatre beside his best friend with his legs curled up underneath him. There was no way he was putting his feet down into the dark where he couldn't see them. He watched as Chief Brody and Quint the shark hunter lowered Hooper in a cage down into the ocean. *Were they crazy? Hadn't they seen the same shark that he had seen?* Their boat was already almost sinking. Water was rising into the cockpit from leaks in the hull. She was sitting so low in the water that the ocean was lapping over the transom! Peter wanted to scream out, *"Just go home! Get a better boat and come back tomorrow!"* but of course he didn't. He sat there watching Hooper go into the water. Slowly, in a shadow, the shark appeared. Peter gasped. It was so big. It seemed to go on forever. It took up the whole screen like a locomotive with teeth, but it glided past the cage with the delicacy of a seagull slicing through the air. Peter pushed himself as deep as he could into his red velvet theatre chair. It smelled like cigarettes. The shark slipped away, dissolving into the murky ocean as quietly as it had appeared. Peter exhaled with relief and felt sweat glistening on his forehead.

With a metallic crash, the shark slammed Hooper's cage from behind. Peter and Charles screamed. Charles tossed their popcorn into the air. Hooper's cage was bent. The shark came back for a second swipe, crashing its torpedo nose into the useless protective metal again and again and again. Bars, joints, and screws twisted and gave way. Hooper pulled out a knife and stabbed at the shark's head but it didn't seem to notice. It pushed harder and faster into the cage. The shark forced Hooper out of the top hatch. Kicking himself through the dark Atlantic as fast as he could, Hooper found safety in the rocks and seaweed on the ocean floor.

The shark rolled and heaved through the water, desperate to shake off the cage in which it was now trapped. Once free, mouth gaping, he disappeared back into the dark depths.

Peter's eyes burned from a lack of moisture but he refused to blink. He wasn't missing a frame.

The shark breached and crashed all three tons of its body onto the transom of the Orca. The boat snapped underneath the great fish like a taco shell. Chief Brody scrambled to brace himself in the cabin but Quint was not so lucky. Realisation spread over the fisherman's face as he slipped toward the enormous maw of the shark. The jaws snapped and Quint kicked. A scream rose out of him low and then piercing. The shark squeezed down and blood erupted from Quint's screaming and gurgling mouth. The ocean turned red. Peter's stomach flipped and for a moment he thought he might vomit. The shark tore down again and in an instant, Quint was silenced. The shark and the shark hunter disappeared into the ocean.

* * *

Alan tried to size up Craig as he walked toward them. He was not happy to see Alan standing at the rear bumper of his truck. Craig hadn't expected to see him and he was not a welcome surprise. Almost immediately, a big smile spread across Craig's face—almost immediately. There had been a split second of recognition and Craig had glared at Alan with the same dark eyes he had on the beach the day before when Alan slugged him. Alan wondered if Judie had caught it. Craig hated him. Alan knew it. Craig was playing the same game as he was; Craig was just better at hiding it.

"Well hello you two," Craig said. "What's up?"

"Alan has invited us sailing," said Judie.

"Sailing?" asked Craig. His eyes narrowed.

"Yes," Judie continued. "Craig, Alan and I talked everything over and we all know the situation. Alan is a very good friend of mine and I want to keep it that way. He does too."

Craig turned his attention to Alan.

Alan met Craig's eyes and picked up his cue. "I'm hoping we can still be friends. There's no way to find out unless we try. I don't want to just be someone you guys nod at as we pass each other on Circuit Avenue. You know what I mean? It's a small island."

"It is a small island," Craig agreed. "So, you propose that we all go sailing? Now?"

"In my family, sailing has always been kind of a cure-all," Alan said. "Even sitting on my boat helps me think. It helps me put things in perspective. I thought maybe if the

229

three of us went out in the harbour, we'd find our way out of this. We'd see where we fit in."

"I know where I fit in," Craig said.

"Yeah, well, maybe I just need to figure out where I fit," Alan said. "What do you say?" Alan stared back as Craig's eyes bore into him. He felt like Craig was trying to figure out what he was up to. He could feel Craig's resistance but he knew there was nothing to be done. Judie wanted to go sailing. Alan was offering the proverbial olive branch and there was no way Craig could refuse without looking like a jerk.

"In that case, let's go sailing!" Craig stretched his smile as far as he could. It didn't convince Alan for a minute but they were going sailing. Alan shone when he was aboard Warlock and he knew it. This was his best chance to get Judie back.

"Oh, that's great!" said Judie. "We'll all have a good time."

Alan liked the tone of her voice. She genuinely sounded excited. If Alan could show them a good time aboard Warlock, Judie would definitely remember what she loved about him. If Craig had a miserable time and blew his Mr Cool cover—more the better.

With Alan in the lead, the three of them headed toward the Chappy Ferry. Alan guessed the wind at around

Alan pointed toward the dock. "You guys wait at the end of that dock over there and I'll come and collect you." He threw his shoes into the dinghy and pushed it into the harbour. Two steps into the ocean, Alan stepped up into the dinghy and settled down onto the centre bench. He began to row.

* * *

Judie turned toward Craig and looked up into his face. "You don't really mind so much. Do you?" She grabbed him by the torso and shook him playfully. "About the sailing, I mean?"

Craig rolled his eyes and chuckled. "Well I'm not thrilled about it to be honest. You and I have a lot to talk about, Judie. I just found out that the production is probably moving to Florida!"

"Florida?" Judie repeated.

"Yes, Florida! They fired the director and they're refiguring the whole movie. They want to know if I want to go with them. A week ago—Christ, three days ago—I wouldn't have even hesitated for even a second but now, you're in the picture and I need to know what you want to do! And I don't want to discuss it sailing the high seas with my new best buddy Alan *fucking* Quaid!"

Judie slipped her arms around Craig and hugged him. "I'm sorry. Alan and I talked at Dock Street and it went okay. I wasn't really sure how he took the news actually. I thought for a minute that he went crazy! He started laughing and I didn't have a clue why. Then he said that he didn't want things to get all awkward between us. He didn't want to say 'let's be friends' if we weren't actually going to be friends. What was I supposed to do? When he suggested we all go sailing to bury the hatchet. What could I say? I had to say yes. Didn't I?"

Craig nodded. "Of course you did. That's why I said yes."

"Well, we're here. It won't last very long. It's windy so we can't leave the harbour. We'll just go sailing and come back and then it will be over. It probably won't take more than an hour. Okay?" Judie glanced quickly at Warlock—the deck was empty. She kissed Craig hard, pulled back and smiled. "I love you."

Craig blushed and smiled back. His first really genuine smile of the day. "I love you too."

15

Charles walked out of the Island Theater and immediately brought his hand up to shield his eyes from the midday sun. The wind had picked up since they had gone into the movie but the sun was strong. Charles looked at his friend. Peter was also shielding his eyes. Charles couldn't make out his friend's face but he could see that his skin was considerably whiter than it had been when they had gone in. Every sign of his early summer tan was gone. Standing in front of the theatre, his legs were shaking. In fact, Charles was shaking too.

"Can we sit down for a minute? Maybe get a Tahiti Treat at Corner Store?" suggested Peter.

"That's a good idea," said Charles. The two of them made their way over to the parkette halfway down Circuit Avenue and Peter slumped down on the same spot where he and Charles had met. "Are you okay?"

Peter nodded. "Yeah. Can you get the sodas?"

Charles nodded. "I'll be right back."

Charles made his way into the dimly lit store and grabbed two Tahiti Treats from the cooler. They were cold and felt good on his skin. Juggling them in one hand, Charles fished his money out of his pocket. He walked between the racks of sun tan lotion and souvenirs up to the same big man who had been at the cash the other day. He handed him his money.

"Is that my friend Peter Morgan out there?"

Charles looked out the door at Peter sitting on the concrete with his head hung low. "Yes sir."

"What's the matter with him? Is he okay? Why didn't he come inside?" The man took the money and made change.

"Oh, he's okay, sir," said Charles. "I'll tell him you were asking after him. I'm sure he'll come in and say, 'hello'," Charles said. There was a slight tremor in his voice. It was the same tremor that was there when a teacher on the schoolyard was grilling him. It sounded like he was getting in trouble. This man's questions were making him nervous.

"Uh huh." The man's tone betrayed the fact that he was nowhere near satisfied. "What have you boys been up to all morning?"

Charles stalled for a moment before speaking. "We saw them filming that JAWS 2 movie down in Edgartown this morning! Have you seen it, sir? They have a shark down there as big as a bus! It's just about the scariest thing we've ever seen. Too much excitement is all. Peter's okay."

"Well you boys take it easy this afternoon. It isn't good to get yourselves so wound up," the man said. He closed the cash drawer with a slam.

Charles walked back out into the afternoon sun and opened both sodas. He passed one to Peter. Peter reached for it greedily and took several big chugs.

"You know that guy in the store?" asked Charles.

Peter shook his head. "No. He's just a nice guy. He gave me a free liquorice that time you and I met."

"Nice or not, the guy is nosy!"

"Nosy?"

"That guy's so nosy he'd smell your farts to find out what you had for lunch!" There was a moment of silence before both boys erupted with laughter. Charles clutched at

237

his belly. All of the nervous energy he had built up watching the movie exploded out of him.

Peter set down his soda so he didn't spill it. "That's pretty nosy!" he said still laughing. He wiped tears out of his eyes with the back of his hand.

"He's worried about you. You do look pretty freaked out," said Charles.

"Do you blame me? You don't look so hot yourself! I saw you shaking in your runners as we walked out of the theatre. JAWS was the scariest thing I've ever seen in my life! Why do people go to movies like that? Holy crap!"

"Didn't you like it?" asked Charles.

Peter stopped for a minute and thought about it. "You know, I guess I did. The shark was the coolest thing like totally ever! Did you see that part when he bit the guy under the water and his leg came off?"

"*And it floated down to the bottom!*" exclaimed Charles.

"Yeah!" said Peter. "I almost threw up when that guy's head popped out of the bottom of the boat though. I didn't think that was going to happen. Wasn't that the scariest part?"

"No. The scariest part was when the shark jumped up at Brody and he said, 'You're going to need a bigger boat!'" said Charles.

"Oh yeah," Peter agreed. "You know what parts I really liked? The parts when the shark was just swimming around and you could see its fin slicing through the water. Those were really cool parts. They weren't too scary but they were still exciting!"

"They reminded me of this morning down on Edgartown Harbor!"

"Exactly!"

"We did it," Charles beamed. "We saw JAWS."

"We saw JAWS!" Peter grinned back at him. "Are you going to tell your folks?"

* * *

With Judie at the helm, Alan hoisted Warlock's sail. The white nylon sheet fluttered as it found the wind. They were heading into the inner harbour. Most of the other boats were tied to their moorings, rolling on the waves, their sails wrapped up in their covers. Cabin doors were closed tight. Nautical groans and clangs sounded across the water under the squawks of the ever-present gulls. The only boat out was theirs. Once the sail was taut, Alan tied off the halyards and took his place at the wheel. Judie gladly relinquished her position and slid further down the orange bench cushion closer to Craig.

"Not ready for Quaid Sailing School volume two?" Alan asked Judie.

Judie laughed. "Not today."

"Have you done much sailing, Craig?" asked Alan.

"Some," Craig called back over the wind. "A buddy of mine has a boat on Tashmoo. We go out every now and again. I'm mostly a truck on the beach guy."

Alan nodded.

"I didn't know you did any sailing," Judie said, twisting in her seat to look at Craig.

Craig just smiled back at her.

"What kind of boat does he have?" asked Alan.

"It's a catboat," said Craig. "Not as nice as this one though. It needs some work. Sailboats need a lot of work—I don't have to tell you that."

Alan laughed. "They are a lot of work," he said. "They say that sailing is the most expensive way to get somewhere for free!"

Judie laughed. "That's awesome," she said.

Alan's chest warmed. It was good to hear Judie laugh.

"Where do you want to go Alan?" asked Judie.

"We're pretty limited," Alan said. "The wind is really picking up. I figure that we'll do the loop down into Katama and then double back. We can't stay out too long."

"That's okay," said Judie. She looked up at Craig and smiled.

"What's your sail made of, Alan?" asked Craig.

"Nylon," Alan said.

Craig nodded. "Good and lightweight."

"It is. Makes it easy to hoist. Especially if I'm going out on a regular basis. No need to work harder than I have to, right?" Alan smiled at Craig. He tried to make it as genuine as he could but it didn't quite hit the mark.

"No. If you're not one who likes to work for things that makes sense. Do you find that you get much stretch in the fabric or degradation from the sun?" asked Craig.

Alan stared at Craig for a moment before answering. Was that a dig? Did Craig just call him lazy on his own boat? Alan looked at Judie. She was looking out over the water and didn't seem to be paying much attention to their conversation at all.

"For the kind of pleasure boating that we do here on the Vineyard, nylon is fine. If the lightweight allows me to work smart, that's a good thing." The sail began to luff and Alan steered closer to the wind. "Sounds like you think you know a little more about sailing then you're letting on my friend."

Craig shrugged. "I read a lot."

241

"I can only imagine," said Alan. "There are a lot of great sailing picture books out there."

Craig opened his mouth for a moment and then closed it. He turned his attention to Judie. "Are you cold?" he asked.

"A little," she said. "but I'm okay."

Craig pulled her closer to him. "Don't worry. I'll warm you up plenty when we get home." Judie sunk into Craig almost disappearing in him. He rubbed her arm to warm her up. Without turning up his head, Craig looked up at Alan and curled up his lips, baring his teeth in a Cheshire Cat grin.

Alan felt realisation sweep over him. All of the blood drained out of his face. His casual grip on the wheel clenched. His knuckles whitened. This race was over. *He's fucked her*, he thought. *He's already fucked her.*

16

The first fork of lightning shot across the sky as Peter pulled open the screen door of his family's gingerbread cottage. He looked up and counted until he heard the rumble of thunder. The storm is close, he thought. He walked inside. His parents were sitting in the living room. His Dad was reading a book and his Mom was reading the newspaper.

"Well, look what the cat dragged in," said his Mom. "Care to tell us what you have been up to?"

"I thought the deal was that you were to come home after you watched your friend film the JAWS 2 scene this morning, bud," said Peter's Dad.

"It was. I kinda forgot," said Peter. "Oh, you guys should have seen it! It was so cool! The shark was *huge*—like, bigger than this room!"

His parents laughed at his enthusiasm.

"Did you get any photos?" asked his Mom. "Nana will want to see that for sure. She loves anything Hollywood."

"I got lots!" Peter said. "Can we go to the drugstore and get them developed?"

"When we get home, bud," said his Dad. "What else did you do?"

Peter fell silent.

"Peter?" his father repeated. "After the shoot was over, what did you and Charles do?"

Peter sighed and slumped down into the pea green chair behind him. "We went and saw JAWS in Oak Bluffs."

"*You what?*" exclaimed his Mom. "Peter, we talked about this!"

"I know Mom," said Peter. "I'm sorry."

Peter's Mom looked at his Dad. "Rob, say something. I hate having to be the heavy all the time."

"What do you want me to say? There's nothing we can do about it now, Carol. He's seen the damned thing," Peter's Dad said. "Are you really all that mad at the boy? I mean, he was going to see it sooner or later. He already read the book."

"Don't remind me," she said.

Peter's Mom looked at him with an expression that he couldn't quite decipher. She didn't look mad *exactly*. She didn't look happy though—that's for sure. Before he could say anything, she rubbed her face with both hands and then ran them through her hair.

"Are you mad at me, Mom?"

"That goddamn shark. What is it about that damned shark, Peter? You couldn't like race cars or Superman—it had to be a giant man-eating shark," she shook her head. "No. I'm not mad at you honey."

"Thanks," Peter said.

"I will be mad at you if you wake up screaming in the middle of the night because you're having nightmares from that stupid movie!" she gave an exasperated laugh. "Then I'll be pissed."

"Were you scared, bud?" asked his Dad.

Peter nodded vigorously. "I've never been so scared in my life, Dad!"

His Mom rolled her eyes. "Great."

"What was the scariest part?" asked his Dad.

"Honestly, Robert! You're as bad as he is!" Peter's Mom stood up. "Go out on the porch. I don't want to hear anymore of this. I'm going to make spaghetti and meatballs for dinner. Okay?"

Peter stood up and headed toward the porch with his Dad in tow. "With garlic bread?" he asked.

"Get the hell out of my house," she said. "...and take your father with you!"

As Peter stepped back onto the porch, the last thing he heard was his Mom muttering to herself, "That goddamn shark..."

*   *   *

Alan did his shot of whiskey and then took a mouthful of Guinness. The sail had been a bust. He had been sure that once he got Judie out on the water, he could get her to see the Alan that she had loved before Craig had shown up. They would get out on the open water and she would see the Robert Redford sailor that had made her laugh; the one she had flirted with over lobster salad at Nancy's. That was before he had figured out that they had already had sex. How could he have been so stupid? Guys like Craig move pretty fast. They don't give a shit about the women they use. They do whatever they can to get their dicks wet. That was all they cared about. They were walking goddamn erections. Craig was going to keep sticking it to her until he got bored and then he'd wipe himself off and stick his dick in someone else. Alan snorted and took another mouthful of beer. He motioned to the bartender for another shot of whiskey. Judie would probably come crying back to him then. She would realise the mistake that she had made and beg Alan's forgiveness. Well, she could go to hell. Alan Quaid wasn't interested in the sloppy seconds of a muscle bound retard like Craig. No way. He wasn't going to give either one of them the satisfaction. There were plenty of women at the Yacht Club who would love to go out with him—girls from good families too. Alan didn't have to keep slumming it with chicks like Judie. *Fuck her.* Alan's second shot arrived and he swallowed it immediately. He asked for another.

*   *   *

"That was brief," Craig said, keeping his eyes on the road as he spoke.

"I know," said Judie. "It was a bit worrisome."

"Are you complaining?" Craig asked. The storm was picking up and the waves were rolling up onto the beach. It wouldn't be long before Beach Road was flooded.

"No, not exactly," she said. "I'm just wondering what happened. He kind of did an about face. Everything seemed okay at first but then it was like a switch was flipped."

"He started chirping me. That's what happened," Craig said.

"What do you mean?" asked Judie.

"What do you mean, what do I mean?" Craig said incredulously. "You were there, babe!"

"I know but I wasn't paying a whole lot of attention to you guys. I love being out on the water and that's what I was focussed on. I remember you guys talking about your friend's boat on Tashmoo and then you started going on about sail material and I kinda zoned out! What did he say?"

"He implied I was an idiot; that I only read picture books," said Craig.

"He did?" asked Judie.

"I wasn't entirely blameless," Craig continued. "I kinda dug at him for not having to work for anything."

"Jesus! Where the hell was I?" Judie shook her head.

"It doesn't matter. The whole sailing thing was a bad idea. When he saw me warming you up, he figured out just how close you and I actually are. He didn't like it. That was the end of the sail."

"I guess it wasn't a good idea at all," said Judie. "I'm sorry."

"It doesn't matter; it's over," said Craig.

"What do you want to do now?" asked Judie.

"I figure I'll drop you off at home then I'll go get some take-out from Nancy's. We'll eat like pigs and screw like rabbits!" Craig looked at Judie for a second, smiled, and returned his eyes to the road.

Thunder rumbled as sheet lightning shot across the dark sky. Heavy rain pelted the windshield as they turned onto Tuckernuck Avenue.

Judie leaned forward and looked up through the glass. "Are you sure you want to go back out in this?" she asked.

"I don't think *want* is the verb that I would use but I don't *want* to starve either," he said.

"I could cook us dinner," Judie said. "I'm not a brilliant cook but I could whip us up some spaghetti and meatballs in a flash."

"Spaghetti and meatballs sounds absolutely perfect," said Craig. "I am sick of take-out anyway." The truck bounced into a pothole and water sprayed across the road. "It's coming down pretty hard. Looks like we're in for a real nor'easter."

"Big storms freak me out a little bit," Judie said.

"Really? Why?" asked Craig. "They're really no big deal."

"I didn't used to be but ever since I spent five days on the island during a hurricane…it turned me off. I used to think they were romantic."

"We can make you think they're romantic again," Craig smiled. "We'll get drunk and run around naked in the rain."

Judie laughed, "You're on." She slammed her hand on the dashboard. "Oh damn it!"

"What?" asked Craig.

"I'm out of wine! We can't have spaghetti and meatballs without red wine!"

"Looks like I'm going out after all."

* * *

With the last piece of garlic bread still in his mouth, Peter cleared the dinner plates from the table. His parents watched him, looked at each other and raised their eyebrows. He smiled at them.

"Thank you very much Peter," his Mother said with an appreciative chuckle.

"Dinner was really delicious, Mom," Peter said. "That was your best spaghetti yet!"

"I'm glad you liked it."

"The kid's right, hon. It was great!" chimed in his Dad. "Why don't you relax while Peter and I clean up?"

Peter's Mom eyed his Dad with a half-smile. "Well, I know why he's being a good boy," she motioned to Peter, "but why are you?"

Peter's Dad leaned over and kissed his wife. "This is your vacation too."

Peter moaned with revulsion. "C'mon! Do you guys have to make out in front of me? It's gross!"

"First of all, we were hardly *making out.* Second, if we didn't do it once in a while, you wouldn't even be here," Peter's Mom laughed.

Peter collected the glasses and brought them over to the small sink that had been fitted into the cottage counter. He turned on the hot water and added soap. What a day this had been. He had been up so early, gone into Edgartown, met his friend Charles, and watched the filming of JAWS 2! Then, he and Charles had taken the bus into Oak Bluffs and they had watched JAWS. It was almost too much to take. Monster shark overload! Peter looked out the kitchen window at the leaves of the rhododendron bush being bombed by the rain. It was coming down hard. They hadn't missed this weather by much. A few hours difference and the whole shoot this morning could have been cancelled. If they hadn't seen the filming of the movie that morning, he and Charles wouldn't have caught the bus to Oak Bluffs. If they hadn't caught that bus, they wouldn't have been walking up Circuit Avenue at just the right time to catch JAWS. His entire day would have changed. Oh, he'd still be having fun. He'd be playing a board game right now with his folks—Life or Monopoly, maybe cribbage with his Dad—but he wouldn't have seen his movie. Even now, when he closed his eyes, he could see every detail of that shark leaping out of the water at Brody as he chummed the water.

"*Peter?*" his Dad shook him gently at the shoulder.

Peter looked up at him, confused. "Yes, Dad?"

"Are you okay, bud? I called you three times!"

"You did?"

"I did. You've also been washing that same cup for five good minutes now. I think it's clean," he said.

"I have?" asked Peter.

"Here—why don't you give me that and go up to bed. Okay, son?" Peter's Dad took the cup from Peter and turned him toward the stairway that led up to the bedrooms. "You've had a long day with way more excitement than you're used to. Get some sleep."

Peter couldn't argue. His eyelids felt awfully heavy and he really didn't want to be washing the dishes. Peter walked toward the staircase, kissing his Mom on the cheek as he passed the table.

The rain filled Peter's room with the *Tap! Tap! Tap!* of a distant marching band. The room was dark but Peter didn't turn on any lights. The dark was soothing. Peter stripped off his clothes, took a clean pair of pyjamas out of his suitcase, slipped them on, and crawled into bed.

Tap! Tap! Tap! Peter saw the man in the red rowboat capsize and the shark pull him under. *Tap! Tap! Tap!* Peter heard the lady with the accent ask if they were really going to close the beaches. *Tap! Tap! Tap!* Peter saw the shark crash through the cage thrusting itself forward to get at Hooper. *Tap! Tap! Tap! Tap! Tap! Tap!* Drums... those marching drums... Peter fell asleep dreaming of the Fourth of July parade in JAWS.

* * *

Judie kissed Craig hard on the lips. She ran her fingers through his mop of brown hair and pulled him in as close as she could. As if she pulled hard enough, she could actually get him inside her mouth. She could smell him—that Craig scent. She had never smelled it before. It was a natural smell, a healthy smell, a sexy smell.

"You're not really going to go back out in this, are you?" asked Judie.

"Yes," Craig laughed. "We're going to get out of bed and get some nourishment or they'll just find us here days later, dead from dehydration and a lack of nutrition."

Judie chuckled. "I'm good with that."

Craig laughed and stood up. He put on his shorts and T-shirt.

"You promised me we would run naked in the rain!"

"Yes, but I want to do it on a full stomach," he said. "Go make me some spaghetti, woman!"

"Oh I see how it is! That's woman's work, is it?" Judie shook her head in mock disgust. "Haven't you heard of the woman's movement?"

"Keep it up and I'm going to have a movement!" Craig stated.

"You're disgusting!" Judie laughed. "Get out of my house and don't come back until you're loaded down with cheap booze!"

"Now, that's my kinda woman!" Craig lifted her to her feet. "Do you care what I get?"

Judie shook her head. "No. Surprise me." She reached for her robe, slipped it on, and tied the belt. "Dinner won't be long. I have meatballs in the freezer. Once they get going in the sauce, it wont take any time at all."

"Sounds delicious," Craig started down the stairs. "Back in a flash!"

Craig opened the front door of Judie's pink cottage and stepped out onto the covered porch. The rain was deafening. Rain pounded the roof of the porch and the neighbour's porches. It hit the roof of his truck and the hood. It was hard to tell the difference between the sound of the downpour and the actual thunder. The campground swirled in oily darkness. The glow of the lampposts cut off by the sheets of rain. Leaves and branches swayed under the weight and force of the water. Craig squinted, standing at the edge of the front step. "Jesus," he said. "Here goes nothing!"

    Craig stepped from the porch and took his first step toward the truck. He heard a crack. Everything went white. Craig fell to his knees and then collapsed face first into the mud.

THE PRESENT

1

Charles pedalled as hard as he could, forcing his black road bike up East Chop Drive. The hill was a killer. The fact that it was at the end of his ride home made it hurt all the more. Moving to Martha's Vineyard was by far the best decision—in his estimation—that he had ever made but it hadn't done much for his waistline. Lobster rolls at The Lookout Tavern, apple fritters at Back Door Donuts, and far too many bottles of Kim Crawford Sauvignon Blanc everywhere, had made all of his favourite shorts either extremely uncomfortable to wear or impossible to get on altogether. Having a wife that stayed fit by going to classes at the YMCA in Vineyard Haven didn't help. She looked great. Even her job as Police Chief of Edgartown kept her somewhat active. It certainly kept her more active than his blogging and writing for various online newspapers. It was all too easy for him to "work" with a donut stuffed in his mouth at the dining room table or with a beer and a burger on the deck of The Seafood Shanty. He could sit on that deck and watch Catboat Charters' Tigress sail through the harbour all goddamn day. There was no use trying to complain about it either. There were people with real problems in the world. He even wrote about some of them. 'Addiction on Martha's Vineyard' had been very well received when it had appeared in The Vineyard Gazette. He was always grateful when someone stopped him on the street to tell him how much they had enjoyed that piece or better yet, tell him that it had helped get one of their loved ones into rehab. When other people in the world were struggling with real problems like that, how was he supposed to complain about having an abundance of seafood to stuff into his face under the hot Martha's Vineyard sun? It was too shameful to even think about. No, instead of wallowing in self-pity, Charles had decided to do something about it. He had bought a bike. He was still sitting down but at least now it hurt like hell and that must be good for something. Trying to put on his favourite Vineyard Vines shorts was like trying to load a shotgun with watermelons; however, a couple of pairs were less uncomfortable than they used to be—it was a start.

Just when he couldn't decide whether his legs were burning more than his lungs or vice versa, he reached the top of the chop and coasted toward the lighthouse. The East Chop Lighthouse was his wrapping up point. He would sit on one of the benches, look out over the ocean, and eat an apple. When he had finished eating and the breeze coming in across Vineyard Sound had cooled him sufficiently, he would walk his bike home. He lived just six houses down from the lighthouse.

The sun was high and the sky was that pure cerulean blue that Charles had never seen anywhere else. The colour was so deep that if he had seen it used in a painting, he would think that the artist had missed the mark—that it looked fake. So much of Martha's Vineyard was like that. The island could be so real that it was unreal. The sky was too blue, the Aquinnah clay was too red, the Chilmark fields were too green, and the Menemsha sunsets were too pink. Everything was all just too real. It was too much. Visitors always commented on it. "How come the sunsets don't look like this in the Caribbean?" or "I've never seen anything like this before." Charles would always want to tell his friends that he told them so, for he had undoubtedly tried to describe these things to them on countless phone calls, or in any number of blogs that he had written, but the island was one of those things that had to be experienced to be believed. It was like those YouTube videos of colour-blind people putting on those special glasses to watch the sunset in colour for the first time. Words just didn't cut it.

Charles propped his bike up against the white picket fence encompassing the lighthouse, opened the gate, and walked toward one of the green wooden benches. There were usually one or two tourists taking photos but today, there was no one. He always liked it when he was alone on the chop. Again, he hadn't a leg to stand on when it came to complaining about tourists. He and Laurie had their own beach house six houses down—he could sit alone by the ocean whenever he wanted—but there was something Zen about sitting alone at the lighthouse. He couldn't quite put his finger on it. It was just oh, so Martha's Vineyard.

* * *

Police Chief Laurie Knickles walked into the Edgartown police station with an Espresso Love coffee in her hand. She took a sip. It was hot and delicious. Laurie tried to remember when she had put the first cup of coffee in her hand but she couldn't. She remembered drinking coffee and smoking with her friends at Denny's during high school;

that was before her move to the island. That had also been the classic ceramic diner mug, exactly like the mugs at The Black Dog Tavern just without the dog. In lieu of the dog, those mugs had read Denny's on the side in that famous red and yellow script. Still, that was a mug. When had she first ordered a coffee to go in a paper cup? Had it been a Tim Horton's in Canada? A Dunkin' Donuts in Boston? She had no idea. All she knew was that it seemed like she always had one wherever she went. It was a permanent fixture.

Laurie smiled at the policewoman behind the front desk. "Good morning, Polly," she said with a genuine smile. "Actually, it's almost lunch now, I guess."

"Hi, Chief!" said Polly. "I saw your husband out on his bike this morning on my way in!"

"He was out there alright," said Laurie. "He's determined to get those pounds off."

"I think he looks just fine," said Polly with slightly more lascivious growl in her voice than Laurie would have liked. "He's a handsome man, your Charles. Besides, I like a man with a little meat on his bones."

The thought of Polly doing anything that would require any man—her husband or otherwise—to have *meat on his bones* was enough to make Laurie toss her cookies. "I hate to disappoint you Polly, but he's determined to get back into his favourite shorts. He says that he's been fat too long and now he's turning fifty. He doesn't want to be *fat and fifty!*" Laurie laughed. "The man is crazy but I applaud his efforts. It keeps him healthy. I wouldn't mind if he was around for a while yet." Laurie stepped into her office and closed the door behind her. She had to force herself to work on the police budget. She was never going to get it done with the door open and Polly outside on the desk. Police work didn't get more tedious than working on the budget and she would take full advantage of any distraction available, even if it meant talking to Polly.

As a general rule, Laurie hated working at her desk, and she had been completely unprepared for the amount of paperwork that went with being a police officer. They sure didn't tell young people that in school. When she had decided to be a police officer, Laurie had imagined herself writing parking tickets, talking to classrooms of children, helping seniors, and saving kittens from trees. Granted, she had been very young at the time. The facts of day-to-day adulthood were all kept very hush-hush. Essentially, being an adult was made up of paperwork, waiting in line, and deciding what to have for dinner. All were time consuming, all were exhausting, and none were mentioned at all to anyone under the age of eighteen. Why spoil the surprise?

Laurie typed her password into her computer and watched it whir to life. She looked at the time in the upper right-hand corner of the screen. It was noon on the dot. Charles would be home soon. She'd give him time to shower, or swim, and eat lunch and then she'd give him a call. If she got lucky, she would time it just before he lost himself up in the attic. Charles was donating some photographs to the Old Sculpin Gallery's exhibit *Martha's Vineyard 1977*. Apparently, nineteen seventy-seven was a big year on the island. It was long before Laurie's time; she didn't know anything about it. Charles was a very different story. When she got home after The Edgartown Council meeting and told Charles about the possibility of the exhibit, he thought it was an excellent idea. She could still hear him, *"Oh! That was a really big year! It will make a really exciting exhibit!"* Laurie just shrugged. "If you say so," had been her response. Between the two of them, Charles was always the one who knew more about their island home. Sometimes it irked her but most of the time, she was really proud of the fact and would brag about him to islanders every chance she got.

Laurie pulled her iPhone out of her pocket and dialled home. Talking to her husband for a few minutes was definitely better than doing the police budget.

* * *

Charles sat down on the hardwood floor of the den. He pushed one of the over-stuffed burlap chairs out of his way to better access the bookshelf behind it. Dragging his finger along the photo albums and picture books, he grimaced. Charles didn't know when he or Laurie had last dusted back here but he would bet a pay cheque that it hadn't been in the past year. Laurie had brought up the idea of hiring a cleaning service a while back but Charles had balked. He had been a lot less busy then. Now that writing was keeping him more occupied, maybe they should revisit the subject. A lot of good people are always looking for work. It wouldn't be hard to get a recommendation.

Fenway The Beagle bound over to Charles, excited to find him sitting on the floor. Floor time meant playtime! Stepping up onto Charles' thigh, Fenway reached his snout up to Charles' cheek and gave it a big lick.

"Aw, Fenway!" Charles laughed. "I love you too buddy, but get down okay?" Charles tried to sound stern but the dog kept licking and Charles kept laughing. The happy sounds had Fenway convinced that he was on the right track, so he lapped eagerly at his owner's face. Charles grabbed Fenway by the torso and vigorously scratched both sides at the same time. Fenway barked in delight and rolled over onto Charles' lap. Charles' phone rang. He reached into his shorts pocket and pulled out his iPhone. It was Laurie.

"Hey Babe," Charles half-laughed into the phone.

"Hey back!" She said. "You sound very happy to hear from me."

"It's not you," said Charles. "It's Fenway."

"I should have known better," Laurie said. "I can't leave you boys alone for a minute."

Charles laughed. "It's true," he said. "Actually, I just sat down to start looking for those photos for the gallery. As soon as he saw me sitting on the floor, Fenway figured it was playtime!"

"It's always playtime with you two. I thought you'd be up in the attic looking for all of those photos," said Laurie.

"I thought I'd take a quick look down here first," said Charles. "Laurie, I think we need to talk about hiring a cleaner again."

"Oh, I'm glad you said something. I chased a pair of rolled up socks under our bed the other day and found enough cat hair to make a brand new cat! You said you would take care of it, and I didn't want to offend you," said Laurie. "I love you babe but I don't think housework is quite your forte."

Charles laughed. "I have to agree. These albums are filthy. Oh, and no offence taken. Do you know anyone?"

"Not off hand, but I'll ask around. I know a few of the guys here use someone. We wouldn't need a lot of help for just the two of us but if someone came in once every two weeks it would make a big difference. You know—dusting, floors, bathrooms. You and I can handle the day-to-day stuff."

"Agreed," said Charles.

"In the meantime, do you think you could run a Lysol wipe over the photo albums and a vacuum under the beds?"

Fenway jumped at Charles again and dragged his big pink tongue over Charles hand and forehead. "Aaawww man!" Charles exclaimed. "Maybe I'll just shave the cat and the dog!"

"Fine," Laurie said. "But wait until I get home. If you're going to try and shave Bubbas, I want to get that on video! That cat is a force to be reckoned with. That'll be worth seeing!" Laurie laughed.

"Did you call for a reason?" asked Charles wiping off his face with the back of his dry hand.

"Nope," Laurie said smugly.

"Then I'm hanging up. Love you," said Charles.

"Love you too," she said.

Charles hung up and looked Fenway in the eye. "Your Mommy is crazy. Did you know that?"

Fenway barked twice for yes.

* * *

With her left foot, April Stevens reached blindly for the parking lot. She knew it was down there somewhere. She should have stepped down out of the van and then once she was standing, turned back in and picked up her bags but she wasn't thinking straight. Her mind was filled with details about *Martha's Vineyard 1977*. The entire show had been her idea but still...

When she had presented it to the board, they had gone for it without hesitation—something she had never seen before—and Clara Skiff and John Pease—two board members that she didn't even think liked her—had recommended that she head up the entire project! She would have the full support of the board of course. She had said yes. What else could she say? She was overwhelmed. April had expected to be included in the organisation of the event, but never in a million years would she have thought she would be spearheading it. Clara and John had always been a little frosty toward April, or at least that's what she had thought. Is it possible that they were setting her up? Was this some grand scheme to get her booted off of the board and out of the Martha's Vineyard Group of Artists? April assured herself that she was just being ridiculous. Even if they wanted to make her look bad, they wouldn't do it at the expense of the Gallery. No, she was over-thinking it.

Everyone had that voice in his or her head. That voice that told them that at any moment, someone was going to discover that they weren't good enough, that they were faking it, and should be kicked out, fired, or removed in some way from the group. Still, she was always hearing about cliques on the island and people playing politics. It was all in her head…wasn't it?

April's foot found the pavement and she asserted herself into a standing position. She took a couple of steps and then pushed the driver's door of the van closed with her bum. She heard a laugh.

"I thought I was the only one who did that!" the voice said. "Here, let me help you with those."

April felt one of the paper Stop & Shop bags lift out of her grip. The sun hit her face and she squinted but not before seeing a mop of blonde hair and the smiling face of her friend, Kathy O'Sullivan. "Oh, Kathy!" she said. "How are you?"

"I'm great! You know me—I'm always good," Kathy said. "What are all these?" Kathy peeked in the bag as the two women walked across the parking lot.

"Oh just some groceries for the gallery," said April. "We all put money in a kitty and then someone goes and picks up coffee, milk, sugar, cups, stir sticks…maybe a treat or two." April fished around in her pocket for her keys. "If I'm honest, the treats are mostly mine."

"I won't tell," said Kathy.

"I try to keep them as healthy as possible," April said. "I really have to lose some weight. Diabetes runs in the family and the doctor is after me."

"Why don't you come for a run once a week with me?" asked Kathy. "We'll have a blast!"

April looked down at Kathy's outfit for the first time. Kathy was wearing running shoes, black spandex pants, and a bright pink tank top with *Do Epic Shit* written across it in big white lettering. It was hard to believe that Kathy was a grandmother. "Oh, I don't think I'm ready for that yet Kathy," said April.

"I'm not a fast runner," said Kathy. "We'll go slow."

"Maybe one day," April said but her tone told both her and Kathy that there wasn't a snowball's chance in hell that she would ever be running the roads of Martha's Vineyard. April reached out her hand and turned her key in the lock. The two women walked inside. April dropped her bag onto the reception desk and Kathy followed suit. "Thank you so much Kathy," April said. "I really appreciate your help."

"No problem at all," Kathy said. "Will I see you at Bob and Brenda's for porch wine this weekend?"

"Definitely!" April laughed. "I will always take you up on *that* offer!"

"Excellent! Back to my run!" Kathy jogged out of the gallery and April closed the door behind her.

April looked around the Old Sculpin Gallery. It filled each and every one of her senses. She never tired of it. April had submitted her application to join the Martha's Vineyard Group of Artists because she loved to paint and she thought it would be fun to make some friends who were likeminded. She had also wanted to join because she absolutely loved the building. There was so much history involved in the Old Sculpin. Her father had owned a catboat when April was young and many of her best childhood memories were of sailing aboard that boat. The Old Sculpin Gallery had been the workshop of Manuel Swartz Roberts—boat builder extraordinaire. Manuel had been known across the globe for his craftsmanship. One of his boats—Vanity—still sailed Edgartown Harbor. Vanity was owned by Martha's Vineyard Museum and was the only floating museum exhibit that she had ever known. April had been out in it a couple of times; she was a beauty. Her father's boat had been a little bigger but being out for a sail brought back a lot of memories. So many catboats had been built in the Old Sculpin but not just catboats. Manuel Swartz Roberts had also designed and built the first Chappy ferry, *On Time*, in this very shop. It was long gone now but the *On Time II* and *On Time III* were built on the same model—with a few adjustments—and are still used today. It was impossible to know everything that had been built in Old Sculpin. When April stood in the gallery, she was sure she could smell the wood shavings that—according to local legend—would get to be more than two feet deep. Each time she entered the building, April took a deep breath. She couldn't help herself. One hundred and eighty years of Edgartown Harbor history lived and breathed in its wooden foundations—in every wood beam, every glass pane, ever hinge, and every nail. April could feel it.

April's thoughts began to wander back toward the exhibit as she sorted through her two grocery bags. While she waited for Charles Williams to bring his JAWS 2 production photographs, she would focus on the disappearance of Alan Quaid. No one talked about it anymore, not like they still talked about JAWS, but Alan Quaid's disappearance had been big news on Martha's Vineyard in 1977. A little unsolved mystery was always a good way to get chins wagging when you were trying to get people interested in local history.

2

Charles set a second stack of albums down on the kitchen table beside the first pile he had trekked in from the den. He pulled out a chair, sat down, and picked up the first album. His heart had dropped into his stomach when he first saw it. He hadn't forgotten about it as much as he just hadn't thought about it for decades. Written across it in faded red pencil crayon was *Amity Island*. He could imagine his friend Peter carefully blocking out each and every letter to make sure they would be evenly spaced. Then, colouring them in an attempt to make them look like the font in which JAWS was written on all of the movie merchandise—red and overly bold. Charles read somewhere that the font was now called 'the JAWS font'. He didn't know if that was true but he hoped it was. Peter had done a good job. Charles remembered receiving the album in the mail. It was the first real package that had come to the house addressed to him. *Master Charles Williams*, the package had read. Charles had held onto the packaging as long as he could but eventually, it had been tossed in the trash. Despite its age, the book was holding together remarkably well. Charles sat back in his chair and ran his hand across the album cover. It was such a distinct feeling, a scholastic feeling—smooth and rough all at the same time. *What was this stuff called? Construction paper? Was that right?* It felt like childhood. It smelled like childhood.

Charles was mildly amazed that the whole album hadn't fallen apart. Peter had punched holes in the cream coloured construction paper—*that was definitely what it was called*—and looped the holes with red yarn to create a binding. As he opened the cover, the brittle paper edges flicked against one another giving the impression that they would tear at any moment but they didn't. The first photos were of Woods Hole and the ferry. What the captions lacked in imagination, they more than made up in clarity. Under the two photos of Woods Hole Ferry Terminal 'Woods Hole' was written in a very neat yet distinctly juvenile script. Charles chuckled at the images. The Cape and Islands gave the impression that nothing had changed in the area for four hundred years but the fact was a lot had changed and changed a great deal. Charles remembered the Woods Hole depicted in these photos, he remembered it quite clearly "like it was yesterday" as the saying goes, but he doubted that his wife would recognise it at all. Laurie hadn't come to the Vineyard until well into her adult years. The terminal building in these photos wasn't even there anymore. The entire space had been reconfigured in an effort to make way for the ever-growing tourism trade. The traffic from the Bourne Bridge down highway twenty-eight to Woods Hole Road had become impossible in the summer months. More and more people were making their way out to Martha's Vineyard and Nantucket for vacation. The islanders complained long and hard about the increasing summer numbers but Charles knew that they would complain even louder if the tourists didn't come—although he never voiced that opinion.

Charles turned the page of the album. In the upper left-hand corner was a photo of the East Chop Lighthouse. The lighthouse in the photo was a rich brown, not the gleaming white that it was today.

"The chocolate lighthouse," Charles said under his breath, smiling.

Beside the lighthouse was a photo of a sign explaining that the site was once a semaphore site privately owned by

Captain Silas Daggett. That sign was another thing that had changed. It had been replaced with one that simply read "Telegraph Hill" with no explanation. Beneath the two photos, Peter's caption was more elaborate. It read, "A semaphore is a system of telecommunication that uses a variety of flag positions to send messages over great distances." Charles remembered the first time he had read this. He had immediately gone to his encyclopaedias and looked up 'semaphore'. It was fascinating. Clearly, his friend Peter had found it interesting too. Peter had been the only childhood friend Charles ever made with whom he could speak about any subject. Charles never had to worry about what Peter was going to think of him for mulling over obscure science, art, or history that he found interesting. Sure, they started with a mutual love of JAWS but it branched off from there. Cameras, paintings, boats, oceans, or animals—no topic was off-limits. He missed that. Charles turned the page again.

State Beach. The memories came flooding back. These were the photos that the two of them had taken together. Using Edith Blake's book as a guide, Peter and Charles had spent the morning running up and down the beach trying to photograph scenes from a movie that they hadn't even seen yet! Was that the day that they finally went to see JAWS or did they see it the day after? Charles couldn't remember.

What he did remember is that trip had been a game changer for Charles. Not just because he finally saw JAWS but also because he had made a really good friend in Peter. The two of them had stayed in touch for a while, quite a while after they had gone home. They wrote each other letters back and forth. He remembered the excitement he had felt receiving a letter from his friend. Kernels of Charles' past popped in his head. Piece by piece, his memory was filling in, forming a bigger picture. These were things that he hadn't thought about in more than forty years. Had Peter and his family left early? It seemed to Charles that they had. Peter had gotten sick or something. Charles didn't think that he had ever known the details. He had been a kid and Peter being sick and eventually getting better would have been enough of an explanation for him at the time. Now that he thought about it though, he must have been pretty sick for them to pick up and leave the island in the middle of their vacation. Who wants to travel with a sick kid? Then again, who wants to live in a tent with one? Wait, no. Charles and his family had been in a tent but Peter was staying in a gingerbread house in Oak Bluffs. Charles hadn't seen it but that's what Peter had told him. There was so much to remember. Charles turned the page again. There it was. The shark.

* * *

April pulled out the framed front page of The Vineyard Gazette and stared at the headline, *Island Son Missing!* April remembered it well. Alan Quaid had taken his boat out in the middle of a storm and was never seen again. The islanders, especially the sailors, had never been entirely comfortable with the story. It just didn't make sense. Going back generations, the Quaids had all been expert sailors. The thought that Alan would have taken his boat out in a storm, didn't quite wash—unless he had been suicidal. Why else would anyone go out in a nor'easter like the storm of seventy-seven? It's just that at the time, suicide hadn't exactly sat right with anyone either. By all reports, the young man had everything going for him. There hadn't been any girl trouble that anyone knew about, and as far as April was concerned, love was the reason most people committed suicide—unrequited love or love gone wrong—but no bereaved young lady ever came forward or showed up at the funeral. If it had been an affair of the heart, some guilt-ridden, pretty young thing would have made an appearance. So what happened? April shook her head and looked at the smiling face of the young, handsome man staring back at her from the newspaper clipping. Young, handsome, and rich—April wasn't buying suicide either. So, why had he taken his boat out on that stormy night? That's not something that you do without a reason. On an island that had more than her fair share, the death of Alan Quaid was one of the better Martha's Vineyard Mysteries. April grimaced briefly and then grinned. This part of the exhibit was going to get a lot of people talking. Just as with everything else on this island, everyone had an opinion, and after a glass or two of complimentary rosé... People talking would ensure that her first exhibit was a success. April's phone rang, jarring her out of her daydream.

"April Stevens," she stated.

"Hi April. It's Charles Williams calling," said Charles.

"Hello Charles!" April cooed. "I was just thinking about you. When should I expect you? I'll put on a pot of coffee."

"Well, that's what I'm calling about," said Charles.

"Is there a problem?" April's tone dropped an octave. She braced herself for a hitch in her plans. She didn't want any hitches.

"No! Not at all. I am going through my photos and I think some of them would have a much more dramatic effect if we blew them up. What do you think? I could get them blown up before I brought them over. Do you really need them today?" asked Charles.

April exhaled with relief. "Oh, is that all. You had me going there for a moment. Charles, I always expected us to do that but I'd like to sit down with you first, so that we can decide together which photos to enlarge. We can have them copied digitally and then decide on the most appropriate size for the available space. Can we do that this afternoon? I'd really like to get moving on this. Say around two?"

"Absolutely. I'll see you then," said Charles.

"Perfect! I'll put on the coffee!" April hung up. She didn't have any photos from the JAWS 2 production except for the few that had been in The Gazette and everyone had already seen those. No one was going to come to an art exhibit that was showing photographs the entire island had already cut out of the front page of their newspaper forty-five years ago. April was counting on Charles' collection. Amateur photos always had a candid quality that gave exhibits a personal feel. The fact that these were photos from the JAWS 2 production was all the better. JAWS had a mystique all its own on Martha's Vineyard. *People will come to see production pics and when they do, they will feel like they're really there*, she thought.

* * *

Eddie Lineback was working alone in the backroom of his Vineyard Haven shop. As Laurel Redington—his favourite MVYRadio dj—talked about on-island music events, Eddie finished wiping the glass he had just set in one of his own handcrafted eleven-by-eighteen inch picture frames. This one was maple with a dark mahogany stain. Eddie almost always worked with hardwood unless a customer specifically requested a soft wood—pine was a common request. He always had some on hand for just such an order. Eddie didn't think much of soft wood for framing as it didn't have the longevity of hardwood and tended to warp over time, but he sure did like the smell of pine in his shop. This customer hadn't been picky about the wood just the finish. He had wanted a dark finish. The photo being framed was the silhouette of Jay Lagemann's Swordfish Harpooner front and centre, backed by a beautiful Menemsha sunset. The photo was a little too generic for Eddie's taste but what it lacked in originality, it made up in colour and natural beauty. It would make a very popular postcard. The photograph had been taken during one of Menemsha's more spectacular sunsets, of that there was no question, but the composition was dull. If the statue had been placed off-centre the photo would have been more interesting—at least to Eddie. Still, the photographer knew enough to straighten out the horizon—that was something. Actually, the fact that he knew enough to capture the moment at all was also something. Most people just walked by blindly unaware and if they took a photo at all, it was a selfie. Eddie hated selfies. This photographer also knew that the oranges and pinks of the sky would be set off perfectly by the dark stain on the frame. Eddie had to give him credit for that too.

Eddie set the photo down and stepped back a few feet. He smirked at his own snobbery. Had he really become that much of a schmuck? Criticizing a photograph of a Menemsha sunset? Clearly, this guy was really proud of his photo. He wanted it framed, didn't he? The guy obviously knew that he wasn't Herb Ritts or Annie Leibovitz; he just got lucky on a beautiful Martha's Vineyard night and took a great picture. Eddie nodded at the photograph in its white matte and its dark frame. "It's not half-bad at that," he said aloud.

The store landline rang and Eddie walked across the room to answer it. He lifted the cordless phone from its charger, pressed the answer button, and brought it to his ear. "Images In Vogue," he said. Eddie hated saying the name of his shop out loud. It was a play on the eighties band *Images In Vogue* and around the time he had opened the shop, Eddie had won a photography competition in Vogue magazine. When it came time to name the shop, he thought it was cool—a sign that he was going places, a sign that told people where it all began. He used to imagine himself explaining the name with a wry smile and a raised eyebrow to excited reporters. They would hang on his every word as he explained his humble beginnings and what it was like to be taking iconic portraits of rock stars, presidents, and royalty, but that had never happened. In fact, he had never left Martha's Vineyard. Photographing the Dukes County Sherriff and his wife was about as exciting as it got for Eddie and that wasn't exciting at all. It looked good in print but the Sherriff and Eddie were both islanders. It's hard to get excited about taking someone's picture when you can remember them farting in gym class. The certificate announcing him the winner of the Vogue competition hung on his shop wall but nothing had ever come of it. Now, he just thought the name of his shop sounded corny and dumb.

"Hi Eddie. It's April. How are you?" A tinny version of April's soft voice cooed through the speaker of the cheap phone.

"I'm great April. How about yourself?"

"Excellent, thank you," April said. "Eddie, I have a job for you but it will need a rather quick turnaround if you can manage it. It's for an exhibit at Old Sculpin."

"I'll certainly try," said Eddie. "What do you need?"

"I'm going to need some photographs digitally scanned, enlarged, and framed."

"How many?" Eddie asked.

"Well, I haven't seen them yet—they should be on their way over now actually—but I'm hoping for around ten."

"How big do you want them?"

"Not huge. I want them to still have a personal feel but large enough to have an impact. I'm thinking eight-by-ten, matted and framed, but I won't know for sure until I see them. What do you think?"

"No trouble at all," said Eddie. "I already have most of the frames, I think. So, it won't take long. I could get them to you in less than a week if I really put my mind to it. As it happens, I'm pretty slow at the moment."

"Oh that's great!" April exclaimed. "Oh—I mean, I'm sorry that you're slow at the moment; I'm just excited that we will be able to work together."

Eddie could hear April blushing over the phone. He laughed. "I know what you mean. When shall I expect you?"

"Tomorrow morning?" asked April.

"Sounds good. We'll see you then. Thank you for thinking of me April. I always appreciate it." Eddie hung up.

Things had been slower than he would like and this job was a good thing. Now that the Menemsha sunset was framed, Eddie didn't really have anything on the books at all. After it was wrapped and delivered, he would double check his inventory and make sure that he had the wood to start making the frames for April's show.

Eddie turned on the phone again and punched in a number. He brought it to his ear and listened to it ring. A deep voice picked up on the other end with a single, "Hello?"

"Hi Craig. That picture is framed and ready for delivery. I'm just wrapping it now."

3

Charles lifted a spoonful of homemade tomato sauce to his lips, blew on it, and then slurped a taste. He gave the thick, hot liquid considerable thought as it rolled over his tongue. *More salt and pepper.* He reached into the cupboard to the left of the stove and pulled out the pepper grinder his aunt had given him for his birthday and the fine sea salt. He added a considerable amount of each before returning them to the cupboard. Charles always cleaned as he went. He discarded tins as soon as they were empty, measuring cups and utensils were immediately put in the dishwasher, and the counters were wiped down continually. It always amazed Laurie that no matter what Charles was cooking or baking, when he put it in the oven, there was never a mess to clean up. You'd swear that he hadn't cooked a thing. Laurie was the exact opposite. Charles always teased her that she would use every pot in the kitchen to make a cup of tea and leave them all in the sink. If pressed, Charles would admit that this was a slight exaggeration but not by much.

Fenway The Beagle strolled into the kitchen. His toenails clicked on the dark wood floors announcing his arrival. He sat at Charles' feet and looked up expectantly.

Charles looked down at his friend. "It's just sauce so far buddy. Wait until I make the meatballs, then I'll have something for you," he said.

Fenway chuffed in disappointment. He stiffened suddenly and his ears perked. He turned his head toward the front of the house and barked. He bolted toward the door as Laurie opened it and stepped inside.

"Well, hello there little guy!" Laurie reached down and scratched Fenway behind the ears. He jumped excitedly at her feet and she laughed. "Okay! Okay! Let me get in the door!" Laurie gave him a gentle push, stepped inside, and closed the front door behind her. She looked across the open area of the main floor and smiled at Charles. "It smells good in here!"

"Not long now," Charles said. "The sauce is done and I've rolled the meatballs. I just have to cook them and make the pasta. Why don't you go have a shower—or maybe a swim?"

"Or both!" Laurie said greedily.

"Sure," said Charles. "You've got time."

"Great!" said Laurie.

"How was your day?" asked Charles.

"Boring," said Laurie. "But boring is a good day if you're a police officer. How was yours? Did April like your photos?"

"She loved them!" said Charles. "In fact, we had a hard time narrowing it down to ten for the show. I had forgotten how many Peter and I had taken—especially of the shark. There were a lot of them both in dry dock and in action. It was pretty cool to see them again. It has been a long time since I sat down and thought about that trip. We had such a good time."

"Does it matter that you didn't take the photos?" asked Laurie.

"What do you mean?" asked Charles.

"Well, you're putting them up in a public show but technically, you didn't take them. Peter did. I mean, I know it's just Old Sculpin; it's not like you're putting them up in the Guggenheim or anything but still..."

Charles stared at her for a moment before speaking. "You know, I hadn't thought of that. I'm not selling them.

I'm not benefitting from this show financially. Old Sculpin is profiting because they will be selling art at the exhibit but we're not selling these photos." Charles thought some more as he rolled the meatballs into the pan. They sizzled. "These photos have been sitting on my bookshelf for more than four decades and they were gifted to me. Legally, that must count for something."

Laurie shrugged. "Probably."

"Oh for crying out loud," Charles said. "Listen to me—*legally*! We're talking about one of my oldest friends. This is a slight overreaction."

"When was the last time you heard from Peter?" asked Laurie.

Charles blushed sheepishly. "It's been a while...a couple of years. He was the last to write and I didn't get back to him. I just forgot."

Laurie stepped up onto the first step of the staircase leading to the second floor. "You know what they say—no better time than the present." With that, Laurie turned and bounced up the stairs with the energy of a woman half her age.

Charles stirred the meatballs as they browned in the pan. It had been a long time since he had written to his friend. They used to write back and forth regularly. Then they emailed and sent Christmas cards and birthday cards.

Phone calls were few and far between. Somehow, the writing was more fun. The anticipation of that next letter, receiving those letters and cards, was far more thrilling than picking up the phone. Both Charles and Peter saw that as lazy and far less interesting. Charles still had every letter that Peter had ever sent him and he was sure that Peter still had his letters too. He couldn't imagine Peter throwing them out. It just wouldn't be him. Charles remembered being a kid and fighting with his parents, getting fired from his first job, and being dumped by his first girlfriend. It didn't matter what was happening in his life, when one of Peter's letters appeared in the mailbox he was elated. Letter days were good days. Charles felt his eyes well up. Why had he let that go? Why had he allowed himself to become too busy for their friendship? That wasn't what he was about. At least, he didn't like to think so.

Fenway head-butted Charles on the leg derailing his train of thought. It caught him off-guard and his knee buckled. Charles looked down. Fenway was looking up at him with impossibly huge brown eyes. His tail thumped on the floor. "You think so?" asked Charles.

Fenway barked two barks for yes.

"Okay, I'll write him after dinner."

*   *   *

Craig Upland stepped down out of his 1977 High Sierra and closed the door with a creak and a thud. In some ways the old truck was showing her age but in others, she was as good as new. Craig had no intentions of trading her in for a newer model. He liked her just fine. They had a connection. Some people understood and respected that; most didn't. It was usually men who understood. Women never did. To them, it was just a beat up old truck. *You can't even plug your iPhone into the stereo so what was the point?* The point was, she still ran like a dream after forty-five years. None of the new pieces of crap coming off the line these days were going to give him that kind of loyalty, that's for sure. She also knew every grain of sand of every beach on Martha's Vineyard. Craig was pretty sure that he could pass out behind the wheel on Norton Point and his truck could find her own way home. Could she use a new paint job? Probably. He'd get around to it one of these days. Bills always seemed to pop up just when he thought he had scraped together enough to spend on her. Never failed. In the meantime, Craig liked his truck so he was keeping her. More important, Judie liked their truck. That was enough for him.

Craig walked across Lobsterville Beach and looked up toward Aquinnah and down toward Menemsha—no one. He had the beach to himself. He pulled off his Slip77 t-shirt and shorts and ran into the water. As soon as the water reached his mid-thigh, he dove and disappeared under the surface.

Craig's strong arms propelled him into the oncoming surf. He knew these waters. He had been swimming the island for more than sixty years. He understood it. He held his breath for the first few strokes and then slowly began to exhale. Craig kicked and pulled his arms in a wide breaststroke until his lungs could no longer bare it. He lifted his face toward the surface and exploded through the rolling waves. Craig opened his eyes and licked his lips reflexively. He loved the salty flavour of the ocean. It was the flavour that tasted the most like home. His childhood home, his parents' house, had rarely felt like a home. There had been happy moments of course, and if he dug deep enough, he could find them, but nothing consistent. He had just as many happy memories in his friends' houses. One was as good as the other. The only consistently happy place in Craig's life, right from the beginning, had been the ocean. He swam in her almost every day. There were days when he couldn't. Nor'easters kept him out, most of the time. Winter kept him out occasionally but not often. His first swims with Judie were among the happiest memories Craig had. Introducing her to the cure-all properties of the salt water, holding her on the beach—those were memories he would never lose. No matter what.

Craig walked slowly onto the sand. His skin was tan and leather. He had the physique of a man twenty years his junior. His beard was grey, his moustache black. His long, naturally wavy hair was more salt than pepper. He thought about cutting it every single day but somehow just never got around to it. Maybe when he finally painted the truck, he'd cut his hair too. It was thick and he could usually keep it in place with a quick run through of his fingers. Air-drying after an ocean swim didn't hurt either.

Craig bent down and scooped his t-shirt and shorts off of the sand and walked back to the truck nude. He opened the driver's side door, tossed his clothes on the seat, and reached into the back for a towel. He dried himself quickly and vigorously. When he was satisfied that he was dry enough, he threw the towel into the back and slipped back into his shorts. Craig stared at his shirt and debated whether he had to put it back on or not. He moved it to the passenger seat. He was heading to Images In Vogue in Vineyard Haven so he was going to need it eventually but for now, he could do without it. He stepped up into the truck, turned the key in the ignition, and pressed his bare foot on the gas. He almost never needed shoes. This was still Martha's Vineyard after all.

* * *

April pulled into the parking lot in front of Vineyard Haven Stop & Shop and put her van in park. She looked over at the constant stream of people going in and out of the grocery store and patted herself on the back for shopping in Edgartown early that morning. "Thank the Lord I don't have to deal with that!" she muttered to herself. April slung her purse over her shoulder, grabbed the tote bag carrying Charles' book, and stepped out into the sea air. She closed the door behind her and headed up toward Main Street and Images In Vogue.

As she walked up the street, she looked around. Edgartown and Oak Bluffs both had so much more going on. There were so many more interesting things happening. Vineyard Haven had great breakfasts—The Black Dog and Art Cliff Diner were on everyone's list of places to go. The Martha's Vineyard Museum was something island visitors had to check off their list. There were a couple of other great spots here and there—Vineyard Vines, LeRoux—but there was something missing. April couldn't quite put her finger on it but there was. Vineyard Haven was the year-round entry point to Martha's Vineyard. It deserved a little spit and polish. The building that had once housed Bunch Of Grapes had sat empty for quite some time and that was dead centre Main Street. Dead was right. Maybe that was all it would take. If the right business went in there—something that would take full advantage of the large patio under the clock—it would make the world of difference. Burying the power lines would make it a lot more pleasing too but who had that kind of money on the island? April laughed at the irony. Correction: who had the money and the interest? The only reason the power lines had been buried on North Water Street in Edgartown was because the wealthy residences got sick of them obstructing their view—or at least, that was the story. April loved Vineyard Haven; she would like to see it get a facelift. They just finished Circuit Avenue and Healy Square in Oak Bluffs. It was time!

April opened the front door of Images In Vogue, ringing the chimes that were attached. She smiled at the old world effect. "Hellooo!" April called as she entered the shop.

Eddie Lineback stepped out of the backroom and was visibly surprised to see April Stevens standing in his showroom. "April!" exclaimed Eddie. "I didn't think we were connecting until tomorrow morning."

"Oh, I know," apologised April. "I am sorry about barging in like this but I wrapped up with Charles much earlier than I expected. I knew you were still open, so I wanted to stop by and talk to you about the photos."

Eddie chuckled. "No problem. I was just working on one of your frames." He went to brush his hands on his pants and stopped. "Just give me a minute to wash up. Okay?"

"Of course! Take your time." April walked slowly around the store, admiring the photographs hanging on the wall. *So talented*, she thought. Martha's Vineyard had been photographed and was being photographed every minute of every day. There was no way she could possibly count how many pictures she had seen of Gay Head Lighthouse, Edgartown Lighthouse, and Wesleyan Grove in Oak Bluffs. Seagulls, Steamship Authority ferries, Inkwell Beach, and Lucy Vincent had graced every book and magazine the world over, she was sure of it. Yet, there was something different about Eddie's photos. Something unexpected. He caught softness where others missed it, and he picked up on hardness that no one else saw. His portraits were natural and his landscapes had humanity. He seemed to be awake for every sunrise but never missing a sunset at the same time. April shook her head. *How did he do it?*

"Okay! Sorry about that," Eddie came out of the back and walked over to the shop counter. "Let's see what you've got!"

"Eddie," April said. "Your photos are truly remarkable."

Eddie smiled. "Thanks April. That's really very kind of you."

"I mean it," she continued. "Every time I come in here I'm just bowled over."

Eddie looked around the store at his work. "I think it's impossible for the photographer to see what others see. I think that is the case for all artists. Even Michelangelo probably looked at the ceiling of the Sistine Chapel and only saw flaws where others saw genius. When I look at my photos, I only see missed light and compositions that could be balanced just a little bit better. You're a painter, April. Do you know what I mean?" He focussed back on April and smiled.

"I do actually, Eddie. I know exactly what you mean," April said thoughtfully. "I often wish, just for a moment, that I could see my work through other peoples' eyes. I would love to know what they see. You know what they say though—careful what you wish for."

The two artists stood in silence for a moment before Eddie turned to April and said, "What did you bring me?"

"Oh! Yes! Well, they're nothing like yours of course but I think they're really quite charming in their own right." April pulled Charles' book out of the tote.

Eddie laughed. "Oh my god! This is awesome!" He tilted his head to get a better look. "Charles made this?"

"Um, no. I think his childhood friend—Oh, I forget the lad's name—made it for Charles, but Charles and this friend took the photos together on vacation back in 1977." April opened the book. "It's fun, right?"

"I love it," said Eddie.

"I made a list of the photos Charles and I decided to use," April said.

Slowly, Eddie began to look through the book. His eyes narrowed. One by one, he absorbed every photo. When he got to the photos of the mechanical shark, he paused. "These are quite good," he said. "There's a lot of energy in these photos."

"You know," said April leaning in. "I thought so too. I mean, I am no photographer—I barely consider myself a painter, not a real one anyway—but I really feel something in these photos." April extended one chubby hand and pointed at an image of the shark. "I love this one. It's almost frightening."

Eddie nodded. "I quite agree with you. You can feel it. The boy who took these must have been terrified when he took them. That energy has been captured completely. I'm really pleasantly surprised, April. I was expecting standard issue tourist snaps. These are so much more…" Eddie trailed off, absorbed in the book.

"Oh, I'm so glad," said April. A genuine smile spread across her face and her cheeks flushed. "So, you think you'll be able to get digital copies of these images without taking them out of the book? Charles was extremely insistent that the book not be tampered with in any way."

"Oh sure," said Eddie. "That won't be a problem."

"Great!" said April. "In that case, I have a list here. Let's go through our selections and you can tell me what you think."

*   *   *

Laurie walked through the French doors that connected the back porch to the den. She was wearing a bright pink and turquoise Vineyard Vines one-piece bathing suit, and drying her hair on a towel. Charles looked up at her when she came in.

"I'm going to write Peter after dinner," he said.

"You know, I was just thinking about that," said Laurie. "He hasn't been here since you two were kids, has he?"

Charles shook his head. "No."

"Why don't you invite him for a visit?" said Laurie.

Charles uncorked a bottle of Kim Crawford Sauvignon Blanc and poured two glasses. He passed one to Laurie and took a sip from the other.

"His photos being in the show are the perfect excuse," Laurie continued. "Plus, I'd like to meet him."

Charles nodded. "That's an excellent idea." Charles walked around the kitchen island and wrapped his arms around his wife. "See? This is why I love you."

"There had to be a reason," Laurie smiled.

4

Peter,

It's been far too long my friend! It's been so long that I can't even remember where we left off. That's not good. I hope you and your parents are all doing well. I'm still living on Amity Island and I'm still married to the Edgartown Police Chief. I'm the envy of all JAWS fandom! Haha! I'm the Lorraine Gary of Martha's Vineyard. She looked a lot better in a tight black turtleneck than I do though…like a lot better.

Speaking of JAWS (and why wouldn't we), they're putting on a multi media art exhibit—I guess you'd call it—at Old Sculpin Gallery. Do you remember Old Sculpin? It's the building on Edgartown Harbor that Quint's shack was based on. Anyway, they're putting on an exhibit that's all about

Martha's Vineyard in 1977! A lot of things were going on here that year including two young kids running around with a camera taking pictures of everything that would stand still long enough! Actually, it's those photos that prompted me to write you. The woman in charge of the exhibit, April Stevens, wants to use some of our photos in the exhibit! Isn't that cool? As you well know, JAWS 2 was a big deal that year and April didn't really have any photos that everyone hadn't already seen. Laurie told her that I happened to have a private collection and she asked to see them—she loved them! April and I just went through them and she's blowing up ten favourites from that album you made for me all those years ago. How great is that?

Anyway, the exhibit is two weekends away and I would really like it if you would come out to the Vineyard for a few days. We will take in the exhibit, tool around the island, and see how all of the JAWS locations have held up. Laurie really wants to meet you too! I promise, she's heard nothing but great things. Well, mostly great things. Okay, she's heard some good things. Ha-ha! I'm kidding. Just come okay? It would be really great to see you.

Your friend,

Charles

5

Eddie Lineback stood in front of his digital printer as it churned out the eight by ten images. He thought that April had been right in not going too big. Sure, if they had gone really big, they could have an incredible impact—especially the close-ups of the shark—but keeping them confined and tight, then placing them in a frame, maintained a certain candid quality. It preserved the photos' intimate feeling. Eddie picked up the first one and looked at it closely. He felt like he was seeing it through the eyes of the boy who took it. He didn't feel like he was at a museum taking in an exhibit of lost Ansel Adams or Herb Ritts. No, a tourist took these photos with an inexpensive camera. They were clear but grainy. They were colour but just barely—

almost sepia. They were charming in the way that old family photos were; the ones where grandpa and dad wore wide plaid slacks, mom wore a skirt suit, and everyone smoked. These photos were in those same washed out greys and ruddy browns, but those plaid-slacked, smoking parents weren't in these photos. They were definitely around when the photos had been taken and when they had come back from the drug store in their paper envelope, those people had looked at these photos to be sure—but they weren't in them. No, the people in these photos—few that they were— were a lot younger and hipper. These people were the youth of Martha's Vineyard. They had long shiny hair and wore cut-off denim shorts, t-shirts, and macramé halter-tops. It was clear that these images had been taken in the mid-to-late seventies. Then of course, there was the shark.

    The photos impressed Eddie. April said that a young boy had taken them. Whoever he was, he had a great eye for composition. His lines were great. His horizons were straight; his subjects were balanced. Each and every one of the photos, whether it was a shark close-up, a close-up of a very pretty girl, or a landscape shot with a couple of people off in the distance, was well thought out. Eddie smiled. He was a fan. He wondered what that kid was doing now. He'd bet a Mocha Motts coffee that whatever the boy was doing, he was in the arts.

* * *

Peter Morgan stepped back from the large canvas to inspect his work. Brush strokes of indigo, cobalt, and Prussian blues created dark images, images of night, heavily forested neighbourhoods. Cold polar white with hues of goldenrod and lemon lit antique street lamps and cavernous black skies—their remote light, the only comfort to the old cottages in the dark wood. The cottages. Streaks of oil-based paint hinted at wood shingled roofs and tongue-and-groove walls. No light emanated through their doors nor through their windows. Their front porches were barely discernible in the shadows. The woods were dark. The cottages were dark. The painting was dark. It was more than dark. It was ominous. The image made Peter uncomfortable. All of Peter's paintings made him uncomfortable. He didn't like them. They haunted him. They always did. From the time Peter first set brush to canvas, each and every one of Peter's paintings made him queasy. They made his heart race and his palms itch. He knew a painting was done when he couldn't stand being around it anymore. When they were done, he rolled them into the backroom of his Brooklyn studio to dry. Once dry, he would send them to the gallery and they would sell them. He never wanted to know who bought them. He never wanted to know where they went. He only knew he never wanted to see them again. Taking in the work in front of him, Peter knew it had to go. He turned away from it, unable to look at it any longer without causing himself physical pain. It was complete. He would email Harry at Williamsburg Gallery and tell him he had another one for him; he could collect it as soon as it was dry.

Peter walked across the studio and opened the fridge. He pulled out a Guinness and sat down at the kitchen table. He took a long swig, filling his mouth and swallowing twice before lowering the can. His heart started to slow and his stomach started to settle. He inhaled deeply and sighed. Tomorrow he would set up his next canvas. He wasn't going to start painting tomorrow but the canvas had to be ready. Why? Why did he do this to himself over and over again? Actually, that was the wrong question. Years of therapy had taught him that. When you want to find an answer, you first have to ask the right question. The question was why did the paintings affect him like they did over and over again? He knew why he kept painting them. Peter knew that his deep-seated need to paint these dark and frightening paintings was actually the hope that one day, he would paint something that didn't scare him. One day, his talents would craft something that he wouldn't find repellent. When he finished a painting he was depleted, almost emaciated, and exhausted. He couldn't imagine ever painting again. He would sleep soundly for a while and eat well. Peter would start to feel good. Then...

Over the next few weeks, as his strength returned, Peter would feel something churning inside him. There was an energy. It was electric. He knew it was another painting but at this stage the colours, the strokes, the canvas, the imagery, they were all mixed with hope. This could be the one. It could all be over. This could be the painting that set him free. This could be a painting of beauty. This could be the first in a long line of his artwork that exhilarated him with every glance. The desperation, the longing, to create such a work would be overwhelming. It would get harder and harder to ignore but at this stage, there was no way of knowing what was bubbling inside him. He could never know for sure. At this stage, it could go either way. The only thing Peter knew for certain was that a painting was coming. The only way to know for sure was to start painting. One day, almost without even knowing he was going to do it, he would pick up a brush. He could be walking out the door, fully dressed for a night out in Manhattan or he could be walking toward the shower, naked with a towel over his shoulder. It would just happen. That would be the end. His fingers would wrap around a long wooden handle and his brush would hit the blank canvas. Like cutting into a healing wound, the bristles would tear through the empty white and release the darkness within. By then, it would be too late. Game over. As soon as he started, Peter would know that this painting was going to be no different than any of the ones that preceded it, but he had no choice except to continue. He had to keep going. Each and every stroke cut and sliced into him like a hunter gutting a deer but Peter was his own prey—alive, breathing, and bleeding. His head would start to scream and his heart would begin to pound. Until he finished the painting, he hardly ate and he would barely sleep. When he did sleep, he was chased by violent nightmares. Once he started, he didn't do anything but paint. It was an exsanguination. He needed the painting out of his system. If he was lucky, the painting would focus on the streetlights or the stars. Peter had figured out that the more light in the image, the easier it was on his system to paint it. He had been painting a close up of one of the antique street lamps. The light had filled almost the entire canvas and it had been comforting, inviting, and soothing. The darkness of the night only crept in at the outer edges. The darkness had hurt like a punch in the stomach. If it were up to Peter, he would have no dark at all but it had to be there. The image was inside him and he had to get every aspect of it out onto the canvas. Dark or light, Peter had no control over the focus of his work. The subject matter was invariably the same. Nightscapes of fairytale images. Antique lanterns hinting at coloured cottages in pitch. In fact, one New York Times art critic had written, "Peter Morgan's works have a Hansel and Gretel quality and we the audience are the titular children. The witch cannot be seen but we know she's there." Peter couldn't argue with that. He knew she was there too.

* * *

April steered the minivan into her driveway on Mercier Way and put it in park. It had been a long day. All she wanted was the leftover tuna casserole that she knew was in the fridge and a good cup of tea...maybe a chocolate digestive or two. As soon as she closed the car door behind her, she could hear Miss Mew howling inside.

"Okay Miss Mew," she called. "Momma's coming." *You must be as hungry as I am,* she thought.

April turned the knob—she never locked the door—and walked in. A thick ball of orange fur twisted and turned between April's legs, simultaneously howling and purring. April kicked off her shoes, walked into the kitchen, and set her bags down on the kitchen table. She moaned with age and fatigue as she bent over to pick up the empty cat dish. "That shouldn't be that hard," she said. Then she remembered the offer from her friend Kathy to go running and thought it might not be a bad idea at that. Kathy had said she would go slowly—take it easy. What did she have to lose…other than forty pounds or so? After the exhibit, maybe she would give her a call. Was Ray Whitaker still offering personal training too? She had seen his ad somewhere? Was he on Facebook? Islanders Talk? Probably. He was such a sweetheart and cute as a button. Hiring him for a session or two would be fun. Maybe he did group training—that would be cheaper. Whatever she was going to do, it would have to be after the exhibit. She had far too much on her plate at the moment but the day's events had really helped her to feel better about things. There was no doubt in her mind that the event would be a success! She still had to talk to Dan and Greg of Cottage City Oysters about arranging an oyster table. That was first priority on her list of things to do in the morning. Island Cocktail Company was all set to cater the drinks. April had never worked with them before but she knew that Plan It Martha's Vineyard, the wedding planners, used them all the time—so they must be good. Plan It had an excellent reputation. A few cocktails, an oyster or two, and a little island history and intrigue would all blend together for a fantastic party! Old Sculpin Gallery would be talking about this event for years to come!

April took a can of cat food out of the cupboard and pulled off the lid. She shook the contents into the bowl and set it back down on the floor. Miss Mew abandoned April's leg and darted toward her dinner. April laughed. "I guess that puts me in my place, doesn't it?" She shook her head. "Crazy cat."

April turned, opened the refrigerator, pulled out a casserole dish covered in foil, and closed the door. A photo held in place by red, heart-shaped fridge magnets caught her eye and she paused. April smiled a weak smile as she traced the man in the photo with her finger. Her eyes moistened. "This was your favourite, Edward," she said. She pulled off the foil and turned on the oven to 275°. "I still only know how to make enough for you and me for dinner and have leftovers for your lunch the next day." April pulled a serving spoon out of a clay pitcher on the counter. "Thirty-five years is a tough habit to break." She broke up the combination of macaroni, tuna, mushrooms, peas, and cheese so it would heat quicker. "I'd put it in the microwave to heat but I know how you hate that—and you're right—it doesn't taste as good. I'm just impatient." April laughed. "You were always the patient one." She re-covered the dish with the foil and slid it into the oven. She looked at Edward's photo on the refrigerator. She took it down, licked her thumb, and gave it a rub. She wiped the photo on her dress and looked at it again. "There. That's better," she said. She narrowed her eyes. "Don't look at me like that," she said. "The cheese has not slid off my cracker—I'm doing just fine. I just miss you. I'm allowed to miss my husband." April kissed the photo before returning it to its spot on the refrigerator door. She secured it back in place with the heart magnets and headed upstairs to get changed.

* * *

Craig turned off the engine and pulled his key out of the ignition. Barefoot, he stepped down onto Main Street, Vineyard Haven and reached into the back for his T-shirt. He pulled it over his head and walked over to Images In Vogue. Other than the usual noises emanating from Copper Wok and Salvatore's, the town was quiet. Vineyard Haven didn't have the bustling nightlife of Edgartown or Oak Bluffs. Down at the harbour, Vineyard Haven had the year round traffic of people getting on and off the island at the ferry terminal. Black Dog Tavern and Art Cliff Diner served up breakfast traffic almost all year. After breakfast though, the summer DINKs tended to move on. The shopping was better in Oak Bluffs and Edgartown; the beaches were better in Menemsha and Aquinnah. While Chappaquiddick, West Tisbury, and Chilmark were calling those who were really looking for peace and quiet. Craig liked staying as close to up-island as he possibly could at all-times. Like any diva, Edgartown was a goddamn pain in the ass most of the time and he'd rather shit glass than have to go back to Oak Bluffs ever again. He came down to Vineyard Haven when he needed to work and sometimes that work meant he made a delivery down-island. It was unavoidable. When he did though—it was in and out. Then he was back up to Aquinnah to the house he and Judie had built with their own hands more than forty years ago. He liked it out there. Nothing changed but the seasons.

The bells over the door chimed as Craig walked into Images In Vogue. The shop always caught Craig a little off-guard. He was in it on a fairly regular basis. Eddie was a good guy; he knew how much Craig needed the work. Yet, every time he walked in he was thrown off his game just a little bit. The store made him feel so good. For starters, it smelled like the ocean. Craig didn't know how or why—he had never asked—but it did. There was a clean, fresh scent. It was like cupping a handful of sea grass under your nose and gently inhaling. It wasn't an air freshener—there was no chemical tang—it was natural and clean. Maybe it wasn't there at all, thought Craig. Maybe the ocean smell was psychosomatic. Everywhere he looked there were photographs of the ocean that Eddie had taken. Small, framed photographs and large photos laminated onto metal or canvas. There were photos of the ocean at peace and violent photos of angry storms. There were seagulls magically suspended in sunset skies over Quansoo Beach, and there were sunrises over Vineyard Sound illuminating Edgartown Light. So, maybe the smell of sea grass was all in his head but Craig didn't think so.

Eddie's photos were proof positive that Martha's Vineyard was a bucolic paradise. It was beaches. It was Amity Island. Rolling farmland held in place by stonewalls. The Vineyard was nothing more than a dreamland for the rich and famous. The flag was a seagull in front of a setting sun. It was Carly Simon's home. Five lighthouses. It was the decompression spot for the nation's Presidents. A life of never-ending lobster rolls, sailboats, and cocktails. The photos on Eddie's walls depicted a Martha's Vineyard that anyone and everyone could visit by merely buying a ferry ticket and walking the gangplank. Yet somehow, Craig had missed that boat. Maybe that was why he liked it so much in Eddie's shop. When he was in Images In Vogue, Craig could see it. He could see the island that everyone else could see. He could feel it and smell it. Whereas out there, on the island that he knew like the back of his hand, it was lost to him.

Eddie came out of the backroom and smiled. "Oh hey man! How's it going?"

Craig nodded. "I'm good. You?"

"Can't complain," Eddie said.

Craig chuckled. "That puts you in the minority."

"Ain't that the truth," said Eddie. "I can hardly look at Islanders Talk anymore."

Craig rolled his eyes at the thought. Craig really couldn't see any redeeming social value in a Facebook page continuously monitored by every single islander. Well, almost every islander. "I don't have the internet," he said.

Eddie froze. His eyes widened. "*You don't have internet?*" he exclaimed.

"Nope," said Craig. "I like being outside and I like books. If there's ever anything I absolutely need to do on a computer, I just go to the library. It doesn't happen all that often. People act like the Internet is the sixth food group but it's not. It's a luxury. You don't die without it."

"No. I suppose not," Eddie said in a placating tone.

"You have that photo for me?" asked Craig.

"Right! I sure do! Come on back." Eddie led Craig into the back of the shop.

Craig looked around. Even in the back, it was a nice shop. Back here it smelled more of woodworking; it smelled of freshly cut pine. It was a good smell—different from up front but very complimentary. Earthy. Eddie picked up a wrapped package and handed it to Craig. "Thanks," he said.

"No, thank you," Eddie said. "You're really helping me out. That reminds me—I'm working on a project now that you could help me with if you're not busy. I'm framing ten photos for an exhibit they're having over at Old Sculpin Gallery in a couple of weeks. It'll be easier to get all ten down there without damaging them if I have and extra body. Nothing major. You up for it?"

"Sure," Craig said. "No problem. What's the exhibit?"

"It's some sort of multimedia project. There will be photographs, artwork—I know she's blown up some front-page articles from The Gazette—clippings and interviews. You know, that sort of thing. I'm not sure what else. It sounds pretty cool. April Stevens, the woman organising it, is really excited about it. Food, drinks—the whole works," said Eddie.

"Sounds like quite the soirée!" Craig laughed sarcastically. "I think I'll pass," he said. "What's the show called? Does it have a specific theme?"

"It sure does," said Eddie. "It's called Martha's Vineyard: 1977."

6

Charles opened the garage door and stepped inside for his bike. The immediate forecast was far from perfect, so he wanted to get out for as much cycling as possible while he still could. He felt good about the progress he had made already toward his weight loss goals. He tried to vary his route now and then but his usual was East Chop Drive to Beach Road, then up Main Street Vineyard Haven to Vineyard Haven-Edgartown Road; once he hit Edgartown, he came back up Beach Road to Oak Bluffs, onto New York Avenue, and home on East Chop. It wasn't crazy long. He wasn't one of these yahoos who had to ride to Aquinnah and back every time he stuffed his butt into his embarrassingly tight biking shorts but it was long enough. It was long enough to work up a sweat, burn some calories, and have a think. A big part of the appeal of cycling for Charles was the thinking that he got done. He did some of his best thinking out on his bike. That had come as a complete surprise. He hadn't always been a bike enthusiast. Oh, he had owned a bike as a kid. He had spun around the neighbourhood with his friends and scraped himself up on a few spills but that was it. When he had outgrown his bike in grade seven or eight, it hadn't been replaced. Bikes just weren't cool enough for high school. By then, his friends were getting licenses and everyone was piling into friend's cars or friend's parents' cars. Four wheels had definitely replaced two on the teenage vehicular scene. You could cram a lot more friends into a back seat than you could onto the handlebars of a bicycle.

    Charles rolled his bike out into the sun and closed the garage door behind him. He clicked his cycling cleat into the pedal and swung his body over the bike as he pushed off. He inhaled deeply as the sea breeze rushed over his face. He smiled. Bikes had changed so much since he was a kid. They had become so serious. What ever happened to banana seats? They were a hell of a lot more comfortable than the current design. When Charles had first taken up cycling, his butt hurt so badly that he could hardly fart without breaking a sweat. Long gone were the days of Peter doubling Charles on his handle bars from Oak Bluffs to Edgartown. Charles chuckled at the memory. A lot of those memories had resurfaced lately. Digging up that book for April had mixed up a lot of feelings in Charles. So had sending that letter to Peter. Charles and Peter hadn't seen each other in over forty years. They had been in close touch for decades after the fact but the more Charles thought about it, the more he realised that even those memories were long ago by almost anyone's standards. Their communication over the last—give or take—fifteen years had been sporadic at best. Did Charles and Peter even know each other? Had they ever? When their communication had been consistent, when they were just kids, mostly they had talked about JAWS. JAWS was their jam! They kept each other abreast of magazine articles and special issues. Charles remembered a particularly extensive letter from Peter about the JAWS 3-D edition of View-Master. That letter stood out because the day before Charles received it, Charles had sent almost the exact same letter to Peter. They had both lamented that there weren't enough shark attack stills or even shots of the shark at all. Charles and Peter had also written each other when they had seen JAWS The Revenge in the theatre. They had both loved it. Charles had loved every minute of each and every note but what had any of them told him about Peter

Morgan the man? He knew he was a painter. How successful a painter, he wasn't sure. How do you politely ask someone if they're making any money? Charles decided that when he got home after his ride, he would Google him. If Peter were experiencing even a modicum of success, the Internet would know about it. Charles had spent plenty of time researching the Internet for various articles as well as personal interest. If there was something, anything about Peter Morgan out there, he would find it. *Was that creepy?* Charles wondered. *Investigating a friend on the Internet?* Charles decided that it wasn't. If for no other reason than he was sure Peter would be doing the very same thing.

* * *

Peter Morgan walked out of Win Son Bakery at Graham and Montrose in Williamsburg, Brooklyn. He headed to one of the metal table and chairs that the restaurant had set up on the sidewalk for their patrons and sat down with his lunch. He had ordered a Double Smash Burger and a latte. He always felt vaguely guilty about ordering such a pedestrian American dish in a Tiawanese restaurant and bakery but he could only eat so much pai gu and drink so much hong oolong tea. Really, when it all came down to it, he doubted that the owner gave a rat's ass what he ordered as long as he paid for it. Peter was a regular. They always greeted him with very friendly hellos and big smiles although they had looked at him a little oddly today now that he thought about it. Win Son was right across the street from his loft. He liked the area a lot and tended not to stray too far from home. Why bother? It was exhausting. He had everything he needed within walking distance of his studio. When he wasn't painting, he ate at Win Son Bakery a few times a week. If he didn't feel like eating at a table on the street, there was always Williamsburg Deli & Grocery on the opposite corner but for the most part, sitting at one of the small metal tables suited Peter. He liked to people watch. There was such a mix—gays, Latinos, Jews, blacks, you name it. What else could you expect from a neighbourhood that was founded by the Dutch, called "Puerto Rico" by the locals, who bragged that it was "Little Berlin" on tourism websites, and served great Tiawanese food? Peter grinned with a mouthful of cheeseburger. He was starving...literally.

Earlier that morning, stepping out of the shower, Peter had caught a glimpse of himself in the full-length mirror that hung on the bathroom door. He needed a haircut and a shave but that was normal. Those things were the first things that Peter lost track of when he was painting. He also needed to cut his fingernails and his toenails—that too, was par for the course. What startled him had been his weight. Peter wasn't sure whether the paintings were taking longer to paint or if the physical effects were just getting more extreme. One thing that was obvious—this painting had taken a lot out of him. He first noticed when he looked down to inspect his toenails, feeling sure they were due for a trim. He was right. They did need cutting but there was something wrong. Peter was confused, unsettled. The nails he was inspecting weren't on his feet. They couldn't be. Standing in the middle of the bathroom, Peter could see the tendons and veins clearly across the bridge of this foot. Every sinew barely contained under its phyllo pastry skin. Peter was a tall man with big feet. He would have considered them quite sturdy-looking, a necessary feature to hold up a man of his stature. The feet he was looking at had no meat on them at all. The arch was extremely high almost completely missing the muscle that ran underneath it. Peter had always been almost flatfooted. The joints in his toes protruded like ball bearings. His nails were not only long but flaking from malnutrition. His calves were so withered that his ankles looked swollen by comparison. Peter's knees were dangerously close to becoming the thickest part of his legs. Legs that had often been compared to tree trunks in the past. Now, behind his penis and testicles, Peter's thighs no longer met at the top. His mound of pubic hair jutted forward over a mound of flesh that protruded in a way Peter had never seen before—was that his pelvis? His hips jutted forward like wings. Peter could count each and every one of his ribs. How had this happened? Shouldn't there have been bells? Whistles? Some sort of internal alarm? People needed food to survive. *They taught us that in school*, he thought. *Hell! Our parents taught us that!* How had his body deteriorated this much without giving him a heads up? How much further could it go before it was too late? Would Peter's heart just stop one day in the middle of a painting because it no longer had the strength to continue? Peter couldn't get the image of himself in the bathroom mirror out of his head. No wonder the Vietnamese cooks had given him such an odd look. They probably thought he was a goddamn junkie. Standing there in his bathroom Peter looked like a prisoner of war being released after years of confinement. Or worse, Peter looked like an exhibit at The Museum of Natural History. How much longer did he have? Frightened, Peter had rushed into his bedroom, found the clothes that smelled the least offensive and raced downstairs to Win Son Bakery. After he finished his Double Smash Burger, he was either going to order another one or head across the street to Williamsburg Deli and Grocery to grab a few things to take home. He had plenty of time to decide. Peter took another bite.

* * *

April stepped out onto the covered porch of the Katama General Store. The day was dark and the rain fell hard. It was the kind of rain that was going to last all day and she knew it. April was an islander, born and raised, and there were certain things that a true islander always knew—weather was one of them. An islander could always tell what was coming and when it would go. April knew that this rain was not going to clear for another twenty-four hours. She took a sip of her hot double-double coffee and squinted up at the sky. *Tomorrow afternoon will be lovely*, she thought. *Tomorrow's sunset will be gorgeous.* That was another thing that islanders always knew—the sunsets after a storm were always the most spectacular. April almost hoped that it would rain the day before the Vineyard: 1977 exhibit but it was really too risky to hope for that. It would be nice to ride on those coattails and get a spectacular sunset down on Edgartown Harbor but really, when it all came down to it, the threat of weather interfering with her turnout wasn't worth it. She would much rather have a week of guaranteed sunshine. The kind of sunshine that made everyone want to be out and about every minute of every day. Best to keep the rain as far from the exhibit as possible.

April dug into her purse and pulled out her car keys. As ready as she could be, she ran toward the van and pulled open the driver's door. She stepped in and heaved the door shut behind her. Drops of water ran across her skin making her shiver. April remembered her grandmother always saying, "Nice day if you're a duck!" but April doubted if even the ducks would be that thrilled with a day like today. She wedged her coffee into the cup holder, stuck her key in the ignition, and turned it over. She reached a little deeper into her bag and fished around until she found a travel pouch of Kleenex. Pulling one out, she dabbed at her face and neck.

"You'd think I'd been swimming on South Beach!" April said to herself in the rear-view mirror. She brushed her blonde hair back from her face and huffed. There was no point in trying to fix it until she got to the gallery. April pulled out onto Katama Road and turned toward Edgartown Village.

By the time April arrived at Old Sculpin, the rain was falling even harder. The sound of the water hitting the windshield and the roof was deafening. It sounded like those automated car washes they had over in America. April had gone through one of those things once when Edward was still alive. They had both hated it. They had gone through one in Boston, out of curiosity, decades ago but they had agreed that the car got much cleaner when they did it by hand and it was a lot more fun too. Not to mention, washing their car in the driveway with a bucket and a hose had to be better for the environment than rolling it at a snail's pace on that conveyor belt being blasted from every which way by water and detergent. How much soap and water did one of those things use for one car? Ridiculous.

April looked out the window at the dark blur she knew to be the gallery. She contemplated turning around and going home—calling today a wash…literally. She bit her lip. Still, she had a lot to do and no one would bother her on a day like today. Bad weather had a habit of making everyone batten down the hatches and hide away until it passed. There would be no interruptions on a day like this. If only she had brought Edward's old slicker or at the very least her wellies. She hated wet feet. Was her rain poncho in the back? The last time she had worn it was at the MV Sharks game. It hadn't been raining like this but there had been a bit of a sprinkle during the seventh inning. *Yes, I think it is back there but how the heck am I going to get at it?* April twisted around in her seat and looked toward the back of the van. She was going to have to get through the front seats and reach back over the back bench—and in a dress! Easier said than done. She rubbed the window and looked around. Even if someone did come by, they weren't going to see her. She couldn't see out of the windows so no one could see in either. Besides, who was going to be out for a stroll in this? The On Time skipper was probably in his shack but he wouldn't come out unless someone wanted the ferry. He'd be sitting in his easy chair in front of the portable heater. He wouldn't have even heard her drive up.

Alright, April decided. *I'm going in! Isn't that what soldiers always say in the movies?* This might not be war but the thought of wedging her backside between the two front seats was equally terrifying. What if she got stuck? Worse—what if she got stuck and someone found her like that? Whimpering for help, her dress up around her waist, and her giant butt wrapped in white double-extra-large granny panties with little pink roses on them exposed for all to see! *The heck with it,* she thought. *At least they're clean.* She could wriggle through the seats, get the poncho, and carry her shoes to the gallery. Then, she could get a lot of work done and she wouldn't have to do it sopping wet.

April undid her seatbelt and turned around in her seat, getting up on her knees as she turned. It didn't look as bad as she had imagined. With one hand on each seat, she pushed herself up and through. She felt her left foot hit something. Her foot was now hot and wet. She had kicked over her coffee. "Damn it!!" she shouted. She let go of the front seats and reached for the back bench. Her body weight was working for her now instead of against her. It was pushing her down through the front seats toward the back. As long as her butt didn't get stuck, she'd be fine. The shoulders of the front seat ground against her tummy. She winced. She felt that sharp pain inside that she felt when she tried to put on jeans that were way too tight. The farther she slid, the more it felt like her skin was going to tear. She cried out. Then, all at once, she was through. April flopped onto the backseat like a sack of russet potatoes. Belly and panties exposed, she struggled to pull her dress down and get into a more civilised position. April started to laugh. Now that she was through and on the back seat, the thought of someone actually coming and peering in the window was hilariously funny. What the heck did she think she was doing anyway? She was not sixteen anymore. She was old enough to have a grandchild who was sixteen! She was not supposed to be rolling around in the back seat of a van with her dress up over her head! April laughed until tears rolled out of the corners of her eyes. She sat up and peered into the front seat. She had kicked her coffee all over the rug. "Aw crap," she said. She decided she would clean it with the steam cleaner on the next sunny day.

    April turned around and reached into the back. Her purple plastic poncho was right on top. She sighed with relief. If it hadn't been there after all of that, she would have been fit to be tied. April pulled the poncho over her head and flattened it against her torso as best she could. She pulled off her shoes. Barefoot—she was good to go. She reached into the front seat for her purse and opened the back side door.

Edgartown Harbor was flooding. April stepped down into water that was already several inches over her ankles. She looked down and watched the water work its way up her hubcaps. No big deal. The harbour always flooded in a heavy rain. She could only imagine what Five Corners looked like right now. She closed the door and walked quickly toward the front door of Old Sculpin.

The rain felt like hail as it pelted her poncho. April squinted to protect her eyes. Wading slowly, she clutched her shoes and purse tightly to her chest, she thrust her feet forward as hard and fast as she could. She was almost there—just a few more steps. A sharp pain shot through her left foot. April screamed and reached out for the handrail that ran up the steps to the front door. Her fingernails dug into the weathered wood. Instinctively, April dropped her shoes and pulled up her foot. It came up in a froth of dirty, red water. A large shard of glass carved into the pad of her foot. It looked like a butcher knife in a holiday ham. Her foot twitched. Blood pumped out of the open wound, over the shard of glass, and streamed into the water below. April reached down gingerly and tried to get a hold of it. It was slippery. Her hands were wet. It was difficult to find purchase. She gritted her teeth. With one quick motion, she pulled it out. April felt it slice through the flesh of her foot. She screamed deep and guttural. She tossed the glass onto the stoop in front of her. Realising that she had been holding her breath, she inhaled deeply, then began to pant. She tilted her head up to try and catch her breath. The pain was blinding. April shook her head. She needed to focus. For the first time since she had gotten out of the car, April looked at the building in front of her. The window beside the front door of the gallery was smashed. All six panes were gone. *That's what I stepped on,* she thought. April looked at the door itself and saw that it was ajar. April was confused. *Why would kids want to break into the Old Sculpin?* Numbness started to creep up her leg. The blood was still pumping out into the harbour. A muddy red river was twisting its way toward Chappaquiddick. She had to get inside. She needed to get inside and lie down. If she could get inside, lie down, and elevate her leg, she could call the hospital. Then she would be okay. April reached for the first step with her wounded foot. As she lifted her foot, her head spun. *Take it easy, April.* She took another big inhale and exhaled through her mouth. Even in the cold rain, she could tell she was sweating. Her bad foot in place on the step, April put her weight on the heel and shuffled forward. Her grip on the railing tightened. She could do this. April half-stepped and half-jumped to get her good foot onto the step. It was a mistake. Her foot slipped out from underneath her. She twisted midair and fell face first into the flooded harbour. April's forehead slammed the cement parking lot with a thud. She tasted seawater and blood in her mouth. Cold water rushed into her poncho.

7

Craig parked his truck on the dirt drive in front of the small log cabin he had built with Judie. It was nothing fancy. It looked just like traditional log cabins have looked since the pioneers landed. Judie's favourite joke was that in one hundred years their cabin was going to look like it was built four hundred years ago. That still made Craig chuckle. She was right. The cabin had a front porch, a door in the centre of the front wall and two windows on either side that faced toward Moshup Beach. The second floor was barely a full floor. The twenty-four gauge steel roof was dark green with two dormer windows on the front side. White chinking sealed the cabin between the logs, which had been milled flat. The chimney on the west side of the roof was for the main floor woodstove. It did an excellent job of keeping the place warm in the off-season. The woodstove also ensured that the place always had a woodsy smell. The island was well storied about folks getting cabin fever over the winter. Isolated, cut-off from the rest of the more populated Edgartown, Oak Bluffs, and Vineyard Haven, some people went crazy without the human connection. Sitting in the peace and quiet with a wood fire, cooking fish that he had caught that day, and talking to Judie was just about Craig's favourite thing to do. He saw people enough when he went in do to odd jobs or stopped at Menemsha Texaco or to pick up some fish from the market—Stanley always gave him a good deal. What more did he need? He didn't have to spend all of his time socialising at Newes From America or even at Chilmark General Store. There were a few things that he would change but for the most part, Craig felt like he was doing okay. At least, he had until an hour ago at Images In Vogue. *Martha's Vineyard: 1977!* What the hell was that all about? What had Eddie said? Photos and paintings? Newspapers? The goddamn island incorporated almost four hundred years ago! Why the Christ did they have to do a retrospective of that year. Craig knew why. A lot of crap went down that year. The island had tried to break from Massachusetts and become its own state, McDonalds tried to get on the island, JAWS 2 did come to the island—Craig had been right in the middle of that—and Alan Quaid had disappeared. Except in print. His handsome, rich, shit-eating grin had been plastered on newspapers all over the country. Apparently, there was nothing else going on in the world. The six o'clock news had chewed every ounce of fat out of that story too. Craig was convinced that if Elvis hadn't died, they'd still be talking about Alan. Craig had always liked Elvis and while he had been sad to see him go, he would always be grateful to The King for leaving when he did. Alan fucking Quaid. It had been forty years and Craig had thought about him every single day. On a good day, he only thought about him once but there weren't all that many good days. Craig had already decided that he was not going to mention the exhibit to Judie.

* * *

The storm had chased Charles home. He got wet in Edgartown but he managed to pedal out of it on Beach Road. It caught up to him briefly at The JAWS Bridge but he picked up his pace and got ahead of it again. He stayed ahead of it for the duration of his ride, skipped his usual rest at East Chop Lighthouse, and the rain hit the driveway as he was rolling his bike back into the garage.

Charles' legs were wobbly. The storm had forced him to ride consistently harder than he otherwise would have. His thighs burned. His chest heaved with each breath. He was uncomfortable and felt like he was over-heating. He took off his helmet immediately. The cool air of the garage felt good. With each breath, Charles felt closer to normal. He closed his eyes for a minute and focussed on slowing his heart rate and breathing. The rain had begun to thunder on the roof like one of those relaxation tapes. It was a comforting sound. Charles sat on the wooden bench he had bought at Chicken Alley and pulled off his shoes and socks. Sometimes, Charles was convinced he could actually hear his feet sigh with relief. Resting his bare hot feet onto the cold cement floor of the garage felt luxurious. He sat like that for a minute before getting up and walking into the house through the side door, leaving a trail of sweaty footprints behind him.

When he opened the door, Fenway barked and ran toward him. His nails clacked on the hardwood and Fenway skidded to a stop by crashing into Charles' shins. Charles laughed. "Easy, buddy!" He reached down and scratched the beagle vigorously behind the ears. "Do you need to go out?"

Fenway barked twice for yes and thumped his tail on the floor urgently.

"Are you sure?" asked Charles. "Do you see what it's doing out there?"

Fenway barked twice again.

"Alright," Charles said. "Your call." He grabbed Fenway's leash and clipped it to his collar. Charles opened the front door and the rain's staccato played full volume. Fenway scurried behind Charles, hiding behind his legs. "This was your idea!" Charles said. "C'mon, we can stay on the lawn but I don't want to find any treats in the corner of the dining room." Fenway looked up at him with innocent eyes. "Well, I hope it was you. If it was Bubbas, I'm going to have to take that cat to the vet. If it was Mommy, then…well…let's just say I really hope it wasn't Mommy. C'mon, let's go." Charles gave Fenway a gentle tug. The beagle stood up, found his courage and headed out the door with a *"Chuff!"*

While Fenway looked for a good spot on the lawn, Charles tried to edge toward the protection of the porch overhang. Not that it made that much of a difference. He was already wet with sweat from his ride. In fact, a walk on the lawn in his bare feet might feel just the thing. Fenway looked at Charles before squatting.

"I'm not looking!" Charles said turning his back on his dog. "God, how did I get such a neurotic dog?" He walked out onto the lawn and dragged his feet through the wet cool grass. He stretched out his toes as far as he could so that he could feel the clusters of long blades run between them. He was right—it was just what his feet needed. The grass was wet and cool and it simultaneously tickled and massaged. Where his feet had been tight and burning, now they were relaxed and refreshed. He was soaked all the way through now. The rain was washing away the salty layer of dust and dirt. Charles tilted his head up toward the sky and let the rain spatter his face. Fenway barked and Charles came back to earth. "Are we good?" Charles pulled out the poop 'n' scoop baggie and picked up the healthy sized turd Fenway had deposited on the lawn. He looked at the dog. Fenway was watching him with great interest. The dog cocked his head causing one ear to flop over his forehead. "You know," said Charles. "I can't make up my mind whether you get a kick out of watching me pick up after you or you're thinking, *What in the name of all that's holy are you going to do with that?*" Fenway barked once and without waiting for Charles, ran back to the house. "Fine," said Charles. "Be that way."

Charles walked up to the front door. He grabbed Fenway's leash so he couldn't run into the house without being towelled off, and turned the knob. Fenway pulled. His front paws lifted off the floor and his back paws scrambled for traction.

"Would you hold on a minute, you crazy dog!"

Charles' phone started ringing and vibrating on the kitchen counter. He looked at the dog and then back toward the phone. He let go of the leash and Fenway ran upstairs.

"Of course you go upstairs," Charles mumbled. "You're probably going to dry off on my bed, aren't you?" He walked to the phone. It was Laurie. "Hey babe."

"What's wrong?"

"I just took Fenway out for a pee and a poop and I'm pretty sure he is upstairs drying himself off on our bed," Charles chuckled dryly. "It's not that big a deal really. I needed to wash the bedding."

"Charles I won't be home right away. There's been an accident," Laurie said. Her voice was low. She was speaking in her cop voice.

"What's going on?" asked Charles.

"Well, we're not really sure," said Laurie. "April Stevens was found face down in the flooded parking lot in front of Old Sculpin just a few minutes ago."

"Oh no! Is she going to be okay?" asked Charles.

"It's too soon to tell. She hit her head pretty hard. I was also told that she lost a lot of blood. I haven't seen her yet or spoken to her doctor. There's a possibility that there was a break-in at the gallery. I'm going down there to check it out."

"Can I do anything, hon?"

"Can you go down to the hospital? April doesn't have any family that I am aware of. Her husband has passed and there are no kids. I don't know of anyone else at least not on island. Do you?"

"No," said Charles.

"I didn't think so," Laurie continued. "If she does wake up, I don't want her to wake up in the hospital all alone. You're at least a friend."

"I don't really know her all that well, Laurie," said Charles. "We've just been working together on this exhibit."

"I know but I trust you. I know that you will say the right things and be comforting. I also know that you will remember anything important if she says anything about what happened to her."

"Got it," said Charles. "Okay, I'll take a quick shower, change, and head right over."

"Thanks," said Laurie. "Charles?"

"Yes?"

"I love you," said Laurie.

"I love you too," said Charles.

* * *

Peter couldn't help but smile at the Puerto Rican music emanating from the nail salon on Graham Avenue.

That distinct mix of Spanish, South African, Caribbean percussion and strings almost commanded every listener to be in a good mood. When he woke up that morning, he decided to have a shower—this time avoiding his reflection in the bathroom mirror—go for a walk, and get a haircut. Going to see Carlos, his barber, was really just an excuse. Walking the streets of Brooklyn, watching the people, hearing the sounds, and feeling the energy was probably Peter's favourite thing to do. A friend had suggested that he buy a bike to make his way around town. It had sounded like a good idea and he picked one up but he didn't like it. The bike got him where he needed to go and it got him there quickly—why anyone had a car in the city was beyond him— but it got him there too quickly. When he was on his bike, it took all of his concentration. He had to focus on not getting hit by cars and not hitting pedestrians. There was absolutely no time to absorb the scenery. There was no time to enjoy the goings on around him. After a month, he had given the bike away to the woman who lived above his studio. Where did he have to be in such a hurry? If he had to go into Manhattan, he was only about a five-minute walk from the L Train and then if he made all his connections, it was a forty-minute commute. In his neighbourhood, he could walk to everything. There was a barber he liked, a drug store, supermarket, deli, you name it. That was the perk of living in the city. You were never want for anything.

Peter couldn't bare to be indoors on a day like today. His grandmother had drilled that into him. When he stayed with her, she was always scooting him outside if the weather was good. She always said that it was for his own good. The fresh air was important. He figured out years later that she really just wanted five minutes of peace and quiet. Peter had been a good kid but needy. He had always wanted validation, reassurance. He supposed he hadn't changed all that much. Isn't that what all artists needed? Regardless of whether or not they were actors, painters, writers, or singers, all artists spent their entire life begging as many people as possible to reassure them that they were good. They needed to know that they weren't wasting their time. Did other professions do that? Did they spend their time wondering if other people approved of their life choices? Peter didn't think so. It seemed like a stretch to him. Then again, other professions weren't piecework designed for mass appeal. Artists only got paid if they sold a piece of art. Singers didn't receive their paycheques until people bought their songs or bought tickets to hear them sing. Writers had to sell books and articles. It was all the same. Perhaps on those terms the desire for constant reaffirmation was warranted. In the beginning, Peter had been desperate to sell just one painting. It had been a dream. One painting would be enough to put coffee, eggs, and milk in the fridge, and fill his cupboard with Mr Noodles at least for a little while. The irony was that now that he had lots of money, more often than not, he was forgetting to eat.

At the barbershop only an hour ago, Peter had watched as Carlos unwrapped the hot towel from his face, lathered his facial hair with warm scented foam, and taken a straight razor to his face and neck. Slowly, expertly, the man had sliced away the ratty beard that had grown during Peter's last painting. As the hair fell away, Peter got a full view of the face underneath. He didn't look good. He didn't look healthy. His cheeks were missing their usual boyish plumpness. A faded sallow had replaced the pink glow that used to dapple his face. Having lost the fleshy caulking that usually filled their sockets, his eyes looked like they were about to cave in or worse—fall out. Carlos had maintained a happy countenance throughout. Peter had been going to him for years so the barber already knew to skip the baseball talk. Peter had no interest in sports. Peter didn't have much of a head for any current events. He was really out of the loop. And even though he had heard the word thrown around at art exhibits a lot, Peter wasn't even sure what a Kardashian was. That was one of the things that

Peter really liked about Carlos—rather quickly, Carlos had figured Peter out.

Peter didn't watch sports; he didn't watch TV shows. Peter did read books but Carlos only read Sports Illustrated. He used to read Penthouse Forum but that was a long time ago. Carlos came from a big family and was working hard at creating another one all his own. Peter didn't have family in his life and loved hearing about it. When Peter sat down to get his haircut, Carlos could talk in minute detail about the antics of his daughters, his wife's almost constant—to hear Carlos tell it—histrionics, and his mother's meddling. They were some of Peter's favourite stories. Peter wouldn't say much and Carlos would stop periodically to ask, "You're sure you want to hear this? You're not bored?" but Peter would reassure him he was enjoying every minute and Carlos would continue. Peter always left the barbershop feeling much better than when he went in and not just because of his hair.

When Peter had walked in that morning, Carlos hadn't said anything to him except "Hey Pete! How ya doin'?" like he always did. Peter wasn't even sure if Carlos had done a double-take when he first saw him. The barber was too professional for that. But after Peter had paid him and the man had tucked his tip into the front pocket of his perfectly pressed slacks, Carlos had patted Peter on the shoulder and with a sympathetic smile on a face much softer than the one he had been wearing through the entire visit, said, "Take care of yourself, Peter." Peter knew what he meant. His eyes had been caring and his voice had been low but really his words were screaming, *"For Christ's sake! Eat something would ya? And get off the junk if that's what your doin'!"* Peter had nodded and smiled. He was also starving. It was a good day to find a seat outside Win Son on the way home. He could go for some Tiawanese. And even though he was still thin enough to see through, he looked considerably less shabby than the last time he had been in there. It would be nice to see the cooks sigh with relief when they saw him. He was sick of people thinking he was a junkie.

*   *   *

Laurie stepped out of her police truck with the pants of her uniform tucked into her Wellingtons. She had originally bought the boots for fishing but once she got out there, she discovered she was a barefoot on the beach kinda girl. It was still raining and down by Memorial Wharf and Old Sculpin, the harbour had flooded almost a foot. She closed the door behind her and started wading toward the gallery in cautious steps.

The front stoop wasn't big enough to be called a porch. It was barely big enough to hold one person. Clearly, the end of the journey, the final step one made when visiting Old Sculpin Gallery, was supposed to be inside the gallery itself at the front desk. Under normal circumstances, Laurie would have done exactly that, like she had done many times in the past. The art community on Martha's Vineyard was extensive and Laurie loved it. She kept well-informed about any and every gallery showing and she attended as many as her work schedule would allow. Charles loved them too. Dinner at a local restaurant and a visit to North Water Gallery, Old Sculpin, or Field Gallery—just to name a few—was just about as good as it got for date night. However, on this visit, Laurie didn't walk directly in. She stopped on the stoop and inspected the broken window to the left of the door. Going on the assumption that this was the point of entry, then most of the glass would be on the floor, inside the gallery, directly underneath the window. April had apparently stepped on a large shard of glass in the parking lot. Was the rest of the window floating around in the harbour? Was her evidence being washed away? In a deluge like this, anything was possible. Laurie decided that not only had she seen all she was going to see under the circumstances but she was also as wet as she could possibly get. She stepped inside.

Once across the threshold, Laurie immediately looked down to her left. The floor was covered in glass and wood. Whoever it was had either thrown something through the window or simply smashed it and used it as a point of entry. Unlike CSI or Law & Order, a lab rat in a white has-mat suit wasn't already tending to the window frame with a small brush. Nor was anyone lifting fibres and placing them in a small plastic baggy for cataloguing. Who had the budget for that? John Q. Public would be very disappointed to find out that police officers didn't take endless walking tours of their own romantically lit police stations, dressed in Armani and Gucci business casual. Laurie turned and walked a little farther into Old Sculpin.

Detective Jack Burrell turned when his boss walked into the main gallery and strolled over to meet her at the front door. "Hey Chief!" he said.

"Jack," Laurie said. "What's it look like?" she asked. Laurie motioned behind her with her thumb in what was the universal symbol for hitchhiking. "Can we get some pictures of that broken glass under the window here?"

"Sure, Chief," said Jack. "I have the camera in my truck. I was just taking a look around to you know, see what's what!" Jack spoke with the exuberance of a teenager. The bounce in his voice insisted that his head bounce right along with it.

"So, what *is* what?" asked Laurie.

"Well," Jack adjusted the uniform hat on his head. He pulled a hanky out of his inside coat pocket and wiped at the rainwater that was still dripping onto his face and hair. "It's kinda weird," he said. "It's actually simple but that's what makes it so weird."

"Show me," said Laurie.

Jack walked Laurie to the back corner of the gallery. The rain thundered on the roof and walls of the old wooden building. The sound was almost uncomfortable. When the wind grabbed at the doors and the window casings, when it pulled at the roof, Laurie actually winced at the noise.

"You see?" said Jack. "This is it!"

Laurie looked up at the wall. The curators of the gallery had taken a front page of The Vineyard Gazette and turned it into a mural. It took up almost the entire back wall. The date was printed across the top in big letters. The copy was from June 30, 1977. Everything else beneath it had been blacked out. Spray-painted out of sight. Wet paint ran down the mural and dripped slowly onto the floor. The room was filled with the smell of aerosol and paint. The chemical tang hit the back of Laurie's throat and sinuses. She brought her hand up to her face in a futile attempt to quell the fumes. "They didn't defile anything else?"

"No, Chief. This is it," said Jack.

"Did they take anything?" asked Laurie.

"At this point, I can't be entirely sure," said Jack. "I'll get an inventory from one of the board members as soon as possible but I can't see any spaces. You know what I mean? There are no holes. If someone came in here, in this rainstorm, there should be an obviously empty space somewhere in the gallery and a wet one at that! There's rain water dripping all over the floor here where the paint has dripped on the floor—this is definitely where they stood—but I don't see water any anywhere else."

Laurie turned around and scanned the floor from the front door to the area in front of the vandalised mural. There were three sets of tracks—including her own—and all three set a direct course from the front to the back. There were water marks all in front of the mural too. Then, back out. She looked around. Jack was right; nothing else seemed to have been touched. "Did you go upstairs?"

Jack shook his head. "Not yet but there are no footprints heading in that direction. I doubt that the stairs will even be wet!"

"It doesn't look like it," said Laurie. She turned back toward the mural and stared at the big black rectangle. "None of the art in here is worth stealing. I mean, it's not like you're going to find any Rembrandts on the walls of Old Sculpin," Laurie said mostly to herself. "But that's the only stuff that means anything to anyone. That's what you would defile."

Jack followed her gaze up to the wall. "I don't follow you," he said.

"Well, if you're a kid and you throw something at the window just because you're a jerk and you feeling like breaking something then fine—end of story. This individual broke in. They brought spray paint with the intent of doing damage. So what do they do when they get in here? After they go to all of the trouble of committing the crime of breaking in? They don't run around spraying everything and destroying as much as they can in the short amount of time allotted to them. They head back to this corner and blacken this particular piece. So, why this piece and nothing else? Especially, when it's the only thing hanging in the gallery from what I can tell, that's easily replaced. Toward that end, blackening out the mural doesn't hide anything. We can just go look it up in the Edgartown Public Library hall of records. I mean, I'm sure that's where Old Sculpin got it."

"Jack nodded. "Oh yeah, you're right."

"We need the front page of The Gazette on June 30th, 1977."

8

Peter Morgan stepped out of Win Son Bakery and Restaurant with an armful of food for the second time in as many days. When he had walked in, the Tiawanese cooks had welcomed him with big smiles and after speaking to each other excitedly in their native tongue, they told him that he was already looking much better. "You cleaned up very handsome!" one of the cooks said in a very heavy accent. "Now, you must eat some more. Yes?" Peter agreed. He told the men that he was quite hungry and in the mood for some of their delicious Tiawanese food. They were elated to hear it. He ordered a large plate of stir-fried pork with garlic chives and black beans. He also ordered a side of medium grain rice to go with it. As he was paying for his

351

order, one of the cooks slipped two complimentary moon cakes into the bag. "We're going to make you nice and fat!" the man said then he filled his cheeks with air and held his arms out in front of him symbolising a large belly. The cook exploded with laughter before walking away. Peter smiled. Right now, nice and fat sounded good to him.

The restaurant had three metal tables, each with two chairs, set up on the sidewalk for their patrons. Peter walked to the table farthest from the front door. Pulling out the chair that faced his apartment building, he sat down and set his well-packed lunch on his lap. He opened the bag and inhaled deeply. The exotic spices of oriental cooking filled his nose and made his mouth water. He reached in for the plastic utensils and the pork and beans, and dug in. The dish was salty, tangy, and delicious. The fattiness of the fried pork was just what his body was craving. Peter could almost hear his brain sending emergency signals for more. He tried to pace himself but it was hard. Each and every bite seemed to wake his senses and as they awoke, they realised just what they had been missing. All of those electric bells and whistles that hadn't gone off while Peter was painting, all of the alarms that hadn't been tripped, were going off like fireworks on the Fourth of July. When he tried to put down his disposable fork and sit back for a moment, he heard voices in his head yelling at him, *"Are you crazy? Keep going!*" Peter found that he had no choice but to keep eating. He felt the energy from the beans and rice coursing through him. He felt nutrients race out to his fingertips. His breathing deepened with every mouthful. He felt a warmth in his groin. Everywhere that life was most important to being human was waking up. His vision sharpened—colour more vivid. Of course, Peter knew that this was all ridiculous. He knew that all of this was impossible, that it was all in his head. It was just his mind encouraging him to keep eating. Still, he couldn't help but feel like Superman first being exposed to the yellow sun of Earth. He felt powerful.

Between paintings, Peter always wondered why he painted at all. He also gave serious thought to never painting again. If he could feel this good between projects, if he could feel this healthy and this happy, wasn't he crazy to ever pick up a brush again? It was like that old joke—the man goes to the doctor and says, "Doctor, it hurts when I do this." The doctor looks at him and says, "Then, don't do that." So, why paint? Would other artistic expression affect him in the same way? If he sculpted, would he be able to sleep, eat, and live like a normal person? The answer was he didn't know. Peter had never tried to do anything else. He had started sketching and painting when he was very young but art hadn't felt anything but good then. He had still lived in Blairstown with his folks. Life was quieter and simpler then. All of the tropes of living in a small town were true as far as Peter could see and they were good tropes. He had played outside with his friends; they had hiked in the woods, creek-hopped, and hung-out at the local diner. He knew everyone in town, and they knew him, so walking the streets at night always felt safe. That little piece of irony always made Peter smirk. Blairstown's only claim to fame after 1980 was that it was where Friday The 13th had been filmed. Whenever he visited his parents, he saw more goalie masks than the average NHL coach. Still, the fact that Kevin Bacon and his friends had been murdered at the local Boy Scouts camp didn't negate the fact that he never felt safer anywhere in his life than in Blairstown. There had been a time when Peter had considered moving back home. He hadn't seen his parents in a while but he knew he couldn't go back now—especially looking like he did. If his mother saw him now, she would have a stroke. He needed to put on weight. He needed to get some colour back in his cheeks. His toenails and his fingernails had to start growing back strong and healthy. His mother had eyes like a hawk. If Peter went back looking anything but the picture of health, he'd never hear the end of it. Peter took the last mouthful of pork and beans then reached for the bag that contained the two moon cakes. It wouldn't have occurred to Peter to buy them but he was glad that the cook had slipped them in. They were a treat.

Peter decided to make a list of groceries that he needed to pick up for the apartment. If he was going to return to any semblance of health, he was going to need to eat some healthy food, not just takeout. He pulled out his iPhone and tapped the Notes app. His screen lit up like the yellow lined foolscap paper of his school days. He sat back to think and took a bite of moon cake. He was going to need fruits and vegetables for sure.

As Peter made his list, he watched the goings on in the neighbourhood around him. The traffic was slower than usual and the sidewalks weren't crowded. He could hear a car horn occasionally in the distance but that was standard for the city. People were at work in the midday and kids were in school. Tourists didn't really wander out his way—they stayed in Manhattan. That was one of the things he liked about being out in Williamsburg.

The sky was unnaturally blue and clouds billowed up in white puffs. There was no rain in these clouds. They were strictly atmosphere. Backdrop. They were the clouds of art. In fact, Peter always called these clouds 'Ray Ellis clouds' because they looked like the clouds in Ray Ellis's paintings. Ellis's sleepy oil paintings of catboats and lighthouses along the Eastern Seaboard were always set against a haze of very distinct clouds—Ray Ellis clouds. Even though most people weren't familiar with the name, they would recognise a Ray Ellis painting right away. Their gentle lighting, soft colours, and feathery brush strokes made them American classics. He was definitely one of Peter's favourites.

Peter turned his head as he caught movement at his apartment building. A young woman climbed out of her window on the fifth floor, the top floor, and stood on the fire escape. Fire escapes were common places for New Yorkers to sit and read on a hot city day or a cool evening in the summer. Some people had their fire escapes decked out with blankets and lawn chairs. Peter had never taken to it. Maybe it was a native New Yorker thing to do. Peter much preferred to get out and enjoy the parks or just go for a walk when he wasn't painting. He recognised the woman. He didn't know her name but he had seen her in the elevator and the hallway. He liked her face. It was a kind face if not a little sad. Quite often when he passed her, Peter would look at her not from the perspective of a neighbour but as a painter. He thought about sketching her. He liked her straight nose and her almond shaped eyes. Her cheeks were faintly freckled and her lips were naturally red. Even from his place on the sidewalk, Peter could make out her features. The wind caught her hair and blew it across her face but she either didn't notice or she didn't care. He liked her long dark hair, her petite figure, and her willowy clothing. There was something familiar in her polite half-smile. That smile that everyone has and keeps just under the surface for acknowledging people in their day-to-day lives. Peter didn't know this girl at all but he liked her. He watched as she stood in case she looked his way. She placed her hands on the railing in front of her. Peter prepared to wave. If she looked his way, he would smile and wave. He watched with his arm at the ready for when she looked up. She didn't look up. The girl jumped. She dove. She used the railing as a fulcrum and tipped over. She went over headfirst. Peter jumped out of his seat and ran toward her. It was over in a second. It wasn't slow like on TV or in the movies. Peter heard her head crack as it hit the pavement. It was loud like a homerun. Blood shot out of her skull like a child jumping on a packet of ketchup. She had already hit the sidewalk when Peter screamed, "*Wait!*" He ran into the street. A car hit his leg. He stumbled but regained his footing and hurried toward the limp body lying on the ground. The girl had landed on top of her head before her body had collapsed limply beside her. Her arms flopped to her side like an abandoned doll. Peter knelt beside her and rolled her to face him. She stared at him. Blood ran out of her nose. Her neck bent unnaturally in the middle. Peter took her head in his hands and he felt the two sides of her skull shift in opposite directions. The top of her head was a flat, ruddy pulp. Bone ground on bone under her ears and face. Her eyes shifted in their sockets. Peter could feel his hands warm and wet. A warm, metallic smell filled the air. He pulled his fingers out of her hair. It looked like he had just crushed a raspberry pie in his fists. There were sirens and Peter wondered if they were coming for her or if they were passing in the distance. Peter couldn't shake her stare. Her left eye drooped down in its broken socket but both eyes were fixed on him. She looked like she wanted to tell him something and Peter didn't want to miss it. *She's Dead.* Her eyes were wide and pleading. She wanted him to know something. *She's Dead.* Peter felt that feeling of darkness, the darkness of his paintings. He felt that feeling of the unseen. He felt that dread, that knot in his stomach. Was this woman trying to tell him what that darkness was? *She's Dead.* Was she going to explain it all away? Peter watched. She didn't speak. She didn't move. Peter felt someone put their hands on his shoulders and gently pull him to his feet. He could hear voices all around him but they were distant and murky. It sounded like he had his head underwater at the public pool. Peter stepped toward the apartment building, braced himself with both hands on the red brick, and vomited his Taiwanese lunch all over the wall.

*   *   *

Charles stood up as Laurie walked down the hall of Martha's Vineyard Hospital toward him. He could tell, even from a distance, that her uniform was quite wet so he walked over to the counter of the cafeteria and fixed her a cup of coffee. She came up behind him just as he finished stirring and he passed it to her.

"Thanks," Laurie said. "How's April doing?"

Charles shook his head. "I don't really know anything. The doctor's still with her."

Laurie sipped at the hot coffee in the paper cup and then nodded her head. "I guess that makes sense."

"What happened at the Old Sculpin?"

"Someone broke in and vandalised the new exhibit," she said.

"The 1977 exhibit?" asked Charles.

"Yes," said Laurie. "The one with your pictures."

"Was anything stolen?" asked Charles.

Laurie shrugged. "We're not actually sure. There's no way we can tell for certain until we get one of the board members to go through the gallery with us and take an official inventory but you know—I don't think so."

"Someone broke in just to trash the place and in this storm?" asked Charles. "That seems weird."

"I know but it doesn't look like theft. There didn't seem to be anything missing. They didn't look like break-in footprints either, you know?" Laurie continued. "They didn't seem to be all over the place; they weren't looking for something. Whoever it was, broke in, went directly back to the exhibit, violated an enormous blow up of The Gazette, and split."

"That's it?" Charles raised one eyebrow and moved his head back incredulously.

"That's it," Laurie said taking another sip of coffee.

"That's weirder than I thought," said Charles.

"So, now I have to decide whether I'm looking for a crazy man...or a moron." She looked down at her cup. "This is really good coffee. Thanks again. I'm soaked. Actually, the first thing that I have to do is go down to The Gazette and find out what was on the page that pissed our vandal off so much that he had to cover the entire image with spray paint!"

"It was that guy," said Charles.

Laurie gawked at him. "That's right! You've been down there! What guy?"

"It was the front page of the issue after that rich guy disappeared in the storm in '77," said Charles. He nodded gently. "Alan Quaid—that was his name. Alan Quaid. He's a big part of the exhibit."

"Why would someone want to black out the face of Alan Quaid forty years after he disappeared? I have to read up on this guy. Do you know anything about him?"

Charles shook his head. "Not really. I think I met him though."

"*You met him?*"

"I think so. I think Peter and I both did. That summer, not long after meeting each other, we met a guy named Alan. It was forty years ago though so, I might be wrong. It doesn't really matter. I mean, even if it was him, I can't tell you anything about him. The day I met the guy I'm thinking about, we were on the harbour—right in front of Old Sculpin actually—and watching them film JAWS 2. My brain was scrambled with rubber sharks. Everyone looks more or less the same in my memory of that day. I can see me, Peter, the shark, and then just people. Oh, there was a girl—a really pretty girl with long dark hair. The only reason I know that is because there is a close-up shot of her in that book Peter made for me."

"Have you heard back from Peter yet?" asked Laurie.

Charles shook his head. "No, not yet."

Doctor Nevin walked into the cafeteria and with a nod of acknowledgement, headed toward Laurie and Charles. He looked like a doctor. His grey hair made a very short halo around the back of his head and his warm blue eyes looked out from behind black horn-rimmed glasses. His average build, his white lab coat that protected his sweater, his tie, and slacks completed the doctor look. But no matter where he was or what he was wearing, Doctor Nevin always looked like he just walked off the set of St Elsewhere, Chicago Hope, or E.R.

"Hello Chief," Doctor Nevin smiled. "Hi Charles. It's terrible weather to be out running around in, but I guess that's why we're here, isn't it?"

"I don't follow you doctor," said Laurie. "What do you mean?"

"Well, if it wasn't for the weather, April Stevens wouldn't be here."

"Oh, that's true," said Laurie. "How is she?"

"She has lost a lot of blood. The cut on her foot is quite deep and the water didn't help. The salt water stopped the blood from coagulating so she just kept bleeding. Then it looks like she either fainted from the loss of blood or just fell and hit her head on the pavement," Doctor Nevin continued. "If Ryan hadn't found her when he did, she would have drowned for sure. We got a lot of fluid out of her lungs and we stitched up her foot and dressed her forehead, but she's not going to feel herself for quite a while."

"Ryan?" asked Laurie.

"The Chappy Ferry skipper," said Doctor Nevin. "Good kid."

"Oh, yes, I know Ryan. He is a good kid," Laurie said. "I guess April's not talking at the moment, is she Doc?"

The Doctor looked at her over his glasses. "No."

"Okay," said Laurie. "I'll check back with you tomorrow. Thanks Doc."

"Ryan told me there was a break-in at Old Sculpin. What did they take?" asked Doctor Nevin.

"At the moment, we're not too sure. I need to get a hold of a board member to go through it with me," said Laurie. "I suppose they're listed on the website."

"I fish with John Pease," said Doctor Nevin. "He's on the board—good guy too. If you want to come back to my office with me, I'll give you his number."

*   *   *

Storms like this always made Eddie antsy. He could never sleep through the night when it was raining this hard. His imagination would get carried away and eventually, he would have to go and check on the store. It wasn't far away. He only lived on Skiff Avenue. More often than not, on a nice day, he would walk to work. In the summer, if he timed it right, his friend Lisa would be in her garden when he walked by and he'd end up coming home with an armful of fresh vegetables. Lisa's garden was one of a kind. It was no wonder she always won prizes at the Martha's Vineyard Agricultural Fair. Eddie looked out the window as he slipped into his yellow slicker and sou'wester. Lisa wasn't going to be out gardening today. It was really coming down. Lagoon Pond Road would be flooded for sure and Five Corners would be virtually indistinguishable from Vineyard Haven Harbor! Eddie decided that the best course of action would be to drive up Skiff to Edgartown Road and come in to town from the other end. Then, he could avoid all of that nonsense entirely. Just a quick drive in to town to ensure that all was well. In his heart of hearts, he knew it would be. It always was. The store was around the middle of Main Street just up from Vineyard Vines so flooding really wasn't an issue. Vineyard Haven sloped down toward the harbour and Main Street was on a hill heading toward West Chop. Any way you looked at it, the rainwater was just going to run right by Images In Vogue. Still, doors could blow open; trees could fall and break windows. Eddie knew a lot of islanders who had sustained quite a bit of damage to their houses, trucks, and businesses at the hands of Mother Nature. It wouldn't hurt to check. The one time he didn't check was the one time something would happen.

Eddie opened the front door and braced himself against the wind and blowing rain. He stepped out, turned to ensure he pulled the door shut tight, and ran to the truck. He jumped in and turned the keys in the ignition. The engine roared to life without hesitation and Eddie eased slowly out onto the deserted street. There was a time when his neighbours thought he was crazy but they were used to him now. They knew exactly what he was doing. That was how things worked on Martha's Vineyard. Everyone thought you were crazy in the beginning but if you hung around long enough, people got used to you and started saying things like "Oh, that's just how Lineback is. That's his way. Pay him no mind." Eddie was sure that his neighbours had almost taken bets on how long it would take him to go out in the storm and check on his store. Everyone else battened down their hatches and waited it out but not Eddie. He would be out in it at least twice. When they had seen him driving out in the middle of Hurricane José they really thought the cheese had slipped off his cracker. He hadn't thought to drive up Skiff that time. Right after making it through the eighteen inches of flooding on Lagoon Pond Road, the winds had lifted his truck off the ground. Only for a second but long enough for Eddie to realise that he had lost control of the vehicle. Long enough to think that he might be flipped or dragged into the harbour. His wheels had made a high-pitched squeal. The body of the truck sounded like Quint crushing a beer can as it hydroplaned all the way into the post office parking lot. Eddie had sat there for a moment to catch his breath and wait for his heart to stop racing. Stupidly, he had still continued to the store and of course, everything was fine. This storm was nowhere near as bad as the hurricane. It was just a heavy rain. Once he checked and made sure that everything was dry and shut tight, he would sleep better.

No one was out. The streets were empty. Eddie turned from Edgartown Road onto State Road and drove back down into town. There were a couple of lights on at The Mansion House—of course there were—but other than that, there were no signs of life. His windshield wipers beat as quickly as their design would allow but it was still difficult to see. Eddie pulled over into a spot on Main Street and shut off his engine. The only sound was the rain beating on the roof of the truck. That tin-roofed cottage sound. He took a deep breath, pulled the keys out of the ignition, opened the door, and made a run for it.

Eddie was at the front door of his shop in seconds. Once under the overhang, out of the rain, he shook like a wet dog and wiped at his face with his hands. He could feel the rain running off the brim of his hat onto the back of his coat. So far, so good. Slowly, his stomach began unknotting.

No windows were broken and the front door wasn't swinging wildly in the wind. Eddie flipped through his keys, found the one he needed, and inserted it into the lock. It turned with a smoothness only achievable through decades of repetition.

When the lights were off, the shop had an ethereal stillness to it. Eddie noticed it every time. He flicked a switch and the single centre track lit up. It wasn't even a quarter of the lights in the store. It was designed to be just enough to light for him to get from the front to the back or vice versa when he was opening up in the morning or locking up at night. All of the rest of the light switches were in the back. This was a good sign. The power was still on. It didn't take much for the power to go out on the island. Eddie had a generator at home, most islanders did, but he didn't have one at the shop. He made his way through to the back following the path laid out by the overhead lights. When he got to the entrance to the back, to his workshop, he opened the door and stopped dead in his tracks. Eddie felt all of the blood leave his face. His arms and hands went numb.

9

Peter woke up screaming. He bolted upright—his chest heaving. Sweat dripped from his brow to his cheeks as he tried to catch his breath. He wiped his forehead with the back of his arm, only to discover that his arm was glistening too. He reached back and felt his pillow. It was hot and soaked. *I could wring it out over the sink*, Peter thought. Sink—that was a good idea. Peter tossed back the wet sheets—*did I wet the bed or is that all sweat?*—and jerkily propelled his thin, naked body toward the bathroom. He turned on the cold water, let it run for a while, and soaked a facecloth in it. He wiped his face and the back of his neck. The cold was sharp at first against his hot skin, but then it eased into refreshing. Peter turned off the tap. He stood in the cool, quiet, dark of his bathroom enjoying the silence. There was a magic hour even in the city between late, late night and early, early morning. It was calm. Then, his dreams came back to him. His head had been clear for a matter of moments, but they found him again and one by one they crept back in like an earwig that, having found the waxy canal on the side of his head, was determined to burrow through his brain from one side to the other. As if dragged by little pincers, Images crawled slowly through his head, making sure that he saw them. He saw the darkness that followed him everywhere he went. This was no surprise. It was the darkness of his paintings. The painful complete blackness that he tried unsuccessfully to purge with every brush stroke. The coloured houses, the dark night, and the white park lights—they were all there but this time, he saw her too. He saw his neighbour. Her head wasn't busted open like it had been after the fall but he remembered blood. Her long brown hair cascading back from her face. Her eyes had been wide with terror and staring at him. She hadn't spoken but her eyes fixed on him with a look that screamed, *Don't you see? Don't you know?* Just as when he had held her head on the sidewalk, feeling it shift and crumble in the bag of skin that held it together, Peter knew she was saying something to him. Her gentle love child looks, her dated hippy clothes, they were all pieces of a puzzle that he couldn't finish. He just stared blankly at all of the pieces feeling stupid and frustrated.

Peter reached for the JAWS cup that held his toothbrush and toothpaste. He placed the contents on the porcelain sink, and filled the cup with cold water. He drained the cup without stopping and refilled it. He drained it again. He gasped with satisfaction. Inspecting the cup he saw that the rim was covered in dried toothpaste. Peter turned on a little hot water and began to rub the cup clean with his thumb and forefinger. He hadn't really considered this cup for a long time. It was just there. He got it on his trip to Martha's Vineyard decades ago. The trip was so fragmented in his head. He had been just a kid. He barely remembered it now. In fact, he hadn't thought about it in ages. He and Charles used to keep in touch. Peter had liked that. There weren't too many people around who still liked to be a pen pal. Charles did though. Charles had been a good letter writer too. Peter still had them all somewhere. They had snuck into JAWS on that trip; Peter remembered that. They had also seen the shark from JAWS 2. Christ, Peter hadn't thought about that in years. When Peter and his family had returned home, his parents had given him this cup. Peter could distinctly see his Dad handing it to him; however, he couldn't see the whole memory. There were pieces missing. His Dad looked upset—worried. Was he worried about Peter? Is that why he was giving him the cup? The memory surrounding the image of Peter's Dad with his arm extended, holding the JAWS cup, wasn't one of excitement. His face didn't flush, his chest didn't warm like they did when happy memories came to the surface. His face didn't crack a smile out of pure reflex. That wasn't his gut reaction to the pieces of this memory. The feelings were fear and confusion. Had it been night time? It felt like it had been the middle of the night. Was that the trigger? Peter was standing in the middle of his bathroom soaked with sweat just like he had been when his father gave him the cup in the first place? Another memory crossed the screen in Peter's head. It was his mother talking to one of his aunts on the blue, high-back couch in the living room. Peter was lying on the floor in the middle of the room drawing like he often was. In fact, it really could have been any day plucked from Peter's childhood and not memorable at all except Peter remembered his mother telling his Aunt that Peter was having night terrors. Peter had thought she was crazy. He had absolutely no idea what she was talking about at the time. Peter knew now that they were a parasomnia. He didn't remember anything of them. Especially, as a kid. He had vague memories of bad dreams and his parents running into his room but other than that—there was nothing. Much the same as his memory of them now.

Satisfied with his cleaning job, Peter refilled the JAWS cup and drank it down. He turned off the tap, put the toothbrush and toothpaste back in the cup, and set it back in its place on the side of the sink. He walked back into the bedroom. His bed was a mess. He wasn't even sure if he had clean sheets to put on the bed once he took these off. He stripped the bed and placed his hands on the mattress. It was wet. Putting dry sheets on this bed would be futile, he thought. 3:45am and it looked like he was up for the duration. Peter walked into the kitchen and put on a pot of coffee.

As the coffeemaker sputtered and gasped, Peter sat down at the table and opened his MacBook. He wasn't even sure when the last time was that he had used his computer. He tried to remember a video or news clip that he had watched on YouTube but nothing came to mind. He couldn't even remember watching any YouPorn. Peter chuckled. He was surprised the computer wasn't covered in an inch of dust. He opened it up and it whirred to life like it had been used only seconds ago. When was the last time that he had checked his email? Peter couldn't remember that either. He clicked on the email icon and the window spread across the screen. There was an email at the top from the gallery; that was good. He'd need to read that one. But it was the second one that really caught his eye. The subject line read: *Amity As you Know Means Friendship* and the sender was Charles Williams.

*   *   *

Looking out over the ocean, Laurie sat in the sunroom of her East Chop home drinking a glass of Kim Crawford Sauvignon Blanc. The rain was letting up and she could see breaks in the clouds a couple miles out over the sound. When asked, Laurie described herself as agnostic at best but when beams of sunlight shone through cracks in the clouds, Laurie thought it looked like God. *We might end up with an incredible sunset. The best sunsets are always after a storm.* Hearing Charles enter the kitchen, she turned and looked in his direction.

Charles opened the fridge and bent down to get a good look inside. "What do you want for dinner?" he called.

Laurie hadn't given dinner a thought. She had been too fixated on the break-in at Old Sculpin and April's health to worry about it. That was pretty typical of their household though. Between the two of them, Charles was the one who was more likely to cook dinner or get the laundry and the shopping done. She teased him about dust bunnies under the bed but the truth was that Charles did a very good job keeping them together. She didn't tell him that enough. "Want to go to Menemsha?" she asked.

Charles closed the fridge and turned to look at her. "For dinner?"

Laurie shrugged. "Sure. Why not?" she said. "I've only had half a glass," she motioned toward her wine glass. "We can take the rest of the bottle with us, grab a blanket, and pick up something from Larsen's. The best sunsets are always after a storm. Isn't that what the islanders say?"

Charles looked out the window at the break in the cloud coverage in the distance. "That's true," he said. He turned to her and smiled. "Are you taking me on a date, Chief Knickles?"

Laurie smiled back, stood up, and walked toward the kitchen. "If you play your cards right, I am. Who knows? I might bring my handcuffs." She winked.

Charles laughed. "Keep them in mind for when we get home. I don't want to end up on the cover of the Gazette being handcuffed by my wife on Menemsha Beach!"

"I'll tell them I'm arresting you for disturbing the peace!" Laurie laughed.

"Will I be disturbing the peace?" asked Charles.

"I hope so," said Laurie. She walked over and wrapped her arms around her husband. She kissed him.

"Are you sure that you want to go to a public place? You're not acting like you want to go out at all!"

"Oh, I know," Laurie said. "But I do really. My mind is spinning about the break in and April and I just want to get out. Sitting on the beach with you watching the sunset, eating a lobster roll, and drinking a glass of wine is as good as life gets. Let's go relax for an hour and do that. Okay?"

"You don't have to ask me twice," said Charles. "I'm always up for a drive to Menemsha with my favourite cop." He kissed her. "Go start the car. I'll grab the picnic basket and a blanket, and meet you out there."

"Deal!" said Laurie. She kissed Charles once more, grabbed her keys out of the key dish on the kitchen counter and bound toward the front door. Getting out of the house was exactly what she needed. Laurie knew that she would still be rolling the case over in her head while she sat on Menemsha Beach but at least she would be *on the beach*. The case would fade in and out of her mind. It would come and go between conversations with Charles, people watching, and—with any luck—the kind of sunset that Menemsha Beach was known for. She had managed to get a hold of Dr Nevin's friend, John Pease. She was meeting him in the morning at Old Sculpin. Together, they could go through the gallery and see if anything was actually missing. Laurie felt like she'd been dealt into a poker game but she couldn't see all of her cards. Knowing whether or not something had been stolen would drastically affect the direction her investigation would take—how she played her hand.

Laurie opened the front door and stepped onto the front porch to find her flip-flops. It would have been smart to bring them in during the storm but it hadn't occurred to her. She was surprised Charles hadn't brought them in but his were out here too. Laurie wasn't sure when they had gotten into the habit of leaving their flip-flops on the porch but they had. During the summer, they were in and out of them so frequently, and more often than not they were covered in sand. Kicking them off and washing off their feet with the hose at the side of the house became standard operating procedure. It was just easier to leave them outside. Laurie wore flip-flops every chance she had. They were a far cry better than police boots. Charles wore his flip-flops when he absolutely had to wear footwear. It seemed as the years went by, more often than not, Charles just went barefoot. Laurie couldn't do that. On the beach was one thing but walking down the street? No way. For one thing, it hurt but for another, it was gross! Laurie couldn't count the number of times that she had sent Charles to wash his feet before getting into bed. By the time August came around, the soles of his feet were black and wouldn't be clean until late October. For someone who wasn't born and raised on Martha's Vineyard, Charles did a fine job of blending in with the natives.

Walking up to their Jeep Gladiator, Laurie inspected the flatbed before getting in. She hadn't put the cover on during the deluge and she was curious to see just how much rain was in it. It wasn't too bad. It had drained well. She was entertaining the idea of sitting in the back on the blanket if the beach was too wet. It might not be such a bad idea. In fact, she could get a couple of folding beach chairs out of the garage and they could do it up right. Laurie turned on her heels and headed back toward the side door of the garage and stepped inside.

All garages smelled the same, she thought. Some stronger than others but it was always the same scent—oil, gas, rubber, and dampness. It was a chilly smell. The combination of the concrete floor and no direct sunlight ensured that the garage was always at least ten degrees cooler than the outside. She was surprised that it didn't heat up in the summer sun but the barrier created by the overhead storage of kayaks, paddles, fishing rods, and snow shoes seemed to keep any heat that built up from coming down. Charles was calling her from the driveway. She eyed the blue folding lawn chairs against the back wall and tucked a couple up under her arm. She took one more look around in case something else caught her eye, before closing the door behind her. Laurie held a chair up in each hand and called out to Charles, "I got the chairs!" She set them in the back, opened the driver's side door, and got in. "I thought we could use them if the beach was too wet to sit on. We could set them up on the flat bed or on the beach."

Charles nodded. "Good call," he said. "I brought your zip-up Slip77 hoodie."

"Oh thanks! Good call yourself!" she said. "Is that it? Are we good?"

"We're good."

Laurie turned her key in the ignition and backed out of the driveway. She leaned forward and looked up at the sky through the windshield. The clouds split open above them. "We should get there just in time."

* * *

Eddie stepped deeper into his workshop. Someone had been through it. Frames that had been drying on hangers were lying on the floor. His desk had been emptied. Folders of photographs had been pulled out of drawers and scattered. A couple of pieces of glass had smashed on the cement. Eddie felt sick. What could anyone possibly want here? Why break into his shop of all places? He didn't do big business. He kept a smile on his face and a positive attitude but anyone in their right mind could tell that he was not rolling in it! He had a small house, an old truck, and a small shop that was in need of redecorating. Why would anyone break in to his shop? *And in this weather?* He didn't even have a safe! He had a cash register but it was up front. He barely kept any cash in it. With that thought, Eddie hurried to the front and opened the cash drawer. There was still cash in it, more than he would have guessed actually. He didn't know how much but maybe a hundred bucks? Fifty bucks more than he would have thought. He never kept that much cash in the till. He didn't have much need for it. Most people paid by debit, or by credit card. Some people paid by check—which was fine if they were islanders—but cash? Never. So why the hell had someone broken into his store? Eddie made his way to the back again. What a goddamn mess. He could feel his scalp itch. He was sweating. His heart was beating like he'd just run a marathon. *Calm down Eddie*, he thought. *Just calm down.* Stepping as carefully as he could, Eddie made his way toward the back closet where he kept his cleaning supplies. He took a deep breath. What could he do? Call the cops? He didn't even know if anything had been stolen. It was far too upsetting to leave it like this. That was impossible. No, the first order of business was to clean up. When everything was organised, Eddie would be able to take stock and see what was missing. He opened the closet and pulled out the broom and dustpan. He'd sweep up the glass, pick up the frames, and then reorganise the photos. Knowing someone had been there, going through his things, was a horrible feeling. He'd never been burgled before—neither at the shop nor at home. He had always heard people talk about it on the news or on cop shows and they always said the same thing. They always said they felt so violated. Eddie had never given it much thought. He had never really processed those words...until now. It was true. He did feel violated. At least, he thought he did. Was this what violated felt like? It was that feeling of being bullied in school. It was the feeling of shame when other kids laughed at you in class. It was also that feeling of walking home through the woods and you don't know how and you don't know why but you're sure without a doubt that you're being watched. Someone had been in Eddie's personal space without his permission, and they had been destructive. That was violation. The worst part of it was that even though it had happened before he got there, maybe long before, he didn't find out until now. Someone had gone through his personal space at some point during the storm but he had just found out now—*Eddie felt violated now.* So, it felt like it was still happening. That was the worst part. It felt like they were still there. Slowly, Eddie began to sweep up the broken glass.

10

The drive out to Menemsha was one of Charles' favourites. It didn't matter which way they went, it was a beauty. It always baffled Charles that almost all of the tourists spent their entire stays down-island. Sure, Edgartown and Oak Bluffs had a lot to recommend them. That's where most of the shopping was and it was where most of the bars and restaurants were, but the island had so much more to offer and there were people who had been coming for decades who had no clue. Charles had even met people who considered the Vineyard to be their second home, in fact their second home *was* on Martha's Vineyard, yet they had never been to Chappaquiddick! He could only shake his head. Martha's Vineyard was one hundred square miles of paradise and most people never saw more than a third of it. As Laurie followed the twists of State Road, Charles looked out over Lake Tashmoo. It was so perfect. The blue water glistening in the distance behind rolling green fields. This was Martha's Vineyard. Stone walls built hundreds of years ago out of rock that had been left by the ice age. There was so much history.

They drove past the sign for Lamberts Cove Road and Charles made a mental note to call their friends Hali and Nate. The four of them hadn't gotten together in ages. He looked at Laurie, considered mentioning a potential dinner date for the foursome, but decided against it. She was deep in thought. It had been her idea to head to Menemsha and the idea was a good one but Charles didn't know how effective it would be. Laurie had admitted to Charles that she was using this little excursion as a distraction and yes, there would be moments when Laurie would be present but they would be fleeting at best. She would catch glimpses now and again of the sunset, she may even taste a bite of one of Stan Larsen's top notch lobster rolls but mostly, her mind would be on the break-in, questions she needed to ask John Pease, and April's physical condition. Laurie was like a pit-bull—once she sank her teeth into something, it was hard to get her to let go.

Houses, stores, buildings of all kinds became few and far between the deeper they drove into West Tisbury proper. Thick woods went on for miles. Branches reached out over the Jeep and the oncoming traffic forming a canopy. Sunlight speckled and danced on the road. Brown leaves leftover from last season dusted up in their wake. Charles reached toward the centre console and turned on MVY Radio. Gerry Rafferty's smooth voice filled the truck. He turned it up. *Winding your way down on Baker Street, Light in your head and dead on your feet...* Charles leaned back in his seat, tilted his head toward his open window, and began to sing along. *Another year and then you'd be happy, just one more year and then you'd be happy, but you're crying, you're crying now...* When the saxophone that made the song a rock classic began to wail, Charles closed his eyes and let it rush over him. For whatever reason, this song was a Martha's Vineyard song to him. He didn't know what it was but there was a vibe. It was a summer vibe. Some songs had summer beach vibes like *Margaritaville* or *California Girls* but some songs were meant for those summer nights. Gerry Rafferty's *Baker Street* was definitely one of those songs.

Laurie turned onto North Road and as the sign reading 'Menemsha' passed her window she said, "I love this song."

Charles nodded without taking his eyes off of the scenery. "It rocks," he said.

Laurie turned down into Menemsha Basin and stopped in front of Larsen's Fish Market long enough to let Charles jump out. "I'll be parked somewhere down at the beach. I'll back in so we can sit in the flatbed. Cool?"

"Works for me," said Charles. He shut the door behind him and looked over at Larsen's. The crowd didn't look too bad. "How hungry are you?" he asked.

"Starving!" Laurie exclaimed.

"Got it," Charles said. He saluted her as she drove down toward the beach. He smiled and shook his head. *When aren't you starving?*

Charles got in line behind three men. He suspected that they were also collecting orders for their partners or families who were off hunting down the perfect spot. He didn't expect the beach to be too crowded. It wouldn't look like a sunset in August but it would still be a good group. The drive to Menemsha from Edgartown or Oak Bluffs was a long one to make without any planning. The storm would have had most people making reservations at Atlantic Fish and Chop or trying to get a table at The Lookout Tavern. The people on the beach tonight would be young couples without kids who could jump into the car on the spur of the moment or people who had summer homes in Menemsha and could just walk to the beach or make the quick drive. Regardless of how many people there were, Menemsha sunsets always put everyone in the best state of mind. It was a good place to enjoy life. Charles placed an order for two cold lobster rolls with slaw, one clam chowder, and one lobster bisque. He also grabbed four bottles of water—there might be some in the Jeep but a couple more never hurt—and a couple of bags of chips. He paid at the cash and waited. His order was pretty standard; it wouldn't take long. By the time he got back to Laurie, she would have everything all set up.

Carrying a large brown paper bag weighted with fresh seafood, Charles headed to the beach. He could see Laurie already. She was in the perfect spot—the last row before the beach, to the left of the lifeguard chair. He could see her sitting with her back to him, looking out over the ocean. Charles knew she wasn't seeing it though. She was back in the gallery staring at the big blacked out mural of Alan Quaid or worse, in her office making notes on what to ask John Pease or April Steven's doctor. However, if there was one thing about his wife that Charles knew for sure, she was a foodie. If a Larsen's lobster roll didn't bring her back to the present—even temporarily—nothing could.

"Here—take this for me would you please?" Charles lifted the bag of goodies up to Laurie.

"Mmmm…what did you bring us?" Laurie asked. When she took the bag she inhaled deeply. "I smell lobster rolls, chowder…*and bisque? Did you get chowder and bisque?*"

"You know…now that I think about it…I just may have," Charles said with a grin. Bracing himself with both hands on the open tailgate, he reached up with one foot and jumped up.

Laurie looked down at his feet and grimaced. "Did you get our dinner in your bare feet?"

Charles looked down and shrugged. "I'm not sure if I kicked my flip-flops off in the truck or left them at home. Did you see them?"

"Ugh," she shook her head. "You're so gross."

"I didn't touch our dinner with my feet. I doubt anyone even noticed," he said.

"You went into a seafood market in bare feet! God knows what's on the floor in that place!"

"I'll go for a swim later. It will wash it away," Charles said.

"You'll probably get eaten by a shark! They'll think you're that stuff in that bucket Brody was throwing in the water." Laurie started to laugh.

"Chum?" Charles asked.

"Yeah! Chum!" Laurie giggled. "That's what they'll call you—Ole Chum Feet—mistaken for dinner by a Great White Shark on Menemsha Beach. Lovely sunset though."

"Are you going to pass me my dinner or what?"

Laurie looked in the bag and pulled out the chowder and the bisque. "Do you want the bisque or the chowder?"

"I figured we could each drink half and then switch," he said.

"This is why I love you," Laurie said and passed him the chowder.

"Right back at ya."

"...Chum feet." Laurie grinned an evil grin.

"You're not funny," Charles said.

Charles and Laurie sat in silence drinking their soups and eating their sandwiches. Charles snuck glances at Laurie to see if he could figure out how much of her was actually here, in Menemsha, with him. To his surprise, she seemed to be there most of the time. She watched kids run by with their beach balls and she watched the seagulls try to make off with potato chips from the Texaco and French fries from Menemsha Galley. As the sun neared the horizon, things began to quiet. It was that same hush that fell over the crowd at the bottom of the ninth inning when the bases were loaded. Menemsha sunsets were always beautiful. The beach was front row seating to watch the sun sink into the open water. But as consistently beautiful as Menemsha sunsets were, nights like these were rare. The storm had broken enough to expose mostly clear skies. Sometimes, storms left grey skies behind, skies that would have to burn off in the morning sun the next day. When a storm blew away and left swirls and swirls of clouds over an open sky, the sunset was magnificent.

Charles glanced at his wife again and he knew she was present. She chewed her lobster roll in silence. The show had her full attention. Above them, the sky was still bright blue, cerulean blue but strokes from celestial brushes had left streaks of glowing yellows and gold. As the sky neared the horizon, it blazed in hues of lemon and tangerine. The clouds, gilded in gold by the disappearing sun, darkened to fuchsia and deep violet. Just above the water's surface, the sky burned the red heat of a stove element. Distant sailboats seemed to defy nature by not bursting into flame. Buoys clanged in the distance. The ocean sparkled every colour while her waves lapped at the sand. When the sun finally disappeared completely, the beach erupted into applause. Charles and Laurie stood in their truck. Families on the beach stood and cheered. People whistled and whooped. Menemsha sunsets. Charles felt his eyes well up.

"That was one for the record books," Charles said. "I'm so glad we did this."

"Me too," Laurie said. She sat back down and stretched in her chair.

"How are you feeling?" Charles asked.

"I feel great," she said.

Charles pulled out his iPhone. "He's coming," he said.

"What?"

"Peter is coming."

*   *   *

Craig watched the sunset through the kitchen window as he scrubbed black paint from his hands and forearms. The sunset was a real corker and lit the entire main floor of the cottage in golden light. The best sunsets were always right after a storm and this had been quite the storm. Between wearing work gloves and spreading out an old towel for the drive home from Edgartown, he had managed not to ruin his truck. If the weather had been better, he would have just jumped into the ocean to scrub up—the combination of sand and saltwater would get rid of anything—but then again, if there hadn't been a storm, he doubted that he would have done such a stupid thing to begin with. The storm coupled with the celebration of Alan

Quaid had simply been too much. When Eddie Lineback had told him about the Martha's Vineyard 1977 exhibit and what it entailed, Craig hadn't been able to think straight. When he left Images In Vogue, he had driven around down island. As the weather darkened so had his thoughts. Alan Quaid. The storm. All those years ago. Without even realising it, he had found himself parked in a driveway on North Water Street at the top of Daggett Lane.

All he was going to do was go down and look. Not knowing was killing him. He just wanted to see what was going on. The exhibit had to be more about JAWS 2 and the secession, didn't it? The disappearance of Alan Quaid had to be nothing more than a sidebar to those more global stories.

In a slicker and wellies, Craig made his way down the hill toward the Chappy Ferry and Old Sculpin Gallery. There was no one to be seen. Even if the shadow or silhouette of someone crossed his path, the rain was coming down hard enough that he wouldn't have been able to make them out. Craig hated storms like this. They brought back chills and a dampness and cold that never seemed to entirely go away. For decades he had tried to ride them out bundled in front of a roaring fire. That helped. Walking down Daggett Lane with rain pelting at his face, water running down his neck and hands, went against every fibre of his being. Still, here he was. He had to know. For Judie's sake, he had to know.

The outer wall of the gallery, on the ferry side, was home to a row of seven windows. Mindful of keeping his distance from the skipper's shed, where the skipper on duty was surely holed up in this weather, Craig started with the back window. It was high and barely accessible. He dragged over an abandoned half-barrel planter and stood on it. The rotted wood cracked under his weight, forcing him to rebalance on the metal rims. Craig wiped at the dirty wet window and peered inside. There he was—literally, larger than life. Craig bent over, lost his balance and fell off of the rotten planter. He vomited. Alan's face, his huge face staring wide-eyed and smiling, no, laughing at him—laughing at Judie. Forty years of emotion rushed up from inside him and his guts wrenched. Reaching out to brace himself against the half-barrel, Craig's empty stomach heaved and heaved. Animalistic grunts and barks hacked their way out of him. Even beneath all of the rain, Craig could feel his eyes watering. Slowly, he stood up and staggered back toward the truck. Two days ago, he had bought three cans of black spray paint for a fence he was working on. They were on the back seat.

It had been a stupid thing to do. He could see that now. Going to Eddie's had been even dumber. He really liked Eddie. Eddie had been good to him, he always threw work Craig's way because he knew Craig needed it. But Craig had needed those pictures. He hadn't really cost Eddie that much. He had broken a couple of pieces of glass but that had been accidental. Craig had left some extra cash in the till to cover it. Mostly, he had just made a helluva mess. Craig had needed those pictures though. They couldn't go up. What if Judie saw them? He took the pictures. He hoped he got all of them. One of the photos was a close-up of Judie. There was so much love in her face. The warmth of her smile. The sunshine in her eyes. Pete had taken the photo. She had really liked that kid. He was pretty sure that kid had been pretty sweet on her too. Pete was a good kid. Craig thought about him a lot. How could he not? Sometimes he wondered what he was up to but mostly, he tried to push him away. An impossible task.

Looking at that picture, it was not hard to see why Craig had fallen for Judie Tate on first sight. Strands of her long brown hair blew across her face. One of them across her teeth and her full lips. She was always pulling hair out of her mouth. Craig thought it was cute. Only her shoulders were in the photo but Craig could see the straps of the white bikini top she was wearing. She had been wearing the same top when they had met. It was such a seventies photo. That natural beauty. The eternal flower child. As risky as it was, Craig was going to keep that photo. Even as self-critical as she was, Judie would like it. If for no other reason, she would like it because Pete took it. Craig was sure of it. The rest of them, he was going to burn in the pit out back.

Craig scrubbed at the paint that remained on his hands. If he couldn't get it all off, he would have to go and see if there was any turpentine in the shed.

*   *   *

Peter walked up the gangplank onto the Steamship Authority ferry. The entire experience was filling him with déjà vu. The train ride from Manhattan to Boston and the bus ride from Boston to Woods Hole had been fine. He had never taken them before. This was the first time he was returning to Martha's Vineyard since he was a kid. Until now, he had always come in the back of his parents' car, so the train and the bus was a very different experience. As soon as he had stepped off the bus onto the parking lot of Woods Hole Ferry Terminal that had all changed. Actually, a lot had changed. The old terminal building that had been right on the water was gone. A smaller structure was on the opposite side of the lot and there was considerable construction underway on the harbor side. Yet, all of these change not withstanding, there was a familiarity in being here. The boats were all new but somehow the same. They felt the same. Perhaps it was just the singularity of the ferry experience. Where else was he going to take boats like this? There were ferries in New York City of course. In fact, there were six different lines with twenty-five ferry piers in The Bronx, Queens, Manhattan, Staten Island, and Brooklyn—the East River Ferry and the South Williamsburg Ferry were right by his place—but they weren't the same. For starters, the aesthetic was different. The New York ferries were exactly what they needed to be. They were big city buses. Steamship Authority borderlined on cruise ship. Peter doubted that islanders saw them that way. These boats were their lifeline and therefore were probably viewed with a certain amount of contempt. A necessary evil. They were on Cape Cod traversing Vineyard Sound not Brooklyn crossing the East River. That made all the difference in the world. The water was blue, not khaki. On a day like today, blue skies and warm breeze, the ferry looked almost pristine.

Peter stepped inside and followed the crowd. Even as a child he would have followed his parents. Now, as an adult, he had no idea where he was going. He passed travellers along the corridor, who had already made themselves comfortable in high-back chairs covered in heavy multicoloured cotton. Peter kept going. He was pretty sure there was some sort of snack bar. Once he found it, he'd grab something to eat, something to drink, and then find a chair outside on the front deck. It was far too nice a day to sit inside.

There was a snack bar. As soon as the corridor opened into a full salon, Peter found himself standing beside it. A line was already forming and Peter quickly took his place. The whole boat spoke to him on a level that he hadn't expected. Bells were ringing in his head and he wasn't entirely sure they were all memory bells. Part of his brain did seem to be saying that he had been here before, that he had taken ferries to Martha's Vineyard before, but other parts of his brain were telling him something else. Something very different. He felt like his brain was telling him that this was the place he had to go. He had felt like that as soon as he had opened up Charles' email and read his old friend's invitation. He knew that he had to go back to the island. He didn't know why but he knew it was true. Deeper still and the most confusing, there was a part of his brain that was yelling at him, screaming to be heard over the memory bells and the directives, but as much as it screamed—it was hard to hear. It just sounded like noise. His instinct was telling him that it was a warning. That made no sense. Floodgates of memories in a place where his family spent many summers made sense. Being told to go and see an old friend with whom he had lost touch made sense. Instinct telling him to run and get as far away from

Martha's Vineyard as he could made no sense at all. All these signals rang repeatedly in his head over and over again.

"What can I get ya?" A large older man, who looked like he should be working the engine room not selling muffins and salads to tourists, stared at him with a look of either impatience or indifference. "Well?" It was definitely impatience.

"How long is the trip to the island?"

"Bout forty minutes," the man said. He pronounced "forty" like "fawty".

"Two Sam Adams and a chowder, please," said Peter. Two beers in forty minutes might just dull the voices at least for a little while. Peter paid the man, slung his bag over his shoulder, and precariously picked up his two beers and his soup. His eyes found the heavy, metal door that led out onto the front deck and he made his way through the crowd.

11

Not only was Edgartown Harbor no longer flooded when Chief Laurie Knickles drove down to Old Sculpin Gallery, the morning sun was warm enough to make dry patches on the pavement. Ducks no longer swam in the parking lot and the docks had once again secured their proper place above the waterline instead of below it. Laurie parked her truck at the base of the stairs that led up the side of Memorial Wharf. The harbour was quiet. The only sounds were the whir of the motor on the Chappy Ferry, the squawk of the occasional seagull, and the clang of the flag against the flagpole. Laurie got out of the truck and took a deep breath of the sea air. It was going to be a beautiful day.

John Pease drove down Dock Street and parked beside the Ferry Skipper's shack. John Pease looked like a golfer. Even if Dr Nevin hadn't told her how he knew John Pease, when she watched him get out of his car this morning, she would have guessed that it was golf. John walked over with a smile and self-assured step that made Laurie think of Cary Grant.

"Good morning, Chief!" John said. "How are you this morning?"

"I'm good, Mr Pease. Thank you. What about yourself?"

"Please call me John," he said. "I know I look like I have one foot in the grave, but I still look over my shoulder for my father when I hear people say Mr Pease!" John extended his hand and Laurie took it.

"Well, it's good to meet you John," said Laurie. John's handshake was warm and firm—confident without being aggressive.

"I'm very pleased to finally be meeting you! I've seen you around of course but I don't like to bother an officer while their working." He let go of her hand and looked around. "You and your team do a fine job keeping our town a happy place to be. Just a fine job."

"Thank you for saying so," said Laurie. "Please, next time you see me or one of my officers, do say hello. That's a big part of why we're here—just to get to know the community."

"That's just fine," said John in that mid-Atlantic accent that was spoken singularly in New England. He looked up to the sky and scanned it from one end to the other. "It's going to be what the old timers used to call 'a true Vineyard day'!" John looked back at Laurie. "I still say it. I think it's such a nice expression. Then again, I'm an old timer!" He laughed at his own joke.

"Oh, you are not," Laurie said and then blushed. She sounded like a schoolgirl flirting. With seemingly no effort at all, when John Pease spoke, Laurie had the feeling that there was nobody else in the world he'd rather be talking to. When he was a young man, women probably chased him around the island. They probably still did.

"Well?" said John. "Shall we go in and see what's what?"

"Yes, I guess we should." Said Laurie. She was grateful to be back on a more officious footing. She couldn't remember the last time she had felt so decidedly feminine while at work. Being around John Pease made a woman very aware that she *was* a woman even if he was at least in his eighties.

"Tell me, how is April doing?" asked John as he walked toward the gallery.

"She's going to be okay," said Laurie.

"I'm glad to hear it," said John. "I'm not surprised. She is in very capable hands. Bob is an excellent doctor. We are so lucky to have him. Most doctors of his calibre would have picked up and ran off to Boston by now but that speaks volumes to his character. Such a good man."

"I don't know him very well—just in an official capacity—but what I do know, I like very much," Laurie said.

John Pease opened the front door of Old Sculpin and stepped inside. Flicking a couple of light switches, he took a quick look around and walked in a little farther. "At first glance, this seems all fine." He reached out and straightened a painting of a catboat sailing past Edgartown Lighthouse.

"That's a beautiful painting," said Laurie.

John nodded. "I'm quite fond of that one myself," he said.

"Who painted it?"

John looked at her with a twinkle. "I did."

"Wow! John, I'm impressed!" she said. "I wish I could paint like that." She blushed again. What was it about this man? She felt like she was gushing. It wasn't like her at all.

"That's very kind, Chief." John stopped and for the first time since he had met up with Laurie that morning, his face lost its smile. His eyes lost their sparkle. "Some people live in a very dark place," he said.

Laurie followed his gaze to the blackened wall mural. He was right. In fact, in all of her years of policing, Laurie didn't think that she had ever heard the criminal element described so succinctly. "That's very true," she said. Then added, "Well put."

John shook his head. Then looked around at the rest of the exhibit. "It doesn't look like anything else was touched though. You didn't find any paint anywhere else, Chief?"

"We didn't," said Laurie. "We just can't be sure whether or not anything is missing."

"To be honest, it doesn't look like anything is," John said. "I'll go upstairs and check the office of course but there is nothing up there of any value. There's no cash left in the gallery. We don't even have a safe. I love Old Sculpin Gallery with all my heart, Chief Knickles but let's face it—it's an old wood shack. Not exactly the smartest place to be storing all of your valuables."

"That's a fair point," said Laurie.

John walked the perimeter of the exhibit and then looked back to Laurie. "The only thing that isn't here is a collection of photographs that was to be hung on this wall." He made a sweeping motion to an empty space opposite the vandalised mural. "However, I'm not entirely sure that they were ever delivered. April was very excited about them. They were digital reproductions from a child's scrapbook if I remember correctly. Something to do with JAWS 2."

Laurie nodded. "Those are my husband's photos," she said.

John's face brightened. "Well then, you know what I'm talking about. That's a funny happenstance…small island."

"If those photos aren't here, where would they be?" she asked.

"More than likely, they just haven't been delivered yet. They'll still be at Images In Vogue over in Vineyard Haven. Eddie Lineback's place. Do you know it?"

Laurie nodded her head. "I know it."

*   *   *

Charles watched the Steamship Authority ferry, Island Home, pull into the dock in Vineyard Haven—a mammoth vessel of white and black steel and a capacity of 1,200 passengers and 76 vehicles. Charles loved the ferries. They were the lifelines of the islands. Everyday, workers, food, and other necessities made their way to Martha's Vineyard and Nantucket via these leviathans. Charles loved riding them and he loved reading about them. This particular ferry had been serving the islands since her maiden voyage in

March, 2007. Her namesake was a sidewheel steamer that served the same route in the latter half of the nineteenth century. One of the things that made Island Home particularly cool was that unlike most of the vessels on the Steamship Authority schedule, she was a double-ended ferry. She didn't have to turn around before entering a slip. The ferries always made Charles smile. They were just so Vineyard.

This time, Charles' stomach was doing flip-flops as he watched his ship come in. His childhood friend, Peter Morgan, was on this boat. He had no idea what to expect. They hadn't spoken, not really, in a very long time. Charles had Googled him and discovered that he was a painter of some repute. His paintings sold very well and for a good price. Did that change who a person was? Weren't all artists supposed to be crazy? Charles remembered his friend having a good sense of humour and an insatiable curiosity. Those two things were what had really connected them as friends. Well, that and their mutual love for JAWS. Still, JAWS would have only gotten them so far. They wouldn't have been able to sustain their relationship—even if it was long distance—for any length of time if they hadn't been able to talk about other things. Charles was sure that it wouldn't take much time at all for the two of them to find the friendship they had built all those years ago. Artists saw things from a different perspective; that's what made them artists. Charles made his living writing. Weren't writers artists? Charles made a living writing but he certainly didn't make the kind of living that Peter made. Without Laurie, Charles would be washing dishes at Sharky's to make ends meet. Martha's Vineyard was an expensive place to live. He'd probably have to wash dishes at The Black Dog and then moonlight at Sharky's. With a pang of guilt, Charles made a mental note to put a little more effort into his housekeeping.

He saw him. At least, Charles thought he saw him. A tall man with a vague resemblance to the man he had seen at gallery openings on the internet, began descending the gangplank. He looked like half the man he had seen in pictures. Charles could feel the horror crossing his face. Was Peter sick? Maybe that wasn't him—it had to be him. He was so thin. Should Charles say something to him? What do you say to someone you haven't seen in forty years? *So, are you dying or what?* That's what it looked like. It was definitely Peter. Charles could see him scanning the crowd. He knew Peter was looking for him. Charles screwed a big smile on his face and shot his hand up over his head. He gave a big wave. Peter saw him almost immediately. His thin lips pulled back over his teeth and his eyes widened. Charles could see every curve of the man's skull beneath his papery skin. Maybe they could stop at The Black Dog for a big breakfast on the way home.

"Peter!" Charles shouted across the parking lot even though he knew full well that he had been seen. Hearing himself calling his friend's name filled him with a warmth that he wasn't expecting. Somehow, hearing Peter's name come out of his mouth while standing only a few metres away from him brought everything together. His smile increased—became more genuine. The screws that he had used to secure it to his face were no longer needed.

"Charles!" said Peter. Only a couple of feet in front of him now, Peter dropped his bag, took his friend's hand in a brief shake then pulled him in for a tight hug. His long arms wrapped around Charles with ease. "It's really good to see you, Charles. Thank you so much for the invite."

Charles could feel his eyes watering. He was overcome with emotion. How had he tuned out his longing for this friendship? How had he let it go for so long? He had missed Peter and he had missed him a lot. He hadn't realised it until just this very moment. For a brief moment, Charles felt like he was ten years old again—standing on Martha's Vineyard with his old friend just moments away from their next adventure on that red Schwinn Sting-Ray bike. "It's so good to see you, man." Charles tried to talk without betraying all of the emotion he was feeling but there was a noticeable warble in his voice.

"I'm so glad I'm here," said Peter. He pulled away from Charles. The two friends looked at each other face-to-face. "Amity, as you know, means friendship!"

Charles laughed. "Yes, it does!" He was relieved to see that Peter's gaunt face was also streaming with tears. As thin as Peter was, his eyes were bright. Upon closer inspection, Peter looked bright and strong. Maybe he wasn't on death's door like Charles had originally thought. Maybe he just needed some fattening up. A few breakfasts at Black Dog and Dock Street followed up with any number of apple fritters from Back Door Donuts would do the trick, no doubt. "How was your trip?"

"It was good," said Peter. "Uneventful—which really is the best you can hope for when travelling."

Charles nodded. "Are you hungry?" Charles tried to catch himself before the entire sentence came out but it was too late. There it was. All he could do now was to act like it was the most casual thing in the world. He would ask everyone that when they arrived on island. Wouldn't he? Charles wasn't actually sure that he would. He looked at his friend to gage his reaction.

Peter laughed. "Wow! Right out of the gate, eh?"

"Christ, I'm sorry Peter. I didn't mean anything by it. I just thought you'd been travelling a long time and you might want to grab something. I didn't mean that you looked like you needed—aw crap—that's not—jeezus. I'm going to stop talking before you decide to get back on the boat." Charles rubbed his face with both hands. He pulled them down slowly, opened his eyes, and stared at Peter. Peter was standing there smiling at him. "You're freaking thin, dude."

"I know," said Peter. "I don't always look like this."

"Are you okay?" asked Charles with genuine concern. Now that Peter seemed to be taking it so well, Charles was grateful that the cat was out of the bag.

"I'm fine," said Peter. "At least, I think I am."

"*What does that mean?*" asked Charles more worried now than ever.

"Physically, I am fine. I just finished a painting and they tend to take a lot out of me. This one was particularly difficult." Peter looked around. "Look, do we have to talk about this here? I mean, you invited me to the island. I assume you have a house?"

"Of course! Come on." Charles picked up Peter's bag and led him to the Jeep.

"You'll be happy to know that I *am* hungry—starving as a matter of fact," said Peter.

"You're right—I am happy to hear that!" Charles laughed as he got into the driver's seat and turned the key in the ignition. "Black Dog?"

"Let's do it," said Peter.

*　　*　　*

April Stevens opened her eyes and looked around as far as she could without moving her head. She was in Martha's Vineyard Hospital. It was dimly lit but she had spent a lot of time in this hospital the last time Edward was sick. She would recognise these rooms anywhere. Was this the same room that Edward had been in? She couldn't be sure. The teal curtains were the same. So were the tan walls but she was sure that they hadn't hired a different decorator for each room, wing, or even floor. The children's ward was probably bright and colourful but other than that, this was probably it.

Her throat was sore. She felt like she would do anything for a cup of crushed ice. Did someone know that she was awake? Wasn't there some sort of bell gadget that chimed at the nurses' station like the pizza oven at Giordano's? There should be. Lying there, April felt like her pepperoni was getting pretty crispy. Maybe she was supposed to press that doohickey that called for the nurse.

That couldn't be right. What if she couldn't call the nurse? Surely, there were people who couldn't move that required assistance. April was pretty sure she could move but she wasn't sure that she should. She wanted to lift her head, get a look around, but she was afraid. Her head felt like a bowling ball that was balanced precariously on the edge of the alley. One false move and she was liable to be knocked straight off her pins. Her head didn't exactly hurt but it felt fragile. Her neck was stiff. She hadn't woken up with that refreshed feeling that she did at home. At home her head rolled around on the pillow looking for the soft fur of Miss Mew's belly. Not this morning. Who was looking after Miss Mew? She really wanted to talk to a nurse. Without moving around, instinct told her that her muscles were tight. Her neck was braced in a self-protective hold. Was she concussed? She didn't remember hitting her head at all. She remembered a lot of rain. She remembered cutting her foot in the flooded parking lot. April could see the huge piece of glass sticking out of her foot. She wasn't aware of any pain in her foot now. Actually, she couldn't feel anything in her foot at all. Where had the glass come from in the first place? She thought hard. Even though she was lying in the hospital bed, she squinted her eyes in an attempt to focus. The front window was broken. The Old Sculpin Gallery door was open and the window was broken. Why would anyone want to break into the Old Sculpin? What about her exhibit? April realised that she didn't even know what day it was. Had she missed the exhibit? That couldn't be. Could it? Pepperoni pizza and bowling with the girls sounded good right about now. April drifted back to sleep.

12

The Black Dog Tavern sat right on the beach of Vineyard Haven Harbor. Built in 1971, the two-storey cedar shingle structure gave the impression that it had been there since Thomas Mayhew had first incorporated the island in 1642. The window frames were painted white and the shingles, worn by the sun and salty sea air, had weathered to a water's edge grey. The interior of the iconic restaurant was no more modern than the exterior. High polished wood with worn soft corners covered every inch. The entire far wall was a brick hearth alight with slow-burning embers. The other walls were wood planks cluttered with the nameplates of long gone Martha's Vineyard tall ships and nautical photos of the area. Wrought iron lanterns lit the room with a weak warm glow but most of the light came from a long row of windows that faced onto the harbour. The wooden benches wobbled either because the legs were uneven or the floor dipped, and the tables were just small enough that patrons tended to hit their knees together when they sat down. It was as if the furniture had been built centuries ago when people were considerably smaller than they were now.

Charles and Peter sat down at a table by the window and almost immediately, a pretty blonde waitress placed two menus in front of them. She looked at Charles and said, "I know you want coffee with milk and a Loretta—eggs over-easy, bacon, and white toast?"

Charles laughed. "Thanks Erin. That would be great."

She turned and looked at Peter. "Would you like a minute to look at the menu?"

"Actually, that sounds perfect. I'll have the same. Thank you," said Peter.

"Great!" said Erin. "That's easy. I'll be right back with your coffees."

As Erin walked away, Peter looked at Charles and smiled. "I take it you've been here before?"

"Once or twice," Charles said with a grin. "The islanders think that it makes me look like a tourist but I don't care—I love this place. As long as they don't need the table, I can sit here and think, drink a coffee, and watch the ferries come and go all day."

"Was this place here when we were kids? It looks like it's been here for ages but everything on-island kinda looks like that. Something must have been built in the last century," said Peter.

"It was here. I don't remember coming here though. My family mostly ate at the campsite. At the time, I thought it was because camping was so much fun but now, I know it was because we were broke," Charles chuckled. "I sure had a good time though."

Peter looked out the window at the harbour goings-on. "That summer that I spent on this island with you was the best summer of my life," he said. "Riding around on that awesome rental bike, being there for JAWS 2, sneaking in to the theatre to see JAWS—it was just the best."

Charles laughed. "So we did see JAWS that summer! I had kind of forgotten."

"How could you forget?" asked Peter. "It scared the hell out of both of us! I don't know how long it took me to go back in the ocean after that but it was a while!"

"Well, you didn't here," said Charles.

"Didn't I?" asked Peter. "We didn't go swimming after that at all?"

"It was right after that when you got sick," Charles said. "Next thing I knew you were just gone. Your whole family just packed up and left."

The sun shone in the window across Peter's face. His smile waned. His skin was almost translucent. He looked like a skull. "I don't remember," he said.

"You must have been pretty sick for your whole family to just up and leave like that. I can see how being on vacation with a sick kid would suck but travelling with a sick kid would be even worse," Charles shook his head. After a long pause, he said, "I was pretty crushed when you left."

"Were you?" asked Peter. He looked down at the wooden table. "I'm sorry."

"No worries. I was just a kid. I was disappointed that's all," Charles looked closely at his friend. There was something going on behind those eyes. Peter had checked out and gone somewhere else. All of a sudden, Charles felt very guilty for bringing up a subject with which Peter was not entirely comfortable. Why though? Everyone got sick. So Peter was sick when he was a kid *forty years ago*! Who cares? Clearly, Peter did.

Erin returned with their coffees, two little silver pitchers, and a white ceramic caddy stuffed with packets of sugar and sweeteners. "The pitcher with the spout is milk and the other pitcher is cream," she said with a smile that felt genuine not just the service industry standard. "Your breakfasts will be out in a minute." She gave Charles' shoulder a squeeze and left.

"Hey," Charles said. "I'm really sorry Peter. I didn't mean to upset you, man."

Peter inhaled deeply. His eyes refocused on the man in front of him and his smile returned. "No, it's okay. I'm the one who should be apologising to you," he said. "You invited me out here and I'm sure you didn't expect me to be such a downer."

"I am really glad you're here," said Charles. "and you're not being a downer at all." Charles poured some milk into his coffee and stirred it with the spoon in front of him. "I do think that there's something bothering you though. You don't have to tell me what it is. I mean, you and I haven't seen each other in forty years and we haven't even communicated in at least ten, but if you do want to talk, I am here. Sometimes, it's easier to talk to someone who isn't a part of your day-to-day life. You know what I mean?"

Peter nodded as he emptied two sugar packets into his coffee and then poured in a heavy dollop of cream. "I do feel like there is something I should come clean about. It happened just before I came and it's a big part of why I accepted your invitation." Peter paused. He stirred his coffee for a lot longer than was necessary. Finally, he tapped the spoon on the side of his mug and set it down on the table. He looked at Charles. "Two days before I left to come here, my neighbour committed suicide in front of me."

*   *   *

Laurie walked into Images In Vogue and looked up as the old-fashioned jingle-bells announced her arrival. It was those little things that made her love this island like she did. As much as some people screamed and squawked on the Martha's Vineyard Facebook page about every little change threatening island life as they knew it—apparently, making sidewalks wheelchair accessible was turning Oak Bluffs into New York City—Laurie could see quaint traditions preserving Martha's Vineyard's old world charm at every turn. As she walked into the shop, Laurie slowed her pace and absorbed each photo, frame by frame. They were glorious. Eddie really was an exceptional photographer. They were reasonably priced too—at least Laurie thought so. She made up her mind to purchase one for the front hall. There was an empty spot over the stairs that had been bugging her for a while and one of Eddie Lineback's photos would be just the thing to brighten up that space.

Eddie walked out of his back room brushing his hands on his jeans. He looked surprised to see her but he smiled just the same. "Hey Chief! I don't think I've ever seen you in here in your uniform before. Are you here on official business?"

"Hey, Eddie," said Laurie. "It's good to see you. I did come on official business. I have a couple of questions that I think you can help me with but now that I'm here, I was thinking about picking up a picture as well. Your work is beautiful, Eddie." Laurie walked farther around the store. She stopped in front of a large close-up of a sandpiper on Lighthouse Beach, the Edgartown Light blurred but distinct in the distance. "I had forgotten how beautiful," she added almost to herself.

"Thanks so much Chief," said Eddie. "I really appreciate that."

"I think I have to have this one," Laurie said motioning to the sandpiper. "Do you deliver?"

"Yes, I do," said Eddie. "I'll send it right over."

"Thanks," said Laurie. "There's no hurry."

Eddie walked over to the photograph and took it down. "What did you want to ask me?" asked Eddie.

"We had a break-in down in Edgartown yesterday," said Laurie. "...at the Old Sculpin Gallery."

Eddie almost dropped the sandpiper photo. "*You did?*" he exclaimed.

"We did," Laurie furrowed her brow, absorbing Eddie's response. "Why so shocked? I mean, I wouldn't think you would expect that sort of thing but you seem particularly…I don't know…invested."

"I am invested," Eddie said. "I'm involved with the Gallery's Martha's Vineyard 1977 exhibit and last night, I had a break-in myself, here, at the store."

"*You did?*" exclaimed Laurie. This time it was Laurie who was surprised.

"I did. It's the first time I've ever experienced this sort of thing and I'm here to tell you, I don't like it. It's really shaken me up if I'm honest," said Eddie.

"Did they take anything?" asked Laurie. "Have you called the police?"

"I hadn't called the police yet. I wasn't sure if I was going to. I mean, they didn't take any of the cash from the till. In fact there's about a hundred bucks in there which is weird. I don't remember ever keeping that much cash just lying around," said Eddie.

"You should still call the police," said Laurie.

"I was just thinking it over when you walked in," said Eddie.

"What did they take?"

"Well, this will knock your socks off actually. The only things they took were the digital blow-ups I made for the

Martha's Vineyard 1977 exhibit. The ones I made from your husband's photos."

"Do you still have Charles' book?" asked Laurie.

"Yes, I do," said Eddie.

"May I have it please?" asked Laurie.

"Of course," said Eddie. "I'll go get it." Eddie hurried to the backroom and popped out moments later with the book in his hands. He passed it to Laurie. "I'm going to have to make all new copies and frames for the exhibit this weekend. I don't have much time."

"You might want to call the gallery on that. April Stevens is in the hospital. She had an accident last night. I wouldn't be surprised if they decided to postpone the exhibit."

"*April's in the hospital?*" said Eddie. "*Is she okay?*"

"Doc. Nevin says she'll be fine but I don't know how long she'll be up there."

"That's awful," said Eddie. "Will you keep me posted, please?"

Laurie nodded. "I'll do that."

"Thank you," said Eddie. "I'll send your photo right over."

"Oh right," said Laurie. "Here, you take Visa right?"

"Absolutely." Eddie walked over to the counter and rang up Laurie's purchase. He took her card and swiped it through.

"Eddie, who knew you had those photos?" asked Laurie.

"I was thinking about that," said Eddie. "I don't think I told anyone except Craig. He's an up-islander who helps me out from time to time. Of course, April knew. I don't know who else."

"Do you have Craig's address and phone number? May I have it?"

*   *   *

"Jesus Christ," said Charles. Peter's statement just hung in the air between them, over their coffees, and the wooden table, and the sweeteners, and the worn metal spoons. All of the standard tavern sounds—the chatter, the scraping of dishes, and the scraping of wooden chairs against wood flooring—all seemed to be coming from somewhere far away. They were faint and muffled. Charles' mouth hung open as Peter's words raced across his eyes like ticker tape, *my neighbour committed suicide in front of me.* Finally, Charles spoke, "I'm sorry Peter. I don't know how to respond to that." It was true. He didn't. This wasn't the sort of thing that just happened once in a while, leaving Charles a bit rusty but with a vague recollection of what he was supposed to do or how he was supposed to act. Quite the contrary. No one had ever said those words to him before and he was completely caught off guard. "No wonder you're shaken up," said Charles. "Christ, I am so sorry that you had to go through that."

"Thanks," said Peter. "Don't worry. I don't think there is an appropriate thing to say in a situation like this. It's not like there's a Hallmark card for the occasion. At least, I hope there isn't." Peter managed a sardonic smile.

"So, you came here to get away from the whole scene?" asked Charles. "I mean, she was your neighbour. I'm assuming it all happened close to home? Oh man, it didn't happen in your home, did it?"

Peter shook his head. "No. It happened outside our building. She jumped..." He stopped.

Charles waited for a moment before speaking. "No wonder you wanted to get away. I'm really sorry that you're here under such horrific circumstances but I'm still glad you're here."

"There's more," said Peter. "but I'm not sure exactly how to articulate it. I've been having these nightmares."

"I'm not surprised," said Charles.

"Sometimes I don't have to be asleep to have them," Peter said. He reached out with one long bony hand as if to pick something out of the air. "I can see them but there's a disconnect between my eyes and my mouth or my mouth and my brain. I'm not even sure. It's like that writing Marginalia..."

"...by Edgar Allan Poe," finished Charles.

"Yes! Exactly! That runs through my mind constantly!" exclaimed Peter.

"Where the confines of the waking world blend with those of the world of dreams," quoted Charles hoping that he was getting the quote right. He loved Poe.

"A Dream Within A Dream," finished Peter.

"Peter, I really want to talk about this. I really do. I think it's important. I think you need to talk about it but I don't think we should do it here. Let's wait until we're back at my place and we have some privacy," said Charles. Cautiously, he reached out and grabbed his friend's hand. He gave it a squeeze and Peter squeezed his in return.

"That's a good idea," said Peter. He looked around at the families surrounding them in every direction. "We would probably scar these little kiddies for life," Peter said.

"Ha! I don't know. These little buggers spend their entire day jumping off the JAWS Bridge. They're pretty tough!" said Charles. He tried to put as much joy into each syllable as he could. He wanted to get as far way from the previous subject as possible…at least for now.

"Wow—people still do that?"

"All day, every day," said Charles.

"That was something we never did," said Peter. "Did we?"

Charles pursed his lips and looked up into his eyelids as if he were skimming a file folder. He shook his head. "No. I don't think so. In fact, I don't think I have ever jumped off the JAWS Bridge. I don't think that's the kind of thing that you forget."

Erin came to the table and set their matching breakfasts in front of them. "Can I get you guys anything else?"

"This looks fantastic!" said Peter.

"I think we're good Erin, thank you, but keep an eye open. Depending on how quickly he gets through this, I might order my skinny friend a second helping of everything!"

"Ha, ha—very funny," said Peter through a mouthful of hash brown potatoes.

* * *

Laurie sat in the basement of the Edgartown Library skimming through the archives of the Gazette. She hated doing this sort of thing. Charles could sit in front of the computer all day and read anything and everything. Laurie was a much more physical animal. She wanted to be out in the real world. Still, these computers were a damn site better than the microfiche of her childhood. Scrolling through that crap researching school projects was enough to make anyone seasick.

Finally she found what she needed. She hadn't even read the date on the paper yet but she knew where she was. Alan Quaid's big smiling face took up the entire right side of the page. Laurie sat back and began to read.

13

April Stevens opened one eye, then the other. She had been in and out of consciousness, not entirely sure if it was over a period of minutes, hours, or days. It felt like hours but she couldn't be one hundred percent certain. She was in Martha's Vineyard Hospital—that much she knew. Everything else was up in the air. When she had first woken up, April had been completely frozen, afraid to move. Every part of her body had felt like a solid piece but worse—something that had been quick-frozen and was likely to shatter into a thousand pieces with the slightest twist or movement. Waking now, she felt much better. Her joints felt relaxed and fluid. Her flesh was breathing, not just her lungs, mouth, and nose but her muscles, and skin. Some parts were sore and some parts were not but all of her felt alive and that was a good thing.

Tentatively, April lifted her right hand and brought it toward her forehead. It moved just fine. Her head hurt, throbbed really. She half expected to accidentally stick a probing finger into an open wound. She didn't even remember hitting her head! Maybe the headache was just a reaction to whatever drugs they had her on. Maybe—nope. April reached her head and found that it was well padded. She ran her fingers along a thick strip of gauze and cotton bandage. She had definitely hit her head and she must have done quite a number on it; that was no Band-Aid on her forehead. April extended her hand out in front of her and inspected her arm. It looked fine—no scrapes, bruises, or bandages. She turned to her left arm and did the same. It looked good too. She tried to wiggle her toes and was very conscious of her toes wiggling on her right foot but she couldn't feel anything on her left. She couldn't feel her toes refusing to wiggle, she couldn't feel them at all. April lifted the blanket and peered down to her foot. It was then that she realised that all of her own clothes were gone. She was wearing a hospital nightie and it was hiked up into her armpits. Embarrassed, April tried to pull the flimsy material down to a respectable position but to no avail. In order to get herself properly situated, she was going to have to stand up and at the moment, she didn't think that she had the wherewithal to do that. April pulled the blanket up to her chin. Where was that nurse buzzer thingamajig? Finding something under her right hand that felt like a TV remote from the 1980's, April pressed a button. Immediately, her feet began to rise. "Oh balls!" croaked April. Her throat was dry and—now that she had tried to use it—sore. She brought the 80's remote up to her face and inspected it. It was the bed control. April squinted at her nightstand and spotted another, smaller, piece of electronics. Maybe that was it. She reached out with her hand and grabbed it. There was no information on it at all. She pressed the button half expecting her face to be snapped into her own lap or the entire bed to be catapulted into the harbour. Nothing happened at all. April pressed it again. Still nothing. She was about to press it for a third and final time when her door swung open and a nurse came in.

"Good afternoon, Mrs Stevens!" said the nurse. "Glad to see you awake! How do you feel?"

April spread her fingers across her throat and pulled them across her skin. Then, she made a motion as if she was drinking from a cup.

The nurse nodded. "Sure. You can have some water," said the nurse in a voice that was soft and not overly saccharine. While April didn't think she sounded condescending exactly, her tone definitely hinted at the fact that it wouldn't take much to get her there. The nurse walked over to the credenza, flipped over one of the cups on the tray and poured from the accompanying pitcher. "Do you want to sit up a bit?"

April nodded.

The nurse picked up the 80's remote and pressed a button. Slowly April started to shift into an upright position. The nurse brought the cup to April's lips and April slurped eagerly.

"Okay, easy does it," said the nurse.

April gulped a bit more before the nurse removed the cup.

"Is that better?" asked the nurse.

April spoke cautiously. "Yes," she said in a tone deeper than her usual register. "May I have a cup of ice, please?"

"Certainly," said the nurse. "I'll go tell the doctor that you're awake and come back with a cup of ice for you. Okay?"

"Thank you," said April. Now that she was upright, April discovered that her room looked out across Vineyard Haven Harbor. It looked like a beautiful day. When the nurse came back, she had to remember to ask her, beautiful or not, exactly what day it was.

*   *   *

Fenway The Beagle jumped up on Peter's lap wagging his tail and barking excitedly. Peter scratched behind his ears and tried to grab him to calm him down but Fenway was having none of it. He wriggled and rolled out of Peter's grasp and ran around his feet.

Charles shook his head. "I've never seen Fenway do this with someone new before. Usually, there's a sniff, a bark, and then off he goes. This is very unusual. He must really like you." Charles leaned down to grab Fenway by the collar. "Fenway! Calm down. You're being crazy!" Charles looked back at Peter. "I can put him in the backyard if you would rather."

"No! Not at all! I love dogs. I love cats too. He'll be fine," said Peter. "He'll get used to me eventually."

"We have a cat too—Bubbas—but I very much doubt she'll give you the same treatment. If you leave your bedroom door open, you might wake up in the middle of the night to find her sleeping on your head though."

"Good to know," said Peter.

"Why don't you go sit over in the sunroom and I'll bring us a couple of drinks," suggested Charles. "What would you like? We've got Kim Crawford Sauvignon Blanc or I think we still have a few Bad Martha's in there somewhere."

"I'll take a Bad Martha's," said Peter. "Although I just had two on the ferry! Maybe I shouldn't."

"You'll be fine. That was over an hour ago and besides, you're on vacation," said Charles.

"I don't want to be a train wreck when I meet your wife!" exclaimed Peter.

Charles laughed, "Laurie's a police chief on a seasonal resort island. You wouldn't be the first person she's met whose gears were more than a little well-oiled!"

"I find no comfort in that statement," said Peter.

Charles walked into the sunroom and handed Peter his beer. "To old friends," he said and held up his own bottle.

"To old friends," smiled Peter. They clinked their bottled and took a mouthful.

Fenway The Beagle ran from Peter's feet toward the front door. He barked and barked. His nails clacked as he skidded across the dark wood floor.

"I think Laurie's home!" said Charles. "I wasn't expecting her until much later."

Laurie opened the front door and Fenway's tail thumped on the floor like the bass on a teenager's stereo. He yelped. "Yes, I see you! Are you Mommy's good boy?"

Fenway barked twice for yes.

Laurie bent over to untie her boots. Once they were off, she walked into the sunroom. "You must be Peter." Laurie extended her hand and Peter took it. "I've heard so much about you; I feel like I've known you for years."

"It's so nice to meet you, Laurie," said Peter. "Thank you for inviting me into your home. It's really very generous of you."

"Charles and I love the company and with the 1977 exhibit coming up this weekend, it seemed the perfect time," she said. "I actually have a few questions for you two. I've been going through this." Out from under her arm, Laurie pulled the book that Peter made for Charles forty years ago and handed it to Charles. "I am going to go and grab a cold drink, then the three of us are going to sit down and talk. I'll be right back."

"Oh my god," said Peter. "The book!" As if reaching out for ancient scripture, Peter extended both hands for the JAWS 2 book and took it from Charles. "I haven't seen this in over thirty years," he said.

"Where's your copy?" asked Charles.

"I'm embarrassed to say that I don't rightly know," said Peter. "I'm assuming that it's packed away in boxes with most of my childhood stuff at my parents' house." Gingerly, he ran his hand over the cover. "I love that feeling, the texture of construction paper. Don't you?" asked Peter. "It really brings back school and being a kid."

"I was struck by the smell of it," said Charles. "It definitely has a scholastic presence. I like it too."

Peter opened the book and fingered the photos on the first page. He stroked each picture as if touch would help to lift the memories contained within. "That summer was so special."

"It really was," agreed Charles.

Laurie walked back into the sunroom and opened up a can of Fresca as she sat down on the over-stuffed sofa. "It seems that it was a very special summer for a lot of people—not just you two," she said.

"What do you mean?" asked Charles. "Because of the exhibit?"

"Well yes, in a way, but more specifically, I mean the vandalising of the exhibit," said Laurie.

"The exhibit was vandalised?" asked Peter. "The 1977 exhibit?"

"You didn't tell him?" Laurie turned to Charles.

"I haven't had time," explained Charles. "We had a lot on our plate."

"Is everything alright?" asked Laurie. She looked at Charles then Peter.

After a moment, Peter spoke up. "I'm not exactly at my best at the moment," he said. "I have recently finished a painting. It was a big one. The painting had a lot of dark in it."

"Dark?" asked Laurie.

"Give him a minute," Charles said in defence of his friend.

"Charles, it's okay," said Peter. "Yes, dark. I find this difficult to explain mostly because I've never tried to articulate it before. At least, not until Charles and I talked. My paintings have been—in my head at least—always the same picture. They probably look like different paintings but with, perhaps, a similar style or theme to an onlooker—in fact I know they do—but they are all the same picture."

"I don't understand," said Laurie.

"Let's say you took a big digital photograph of a flower garden. Okay?"

Charles and Laurie nodded.

"Okay, well, sometimes my mind zooms in and shows me the roses, some days it zooms in and all I can see are the hydrangeas. The next time it will simply be the dirt between the rows but in my head, it is always the same garden. I am always painting the same picture whether it looks like it to you or not," said Peter. He sat back in his chair and took a mouthful of Bad Martha's.

"So, I assume you don't paint flower gardens really," said Laurie.

Peter smiled. "No, I don't."

"So, what do you paint?" she asked.

"I'm not exactly sure," Peter said. "I think it is a place from long ago. There are streetlights but they're old. You know, like gaslights. They're always lit because my paintings are always set at night."

"That's the dark?" asked Laurie.

Peter nodded. "Yes. What part of the scene I am painting will determine how much dark is in it. If it's a close-up on the lanterns then the dark will be minimal, off in the corners but sometimes, the lights are off in the distance and the dark is front and centre. The more dark there is, the more the process of painting takes out of me. Each and every stroke of darkness—blackness—takes a physical toll on me. There is something in that blackness, in that darkness, that is reaching out for me. It's drawing me in. It's trying to consume me. When I'm working, the painting will be all I can see, hear, or do. It's like my brain knows how hard the painting is on my body and it does everything it can to get me through it as quickly as possible. By the time I am done or my painting is done, I am never sure how long it has been since I have eaten, or slept, sometimes I have soiled myself and not even realised it." Peter looked away from Laurie unable to look her in the directly in the eye any longer. "Everyone in my neighbourhood thinks I'm a goddamn junkie." Tears dampened his cheeks and he tried to wipe them away casually.

"Peter..." said Charles. He tried to sound reassuring. Charles tried to imply that nothing could be further from the truth but he fell short. Fleetingly, Charles had wondered the same thing when Peter had walked down the gangplank that morning.

"No, they do Charles," Peter reaffirmed. "I disappear for a month at a time and when I show up again, I look like I haven't slept or bathed in weeks and I've lost about forty pounds. What would you think? Don't forget—it's New York City to boot."

"Peter," said Laurie. "May I ask you a question?"

"Why paint?" asked Peter.

"Well, yes!" said Laurie. "If you feel like it's killing you, then why paint at all?"

"It's a valid question and it's one I have asked myself over and over again," Peter said. "First off, the easy answer is because I'm a painter. The second answer is much closer to home. It rings truer somehow. Every single time, I tell myself, this time it will be different. This time, I'll put my brush to canvas and colour will come out. This time, I'll paint and the subject will be drenched in sunshine. There will be green grass and blue water. I always think that the next time will be different. Then each and every time, as soon as I start, I realise that I'm still in those dark woods. Those same antique lamps light me as I walk among the small, unlit coloured houses. I'm always there."

"Coloured houses?" asked Charles.

Peter nodded. "In the woods there are all of these little houses painted different colours. They're not like real houses, they're small."

"Doll houses?" asked Laurie.

Peter shook his head. "No, they're big enough to walk into they're just small, ornate, coloured houses."

"Peter," said Charles. "Those are the gingerbread cottages in Oak Bluffs. You've been painting Wesleyan Grove! At least, it certainly sounds like Wesleyan Grove. You and your family stayed in one during the summer of 1977!"

* * *

Craig snapped a picture frame over his knee and tossed it into the fire blazing in the backyard fire pit. He and

Judie had put in the pit even before the house was finished. Initially, they had used it to burn off garbage and unused wood during the build. Then, they had kept it and cleaned it up to enjoy in the evening. Chappaquiddick's East Beach was far enough from the town lights to be good for stargazing but nothing beat Aquinnah. They were so off the beaten path that each and every star seemed close enough that you could reach up, grab it, and put it in your pocket. Judie always did that. She would reach up and take a star from the sky and say, "I'm going to save that one for later." Then she would turn and smile at Craig, her face glowing orange in the firelight. Being on this island was the best thing for her. It was where she positively glowed, she shone. Some people thrive in the city but others need nature. When Craig and Judie first met, Judie had already figured this out for herself. She had come back to the Vineyard from New York because she knew the city was not for her. Every time Craig looked back on that period of their lives, he felt a punch in the gut. Guilt punched him in the stomach harder than anyone in a bar fight ever had. There had been extenuating circumstances but even still, they should have found another way. He should never have forced her off the island.

Normally, Judie would join Craig for a bonfire. He would start piling up odds and ends that needed to be destroyed. It was easier and cheaper than going to the dump. They never burned things that were going to harm the environment—just paper, cardboard, wood, etc. When the fire was lit, and Craig had it stoked and burning smoothly, Judie would come out through the backdoor. If it was summer she would show up with two bottles of beer. If it was spring or fall, she would have two freshly brewed coffees with a little something extra poured in to keep them warm.

    Craig was doing this fire alone. Judie couldn't join him for this one. Craig had lit this fire to get rid of the pictures. One by one, he would tear them up, break down the frames and burn them all. He wasn't sure what he was going to do with the glass yet but he'd sort that out when the time came. He could drop them off at Chilmark General Store or outside Alley's. If he went early enough and just propped them outside the door, someone would take them. There was no shortage of photographers, craftsmen, or hobbyists on the island. Any number of people would grab them and take them home.

    The frames went up quickly. All of Eddie Lineback's hard work, blackening, then burning in dancing spears of white and yellow gold. Craig felt badly about Eddie but that couldn't be helped. Craig wondered if Eddie would even report the break-in. Eventually, Eddie would put it together that the photos were gone but there was money in the till. All Craig had really cost him was time. It had to be done. Craig just couldn't let those photos go up. How could he? How could he go back there? It was all so long ago. He had never understood people's fascination with the past. They called it nostalgia. Craig thought it was a load of crap. It was much healthier to move on—move forward. Once the fire was gone, that would be that. This fire would burn hot and quick. In fact, it was close to finished. Craig would be done with this in no time at all. He was burning nine of the ten photos he'd taken from Images In Vogue. He knew it was a dumb thing to do but there was just no way he could burn up the portrait of Judie. That fresh beautiful face and wide smile. There was just no way. He had to keep it. He would just have to figure out a way to explain it to her that's all.

14

"Charles, which photos did you and April select for the exhibit?" asked Laurie. "Do you remember?"

Charles nodded and swallowed a mouthful of Bad Martha's. "Sure. May I see the book for a minute, Peter?" Peter passed the book to Charles, who then turned it to face Laurie and Peter. Slowly, he went through page by page and pointed out the photos. "We picked out these three close-ups of the shark, these three of the production team filming out in Edgartown Harbor, these two of the trucks and the sign blocking the road, and then this one of—"

"Judie," said Peter. He sounded like he just turned the corner in the supermarket and bumped into an ex-girlfriend. Peter felt his stomach twist.

"That's right!" Charles said. *"Her name was Judie!* I was trying to remember it earlier but I couldn't quite get it. Judie... She was your neighbour that summer."

"My neighbour..." Peter said in that same shocked and breathy tone. "Christ, she could be a double of my neighbour," Peter looked at his beer, grimaced, and pushed it away. With both palms, he rubbed at his forehead as if he was trying to rearrange his thoughts until they made sense to him. He pressed hard trying to fix what was going on inside his head. "Judie was my neighbour?"

"Peter, are you okay?" asked Laurie.

"Yes," said Charles. "In Wesleyan Grove, in the gingerbread cottages."

"I'm going to get you a glass of water," said Laurie. She got up and hurried to the kitchen.

"She looks just like my neighbour in Brooklyn," said Peter.

"The one who..." Charles trailed off.

Peter nodded. "The one who jumped. Yes," Peter stared at the photo of Judie's smiling face. Her long brown hair blowing in the Vineyard breeze, so young, tan, and pretty. *Neighbour? Judie had been his neighbour?* Peter could feel the darkness of his paintings creeping in along the periphery of his sight. It was crawling across his line of vision to block out Judie's photograph. The darkness was trying to push Judie out of his mind for good, but she was there now and she was there to stay. Judie was in his head and she was trying to find the place she belonged. In the back of his head, Peter could feel memories struggling in the deep, black strap molasses of his brain where he had stuck them decades ago.

He saw his young, pretty neighbour in Brooklyn lying in the bloody, pulpy mess of what had been her brain and blood and tissue. He saw her lying there in his hands, staring at him with her misaligned eyes in their broken sockets. Peter thought he had felt her trying to tell him something. She had been reaching into him. Her face had been reaching in and pulling at those same memories that he felt pulling at him now. But what if he had been wrong? What if it had been the other way around? Had it been his memories that had reached out to her? Had his own brain recognised something from its past in that young girl's smashed and bleeding face? Had his exiled memories looked out and seen their own reflection? If so, how much of his subconscious had played a part in getting him here on Martha's Vineyard?

"Peter?" Laurie said in a firm voice. "Are you okay?"

Peter came back to the present. Charles and Laurie were staring at him with matching looks of deep concern.

Laurie held out a glass of ice water. Peter accepted it and took a couple of mouthfuls. It felt good.

"Do you want to lie down?" asked Laurie.

Peter shook his head. "No, I'm okay," he said. "Thanks for the water. It feels good." He took another mouthful.

"Your neighbour who committed suicide," said Charles. "Looks like this woman, Judie?"

Peter nodded. "She does. I'm starting to wonder if that's why I'm here."

"What do you mean?" asked Laurie.

"Charles, I don't remember much about that trip," said Peter. "The only parts that I remember are the parts with you. It's like there is a construct in my head of what that trip was and the closer I look at it, the more I realise that it's full of holes. That the trip could not exist the way I remember it. I mean, don't you think it's strange that I should remember taking pictures of the JAWS 2 production but nothing of where I stayed? Or that I remember riding around on my bike with you but until this very minute, I had completely forgotten about this woman—Judie—who was my neighbour or her boyfriend? They were such a huge part of the trip!"

"Boyfriend?" asked Laurie. "Who said anything about her having a boyfriend? Did I miss something?" She looked at Peter, then Charles, then back at Peter.

444

"Yeah," Peter said. Judie had found where she belonged in his head. He could see her now on top of Memorial Wharf where he had taken the photograph. "She had a boyfriend. His name was Craig."

"Craig?" asked Laurie.

"Yeah, and there was another guy too," continued Peter. "His name was Alan."

*   *   *

Eddie Lineback walked through the halls of Martha's Vineyard Hospital looking for April Stevens' room. Unlike the frenetic energy of big city hospitals, Martha's Vineyard Hospital had a quieter more positive vibe. If you had to be in the hospital, Eddie figured this one wasn't bad at all. He was carrying a bouquet of flowers that he had picked up at Morris Florists on State Road. It was an assortment of blooms in varying shades of white and yellow. Eddie knew there were a couple of roses in there and quite a few daffodils but after that, he was lost. He liked the bouquet though, and he remembered reading somewhere that yellow flowers were for friendship among other things. That was good. He didn't want it to seem weird or to make April uncomfortable. Eddie was pretty sure he was over-thinking it but he really didn't want April to think that he was trying to get into her pants. Eddie cleared his throat and knocked on the door.

"Come in," April called.

Eddie walked tentatively into the room and was relieved to see April sitting up and looking more-or-less like her old self. He always found it uncomfortable and awkward to act all happy and casual when someone was lying on a bed with tubes sticking out of their face and arm or with a limb or two in a sling. "Hey April!" said Eddie softly. "How are you feeling?"

"Oh Eddie! Look at those flowers! Are those for me?" April inhaled dramatically. "Oh, they're just lovely!"

"Well, I thought they might cheer you up," Eddie said. "Besides my Mum always told me never to visit someone in the hospital empty handed." Eddie set the bouquet down on the bedside table.

"Oh, I can already smell those roses!" squealed April. "These sure have given me a lift!"

Eddie smiled. "I'm glad," he said. "Why are you feeling so glum? I know you're in the hospital but you're going to get better. In fact, I walked in here and was happy to see you look almost your usual self. What's the doctor been telling you?"

"You're right," April said. "I have to remember to count my blessings. Doctor Nevin, and that boy Ryan at the

Chappy Ferry, have saved my life and that is a blessing. I don't feel all that bad. It could be much worse. No, funnily enough, I'm not feeling down about my health. I cut my foot and bopped my head off the parking lot. You're right—I'll heal just fine."

"So what is it then, April?" asked Eddie.

"It's the exhibit. This was to be my first exhibit that I handled all by myself and now look at me," said April. "I can't very well host the Martha's Vineyard 1977 exhibit like this, now can I?"

"No, I suppose you can't," agreed Eddie. "You won't be better in time?"

"The doctor doesn't think so," said April. "When I woke up, I wasn't even sure what day it was. I know now and I feel fine but Doctor Nevin says that hosting the exhibit will be too much for me." April reached up and patted tentatively at her bandaged head. "I don't want to risk coming back in here. I mean, it's a lovely, well-run hospital, but it's still a hospital."

"Have the police come and talked to you yet?" asked Eddie.

"The police?" asked April. "No. Why would the police want to talk to me?"

"About the break-in at Old Sculpin," said Eddie.

"The break-in!" exclaimed April. "I remember the front window being broken," she said. "I think that's how I cut my foot but I figured it was just kids out goofing off. There was a break-in? Why?"

"To be honest, I don't know," said Eddie. "I think it had something to do with the 1977 exhibit though."

"What makes you say that?" asked April. She struggled to sit up a little straighter. Eddie had her full attention.

"Chief Knickles came over to Images In Vogue and while she didn't get around to asking me the questions she wanted to ask, I get the feeling it was about the exhibit," Eddie said.

"Why?" asked April.

"Well, she led in by telling me there had been a break-in at the gallery, but then I told her that there had been a break-in at my shop. That derailed her completely but she was very interested in the fact that the only things stolen—that I could see—were the photos that I had blown up and framed for you from Charles' book," Eddie sat back and put his hands on his knees. "I'm starting to feel like Sherlock Holmes. I've been trying to put the pieces together all day!"

"The thief took our photos? Why?" asked April. "That doesn't make any sense."

"No, it doesn't," said Eddie. "So, part of the reason I was coming to visit was to see if there was going to still be an exhibit at all."

*   *   *

"Craig?" asked Laurie. "Her boyfriend's name was Craig?"

Peter nodded. "I'm sure of it."

"Yes," confirmed Charles. "I remember him too. Big, hairy, handsome kinda guy. He kinda scared me when we were kids actually."

"Why?" asked Laurie. "Was he a jerk?"

Charles shook his head. "No, not at all. Quite the contrary, I think. He worked on the production of JAWS 2. It was him who got Peter and I down to see the shark. I think he was really nice."

"Then why were you scared of him?" asked Laurie.

"I think he was just a really big guy, oozing testosterone, and I was intimidated like most little boys would be," said Charles.

"Was he an islander?" asked Laurie. "Do you know?"

"I didn't know anything about him except that he worked for Universal. I don't think he did anything technical. I seem to remember that he just did grunt work. So, there's a good chance he was hired locally. Why?"

"There was a break-in at Images In Vogue last night too. The only things stolen were the photos blown up from your book. Those photos were to be used in an exhibit that was vandalised last night. I haven't had a chance to talk to April Stevens yet but I did talk to Eddie Lineback over at Images and he says that the only people who knew about the photos being in his backroom were April Stevens and his delivery man," said Laurie.

"So, who's his deliveryman?" asked Charles.

"Some guy in Aquinnah *named Craig*," said Laurie. "Now, you guys are telling me that you knew a guy when these were taken *named Craig?*"

Peter held up the construction paper book and pointed to a photo he had taken forty years ago on State Beach. "Look—those three people on the beach? That's Craig, Alan, and Judie."

Charles and Laurie leaned in for a better look.

"That's them," said Peter.

15

Laurie drove past the turn-off that she and Charles had taken to watch the sunset in Menemsha and continued on following the signs to Aquinnah. While it had been bright and sunny down-island, up-island was darkening under heavy clouds. It was definitely going to rain and by the looks of it, eventually the rain would make its way across the entire island.

Laurie loved Aquinnah but her job and her life kept her busy and she very rarely made the trip—very few down-islanders did. That worked both ways. The friends that she had, who lived in Menemsha and Aquinnah, all rolled their eyes and cringed at the thought of having to go Edgartown or Oak Bluffs. Being a washashore, Laurie had found it odd at first that there was such a divide. It had surprised her. Laurie had grown up in Toronto, Canada—a city of seven million people if you included the suburbs—and crossing Martha's Vineyard hadn't seemed like such a big deal when she had first moved there. But life gets in the way. While she loved the views from the deck of the Aquinnah Shops Restaurant and walking Moshup Beach in the morning, the longer she lived there, the rarer her trips up-island became. Laurie felt that was a real pity. As much as she loved down-island life, up-island had a magical, almost pristine quality. For miles and miles, Chilmark and West Tisbury felt like they hadn't changed a leaf in hundreds of years. These western parts of the island gave the impression that the British landed with Thomas Mayhew, ploughed enough of the land to dig up the stones required for the stonewalls, and then just disappeared. Acres and acres of open fields, lined with centuries-old walls, rolling across Martha's Vineyard without a person to be seen. Pine and scrub oak clustered here and there but for the most part it was vast open fields leading across the rocky terrain to the ocean. On an island, everything led to the ocean.

    Laurie could certainly see why someone would want to live out here; however, it was a bit too isolated for her. She needed some human connection, not much but some. For the right person, it would be paradise. Someone who wanted to be alone with their thoughts, someone who didn't want people digging into their private life. The townships on Martha's Vineyard were certainly not short of busy bodies. It was really hard to keep a secret in Edgartown, Vineyard Haven, or Oak Bluffs but in Aquinnah an islander's privacy had a fighting chance.

Laurie figured that Craig was just such a person—quiet and private. She was having a hard time remembering his last name. Her eyes watched carefully as she took a curve past Squibnocket Road—Laurie loved Squibby. It was one of her favourite beaches but she hadn't seen it in years—then she glanced at her notes on the dashboard. Craig Upland, his last name was Upland. After her talk with Charles and Peter, Laurie had called the station and asked Jack to fill her in on everything they had. There wasn't much. Apparently, his Father had been a local doctor but that had been way before Laurie's time. Both parents were now deceased and Laurie didn't know of any living relatives. Craig had been busted for pot when he was a kid. Big deal. That wasn't exactly an exclusive club—especially, in the early seventies. Now, he lived in Aquinnah off of Lobsterville Road, not far from the beach, with his wife, Judie. When Laurie had heard that his wife's name was Judie, she had decided it would be worth the drive out for a visit. The Judie in Charles' book must be the Judie he had married. There were too many bells and whistles going off here. The only thing defaced in the exhibit was a photo of Alan Quaid, Craig was Eddie's deliveryman, and there were photos of Alan, Craig, and Judie together in Charles' book. The whole *Judie being a dead ringer for Peter's deceased neighbour and the possible reason,* at least on some esoteric level, *for Peter's being on the island* was a whole other kettle of fish. Laurie had decided to let Charles sort that one out. Peter was his friend. Right now, she had a theft, two break-ins, and a vandalising to deal with. This visit out to Craig Upland's might just sort the whole mess in one fell swoop.

The one thing that Laurie couldn't sort out was why? It was all just so petty. It didn't solve anything, at least not that Laurie could see. What would painting over a photo of Alan Quaid solve? It was so easily replaced. What would it accomplish to break into Images In Vogue and steal the framed images that Eddie had taken from Charles' book? Just like the image in Old Sculpin, they were easy to duplicate. In fact, now that Laurie thought about it, Eddie probably still had the digital copies on file. He could literally print out another copy of each of them in five minutes. If Craig was behind all of this, he clearly wasn't a digital age kinda guy. In fact, Laurie should have asked Eddie to print off copies while she was in the shop. She really had to catch up with the digital age herself. She did have an iPhone though, that was something. Baby steps.

State Road twisted under trees and through underbrush that was broken up by the occasional dirt driveway leading to unseen properties nestled back far from traffic. As she neared a sign that read Lobsterville Town Beach, her navigation system called out, *Turn right down Lobsterville Road.* Laurie hated her automated navigator. She found it jarring. She had to admit though, while she found it completely useless in town, out in the boonies of Martha's Vineyard where half of the roads didn't have street signs let alone street numbers, it made things a lot easier. Laurie made one more turn under the instruction of the navigation system before it announced that she had reached her destination.

* * *

Across from Oak Bluffs Harbour, beside Sunset Lake, Charles and Peter walked down Lake Avenue toward the heart of town. The air was getting heavy—heavy enough that a storm felt imminent—but for the moment at least, it was a beautiful afternoon. After Laurie had left for Aquinnah, Charles had suggested that they go for a walk into town. It wasn't all that far from their place on East Chop and they would have plenty of time to sit around the house after the storm hit.

    Peter hadn't been on the island since they were kids. The two of them had spent a lot of time in Oak Bluffs once upon a time. Some things were still the same but a lot of things weren't. When Charles had suggested that they go for a walk up Circuit Avenue, maybe over to the park, Peter had shown more than just a little interest. He was excited about it. In fact, his reaction had surprised Charles. He thought Peter might be hesitant. It was clear that being on the island again was stirring up a lot of emotion in him, mostly positive but even some of the positive emotions were stressful. For instance, it had clearly been stressful when Peter realised that his neighbour who had committed suicide was the spitting image of Judie his childhood neighbour from Wesleyan Grove. Exactly how big of a role that had played in getting Peter to the island, Charles wasn't sure, but the human brain was capable of some pretty amazing things. It wasn't that much of a stretch to believe that Peter had buried all of his memories from that summer. Charles just didn't have a clue why he would. All of Charles' memories from the trip were great! That trip was the kind of summer adventure around which Bruce Springsteen would build a song or Mark Twain would build a novel, but Charles and Peter hadn't been together all day, every day. There had clearly been more to Peter's trip than Charles realised. It all left Charles with one question gnawing at his brain—why had Peter and his family up and left in such a hurry?

Regardless, was it such a stretch that these buried memories would be triggered to the surface by a traumatic event like the suicide of Peter's neighbour? If so, If these memories were swimming to the surface because of the death of that woman and she looked like Judie, would the memory Peter had been buried all this time have something to do with Judie? Didn't that only make sense?

"I think I could find a place along this strip and watch the world go by all day," Peter said.

Charles nodded. "I do that sometimes. I'll have a list of things that I'll need to get done, then the next thing I know, I pass on the bus and I'm on Nancy's upper deck, pulling out a chair, parking my butt in the sun, and ordering a margarita."

"Nothing wrong with that," said Peter.

"The thing is on this island," continued Charles. "It seems to be a completely acceptable excuse!" He laughed. "I've never lived anywhere that you can say, 'I never made it past the patio,' and have it accepted as a legitimate reason for not getting anything done."

"Is that what they call, 'being on island time'?" asked Peter.

"That's it exactly," said Charles. "That's Nancy's over there." Charles pointed to the large restaurant on the harbour with the deck sprawling across the entire second floor.

"Was that there when we were kids?" asked Peter.

"Yes and no," said Charles. "Nancy's was there but it was barely more than a burger stand. It was a little white building with an order window in the front. You placed your order and ate outside."

"Did we ever go there?" asked Peter.

"I don't think so," said Charles. "I don't really remember us eating meals together. I remember going home to eat with my parents at our campsite. You and I hung out between meals."

"That sounds right," agreed Peter. Peter's head turned upward and his eyes scanned the large yellow building that loomed on their right. "This is the theatre, isn't it?" said Peter with excitement. "This is where we saw JAWS! That I remember!"

Charles laughed. "This is it, alright! It's not open at the moment. It's kind of lapsed into disrepair." He grimaced.

"That's sad," said Peter. "This was a really beautiful theatre from what I remember. It was really old school. Red velvet, wood, a balcony. We sat in the balcony remember? Holy crap, I wasn't entirely sure I was going to live through those two hours. I was absolutely terrified for the entire time."

"You and me both!" said Charles. "When Ben Gardner's head popped out of the bottom of his boat, I almost jumped right on top of you!" Charles laughed and Peter laughed along with him. "I don't think I peed myself because I had shorts on, but let me tell you, it was close…very close."

The two men turned the corner and headed up Circuit Avenue. The street was busy with tourists. Music pumped out of The Ritz on one side and Flavors on the other. People laughed and talked, walked in and out of shops, or just relaxed on benches, drinking cool drinks, under various parcels of shade.

"Is the arcade still up here?" asked Peter.

Charles nodded. "It is! It's different but the same—you know what I mean? It looks different because games are so different but it still has the same feel."

"Is that little store on the corner still there? The one where you and I met? What was it called?" Peter asked.

"The Corner Store?" Charles laughed. "Yep! It's still there and it's exactly the same. I wouldn't be a bit surprised if you could find something on those shelves that has been there since 1977!"

"Don't tell me that old guy still works there. He must be dead by now," said Peter.

"He's still alive but he doesn't work there anymore," said Charles.

"He's still alive?" exclaimed Peter. "That was forty years ago! He must be one hundred and twenty by now!"

"Not quite," said Charles. "I think he's ninety-five. It was in the paper—small towns." He smiled.

"I love that," said Peter. "You'll never open the paper in New York to see a column titled, *Remember that old guy from the store? Well, he's ninety-five.*" Peter's eyes scanned up and down the street with a look of admiration. "It's too bad too. There's such an element of humanity in a small town that you lose in a big city. This is such a healthier way to live."

"Ironically, it's only a healthier way to live if you're healthy," said Charles.

"What do you mean?" asked Peter.

"Well, if you get sick or need to see a specialist in the city, you book an appointment and go," said Charles. "Here, we have to book an appointment sometimes in Boston. Then we have to book the ferry, book a car or a bus, possibly a hotel room—it's complicated. Living on an island is not always easy."

"I never thought of that," said Peter.

"Neither did I until I lived here."

They passed Sharky's bright and colourful sign of a shark wearing sunglasses and a sombrero, and drinking a margarita. Then, Charles detoured to the right, and walked down a short alley.

"Where are we going?" asked Peter.

"I want to show you something," said Charles.

The area grew thick with trees and shrubs before opening up onto row after row of the small, multicoloured cottages of Wesleyan Grove. Houses of blue, green, pink, brown, white, and orange stood shoulder to shoulder all trimmed with delicate wooden lace. Flowers of every colour grew out of gardens, bushes, and window boxes. Old trees, heavy with leaves, clustered in the centre of the campground.

Peter walked in gingerly with the trepidation of a child. "It's my painting," he said.

* * *

Laurie got out of her black and white SUV with Edgartown Police written across the sides in big bold lettering. According to her GPS, she was at the home of Craig Upland and Judie Tate. The house was modest, pretty, and typical. Once around the trees and shrubs that separated the home from the road, the driveway opened up into a dirt circle in front of a one-and-a-half storey cedar shingle home topped with a slanted roof and dormer windows. An old Chevy Blazer was parked in the drive in front of the grey main door of the house.

Laurie watched the windows—two on the main floor and two on the second—for movement. More often than not, when she drove up to houses in the country, she would see movement at one, if not all, of the windows. Visitors were usually few and far between in places like this. The sound of her tires rolling up the drive was usually enough to perk the interest of anyone who was home. The old truck made it look like someone was home. How many vehicles were these two likely to have? The house was small and while it was pretty and well maintained, it certainly wasn't new. It might not be as old as the truck but it was close. No, with gas prices being what they were, Laurie didn't think that Craig and Judie were going to be squandering money on a second vehicle. So, where were they?

Laurie closed her driver's side door quietly. She wasn't trying to sneak up on them exactly but she wasn't trying to make a big deal of her presence either. Something in her gut told her that she wanted to act casually. She stepped up the two steps that led to the front porch and then knocked on the front door. She gave a solid knock. She was here, there was no use trying to pretend that she wasn't. There was no answer. She knocked again. Laurie listened carefully for noises coming from inside the house. Was there someone shuffling around inside? Did she hear whispering? No. She didn't. There was silence inside. Laurie walked back down the steps and turned to look up at the second storey. There were no lights on and still no sign of movement behind any of the white curtains. The truck was here though. If this was Edgartown, Oak Bluffs, or Vineyard Haven, Laurie could assume that they had gone for a walk or gone to a restaurant, or swimming—anything really—but out here there wasn't a lot to do within walking distance. Laurie wasn't even sure where you would buy your groceries if you lived out here. Lobsterville Beach was the closest beach and it was certainly doable on foot, but it was a bit of a hike. Laurie began to make her way around to the back of the house. There was the faint smell of wood smoke. It wasn't strong enough to be from a fire still burning and it wasn't smoky enough to be from a fire burning far away. It was the smell of a fire that had burned recently but had been doused. It was the smell of charred wood.

    Craig Upland sat under a white lilac tree wearing nothing except a pair of well-worn denim shorts. Laurie watched him momentarily from a distance. All of a sudden, she had the feeling that she was intruding. She felt uncomfortable. Craig's lips were moving and when she focussed, she could hear that he was talking quietly but to whom? The tree he leaned on stood alone in a small clearing. In his hands, he pulled at a piece of grass or a dandelion—Laurie couldn't quite see—but what she could see was that he certainly wasn't holding a phone. Craig was alone and most definitely talking to himself.

Laurie cleared her throat.

Craig leapt to his feet with an agility that would have been impressive for a man half his age. He stared at Laurie first with wide eyes of fear, then they narrowed and his face flushed with anger.

"Mr Upland?" said Laurie. "Mr Craig Upland?"

"Yes," said Craig.

"I'm Police Chief Laurie Knickles of the Edgartown Police Department," said Laurie. "May I ask you a couple of questions?"

"You're a little off your beaten path. Aren't you, Chief?" asked Craig without smiling.

"Yes, I suppose I am but we had an incident down in Edgartown and another over in Vineyard Haven and I just thought you might be able to help me with a few details," said Laurie.

Craig shrugged. "Ask your questions but I don't know what I'll be able to do for you."

"Would you be more comfortable if we went inside?" asked Laurie.

"No," said Craig. "Why?"

"Some people prefer to sit in a more formal setting when they talk to the police," Laurie said. "That's all."

"Don't you mean that the police prefer people to sit in a more formal environment when they're questioned?" Craig asked. "Officer, if you have questions for me, go ahead and ask them. I'm fine right where I am. In fact, this is my favourite spot. This is where I spend most of my time."

"You're an islander, Craig" said Laurie. "Is that right?"

Craig nodded. "Yes," he said.

"Do you know Eddie Lineback?" asked Laurie.

"Sure," said Craig. "I work for Eddie sometimes. Deliveries mostly."

"Have you made any deliveries for him lately?" asked Laurie.

"Yes, I made a small delivery of a framed photo," said Craig. "I don't remember where exactly but Eddie would know."

"Did you know that there was a break-in at Eddie's shop?" asked Laurie.

Craig stared directly at Laurie, eye-to-eye. "No, I didn't. I haven't been down-island since I made that last delivery for Eddie."

"Do you know Mrs April Stevens?" asked Laurie.

"I think she's one of the members at Old Sculpin Gallery," said Craig.

"And how do you think you know that?" asked Laurie.

"Eddie mentioned her to me when he was asking me about working a job for him," said Craig.

"What was the job?" asked Laurie.

"He wanted me to deliver some framed photos to the gallery for one of their exhibits," he said.

"Did you do it?"

"I told you—I haven't been down-island since I delivered that one photo for Eddie," said Craig. "Is that it?"

"Yes," said Laurie. "That's pretty much it." Laurie turned to go back to her car but then stopped and turned back to face Craig. Craig had started to sit down when Laurie turned to leave but when she turned back around, he straightened again, eyeing her warily. "There is one more thing actually Craig," Laurie said, feeling just a trench coat shy of Columbo.

"What?" asked Craig.

"Do you know Alan Quaid?"

16

"What did you guys talk about on the walk home?" asked Laurie.

"Not much," said Charles. "I tried to ask him about what happened and I got nothing. So, then I tried to talk about our time hanging out as kids. I even tried talking about JAWS but I didn't get much. All I got were a couple of smiles, or one word answers."

"Where is he now?" asked Laurie.

"As soon as we got home, he went upstairs to lie down," said Charles. "I haven't heard a word out of him since."

Laurie poured a glass of Kim Crawford Sauvignon Blanc for herself and another one for Charles. Before bringing them into the den, where Charles was waiting not just for wine but for answers, she stood and watched the storm coming closer through her kitchen window. It was the storm she had seen hints of when she had been up-island. Now, those clouds were rolling across Vineyard Sound bringing the rain with them. Being on East Chop, on beachfront property, she had an unobstructed view.

Laurie loved her home. She had worked hard for it. There had also been a certain amount of luck involved. She had come to Martha's Vineyard at just the right time. The housing market had dropped and that had meant a lot of trouble for a lot of people across the country but not for people who were moving in from a more stable economy and looking to buy property. Almost the entire world had been affected by that crash. Only a few countries had managed to get out unscathed. Canada had been one of them. Yes, she had been lucky and not a day went by that she didn't count her blessings at least once or twice. Running a police department in a small town was just her speed. Having a husband as supportive as Charles wasn't more than she ever dreamed of having but it was certainly more than she ever expected. Laurie had always assumed that being a female police officer precluded any chance she had at having a stable long-term relationship. For the first half of her adult life, that had been true. Reconnecting with Charles changed all that. Their love for Martha's Vineyard coupled with their love for talking through a puzzle over a glass of wine had started them on a journey that showed no sign of coming to an end. They were still learning. They were still discovering. Being in a relationship was like being in a never-ending game of show and tell. Right now, Charles was showing Laurie his friend Peter. Laurie had heard Peter's name almost from day one but she had never met him. Actually, other than Charles' family, Laurie had met very few people from Charles' past. Their wedding had been small and it had been on-island. Laurie hadn't invited any of her childhood friends either. She wasn't really in touch with them anymore. As a woman, Laurie found it difficult to maintain close relationships with friends once they started having children. Laurie didn't have kids and didn't wanted any. She never had. That changed the dynamic of friendship. When Laurie was pretty sure she would rather take her own eye out with a melon-baller than have another conversation about the trials and tribulations of breast feeding, she knew it was time to get new friends.

"Laurie?" called Charles. "Are you alright?"

"Huh?" Laurie blinked a couple of times as she tried to return her focus to the scenery in front of her. "Oh, I'm fine. Sorry about that."

"What were you thinking about?" asked Charles.

"Friendship mostly," Laurie said. "Peter's being here has had me thinking a lot about friendship." She walked into the den and passed Charles one of the glasses of wine.

"What about friendship?" asked Charles.

Laurie sat cross-legged in a big chair that faced out over the ocean. "How we grow apart from the friends of our youth. How making friends as an adult isn't easy." She took a sip of wine. "I mean look at us—I'm not in touch with any of my high school friends and Peter is the first friend of yours from childhood that I've ever met and he's also the only one that I've ever heard you talk about."

Charles nodded. "That's true. Why don't you talk to your friends anymore?"

"I always tell myself that it's because they had kids. That changes everything if you're a woman. I always feel guilty for not wanting to listen to them talk about diapers and midnight feedings. It also kills me to act like their kid is the most beautiful or smartest kid I've ever seen, when in actual fact I think each and every one of them looks like an Easter ham in short pants," Laurie said taking another sip of wine.

Charles laughed. "Don't be too hard on yourself. They probably felt less and less interested in hearing about you going out for a dinner date or going fishing in Aquinnah." Charles reached over and squeezed his wife's foot. "You just grew apart. It happens to everyone."

"Yeah, I know," said Laurie. "It's a little sad."

"Well, don't look at it that way," said Charles. "It's human growth. If the people in our lives didn't change over the years, there's a good chance that we wouldn't change either and that really would be sad. Learning new things changes how we perceive the world and the people in it. Movies and books turned me into a writer; they turned Peter into a painter. Everyone is different. So don't be so hard on yourself. You never have to look too far to see how good you've got it."

"Actually, that's what got me started, I think. I was thinking about how lucky I am. The home I have… and my husband." Laurie reached out for Charles' hand. Their fingers intertwined. "I love you."

"I love you too," said Charles. "You know, speaking of Peter's paintings, I think he and I had a bit of a breakthrough today."

"Why? What happened?" asked Laurie.

"We went for a walk down to Circuit Avenue. You know, just to see what we could see," said Charles. "He and

471

I spent a lot of time there together and he wanted to see what had changed and what had stayed the same. He wasn't even sure what he would remember but it was a nice day for a walk—so what the hell, right?"

"Absolutely," said Laurie. "What did he think?"

"We had a great time," Charles said. "He was sad to see the Island Theater was in such a state."

"We're all sad to see that," Laurie interjected.

"But the arcade was still there and so was The Corner Store where we met. That was cool," said Charles. "Then, we went to Wesleyan Grove."

"I was wondering if you were going to say that," Laurie said. "What did he think?"

"I wasn't sure at first. I'm still not sure to be honest," said Charles. "I didn't say anything. I just turned down that alleyway beside Sharky's and let him follow me in. I figured, if I was wrong, I was wrong."

"And?"

"He walked in like a dog or a cat walking into their new home for the first time. His eyes were wide and his head kind of darted back and forth. He took in every house, every tree. I was a bit afraid that it was going to be too much for him but he said, *This is my painting!* He sounded excited about it but a little scared too. It definitely scared him but I could tell by the way he kept moving forward that he wanted to be there, that he needed to see it. We just walked around the circle—you know that path that wraps around the tabernacle—and I just let him lead the way. Then he stopped in front of a pink house and a dark turquoise house. He froze in his tracks. He stared at the houses in silence for quite some time until finally I called him. I just said, 'Peter?' and he said, *I want to go home.* So, we came home."

"That was it?" asked Laurie.

"That was it," said Charles.

*   *   *

April Stevens sat in her hospital bed and watched as the storm rolled in closer to Vineyard Haven Harbor. While the sun was still shining across State Road, the sky and the sea about a half a mile out were very dark.

April was crying. In her right hand she held a tissue—not one of the cheap hospital tissues but a good one that she had retrieved from her purse. She dabbed at the corners of her eyes with it to prevent her tears from rolling down her face. This was supposed to be her moment. This show was going to prove that she could do it. *Martha's Vineyard 1977* was going to show her island home that she could put together an art exhibit that they would all be talking about for seasons to come. At least, they would all be talking about it until her next one. This was supposed to be her first. April had planned *1977* down to the very last detail. It was going to be perfect. Now, it was all for naught. Not only had someone broken into Old Sculpin but someone had broken into Images In Vogue too. Poor Eddie. April knew that he worked on a shoestring budget. She knew that he had already spent time and money on the materials to print out the photos and make the frames. Old Sculpin was insured but April wasn't sure if the insurance company would cover Eddie's images because they were in his workshop. If they had been stolen out of Old Sculpin that would be a different story but they hadn't been. Eddie was such a nice man. Who would want to break into those two galleries and who would want to vandalise her exhibit? People were crazy. There was just no way around it. At least once a day she bumped into someone who had lost at least half of the stuffing in their comforter and now one of them had run amok in her life. *Well, enough is enough,* thought April.

"As sure as the Good Lord tested Abraham, the good lord will test us," April said to herself. "And if this is a test, so far, I'm failing it."

April leaned over and picked up her purse from the bedside table. Eddie's flowers were on the table. She smiled. No matter where she was, flowers made her happy. She plopped her purse down in her lap and fished around in it until she found her notepad and her pen. She flipped the pad open to the first blank page and wrote 1977 REGROUP across the top in big capital letters. She placed the tip of her pen to her lips while she had a think. What exactly did she need to do to make *Martha's Vineyard 1977* happen on time as planned?

*   *   *

"What about you?" asked Charles. "How did you make out in Aquinnah?"

"First of all, I would never have found the place if it wasn't for my navigation system. Thank God for GPS," Laurie said.

"I thought you hated that thing," said Charles.

"I'm still not a fan," she said. "but when you're out in the middle of nowhere—especially on this island where they don't even bother to mark the roads—it comes in handy," Laurie said.

"Okay, so you got there," said Charles. "What did Craig have to say?"

"Well, I didn't really get anything tangible but I didn't really expect to either," Laurie said. "I just wanted to go out there and talk to Craig and ask him a couple of questions. I wanted to put a face to the name."

"How did it go?" asked Charles.

"Oh, he's our guy," said Laurie. "That's for sure."

"What makes you say that?" asked Charles.

Laurie laughed. "Well, he did not want me there. That was painfully obvious but that doesn't necessarily mean anything. A lot of people don't want the police sniffing around their property on this island. Some people have illegal tenants, some grow pot, some build without permits—on this rock, there are countless reasons people want the police to stay far, far away."

"So, what makes Craig stand out?" asked Charles.

"Just as I was leaving, I asked him if he knew Alan Quaid," Laurie said. "His very tanned face went white. His aggressive attitude faltered. And then he lied—he said no."

"Really? He said he didn't know Alan Quaid?" Charles asked. "That was dumb. Everyone who was here in the 1970's knows who Alan Quaid is. That would be the same as saying he'd never heard of Ted Kennedy and Mary Jo Kopechne! The disappearance of Alan Quaid was big news around here for a long time."

"Not only did I recognise him from your photos, to his credit he hasn't changed all that much. It was the way he said answered too," continued Laurie. "He kind of stuttered it out." Laurie took another sip of wine.

"What about Judie, his wife?" asked Charles.

"That was another thing that was weird. I didn't see her," said Laurie.

"Couldn't she have been in the house?" said Charles.

"Well, yes. Of course, that is entirely possible, but if I wasn't a cop and a police car rolled up to our house, and a cop was talking to me in our backyard, wouldn't you come out to see what was going on? Wouldn't you at least come to the window for a look?" said Laurie.

Charles nodded. "Yes, I would—especially, if I lived out in the bush."

"That's just it. I was going to ask him about his wife but I got the feeling that we were completely alone. In fact, it felt like Craig had been alone out there for a long, long time."

* * *

Standing quietly in the dark, Peter listened to Charles and Laurie from the staircase landing. The Craig that Laurie had gone out to visit that afternoon was the right one. He was the Craig that Peter had known on his trip to Martha's Vineyard as a kid. There was a dark, tight, and twisting knot in Peter's gut that told him, without a shadow of a doubt, that he needed to see Craig. Seeing Craig was the reason he was on Martha's Vineyard.

17

Peter was lying in bed, listening to the storm, when he heard Charles and Laurie come upstairs, walk down the hall, and close their bedroom door. The wind howled across the sound, forcing the waves to crash against the shoreline. Rain pelted the window in an unsettling staccato. Peter saw a storm as nature's way of telling you that everything was not okay. That there was something wrong. Everything about a storm was disruptive and invasive. It was Mother Nature trying to correct an imbalance. She was trying to thin out a heavy sky, fill a depleted sea, or wet a dried out forest. A storm was surgery. It was hard and cutting. A big storm was always something that required a period of recovery, a rest. Peter didn't like storms. As far back as he could remember, they had scared him. Fractions of one storm in particular had begun slicing into his memory like a scalpel that afternoon. It was a memory that was carving through his consciousness leaving shredded openings that Peter could peer through and see bits, pieces, guts of his past, parts of himself that he hadn't seen for a long, long time. He could see the storm. He could see his paintings.

It was dark. The images that he was seeing sliced open in front of him, inside of him, were dark. It was *that* dark. He was watching with his eyes like movies in a theatre, but the scene he was watching was happening deep down inside. He hadn't known that until just this afternoon. He hadn't known that the paintings he had been creating were an actual part of him until just a few hours ago. Oh, he had known that he was responsible for his own work. Peter knew, like any artist did, that his brain was guiding his hand, telling him what to paint. His brain selected the colours and the light and the images that he put to canvas but what he hadn't known or refused to know was that the images he painted were a part of his own memory. That one giant photograph that was in his mind—the one that came out in painful shards cutting into him with every stroke—that photograph, he had taken himself. He had taken it that summer on Martha's Vineyard just as surely as he had taken it with the camera that his Nana had given him for his trip. All of the photos glued into the book that he had given Charles were just like this one. They were just as real and captured the same time on the island, but this one photo that he had tucked away in the back of his own private camera case was far more vivid and far more powerful.

He could see the whole thing now. Peter had always known that all of his paintings were pieces of the same puzzle. Painting them had been the only way his brain knew to get those particular pieces out of his system. With each work, he had removed a little bit more of the puzzle, and with it, a little bit more of the darkness that it held but he had never been able to see the front of the box that it came in. He couldn't see the big picture. Now he could. Charles had unwittingly walked him right into it this afternoon.

When they had walked up Circuit Avenue, Peter had noticed a lot of changes that had taken place over the last four decades. A lot of things had stayed the same too. When Charles had veered from the road and walked him into Wesleyan Grove, it was as if time had stood still. Peter was sure that there were leaves hanging from branches that he had painted twenty years ago. Each and every leaf hung there, waiting, waiting for him to return. Lampposts that had shown him mercy, casting light as he painted, stood there now stoic and unwavering. Each and every gingerbread cottage rested back on their laurels presenting their striped and spotted faces, their multicoloured eyes and mouths watching him as he walked by. Then, there had been those two homes in particular. He had forgotten all about them. He had seen the teal, orange and white house first. Such funny colours to blend together on a home, he had thought. That was the first thing he remembered when he stopped in front of the porch. Peter had remembered that he had thought that as a boy and how he had been grateful that his parents hadn't rented the pink house beside it. That was right, they had rented the turquoise house as a family. He could see it. He could see inside it. He could see his white room with its high ceiling and its gauzy curtains. He could see the fan that forced the heavy, summer air to circulate. Peter remembered it was hot and he had slept on top of his covers. He could see the white y-front underwear that he wore to bed that summer.

    Peter also saw the pink house. It was all pink, varying shades of pink but all pink nonetheless. The pink house scared him. The pink house was where she had lived—Judie. The girl who was smiling in his photograph; the girl who looked so much like his neighbour. When Peter looked at the pink house, the pink of the house intensified to red and he could see his neighbour's blood on his hands. His hands were sticky and caught in the thickness of her long,

481

bloody hair and crumbling skull. That's where it was all coming apart, falling apart like the girl's eye sockets and skull. Peter's memories of his childhood vacation were intermingling with the recent memory of the dead girl on the sidewalk and he didn't know why. Every time he tried to separate them, tried to pull them apart, all he could see was his own fingers pulling through her hair. His stomach twisted and tied into knots. He felt his insides blacken like cancer. He felt like he was painting. But that was Judie's house. He could see her in the rain—Craig was with her. *That* little image peeking through the shredded memories scared him the most of all. He could see the rain, he could see the pink house, and he could see Craig and Judie. Peter also knew that coming to Martha's Vineyard had very little to do with rekindling an old friendship. He was on-island to expose the last photograph that he had taken on that trip.

Peter got out of bed and got dressed. He opened the bedroom door and listened in the hallway. The only sounds were those of the storm outside—the wind whistling through the few windows that were still open and the rain pelting the roof, and the side of the house. He could hear the waves, heavier than normal, crashing the shore all up and down East Chop. Once he was sure that he was the only person awake, he slipped completely out into the hallway and closed his door behind him.

His sock feet made nowhere near enough noise to be heard over the rain. The wooden stairs were strong and barely creaked. Once on the lower landing, he sat down and pulled on his shoes. When he stood, he picked up Charles' yellow slicker off of the coat rack and then paused. He had made up his mind upstairs but now that he was faced with it, he hesitated. Finally, Peter took a deep breath and lifted Laurie's keys from the key rack.

Peter opened the front door and closed it as quickly as he could. He squinted as he faced into the wind and rain. The storm was stronger than he had realised. He ran toward the police truck and pressed the unlock button on Laurie's fob. The SUV beeped into life. It was loud and the high-pitch of the beep cut through the storm enough to make Peter wince. He looked up at the second storey of the house to see if he was being watched. There was no one. The windows were dark and empty. Charles and Laurie's bedroom faced the ocean; there was no way they could have heard anything over the wind. If they did, there was no reason why they wouldn't think that it was one of their neighbours.

Peter slipped into the driver's seat. He stuck the keys in the ignition and turned. The engine rumbled under the hood. The lights came on in the cab and the headlights lit the silver sprays of rainwater in front of him. Peter wasn't sure if he had broken any laws yet but if he hadn't, his toes were definitely on the line.

The screen on the dashboard lit up with several options. He tapped the navigation app and then tapped *My Destinations*, followed by *Destination History.* The most recent destination in the drop box was an Aquinnah address. That had to be it. That had to be Craig and Judie's house. Gently, Peter pressed his foot down on the gas pedal and turned right toward Vineyard Haven. He had definitely broken a law now. He just hoped that he would get the truck back before Laurie and Charles woke up.

* * *

Craig stoked the fire with the metal poker. Then, he reached for another log from the pile stacked high beside the hearth, and threw it on. The storm had brought a chill into the air but a healthy fire would be just enough to take the moisture out of the air and keep the house warm.

He was unsettled. There had been a time when Craig really liked storms but that had been a long time ago. Now, they chilled him right through and he didn't like them at all. He used to like going to watch storms at South Beach. He would sit in his truck with a bottle of Jack Daniels and the girl of the week, and the three of them would watch the storm crash against the beach. But that was a long time ago, that had been before Judie. Judie didn't like storms either. So much changed back then. So long ago. Craig thought he had put it all behind them. Everything had been so quiet for so long—decades. Now, those goddamn people over at Old Sculpin had decided it would be fun to dig up Alan fucking Quaid and all that he represented. 1977 was forty-five goddamn years ago! Who gave a rat's ass about what happened back then. Nothing could be changed now. What's done is done. Wasn't that how the saying went? People never stopped to think about who they would be hurting when they started dredging up memories that had long sunk to the bottom.

He hadn't helped. Craig knew that now. Hell, he had known that as soon as he had driven home the other night. He had just been so angry, so upset. That face—Alan's fucking goddamn face—blown up like a matinee idol for all the island to see. Wasn't it bad enough that they had lived through it all in 1977? Craig guessed that he had been the only person in America, maybe in the whole world, who had been happy that Elvis Presley had died. Oh, he loved Elvis as much as the next guy but the death of The King had distracted the country, and more importantly, this island from the disappearance of Alan Quaid. Now, he had come back—*Larger than life*—and Craig had gone and made it all worse. By panicking and acting out of anger, Craig had drawn attention to the exhibit and more importantly Alan. If he had just left well enough alone, the exhibit would have passed everyone by and that would have been that. But no, he had to go in like a bull in a china shop and start smashing and tearing down everything in sight. Now, the cops had been out. That goddamn cop had even asked him if he knew Alan Quaid and—*because he hadn't been stupid enough already*—he had said no. No! He had said no.

The cop knew he was an islander. She knew that he had grown up here. God knows what else she knew about him. Craig didn't know where the cop—what was her name? Chief something from Edgartown—was from, she wasn't an islander. If she was from the island, Craig would have known her. She looked like she was about his age. Regardless of where she was from, if she was the Police Chief in Edgartown, she would know that every islander knew who Alan Quaid was. His disappearance was even in the Martha's Vineyard Museum! Alan was as much a part of the island history now as Nancy Luce, John Belushi, and Carly Simon. When it all came down to it, that was Craig's fault too but what else could he have done? He was just a kid. They were all kids. Actually, one of them really had been a kid. Pete had just been a little guy. Pete…his shark guy. How old had he been? Ten?

*   *   *

A fork of lightning lit up the sky over Vineyard Sound, waking Charles with a start. Fenway The Beagle buried his nose in the back of Charles' knees and whimpered. Ever since they had adopted him, Fenway had been scared of thunder and lightning. Who could blame him? There were people who were scared of thunder and lightning. Even though there were scientific explanations that lay fears to rest in almost everyone, some people just didn't like it. So who could blame an animal that had very little understanding—as far as Charles could tell—of weather systems? Charles sat up, grabbed Fenway around the middle, and dragged him up to his chest, so they were spooning. Fenway gave Charles an appreciative lick on the cheek before resting his head on the pillow. Charles made a mental note to wash the bed linens in the morning. They were due for a wash anyway, and now his pillowcase would be covered with dog drool.

Charles wondered how Peter was sleeping through the storm. Actually, he wondered if Peter was sleeping at all. He had gone to bed immediately after returning from Oak Bluffs. He hadn't even had dinner. Charles wasn't sure exactly what he had expected by taking Peter into Wesleyan

Grove but he had thought it would be a revelation for him. From his description, there was no question in Charles' mind that Peter had been painting Wesleyan Grove all these years. Charles thought that finally seeing it would be a huge weight off Peter's mind. He thought Peter might have what they called 'a moment of clarity' and that a lot of the blanks he was having surrounding his past—their past actually—would be filled in and that had to be a good thing. Didn't it?

Charles did think that he had filled in some gaps for Peter. He had definitely recognised the campground. As he entered, he had said, "It's my painting." Peter had walked around slowly taking in every blade of grass, every flower, every tree, every house. Those houses. There had been something very special about those two houses where Peter had stopped. Charles could only assume that one of them had been Peter's family's rental house but the sight of both the blue house and the pink house had absorbed Peter. He had looked back and forth from one to the other as if one of them was going to move and he was afraid of missing it. Then, they left.

Had it been too much for him? Charles wondered if he should have given Peter a heads up before taking him in. Peter hasn't been exactly stable since he arrived—that much was obvious. Maybe taking him in there unprepared had been a crappy thing to do to his friend. Shoulda, woulda, coulda—hindsight was always twenty-twenty.

Gingerly, Charles pushed Fenway toward Laurie and got out of bed. He had to pee and the more he thought about Peter, the more he wanted to take a quick peek in and make sure he was okay.

Charles padded down the dark wood floors of the second storey toward the guest bathroom. He hated using the en suite in the middle of the night. Half the time, he woke Laurie up and he knew that she had a hell of a time getting back to sleep once she was awake. The bathroom in the hall was just as nice and it was right beside Peter's room. Once in the bathroom, Charles closed the door behind him to muffle the noise, although he was sure the storm was doing a fine job of that already. When he finished, he waited for the sound of the toilet to subside before turning out the light and stepping out into the hallway once again. He paused at Peter's door. It was silent. He had to be asleep. Charles thought twice about opening the door. He felt like an overprotective mother. Actually, he was a concerned friend. There was nothing wrong with checking in on a friend. Charles placed one hand on the door and one hand on the knob. He twisted the knob slowly and opened the door wide enough to poke his head in. The bed was empty. Charles opened the door a little wider. The room was empty.

Charles cleared his throat. "Peter?" he whispered. Nothing. Then a little louder, "Peter?" Silence.

Charles swung the door open and took a quick look around. The room was definitely empty. Peter's suitcase was propped open on the dresser. His clothes were still there so, he hadn't run away in the night. *He skipped dinner,* Charles thought. *He must be down in the kitchen, making himself a sandwich or raiding the refrigerator.* Charles decided to go downstairs to make sure he was alright. As he walked past the window, Charles looked out over East Chop Drive, their front lawn. Their drive caught his eye. The Jeep was the only vehicle parked out front. Laurie's Police Unit was gone.

* * *

Peter drove shakily along the muddy roads of Aquinnah. He was frankly surprised that he had made it as far as he had. The weather up-island was a lot worse than it was down-island. Parts of the road had flooded out and the other parts were slick with rain and mud. Visibility was next to zero. There were no streetlights out this way and even the high beams on Laurie's police cruiser barely carved a path to follow. Peter figured if something was in his way, he was going to see it just in time to hit it. He had already narrowly missed two trees on a couple of particularly sharp turns.

Peter didn't see how anyone could drive out here. Even if they were familiar with the island, even if they had grown up here, driving in this weather was stupid. Which, Peter realised, was exactly why he hadn't passed a single soul. That was definitely a good thing. Someone might drive by and get enough of a glimpse to realise that he didn't look anything like Laurie and call 9-1-1. Peter couldn't believe that he had taken Laurie's truck—*Jesus, he had stolen the Police Chief's truck!* Not only had he broken the law but he had betrayed the trust of his oldest friend and his friend's wife. They had welcomed him into their home and this was what they got in return. Peter wasn't even sure if he had a valid driver's license. There was a distinct possibility that it had expired but he wasn't sure. Peter didn't know if that made the whole thing better or worse. All he knew was that he needed to see Craig. He needed to talk to him now. The only way that he could do that was to take Laurie's truck. It was the only vehicle with the directions to Craig's house programmed into the navigational system. With any luck, he would be back before Charles and Laurie woke up.

*   *   *

"*He stole my truck?*" screamed Laurie. She threw back the covers and leapt out of bed. "*Are you kidding me?*"

Fenway the Beagle started running in circles on the bed and barking. "What is he trying to pull?" Laurie yelled. "Who steals a cop car in the middle of a rain storm to go joy riding?"

"Calm down," said Charles. "Please, just stay calm!"

"Charles for Christ's sake, I'm the Chief of Police! I can't have my houseguests taking my police vehicle!" Laurie picked up her uniform from the wingback chair beside their bed and pulled it on. She rubbed her face with both hands. "Oh my god, I can't believe this is happening. I'm getting dressed for work but I don't even have my goddamn truck!"

Charles grabbed a Black Dog sweatshirt and a pair of Vineyard Vines shorts and threw them on before Laurie had too much time to get ahead of him. "The Jeep is still there. Couldn't we go after him?"

"You know where he went?" asked Laurie. "How do you know where he went?"

"There's really only one place he would go," said Charles.

Laurie stared at him for a moment before speaking. "He went to see Craig Upland," she said. "That's why he took my truck. I programmed the address into the navigation system. It will take him right to him."

Charles nodded. "I'd say that was a pretty good guess," he said. "Being in Wesleyan Grove jarred a lot more loose than he wanted to tell me. Peter stayed in Wesleyan Grove in 1977. Craig sabotaged the 1977 exhibit. They both knew Alan Quaid," Charles continued. "Peter is remembering more, and more, and he just went to see the only man on the planet who can help him."

Laurie led the way downstairs and put on her boots.

Charles put on his wellingtons and reached for his slicker. "Aw crap," he said.

"What?" Laurie asked.

"I think Peter stole my slicker."

18

Craig lifted his head from his book and listened. He thought he had heard a car engine. He looked toward the front windows of the living room without getting up from his chair. The sound was gone. All he could hear now was the crackling of the pine and oak logs on the fire and the wind and rain outside. No one would be out in this weather; no one with half a brain anyway. He went back to his book. Craig loved Agatha Christie. Her books weren't too long and her plots were terrific. Craig had read enough of them now that sometimes he could figure out who did it but not often. More often than not, there was an exciting reveal at the end—that was his favourite part. They were always a good story. Craig heard it again. There was definitely a car engine revving outside. More than that, stronger than that, it was the engine of an SUV or a truck. Headlights flashed across the front windows. Craig leapt from his chair and hurried to the front door. He opened it and stepped out onto the front porch. He squinted through the heavy rain. *The police were back? In this?* He thought. *In the middle of the goddamn night?* There was something wrong. The police just didn't do this sort of thing. The truck stopped and the lights went out. Craig waited on the porch, where he was protected from the rain. He watched the truck, not sure what to expect at all. He was leery but more than that, he was curious. The driver's side door opened and a tall figure in a yellow slicker stepped out. The driver closed the door with a slam and ran for the protection of the porch. Craig debated going back inside. This was not the Police Chief who had been there that afternoon. For starters, Craig was pretty sure this was a man and he was about a foot too tall. This guy made it from the truck to the porch in about three long strides. He ducked as he stepped onto the porch. The man reached up and pulled down the hood of his slicker.

"Craig," the man said.

The man was thin, too thin. He looked like he should be in the background of an infomercial while some low-grade star begged for donations. Still, there was something about

495

him that looked familiar. Even the voice rang a bell. It wasn't quite right but there was something in it. There was a tone that jarred Craig's memory. It made the hair on the back of his neck stand up.

"Craig," the tall man repeated.

"Do I know you?" asked Craig. He could feel his muscles begin to tighten. His forearms thickened and his shoulders drew back. He didn't know if he was going to have to knock this guy off of his porch but if he did, he was ready.

"Craig, it's me. It's Pete."

Craig felt his stomach drop. His shoulders rolled forward and his arms went weak. For the first time, Craig felt his age. He felt tired and old. He stared at the tall, gaunt man standing on his porch and tried to place the face of the healthy young boy over the sunken eyes and the sharp cheeks. He was there. Craig could see him. Just barely, but he was there. "Jesus Christ! Pete! How are you?" Craig opened his arms wide and stepped forward to embrace his young friend.

Peter hesitated and stepped back out into the rain.

Craig stopped and dropped his arms. He furrowed his brow. "Are you alright?" he asked. "I mean, you don't look so good Pete."

"I need to talk to you," said Peter.

"Why don't we go inside where it's warm...and dry." Craig stepped back and opened the front door. He stepped aside to let Peter go first.

Peter stepped inside cautiously.

"Let me take your coat and you can go sit by the fire," offered Craig.

Still looking around the room, Peter took one of the chairs by the hearth.

Craig went into the kitchen and returned with two glasses of ice and a bottle of Jack Daniels. He set all three down on the ottoman between the two chairs, and took the chair opposite Peter. He poured two fingers in each glass and passed one to his young friend. "Cheers," he said.

"Cheers," repeated Peter.

"So, why are you here?"

*　　*　　*

Peter took a mouthful of whiskey. It burned all the way down. His belly felt hot. His head was hot. He was doing his best to assess the situation but he was doing a poor job of it. In Williamsburg, Peter had felt like he was losing control of his life. His health was slowly slipping away from him. Each painting was getting harder and harder to paint. He was sure that they were killing him piece by piece yet, he knew he was unable to stop. It was beyond his control. Then his neighbour had jumped—died in his hands. She had reached into his soul, into a part of him that he had buried decades ago, and dredged something up to the surface. That had led him back to Martha's Vineyard. Peter had thought he was escaping, just like everyone else did, to the idyllic island, but that was not the case. When he had seen Judie's face, more lagan bits of memory had come to the surface. Wesleyan Grove had been the corker. The bloodied dead face of his neighbour, Wesleyan Grove, the storm, Judie's smile in the photograph: they had all led him here to Craig's house. Now, that he was here, he had no idea what to say.

Craig stared at him expectantly. "Well?" he asked.

"I'm not sure," said Pete.

Craig took another mouthful of Jack Daniels and refilled his glass. "Pete, it's been forty-five years. Now, you show up on my doorstep in a cop car in the middle of the night. I can't believe you're here to see how I'm doing."

Peter stared at him, desperately trying to formulate his thoughts into a coherent sentence.

"You don't look healthy," Craig said. "Are you alright?"

Peter nodded. "I'm okay," he said. "I just haven't been eating very well lately. Give me a week and I'll look better."

"At least, you're talking now," said Craig. He paused before continuing. "I thought we decided that you wouldn't come back."

Peter felt another blade slice through his memory. *You can't come back here—not ever!* "I d-don't remember."

"You don't remember?" asked Craig. "What don't you remember? Sorry, that's a stupid question. What do you remember?"

"I've been painting—that's what I do now; I'm a painter—and I've been painting these paintings that are all bits and pieces of the same image. They're all nightscapes. They're stormy and dark. And there are these houses in the background. I didn't even know what they were until Charles showed me Wesleyan Grove today. I saw them—*I saw my painting!* Then I saw the house where I stayed with my folks and I saw Judie's house!" Peter wasn't sure but he thought he saw Craig wince at the mention of Judie's name. "Seeing them scared me to death. I could feel the darkness inside me that I feel when I paint. I could feel the anger, and the fear, and the hatred, bubbling up inside and leeching out of my skin. I don't know what it is. It feels like death. I know that I was supposed to come back. Parts of my memory are coming back but I don't know what they mean. So I don't even know what questions to ask. All I know is

499

that I had to come see you. I need to know what happened and you and Judie are the only ones who were there."

Craig stared at Peter with intense eyes. His lips were thin and tight. He finished his second glass of Jack without taking his eyes off of Peter. "Can't you just go away?" he asked. "Can't you just leave it alone?"

"It's taken me forty-five years to get here," said Peter. "I have to know."

Craig breathed heavily through his nostrils. His chest heaved up and down but nothing else moved. He sat like that for what seemed like an eternity to Peter. Then he stood up and walked out of the room toward the kitchen. Peter heard the back door open and Craig went outside.

Peter had no idea what to expect. Part of him wanted to run. Part of him thought that Craig was right, that he didn't need to know and that this was all a big mistake. If Peter left now, things would stay as they were. They would stay as they were and that would not be good. Peter wouldn't be able to take it. If things stayed how they were, he would be the next one jumping over the fire escape in Williamsburg, Brooklyn. As terrifying as it was, Peter needed to know what happened forty-five years ago. His mind knew it. His body knew it. Peter's body felt like it was made of lead. He felt like he wouldn't even be able to lift his glass to his lips if he wanted to. All he could do was sit there in the light of the fire and wait for Craig to return. He was too afraid to shake. He felt like staying absolutely motionless would keep things the same for as long as possible. Peter didn't dare move.

The back door slammed in the wind and out of the dimly lit back of the house, Craig came back and walked right up to Peter. He leaned forward and placed something cold and damp in Peter's lap. Peter looked down. It was heavy, large, and oddly shaped. It was round but it had sharp spikes jutting out in all directions. It was pink. It was a conch shell.

Peter sat there staring at the shell in his lap as Craig reclaimed his seat and poured himself another Jack Daniels. Peter's head twisted slowly around as his eyes took it in from every angle. Finally, Peter lifted his hand from the armrest and placed it over the conch. The exterior was rough and flaky. The interior was smooth and polished. As soon as he touched it, he felt energy course into his hand. He felt it course up his arm. Peter felt like he had stuck his finger in an electrical socket. His eyes widened and his back straightened. More than anything, he wanted to take his hand off of the conch. He wanted to thrust the conch off of his lap and onto the floor. He didn't want it on him, he didn't want it near him. All of a sudden, Peter thought that this whole thing was a bad idea. He wished he was back in his studio in New York, safe and alone in the dark. But he wasn't. He was on Martha's Vineyard. He was on Martha's Vineyard and more memories were bubbling to the surface. The storm was back in front of him, inside of him. He was there. Not the storm here and now but *that* storm, the storm of his paintings, the storm of 1977.

*   *   *

Peter woke up in his room in the gingerbread cottage his parents had rented for the summer. He was sweating. The room was hot but that wasn't why he was sweating. He had a nightmare. He had been dreaming about the shark, not a real shark, the shark in JAWS. His breathing was heavy. He couldn't remember the dream exactly but the shark was there. It was big and there had been screaming. Lots of screaming. He could still hear it. Peter threw back the covers and got out of bed. He didn't want to wake up his Mom. If he did, he would just get in trouble all over again for going to see the movie in the first place. He had loved it but at this moment in time, right now in the middle of the night, he wished he hadn't seen it either.

Peter stripped off his pyjamas and found a dry pair. He pulled the covers off his bed and threw them on the floor. Lightning flashed in his bedroom window and Peter jumped.

Most of the time, Peter thought storms were cool, but right now, he just wanted quiet. He could still hear the screaming.

He could hear screaming.

Someone was screaming.

Peter walked over to the bedroom window and pressed his ear against the screen. It was coming from next door. Through the rain, through the wind, Peter could hear muffled screams coming from Judie's house. Were they just joking around? Judie had been making noises kinda like that when Craig was carrying her over his shoulder. Were they just horsing around? Peter's heart was racing in his chest. It was pounding. His stomach flipped. It didn't sound like horsing around. Peter stood still and brought his hands up tight to his body. Should he wake up his parents? He didn't want to get in trouble. But what if she needed help? Peter decided to go and take a quick peek inside Judie's window and see. If he took a quick look then he would know if she needed help, and he could get his Dad if he needed to. Maybe he could help her on his own and he would be a hero! Maybe she would kiss him again.

Peter tiptoed down the stairs to the main floor. He crossed the main room and opened the front door. The door was light and easy. The screen door screeched in its hinges. Peter stopped to listen for his parents but heard nothing. He closed the door behind him and made his way across the porch toward the house next door.

The screaming was louder now. Peter's scalp prickled under his hair. Maybe he should go get his Dad. He was only a couple of feet away. The window of Judie's living room was open—Peter could see it. He would just take a quick look.

Peter stepped over the railing of his porch and down onto the wet grass. He pushed back the branches of the bush on Judie's property, scratching himself in the process. He was right in front of the window now. He was so close that his breath was fogging up the glass. Peter wiped the fog away, cupped his eyes, and peered in.

Judie was on the couch. Her top was pulled half off and she was naked from the waist down. Alan was on top of her, pushing, and thrusting himself into her. He was bracing himself up with his right hand and trying to cover Judie's mouth with his left. Peter felt sick. This was sex. He knew that. But this wasn't right. Judie was crying and grunting. Alan pushed and pushed and every time he did, Judie cried and grunted again. She was trying to speak. Peter heard her say 'Please'; he heard her say 'Stop'. She was saying stop but he wasn't stopping. Why wasn't he stopping? Peter started to cry. He could see her lower belly, below her belly button. He could see hair matted and dark. She was bleeding. Alan was *hurting her so bad. God, why didn't he stop? He wanted her to stop!*

Peter pulled back out of the bush, bent over, and threw up. He wailed out and ran. He ran around the porch of Judie's house onto her front lawn. She was screaming again. He could hear her screaming. He could hear Judie screaming. The first girl to ever kiss him was screaming. Peter stumbled back and tripped. He fell in the mud. He scrambled back up and realised that he had fallen over Craig. Craig was lying face down in the mud. He had to wake up. Craig could help! Craig could fix this. He could make her stop screaming. Peter pounded on Craig's back but he didn't get up. With both fists, Peter hit him again and again until Craig moaned and turned his head. He choked and gasped.

"Craig!" Peter yelled in his ear. "Craig! Get up! He's hurting her!"

Peter got up and ran toward Judie's pink house. He ran up the stairs and pulled open the screen door. The screaming was so loud now. He pushed open the wood door and ran into the living room. He was feet behind Alan and Judie. They didn't even hear him come in. Peter grabbed a large conch shell from the table beside him with both hands and lifted it high over his head. With every fibre of strength that he had, Peter brought it down on Alan's head. He felt it hit and then, he felt it go in. The shell lodged in Alan's skull and *immediately, he stopped thrusting. Blood shot out of the back of Alan's skull like a fountain in a park. A vivid red spray shot across the white interior of Judie's home. Peter pulled at Alan's shoulder and rolled him back. Alan's feet were still tangled in his pants, his shirt was pulled up to his nipples. His erection, covered with Judie's blood, pointed to the ceiling as his body crumpled to the floor.*

Peter stared at Judie's naked body. Her legs were splayed and her vagina was sticky and red. Her torso convulsed as she cried. Through spatters of Alan's blood, she stared at Peter with pleading eyes. Alan had hit her. It was obvious when Peter looked directly at her. Crying, He wanted to look away. He wasn't sure what to do. He felt embarrassed and ashamed.

Judie tried to fix her shirt. As if fixing her shirt would make everything better. But nothing could make any of this better. Judie couldn't cover her bleeding privates, Alan's blood in her hair, her torn underwear, or her puffy and swollen face.

Peter walked over to the other end of the room, picked up a blanket off of a chair and opened it up. He brought it over to Judie and held it out for her to cover herself. She tried to speak but her chest was heaving. Her breathing—panicked. She was sobbing. Peter didn't know what else to do. He tried to comfort her by stroking her hair, but his hands were covered in Alan's blood. It dripped into her hair. The blood slickened, twisted, and tangled his fingers in her hair. She starred at him as he did his best to pull them free. He tried to read her thoughts but he just didn't know. He wished he had run for his father.

The front door opened and Craig walked in. Peter looked up at him and started crying again. Craig stood there, first looking at Peter, then Judie, then Alan on the floor. He hurried over to Peter and hugged him hard. Peter cried into Craig's muddy shoulder until he couldn't cry anymore.

"Pete," Craig said. "Can you hear me?"

Peter nodded.

"We're going to take off your pyjamas. Okay?" said Craig. "You're covered in blood. I want you to take them off, leave them here, and go home."

Without a word, Peter stood up and stripped off his pyjamas. Then, he walked naked to the front door. Just before he left, he looked back and saw Craig holding Judie as tightly as he had ever seen anyone hold another person. They were both crying.

19

Craig poured another two fingers of Jack Daniels in each of their glasses. He sat in his chair and watched Peter sit on the opposite side of the hearth and cry. The Jack Daniels was supposed to make him feel numb. It was supposed to take all of this away but it didn't. He could still feel it. This evening hadn't been as cathartic for him as it had been for Peter. For Craig, it had always been there. He wasn't digging up suppressed memories and going all Freudian in the middle of Aquinnah. Instead, Craig had taken all of those memories and lived with them. He lived with them everyday.

Peter looked up at him and then down at the conch shell. "So, I killed him?"

Craig cleared his throat. "I don't remember it that way. I remember that you saved Judie's life...for a while anyway."

Peter set the conch shell on the ottoman in front of him with the Jack Daniels, then rubbed his hands vigorously on his pants. "Where is Judie."

Craig stared into the fire. "Judie never got over what happened, not entirely. She committed suicide not long after we built this house."

"I'm sorry," said Peter.

"I thought we would be okay," said Craig. "Out here, in a new place, far away from where it all happened. There was no need for us to go to Oak Bluffs. Aquinnah feels like the end of the world most of the time. That's what I like about it. Judie liked that about it too."

"What happened to Alan?"

Craig took a deep breath. "Judie didn't want to go to the hospital. She didn't think it could be kept quiet. She was probably right. This island is terrible for gossip. There was no way that all of those nurses could have kept their mouths shut about a rape in Oak Bluffs. I took her upstairs, made her as comfortable as I could, and wrapped Alan in garbage bags. I tossed him in the back of the truck and drove down to Edgartown. The storm was bad. Brutal. Worse than this one. They had shut down the Chappy Ferry for the night, so I got into a rowboat and made it out to Alan's sailboat tied in the harbour. I opened all the hatches, unwrapped him, and started motoring us out as far as I could. I got us just past Cape Poge, untied the sail, hoisted it about halfway until the wind took it. Then, I jumped. I nearly died that night. The only thing that kept me going was the thought of Judie lying up in her bed alone and crying. I couldn't take it. I probably would have drowned if I didn't know just how badly she needed me. The wind of the storm pulled the boat out to sea but the tide was coming in, it helped me get back to Chappaquiddick. I walked the beach back to the inner-harbour and then swam back to my truck."

"Nobody came asking?" said Peter.

"There was no immediate connection," said Craig. "Nobody had really seen us together. JAWS 2 Production slowed while they hired a new director. That gave me time to clean and paint the inside of Judie's place. When production moved to Florida a couple of days later, we went with them. When we got back, we sold the house, and bought the land here. Judie liked the building of the house—it gave her a focus—but as I said, she never really got over it."

"I'm really sorry," said Peter.

"Yeah me too," said Craig. "I buried her out back and planted a white lilac tree at her head. That was her favourite. Most of the time, I don't feel like she's gone. I think she's still here. I talk to her all the time. Probably sounds crazy."

"I don't think so," said Peter. He looked down at the conch shell and grimaced. "Why did you keep that?"

"I don't know. At first, it was too hard to wrap in the garbage bags. It kept cutting them open. Then, I didn't want the cops to find it and figure out that it had killed Alan. So, I hid it. Then, it just seemed too important to get rid of it. Stupid, I know."

Craig watched as Peter reached forward, picked up the conch, and threw it in the fire. The two men sat in silence for a long time.

20

John Pease stood just inside the door of the Old Sculpin Gallery. The day had started with a sunrise full of colour, and the day had crested into a clear blue sky and a light breeze. It was a true Vineyard day. His custom-tailored, blue and white, seersucker suit was immaculate—as were his yellow bow tie and matching pocket square. John felt good. When April had called and asked for his help in ensuring the *Martha's Vineyard 1977* went on as planned, he had jumped at the chance. He liked April a lot. It had broken his heart when he heard she had an accident that was going to keep her from hosting the event after all of her hard work. Especially, seeing what an excellent job she had done! He would be recommending to the board that she helm another project as soon as she was up to it. With a few adjustments, the exhibit looked great. There hadn't been time to replace the large blow up of Alan Quaid but John didn't care for drawing that much attention to a tragedy anyway. They had expanded the JAWS 2 coverage and focussed on some of the politics that had taken place at the time. Eddie Lineback had replaced the photos but instead of frames, he had mounted them on rough boards. Quite frankly, John thought the frames would have been lovely but the rough edged bare boards matched the barge in the pictures that carried the shark to-and-fro. It gave the whole thing a very authentic, retro feel.

A silver flatbed Jeep pulled up beside Memorial Wharf and John gave a hearty wave. "Charles! Chief Knickles! We could not have asked for a more glorious day!"

Charles and Laurie walked toward John with big smiles. "Hi John," they said in unison.

"Chief Knickles it is lovely to see you dressed as a civilian. A beautiful woman shouldn't be encumbered by all of that hardware," John winked a warm smile at Laurie. "Come inside and have a look around. We've spruced things up a bit since you were last here."

Laurie chuckled, "Thanks, John."

Charles looked at Laurie. "Are you blushing?"

John laughed and turned back out toward the parking lot just as a van pulled up right in front. Eddie Lineback hopped out and ran around to the passenger door. He opened it and helped April down. He took her handbag while she got organised on her crutches, and handed her bag back when she was ready.

"I'm going to go park the van," said Eddie.

John hurried down the stairs as Eddie drove away and met April on the concrete. "May I give you a hand, April?"

"Oh, no! Thank you so much John but I have to get the hang of these things. I'm not too bad going forward in a straight line." April looked ahead at the gallery. "I might have a time of it on the stairs though."

"No problem, my dear," John said. "I've got you." He helped April up with ease.

Wide-eyed, April looked up at John and clutched one of his hands in hers. "How does it look?" she asked.

"You did a marvellous job, April," said John. "Just marvellous. As soon as you're ready, we're going to have to get you to organise another event!"

April beamed and went inside.

John turned back toward the sun and Edgartown Harbor. *Yes*, he thought. *It was going to be a true Vineyard day!*

*   *   *

Peter opened his bags from that morning's shopping trip to Vineyard Haven. He pulled out a treated canvas and a small collection of paints. He spread out an old t-shirt on the floor to protect it and propped the canvas up against his suitcase.

Craig was in jail. There had been no way around that. At least, Eddie wasn't pressing charges. The police had arrested him strictly on the break and enter at Old Sculpin and the vandalising of the exhibit. When it all came down to it, he hadn't really damaged that much. He had broken an old window, which he had already agreed to replace and he had spray-painted over a blow up of a newspaper. He would pay the damages and that would be that. Peter would bail him out as soon as he could. Craig had done so much for Peter already.

Peter was trying not to think about the goings-on the night before. When Charles and Laurie had shown up in Aquinnah, he had been as surprised as Craig. Craig had confessed to the damages at Old Sculpin and Laurie had arrested him. Peter had gone back to East Chop with Charles in the Jeep. By then, the storm had subsided, and driving home had been far less treacherous than the drive out. Peter had told Charles everything. He didn't know if he should have but he did. It just came out. Charles was his friend and it all came out. When they got back to Charles' house, Charles said he was going to have to tell Laurie. For Christ's sake, Peter had stolen her truck—that alone warranted an explanation. Charles didn't know how the past was going to play out for Craig or Peter but the three of them—Charles, Peter, and Laurie—were going to have to sit down and Peter was going to have to tell the whole story to Laurie, officially.

There was no statute of limitations on manslaughter in Massachusetts, but there had been extenuating circumstances, and Peter had been a child. It was hard to know what would happen. Was there even any evidence to support Peter's story at this point? He was actually looking forward to sitting down with Laurie and putting the whole thing behind him once and for all. That morning, when Peter woke up, Laurie and Charles had already left for the exhibit and they were still gone. Whatever was going to happen was going to have to wait.

Peter opened all of the colours of paint and squirted dabs onto the clean, new palette. He took a brush and mixed some colour until he had it to his liking. He pressed the brush to the canvas and pulled it across. Bright green. The bright green of spring flowers glowed out of the brush.

The energy from the brush, to the paint, to his arm, exhilarated him. He did it again. Bright green with a hint of yellow streaked beside the first stroke. His chest puffed up with joy. He reached for another brush, rolled it in colour, and pressed it on the canvas. Pink, petal pink—the colour of roses under a midday sun. Peter could feel tears filling the corners of his eyes. He started to laugh. Painting just felt so good.

THE END

Also by

Crispin Nathaniel Haskins:

The JAWSfest Murders

Deadly Catch

White Shark

Pretty Vineyard Girls

Dead And Buried

Manufactured by Amazon.ca
Bolton, ON